Praise for *Toured to Death*

"Toured to Death, the first book in Hy Conrad's Amy's Travel Mystery series, is a deftly constructed puzzle—fast-paced, entertaining, and a mystery lover's treat. Conrad's signature wit and talent for complex, three-dimensional characters shines through in this clever mystery within a mystery."
—John Clement, co-author of the Dixie Hemingway series

"An absolutely wonderful mystery, served just the way I like—with heart and humor."
—Tony Shalhoub

"Smart, snappy dialog and fun, likable characters keep this series debut moving right along."
—*Library Journal*, starred review

"What could go wrong on an inspirational mystery tour where the game of murder turns deadly? How about . . . everything. Fasten your seat belts and prepare to be entertained!"
—Maddy Hunter, author of the Passport to Peril series

"Fast-paced with an appealing international flair, this story will likely cross gender and genre lines, appealing to both men and women as well as to readers of more than just cozies. Characters with plenty of flaws offer enough red herrings to keep the ending a surprise, even for seasoned mystery fans. A delightful new series."
—*Booklist*, starred review

Also by Hy Conrad

Dearly Departed

Published by Kensington Publishing Corporation

Toured to DEATH

HY CONRAD

KENSINGTON BOOKS
http://www.kensingtonbooks.com

KENSINGTON BOOKS are published by

Kensington Publishing Corp.
119 West 40th Street
New York, NY 10018

All Kensington titles, imprints, and distributed lines are available at special quantity discounts for bulk purchases for sales promotion, premiums, fund-raising, educational, or institutional use. Special book excerpts or customized printings can also be created to fit specific needs. For details, write or phone the office of the Kensington Special Sales Manager: Attn. Special Sales Department. Kensington Publishing Corp, 119 West 40th Street, New York, NY 10018. Phone: 1-800-221-2647.

Kensington and the K logo Reg. U.S. Pat. & TM Off.

ISBN-13: 978-1-61773-680-3
ISBN-10: 1-61773-680-5
First Kensington Hardcover Edition: February 2015
First Kensington Mass Market Edition: January 2016

eISBN-13: 978-1-61773-681-0
eISBN-10: 1-61773-681-3
Kensington Electronic Edition: January 2016

10 9 8 7 6 5 4 3 2 1

Printed in the United States of America

PROLOGUE

The fussy little man held out a legal-size manila envelope. Fanny Abel accepted it, weighing it in her hand. "That's it?" Disapproval tinged her words. More than tinged. After all, this was Fanny. "It can't be more than thirty pages."

"Forty-three. But it's double-spaced." The man actually seemed amused. Fanny wondered if she might be losing her touch.

She tried again. "This is supposed to keep our mystery fanatics occupied for the next two weeks? For all the money we're paying you . . ." She let the words dangle.

"I e-mailed a copy to your daughter in Monte Carlo. It's all she'll need to start the game, I assure you." There was a certain condescension in his calm, as if he were explaining things to a very dense child. It was a trick Fanny recognized from her own arsenal. This guy was good. "She followed my previous packet of instructions?" He tilted his head quizzically. "If not . . ."

"Of course she did." Fanny hated not being in control. Unlike her daughter, she had rules to avoid such situations. Rule number one? Never do business with people you didn't know during your husband's lifetime or to whom you aren't related, preferably by blood. Otto failed on both counts. She had known him for only . . . how long? A minute? Two at the most, since the eccentric figure had walked through the door of their Greenwich Village travel agency.

Owlish was the word Amy had used to describe him— the small stature (no taller than Fanny herself), the pearlike shape, the thick, round glasses that tried their best to add substance. Fringes of white, wispy hair wreathed his face. If Fanny squinted, they could be feathers.

Otto was decked out—*dressed* didn't do him justice— in a suit of gray wool tweed. The cut was almost Edwardian, so old-fashioned it could almost be trendy, some London design that had yet to make it across the Atlantic except for a few isolated outbursts, like the arrival of a flu strain. But the material showed signs of age. Food stains peppered the sleeves. And the details were of such poor quality that Fanny decided the suit had never been fashionable.

Fanny resented that Amy couldn't be in two places at once. Any considerate daughter would figure out how to be in Monte Carlo, dealing with the tour, and in New York, dealing with this strange animal that she'd discovered in some article and then tracked down on the Internet.

The illusion of a ruffled breast was accomplished by a wrinkled white shirt accented by a clip-on bow tie that bobbed so dramatically when Otto spoke—so irritatingly hypnotic—that it had to be deliberate. Intimidation by annoyance, an advanced ploy that she herself rarely dared.

"The entire game is written and ready to play." Bob, bob, bob. Fanny had to force her gaze down to the envelope. "Every day your daughter will receive new instructions. All taken care of." He was reaching across and tapping at the final invoice, paper clipped to the corner.

"What about the ending?" Fanny contorted her own squat frame, hunching down and trying once again to force her opponent into eye contact. "Shouldn't we know how it comes out? You know. Killer? Motive?" With a bit of eye contact, she might just regain her footing. "What if no one can solve it or if a clue gets lost? Amy says she would feel more comfortable . . ." Were his eyes peering up at hers through the bushy eyebrows? She couldn't tell.

"That's not the way I work. You'll notice the item listed as 'assistant fee.'" Another reach and a tap, and this time Fanny couldn't help glancing at the invoice. The glance turned into a gape.

"Oh, my lord!"

Otto chuckled. "My assistant will be keeping tabs on the tour, at great expense to me and greater expense to you. Amy didn't advise you of this?"

"Yes, of course. But . . ." *But such an expense.*

"Mrs. Abel, I have been constructing mysteries for nearly thirty years. The best of the best. And no one knows the ending beforehand—not the organizers, not the actors, no one. I once designed a game at which the vice president was in attendance. And if I won't tell the Secret Service, I certainly won't tell you." Here he preened, smoothing back his head feathers with a fat left claw. "As for something going wrong . . . My assistant will be onsite, observing every step. You don't need to know anything more."

"Well . . . I guess that makes it okay." Fanny straightened the tan, pleated blouse that Stan had told her—in one of those rare romantic moments when her late husband knew he had to say something—so perfectly set off her auburn pageboy. Now, three years after his death, the blouse, a bit tattered around the cuffs, was still her first choice out of the closet. With a sigh, she opened the center drawer of the Chippendale-style desk that had once stood in the corner of Stan's den, took out the company checkbook, and began to write.

Why couldn't Amy have opened a normal travel agency? Between them they knew enough New Yorkers seeking European culture or sunny beaches. But no. Despite Amy's timid nature, she'd wanted to specialize in the exotic. Amy's Travel. Simple but personal. Fanny liked it.

Their agency would be different, Amy had vowed, shunning the usual low-risk, high-volume stuff. The Internet had already destroyed that end of the market. No, they would concentrate on customized excursions.

Fanny suspected the idea had been inspired by Amy's fiancé. Eddie McCorkle, bless his soul, had been the adventurous half of the relationship. He had always been dragging Amy someplace new, talking her into a trek on the Inca Trail instead of a walk on a Caribbean beach. Amy would fret for weeks beforehand and wind up loving every minute. They'd even fantasized about writing travel books. To work together, to travel and see new things. Someday.

Someday had ended two years ago with Eddie's death, just a week after he'd popped the question.

Stan gone and then Eddie in less than a year, leaving a widow and an almost widow, both of them too young not to start over. But was this the way to start? Fanny wondered. It was as if Amy was pushing herself to become someone else.

The Monte Carlo to Rome Mystery Road Rally—

Fanny knew she didn't like this name—was a perfect example of the new Amy. A high-risk, high-profile venture that put them at the mercy of the bank—and of an eerie bird of prey named Otto.

"What if something happens to your assistant? He or she or whatever. God forbid you should divulge the sex."

Otto's grin was unnecessarily rude, considering that she hadn't finished signing the check. "If my assistant should unluckily be hit by a bus, then I shall personally take over the game. No extra charge." He eyed the checkbook. "That's Ingo, i-n-g-o, an anagram for *goin'*, which is what I must be doin', my dear. Thank you."

She wrote as slowly as she could.

Otto took the 1 train from Christopher Street to Times Square. From there it was a short walk to the dingy two-room depressant that had been home ever since his bedridden wife had gone on to her much-deserved reward.

Their life had been a simple one. Mary Ingo had brought in a regular paycheck as a Brooklyn borough clerk, while Otto had written a succession of unpublishable mystery novels. The response from literary agents was always the same—good, twisty plots; poor character development. It was only a matter of time and luck before one of the agents, a member of the same church, asked Otto if he could write a mystery game for a charity event. After the rousing success of *The Deadly Communion Wafer,* one thing led to another.

It was on the day of Mary's funeral that he placed on the market the Brooklyn row house that he'd been born in, married in, and grown old and stout in. Over the following week, the sanitation department carted away dozens of pieces of heavy walnut furniture left out at the curb. Otto was throwing out anything and everything that might remind him of that unhappy eternity. And although his simpering niece—his wife's niece, actually—had begged him to save her the photo albums and the dinette set, out they had gone with the rest. His books—the research books, the classic mysteries from which he mercilessly stole plot twists, plus the prized bound scripts from his own games—all of these went with him.

Along Eighth Avenue, a breeze stirred the street debris into curbside cyclones. Otto joined the crowds elbowing past the cheap storefronts that asserted their stalls halfway out into the bustling sidewalk.

Ignoring the chaos, Otto concentrated on the game he'd just delivered, mentally reviewing the twists and turns, imagining the players' reactions and pre-guessing their second guesses. Designing mystery games was a specialized skill. But within this nearly invisible world, Otto was a living legend. Who else could have carried off The Guggy Murders, a charity event at the Guggenheim that had four hundred of New York's wealthiest racing up and down the spiral ramp in gowns and tuxedos, trying to discover who was impaling the museum staff on a slew of "priceless" mobiles?

A block south of the Port Authority Bus Terminal, Otto used his key on a reinforced steel door and began to wheeze his way up four flights to the mystery king's lair. One step at a time. Arduous minutes later and he was depositing his overstuffed body into the deep, form-fitting depressions in his overstuffed sofa.

It was only as his own gasps were fading from his ears

that Otto realized he wasn't alone. He glanced up at the outer door, the door that he, in his oxygen deprivation, had neglected to shut behind him.

On the two windows that faced Eighth Avenue, the blinds were lowered, permitting a few slivers of dusty light to squeeze between the venetian slats. Otto had not yet switched on a lamp, and the naked bulb dangling from the stairwell ceiling turned the figure into the blackest of silhouettes. The figure glided in and closed the door, plunging the living room into darkness.

The owl's eyes blinked and adjusted. Among the shadows, a profile, and then the outline of eye sockets, cheekbones, and a mouth came into focus. The face was vaguely familiar. "What are you doing . . ." He stopped when he saw the gun. "Oh, my."

Otto regarded the firearm with a curious eye. He knew his guns—and his bombs and his poisons and just about anything else that could maim or kill. Even in this light, he recognized it as a .22 pistol with a silencer, a muffler, as the English called it, screwed onto the muzzle.

Good choice, he thought in an oddly dispassionate way. A silencer would be useless on a revolver due to the gaps around the chamber, from which air, and therefore noise, could escape. The smallness of the .22 and the fact that it was a pistol meant that the explosion would be minimal. Just the kind of weapon he himself would have written in.

"The walls are very thin," Otto panted. "My neighbors are nosy." He wondered if he had enough breath left in him to scream. At the same time, he was fascinated by his assailant's face. So familiar, yet not. "What do you want?"

The intruder didn't reply. Not a good sign.

"I have a few hundred dollars." But he instinctively knew money wasn't the object. "I have a credit card." He didn't. At this point he was just looking for a response.

The figure didn't move but seemed to be waiting—nerveless, emotionless. Waiting for what? The only sounds in the stale, greasy room were Otto's labored breaths and the normal abuse from Eighth Avenue: the blare of taxis as they jockeyed for position by the Port Authority, the rhythmic *clunk-a-clunk* of tires passing over an ill-fitting construction plate. It was during one of these *clunk-a-clunk*s that the figure fired.

Otto had read about thousands of fictional deaths, had personally staged dozens of them, but had never before been on the scene of a real murder. In his rare moments of self-doubt, he had wondered if his re-creations might be too clichéd or unrealistic. Did shooting victims really convulse with the impact, then go limp in their chairs as the life drained out of them?

Yes, they did. And with a certain degree of satisfaction, he convulsed and slumped and drained. *Of course, I could be reacting this way because that's how I think I'm supposed to,* he thought, then discarded the notion. *No, this is accurate, as far as I can tell. I should be spending my last moments thinking up a deathbed clue, shouldn't I? Some clever, unmistakable lead . . .*

He slid from the sofa to the floor, leaving a smeared trail of red against the dirty corduroy cushions as he fell to his knees and collapsed forward. His brain was far too woozy now. Besides, he truly had no idea who had killed him, which was annoying on both a personal and professional level.

Otto's next thoughts were of the regrettable differences between factual and fictional murders and how, even discounting his current situation, he much preferred the fictional.

I wonder if this will ever be solved, he mused dryly. *How very like me to leave a murder mystery in my wake. How fitting.*

PART ONE

AWAY GAME

CHAPTER 1

"How can you dictate my menu?" Emil Pitout snatched the printed card from Amy's hand and inspected it. "You are a chef perhaps?" The doughy man in the apron smirked—a needless smirk, since his tone was expressing it nicely. "Do you have a Michelin star you neglected to tell me about, eh? My apologies."

Amy didn't take offense. She was too busy mentally translating the rapid stream of French and trying to phrase her own response. "I'm not a chef, Emil."

"You must be. Perhaps you wish to cook tonight? I don't want to jeopardize your menu with my clumsy efforts." Or at least Amy thought the word meant *jeopardize*. Something close.

Emil stopped to read the card. "Not bad," he said grudgingly, as if he'd never seen it before. "But why must the dishes be just so?" The menu slipped from his fingers, drifting to the white tile floor. The entire kitchen was white and chrome and shining, like a surgical theater.

Amy hated arguing. She wasn't good at it, even worse in French. Her usual ploy was to surrender. It tended to cut short the inevitable bloody defeat. Only this time she couldn't.

"Because they must," she ventured, bending down to retrieve the menu. "Emil, you've had this for a week. If there was a problem, you should have e-mailed me. It's a simple dinner, nothing out of season. A fish soup, coquilles Saint-Jacques d'Étretat . . ."

Emil snatched at the menu again, but Amy pulled it back. "You have been to the market? I came late this morning—five o'clock—so I probably missed you. The haricots verts were perfection. They would have thought me mad if I didn't buy them." He pointed to a basket of the greenest green beans Amy had ever seen.

She was finally getting the point. "You want to substitute a vegetable."

"The other, it was passable." Emil shrugged, pointing to a basket of equally green broccoli heads. "But to take these poor fellows and then to pass up the haricots verts . . . What is the problem with one substitution?"

Amy honestly didn't know, but she had her instructions. "Emil," she pleaded. "We are occupying sixteen rooms. And we paid a good deal extra to reserve the whole restaurant." She was sounding like a pushy businessman. Even worse, an American.

"You think this is about money?"

Well, yes. "Of course not."

"It's not about money."

"I'm sorry. No artist likes being told how to perform. The green beans look fantastic."

"Look? Ha." And in a smooth motion perfected over years of stuffing capons, he slipped a bean between his adversary's teeth.

"These are American tourists," Amy mumbled as she

crunched. "Which is not to say they don't appreciate food. Mmm, delicious. But they won't mind something not quite so perfect."

"You think it matters who I cook for? You think I walk out into my dining room and say, 'Oh, these people, they won't appreciate my food. I will serve them crap'?" Actually, Amy had been to Paris bistros that made this scenario sound plausible. "Americans come in, and they ask, 'How is this cooked?' 'What vegetable comes with that?' 'Can I have this instead?' "

"Well, they are the ones eating."

"They get the vegetable I decide goes best. It is part of the whole."

"Emil." Amy pushed her glasses back up on her nose. "If it were up to me, I would love green beans. But these are my instructions. People must sit in certain places and do certain things. I don't know why. Will this be a clue? I don't know. Will something be poisoned?"

"Poison?" Emil gaped in mock horror.

"You know what I mean."

"You are going to poison my food?"

"Emil, please."

"I call the police."

How do you say 'get off it'? "I have told you over and over. This dinner is part of a murder mystery game. I can't change a thing."

"Even pretend poison, I will not allow. . . . That thing that tastes of bitter almonds?"

"Cyanide. No. No pretend cyanide."

Emil huffed. "You should not play games with food."

For Amy, the ensuing compromise felt like a victory. At least she hadn't caved completely. The haricots verts, they agreed, would be a side dish, in addition to the

broccoli. She just hoped that Otto Ingo's entire mystery
didn't hinge on the absence of green beans at the opening night banquet.

It was a few minutes past noon on a cloudless day in
mid-September. Amy Abel had changed into a crisp
white blouse, lime-green clam diggers, and her favorite
white and green espadrilles. Taking a deep breath of
sea air, she strolled down the front steps and turned left
onto avenue Saint-Martin.

The small luxury hotel had been hard to find. According to Otto's specifications, it had to possess a terrace
opening directly onto the dining room and should, as
much as possible, resemble a private home. Deluxe accommodations in Monaco tended to be large affairs.
The smaller, homey hotels were generally of a lower
grade, something that might have been all right with
Otto but that would not have suited Amy's clients.

Salvation had come in the form of the Hotel Grimaldi,
an eighteenth-century mansion on the spit of land known
as Monaco-Ville. Halfway between the oceanographic
museum and the cathedral, the Grimaldi was in a district
filled with ancient squares and serpentine alleys, hardly
the center of jet-set action. But this tiny gem was posi-
tioned right next to the seaside cliffs. And the view from
the terrace was as good as you'd find at the Fairmont
Monte Carlo.

Amy had left her to-do list back in her room. This was
meant to be a break. *Perhaps lunch at an outdoor café,* she
thought as she wandered away from the crashing waves.
Emil was in his kitchen; the guests were all checked in;
the actors would be needing her for the rehearsal in the

dining room, but that wasn't until three. Before she knew it, Amy had mentally re-created the to-do list.

She'd barely traveled at all since Eddie's murder. Could it be almost two years? Time had glided by in a haze of despair. It had all been so senseless, so random. Hundreds of times she had gone over—still went over— the events of that Saturday night in early November. If only they hadn't had that fight. If only Eddie hadn't gone out for a walk. If only he had stormed out five minutes earlier or later or hadn't turned down Minetta Lane. All the millions of little forks in the road, the in- consequential moments you never gave a second thought to until they heartlessly, mechanically clicked into place and destroyed your world.

Amy knew this was all part of not letting go. But how could she let go? It had been the beginning for them, a burgeoning world of inside jokes, of quiet, cuddly morn- ings, and little traditions . . . all gone in an instant.

Amy tried to focus on the modest glories of the neigh- borhood, on the neat rows of window boxes, on the brass railings glowing richly in the sun. Which was worse? she wondered. Thinking about Eddie or obsessing over the game?

This rally had been her brainchild, combining her two great loves, travel and mysteries. The idea had come to her fully formed after she'd read a *New York Times* article about a mystery event at the Guggenheim.

Mystery parties were not new. They had been around for decades and usually consisted of a poorly written mystery, two hours of half-drunken role-playing in someone's living room, and a disappointing solution that didn't quite make sense.

But what if you could make it bigger and better?

What if you fully immersed the players, took them on a journey, and made the mystery last for weeks, not hours? This Otto Ingo, barely mentioned in the *Times* article, seemed to be just the kind of man to approach about her idea.

Amy had assumed there were others like her, but with money: mystery lovers willing to pamper themselves to the tune of two weeks and many thousands of dollars. So she'd gone out on a limb, getting in touch with Otto, arranging the tour, creating the brochure and the Web site, all on her own. Well, not quite on her own. Her mother had been loyally at her side, to complain and tell her they were headed for disaster.

The rally had filled up quickly, much to Fanny Abel's amazement. If everything went right, the Monte Carlo to Rome Mystery Road Rally would put their little agency on the map, giving it a distinctive niche in the cutthroat travel market.

If things went wrong . . . For a woman who hated risk, who had moved back in with her mother rather than live alone, Amy was taking the risk of a lifetime. She was painfully aware that there was no other tour operator sharing the downside. And that was the reason why she kept reviewing her mental checklist.

Amy turned down a narrow pedestrian lane. The air was balmy, with that distinctive resort smell—coconut oil and citrus and aloe. Strolling in the welcome shade, she was jostled by the amiable tide, a couple here, a trio there, a small roadblock of Germans hovering around a particularly cheap postcard rack.

This scent, so suggestive of languid, half-forgotten vacations, was it seeping out of the rows of plastic bottles in the souvenir shops or evaporating straight off the tourists? Perhaps it was part of the atmosphere, the result of so many decades of slathered, half-naked bodies leaning against porous limestone columns or dripping their fragrant sweat onto the cobblestones.

The late summer sunlight met her at each corner, teasing her with its heat, only to retreat once she ventured on to the next block. Farther down, at the end of the block, Amy could see the shadows disappear, and knew that she was approaching a square. *Good.* She hadn't forgotten.

Dominick's was one of several cafés that poured their tables and umbrellas out onto place Saint-Nicolas, a picturesque square whose centerpiece was a statue of the somber Christmas saint. The old man peered down from the top of his lazy fountain, the water barely dribbling from the four lion heads that sprouted just below his feet.

They had eaten lunch at Dominick's on their very first trip, a three-week extravaganza fueled by sex and excitement and next to no money. How many more places would she find from their travels? Not that she was looking.

Amy settled into a white plastic chair at a red plastic table. She asked the waiter for a *croque-monsieur* and an Orangina and was surprised at how quickly the order arrived. That was the one advantage of coming here in high season. The cafés did their best to churn the tables.

Amy took her first bite, then turned her chair to get the best view. Only gradually did she become aware of a couple, an older woman and a younger man, staring at her from under an umbrella of the adjacent café.

Amy didn't consider herself the type to draw stares. True, she was tall and slim—not model slim, but close— with a five-foot-ten frame inherited from her father. In all other ways her looks were remarkably unremarkable. In her early thirties, an ordinary age, she possessed brown, slightly wavy hair cut to shoulder length and pulled back into a chignon. Her nose, mouth, ears, and brown eyes were equally ordinary. Eddie's best friend had once described her as the prettiest girl in the office. And although Amy had never worked in an office, the description rang true.

Her one extravagance was the eyeglasses. She loved them and felt they added some much-needed definition. A visual signature, with unlimited variety. Since childhood she had thumbed her nose at contact lenses. And the very idea of LASIK surgery . . . Her current favorite was a pair of Lafont sunglasses, with round tortoiseshell frames, and she was wearing them now.

Amy tried not to stare back but couldn't help glancing their way. And then it came to her. "Ms. Davis," she said in a flash of recognition. No wonder they'd been staring. "Excuse me. I was daydreaming." She tucked fifteen euros under her ashtray, took her plate and glass, and went to join them.

"Oh, you didn't recognize us. Admit it," the woman purred.

"No, I did."

"I forgive you." Georgina Davis flourished an outstretched hand, as if to embrace her approach. "I barely recognized you myself. Your glasses are different." She laughed in a pleasant, self-deprecating way. Her gold bracelets jangled as she moved an elegant crocodile purse an inch closer to her iced tea, her best effort to make room at the small table.

A British friend had once suggested that while some cultures might be obsessed with birth, education, or other barometers, in America things were more elemental. Beauty, youth, and money. This was how a democracy judged its people, he'd said, which explained why most U.S. magazines printed photographs of their subjects, found a way to mention their age, and always gave some hint of how well off they were. Amy had been appalled by the observation but now found herself using it to evaluate the two people seated around the curve of the table.

Georgina Davis was third-generation money, grand-daughter of Davis Buttons, Inc., and worth a comfortable hundred million. A well-preserved sixty, Amy estimated, and probably ready to deny it.

In the final category, Georgina lost more of her democratic prestige. A soft aurora of strawberry hair did its best to soften a jaw that could be unkindly called lantern and a cleft in the chin too deep and heroic to be labeled a dimple. On a man it might be considered a strong face. A man at least would have had the option of cloaking it with facial hair. On a sixty-year-old woman, however, all you were left with was the odd impression that you were always catching sight of her from the wrong angle.

Her companion, Marcus—from her time with the travel documents, Amy recalled an Hispanic last name—rated much higher in the two less critical areas. He was about Amy's age and perhaps an even six feet, not tall enough for her to wear decent heels in his company, but . . . Why was she even thinking that? His face was long, with largish features—an aquiline nose and over-size ears partly covered by hair. He had a wavy, shiny jet-black mane, which complimented his olive complexion. Good hair and a killer smile.

"Marcus Alvarez," he said, flashing a smile and extending a hand. "I'm Georgina's companion." His accent was American.

Amy's brow furrowed at the old-fashioned term. She had thought Georgina was traveling alone. "Companion as in friend?" The hand shaking hers was strong; the skin tanned and nearly hairless.

He laughed. "As in that's my job."

"Marcus, honestly!" The heiress's face reddened, the color clashing momentarily with her hair.

"Sorry, Georgie." He turned to Amy. "Back in Palm Beach I'm Ms. Davis's personal assistant. But ever since we got here, people have been asking what she's up to that she needs a personal assistant."

Amy felt vaguely disappointed, the same way she would be to learn that a gorgeous man was a model or a well-built man a personal trainer. Marcus's charm and style didn't seem to count for as much when they were part of his job description.

"I've always had someone travel with me," Georgina said, "ever since the age of chaperones—which was not that long ago." A pout caused her stretched hairline to inch down toward her plucked eyebrows. "Why can't we settle on *friend*? Aren't we friends? Or am I some pathetic crone, forced to hire a companion? Is that what you want people to think?"

"I'm sorry." His apology sounded sincere, if still playful. "From now on we're two dear friends."

"Thank you." Georgina sighed dramatically. "Now, hunt down the waiter, pay the bill, find me a couple of aspirins, American made, and get hold of a cab. Please," she tossed in for friendship's sake.

Marcus curled his lips in a grin that only Amy could see, then did as he was told.

Georgina settled back into her plastic chair and smiled warmly. "All right, tell me. What exactly is a mystery race? I know it's all in the brochure. But who reads?"

"It's not a race. It's a rally," Amy explained. "Getting to the finish line is only one part. You'll play in teams, with every team representing one suspect in the story. One team plays the victim's wife, one plays his son, et cetera. Six teams, four players on each team. Every morning you get clues, and then you start racing."

"Like that TV show," Georgina said. "*The Fabulous Race.*"

"*The Amazing Race*, yes. Except it's not just about getting there first. As you go along, you pick up clues to the mystery. It'll become clearer as we go along."

"I'm sure it will."

A minute later Marcus emerged with a glass of water and a travel-size bottle of Bayer scavenged from his camera case. "The waiter is getting a taxi for us. Are you all right? Did you want to go back to the hotel?"

Georgina nodded as she gulped down three aspirins and sipped the water. "I'm a little tired from the flight. And I do want to be at my best for the banquet." Even though the table was just a few inches away, she handed the glass to Marcus. "You don't have to come with me, dear. If you and Amy wish to go off and see a little of Monaco . . ."

"Yes, I think so," Marcus said, accepting what was only a begrudging offer of freedom. "That is, if Amy isn't too busy."

"Oh, Amy must have dozens of more important things . . ."

"As a matter of fact, I'm free." Amy couldn't resist contradicting an entitled heiress. "I'd love to show Mar-

cus around. It's just about the only country that lends itself to a walking tour."

"Good." Georgina pushed herself to her feet, wob-
bling ever so slightly for effect. "I'm sure I'll be all right."

"Of course you will," Marcus said.

They remained firmly oblivious to Georgina's ma-
nipulations, walking her through the café, depositing
her into the taxi, and waving her on her way.

"It does her good now and then," Marcus whispered,
his breath tickling Amy's ear. "So, where are we going?"

CHAPTER 2

The Exotic Garden was a short walk away, occupying a cliff-side block not a hundred yards from the nation's western boundary with France. *Exotic* might be too exotic a word, Amy half apologized. It was a cactus garden.

They entered from the top, stopping to take in the landscape of succulents laid out below, a palette of greens and grays in every imaginable shape—round and spiked, flat and tall, modest and extravagant. A series of wooden footbridges wound through the cacti, making the steep ground passable and eventually leading down to a single exit onto the boulevard below. The winding paths constantly broke off, then wove back on themselves, giving access to every part of the sloping garden and making it all seem much larger than a single residential block.

Down below, a German guide led a small cadre of tourists. As they walked, he pointed out plants of interest, speaking in slow, heavily accented English, which carried up the slope. His charges nodded in response, occasionally breaking off to talk among themselves in fast bursts of Spanish. Amy had seen this before, the use of English as the new Esperanto, the common language of a shrinking world.

"I wonder what the story is there." Marcus leaned into her with pleasant familiarity.

"They couldn't find a Spanish-speaking guide."

"Hmm. A bit like *Madame Butterfly*."

"*Madame Butterfly?*"

"You know. The opera. Japanese girl and American boy. Somehow they find a common language in Italian."

Amy chuckled. "You're right. I never thought how illogical that was."

"Well, not for the Italians."

They wandered away from the tour group, down the leftmost path. Nearly the entire principality lay nestled at their feet, a neat, flower-bedecked world. At the foot of it all was a yacht basin flanked by two ribbons of thin sandy beach. And just beyond the harbor and the beach was the blue-green Mediterranean, sparkling merrily in the sunny distance. Amy imagined she could hear the rhythmic surf.

The moment seemed perfect. The weather, the view, the slightly salty breeze. "What do you think of Monaco?" she asked, distrusting the quiet perfection.

"It's nice."

"Nice?" She remembered being here with Eddie, just a few blocks away, looking at real estate windows, gasping at the prices as they fantasized about living in the Mediterranean principality.

"A bit artificial, don't you think? Like Epcot Center. Everything so controlled and condensed, but with the illusion of size."

Amy was a bit thrown. "Well, you have to admit it works. I mean, as a country."

Marcus turned from the view. "It's a tax haven the size of a few dozen football fields. Of course it works."

He was smarter than she had given him credit for. Opinionated and educated . . . and sexy. She phrased her next statement carefully. "You're not the kind of man I would imagine as . . . you know, a companion."

"We're not sleeping together, if that's what you think. And I'm not gay. Most people think one or the other."

"It n-never crossed my mind," Amy stammered. "Why do people think you're gay?"

"I don't know. Maybe because I don't drink beer or watch sports."

"Plus, you have great hair and a good fashion sense."

"That's an anti-straight cliché, Ms. Abel, but thank you."

With a lazy, comfortable shrug, he turned back to the view. Below them, the German and his Spaniards had exited and were heading toward their tour bus. The two Americans were seemingly alone. Marcus had leaned his body into the railing and was in the process of pushing himself away. It was an unthinking rocking movement, almost like a stretch. And it probably saved his life.

The stone came from behind and lobbed past his face, just missing the railing as it breathed its weighty threat in a rush of air. Visually, it was a blur, a coconut-size object arching within millimeters of his hair, smashing into a nest of prickly pears two levels below.

The shock alone was enough to throw Marcus off balance. He fell to one side and back, twisting an ankle as he collapsed. "Augh." He turned and glanced up the rocky slope. "What the hell?"

Amy's glance followed Marcus's. There was movement up there among the cacti, a shadow retreating through the gray and green stalks. "Someone threw a rock."

"I'm all right. Go."

"Go where?"

Marcus pushed her helping hands away. "Go see who it was."

"Who it was?" Amy's feet remained rooted, her mind numbed by the unexpected.

"Don't confront him. Just look."

"Umm." Amy didn't know what to say or do.

"What are you waiting for? Go. He's getting away."

With a quick pivot, Amy hurried back up the path, swinging herself around a railing, then twenty feet up another incline and around a second railing. From here she had an unobstructed view of the next few turns. Whoever had been there was gone.

Amy returned, the sound of espadrilles on gravel crunching loudly in her ears. "Maybe it was an accident," she said. Marcus didn't look happy. "Are you all right?" She extended her hands again.

Marcus refused her assistance. "An accident?" He reached up for the wooden railing but was too far away.

"Let me help."

"No, I'm fine." He waved her away. Their hands never touched, but it felt almost like a slap. "You were right not to go. It might have been dangerous."

"I did go. He was already gone."

Marcus finally grasped her hand, pulling Amy off balance and down as he pulled himself up. He hobbled past her up the twisting incline. "I could've been killed."

"It was probably some crazy kid."

"Well, that makes it fine."

"Or an accident."

Amy crossed to him, and they leaned over, staring at the weapon, a lethally large stone in a prickly pear setting.

"That's one strong kid," Marcus growled. "And it was thrown, not dropped, not dislodged."

"I couldn't have caught him, anyway," Amy said.

"I didn't ask you to catch him." Marcus abandoned the postmortem and placed a hand on Amy's shoulder for support. Together, they made their way down the path toward the exit. Without a word, they passed the rock and kept going, the blue-green scenery now wasted.

"I'm just not good in emergencies. I freeze up."

Had it just been freezing up?

Unsettling memories flashed. The time she had been bullied on the school playground and had pretended to be sick for the next two days. The time she'd been robbed in Central Park, when she could have run away but didn't. And the big memory—Eddie's attack and her delay in calling 911, which didn't make any difference, no difference in the world, because he was already dead.

Awkwardly, they walked, like an elderly couple out for a pleasant but difficult stroll.

"I should have gone after him."

"That's okay," Marcus said and winced as his foot hit an uneven patch of stone.

CHAPTER 3

As the afternoon progressed, a line of clouds began forming over the nation, and by eight that evening, a warm but threatening breeze wafted its way in from the Mediterranean. The air was still comfortable enough to allow Amy's guests to mingle out on the stone terrace. An open bar had been set up near the doors to the dining room, and that became the centerpiece of the festivities.

Fashion-wise, Amy was always torn between the needs to stand out and to fit in. Her black evening dress seemed to tread the line perfectly, a stylish, strapless Donna Karan from last year's collection, bought recently at an outlet store. The glasses were also Donna Karan: black on orange, with rectangular frames.

Leaning against the marble balustrade, she nursed a well-deserved Campari and listened to the waves, trying her best not to think about the clouds.

All twenty-four guests were dressed formally in honor of the rally's opening night, or perhaps in honor of the fictional Daryl Litcomb and his dinner party.

Two hours earlier Amy had slipped the mock invitations under each door, requesting them to spend the evening at the industrialist's home and setting the time and place, 7:30 p.m. on the terrace. This was their first hint about the mystery's plot, and although the details on the engraved invitation were almost nonexistent, they still managed to pique everyone's imagination.

A dozen theories were already in circulation. "Daryl Litcomb is obviously the victim," a toothy, heavyset woman was telling her friends.

"I'm suspecting his wife," came another knowing comment, even though Daryl's marital status had yet to be revealed. "Is Litcomb an English name?"

At 8:05 p.m. Amy strolled to the French doors and raised her hand to the maître d'hôtel. Fire at will. The seven actors hidden in the shadows of the dining room also noted her signal and tucked their scripts into assorted purses and pockets. Amy scurried to the bar and replenished her Campari, this time with soda.

A well-timed crack of real thunder subdued the half dozen conversations, and it was during this lull that a high-pitched laugh erupted from one of the dining room actresses. It was followed a second later by an angry shout, delivered by a male voice, then several loud and colorful insults.

A curious excitement rippled through the guests as they gravitated to, then crowded around the French doors. Suddenly, a chandelier illuminated the room's central round table, spilling enough light to include all seven performers, also dressed formally and ready for dinner. The guests broke out in applause, heralding the official start of the Monte Carlo to Rome Mystery Road Rally.

Amy watched and listened, as attentive as her clients. This morning she had been unnerved to learn that most of the dialogue would be ad-libbed, following Otto Ingo's plot outline, with only a few key pieces of information recited verbatim.

As the actors eased into their roles, Amy found herself pleasantly surprised. The majority of them were Americans, recruited by a Paris casting agent. During their few hours of rehearsal, they hadn't seemed to take the job seriously. Jokes had flown, mostly at the expense of the plot. Critical lines had been flubbed. And no one had stayed in character for more than a minute. Amy had been within an inch of getting up the nerve to yell.

But now that the costumes and lights were on and an appreciative audience stood in the doorway, the cast came to life, imbuing Otto's hackneyed scene with as much life and realism as the average TV drama. Not high art, certainly, but at least a level of competence with which their viewers seemed comfortable.

The plot began simply enough. Daryl Litcomb, an American businessman, had invited several guests to spend the weekend at his Monte Carlo estate. The exposition came fast and blunt, with lines like, "Well, if it isn't the legendary soap opera star, Bitsy Stormfield."

This prompted a similarly contrived but information-packed reply. "Stew, dear. I see you've already had a drink. Being Daryl's business partner must be the perfect job for a lush."

The audience readily forgave the clunky dialogue and probably appreciated the broad personalities and names: a diminutive but excitable actress named Bitsy Stormfield, an alcoholic business partner named Stew Rummy.

Otto obviously knew his business. Subtleties were harder to remember, and at this stage in the game

there was a lot to digest. Several of the players had
pulled notepads from the folds of their formal wear
and were writing down anything they thought might
prove helpful.

In the space of ten minutes, the six future suspects were
introduced, with their names and relationships to Daryl
repeated several times. Members of the household included Daryl's unhappy wife, Dolores; his faithful secretary, Fidel; and Price, the millionaire's spendthrift son.

The weekend guests consisted of just three. Bitsy and
Stew were old friends of the family, as was Dodo, an eccentric, middle-aged heiress of dubious mental capac-
ity. Dodo Fortunof, perhaps the most inspired of the
names.

Three men, three women. Three household members, three outsiders. The mystery's demographics had
been constructed with the same precision as everything
else.

As the dialogue progressed, the actors drifted to
their places at the round table. Dolores rang a silver
bell, and a butler and maid responded, entering from
the kitchen with a soup course. The theatrically bright
lights dimmed, and the first scene was over.

There was only a smattering of applause, as if the
guests were reluctant to admit the unreality of the
scene. Amy and the maître d' then went about the task
of seating them at four rectangular tables surrounding
the circular one. The waiters were already busy serving
up an identical first course, a *soupe de poissons* rich with
saffron and fennel. Amy found her spot at one of the tables, suddenly realizing how little of her lunch she'd actually eaten and just how famished she was.

"Very exciting," Georgina murmured. Ever since sitting
down, the heiress had been uncharacteristically quiet.

Now she placed aside her soup spoon and leaned into
Amy. "And such an interesting story." Both sentences
were delivered in a flat tone that gave the impression of
things left unsaid.

"Glad you're enjoying it."

"I wonder where he got his ideas, the person who
wrote this."

"His name is Otto Ingo," said Amy. "He's the best in
the business. Although he does seem to like his clichés."

"You're too cruel." An amused reprimand, but delivered with the same flatness. And then the tone was gone,
replaced by Georgina's usual carefree lilt. "Did this Otto
know who was coming on the tour? I mean, was he given
our names?"

What an odd question. "Uh, no." Amy paused as a slim,
silent waiter circled their table, collecting bowls. "Otto
was working on this before I made the first booking. He
never even saw a guest list. Why do you ask?"

"No reason." The lights were dimming now, like the
houselights in a theater.

The spotlight had again come up on the central table
as the seven actors wiped their mouths. Their first few
lines were drowned out by the sound of two dozen chairs
scraping across the floor as the players rearranged themselves for a better view.

Scene Two consisted of more heavy-handed exposition, this time focusing on Daryl's social and business
life. Innuendos of love affairs and crooked deals splat-
tered wildly around like loosely packed shotgun pellets,
hitting everyone and everything but causing little damage. Meanwhile, the butler and maid delivered shell-
shaped dishes. Scallops in a garlic cream sauce.

As the cast members gazed down at their new course,
Dodo launched into her monologue, a comic speech

loosely outlined by Otto and elaborated on by an imaginative actress.

"My third husband could never eat seafood," she announced, toying with her scallops. "Which was odd, considering he was Swedish and those people just seem to live on fish. Most everything affected Lars's stomach, poor dear. He would have the most appalling attacks of gas, like nothing you've ever smelled. How to describe it . . ."

"Don't," murmured her hostess. But it was useless.

"Have you ever had a skunk spray your compost bin? That happened to us on Martha's Vineyard. *Très* pungent. It was like that—with perhaps an added hint of rotten cocoa beans." Dodo sniffed the air, as though her description had magically re-created the aroma. She went on for another two minutes, and by the end of her unappetizingly explicit speech, Daryl Litcomb had stopped eating, a pained, faraway expression etched on his weathered face.

"Honey?" Dolores Litcomb leaned across the table and touched her husband's sleeve. "Is everything all right?"

"Yes." Daryl's voice was hollow. "I mean, no. I'm not feeling well." He looked up at his guests, and it was like he was seeing them for the first time. "I'm sorry, people, but you'll have to excuse me." And with no further explanation, the tall, lumbering man rose from the table and stumbled off toward the hotel lobby—or, to maintain the illusion, the front hall of his home.

"The scallops are poisoned," Georgina whispered, first to Amy, then to her other tablemates. "The scallops are poisoned."

"I don't think so," Amy said as she pointed to the central table.

Georgina followed Amy's gaze. "Oh. I guess this isn't going to be so easy."

"I hope not," said Amy.

Back at the spotlit table, Stew Rummy and Fidel were busy. They had divided the remains of Daryl's appetizer, scooping the round, creamy morsels into their own dishes, and now they were devouring them with systematic diligence. It was an uncharacteristic act, wildly out of place for both the men and the setting. But it served admirably, laying aside any theory about poisoned shellfish—for the time being.

Three more courses and three more scenes followed. The seven characters spent the time exposing the subtler facets of their one-dimensional personalities, and it was here, with most of the essential information already dispensed with, that the actors could shine. Humorous touches abounded.

Amy was relieved to see how much her guests were enjoying themselves. A little competition, a little faux danger, a little—very little—story. Their bodies were relaxed; their faces animated. *Like children,* she thought. *Wealthy, powerful children who can put aside their own lives for two full weeks and escape into a murderous little game.* Did she really envy them? *Yes,* she decided. She did.

Throughout the meal, Dolores Litcomb grew increasingly concerned. Finally, during the fruit and cheese, she excused herself from the table, promising to be back in a minute. "I just want to go check on Daryl."

The sumptuous meal, combined with cases of French wine, had numbed the few remaining inhibitions of the formally dressed detectives, and Dolores's departure was accompanied by a chorus of drunken catcalls.

"He's dead, honey."

"You need an alibi. Take someone with you."

"Don't scream."

"I want a good scream."

The actress ignored these intrusions from the fourth wall and disappeared into the Hotel Grimaldi's lobby.

Her return was timed to coincide with the arrival of dessert. The lack of a scream and the absence of blood on her dress disappointed the crowd's Grand Guignol faction, but there was good reason. Daryl, it turned out, wasn't dead. Just missing.

"He's not in his room," Dolores said. "The servants are checking the grounds, but . . ." And here she collapsed into her chair. "His room is a shambles, things thrown everywhere. What in the world could have happened?"

"He's been kidnapped," the TV soap star said.

"Nonsense," the drunken business partner blustered. "It's a big house. He's probably tucked away in some corner, reading a book."

The other actors, some with authentic reluctance, pushed aside their strawberry tarts. Each one had similar words of comfort. A proposal was made to cut short dinner and search the entire mansion.

"I'll check the wine cellar," Stew Rummy volunteered brightly and got a laugh.

As the actors made their way, Amy stood and applauded, signaling the end of the evening's performance. During the ovation that followed, the spotlight faded, the general lighting was bumped up to reading levels, and a cadre of waiters set about serving the players their own strawberry tarts, each one carefully delivered to a specific place setting.

"I'd like to thank the Litcombs and their guests for providing us with such an enjoyable dinner." Amy had taken a stance behind Daryl's empty chair. Making speeches embarrassed her, but they were part of the job. "And now I suppose you'd all like to know how this game works." She was grateful for the few chuckles and the rag-tag remnants of applause. "Good. As you know, this is going to be a team effort. Each team will represent one of the characters, except Daryl, of course, who is missing."

"And presumed dead," a male voice blurted out from table three.

"Not necessarily," Amy admonished. "We'll know more in the morning." Then she went on to explain the rules.

They would be divided into six teams of four each. Tonight in their rooms, each player would find a packet of information explaining their character's secret relationship with the missing industrialist. All six characters had some guilty secret they were hiding from the others. Naturally, this information had to be kept private and could be discussed only with members of one's own team.

Tomorrow morning each team would elect a captain, someone who wasn't afraid of a little role-playing, since he or she would be physically representing that team's character for the rest of the game.

"So, who the hell are we?" the same person demanded.

"Glad you asked." Amy smiled, feeling just a little more comfortable. "I don't mean to destroy your enjoyment of tonight's dessert, but before you polish it off, I might recommend a closer examination. On the inside crust of each tart is a number between one and six drawn in blue food dye." The last words were almost drowned out by a clattering of plates and forks.

Amy could see Georgina, her plate held at eye level, lifting the tart and peeking underneath. "No, no. The inside crust," Amy explained. "Under the strawberries.

And let this be your first lesson. For the next two weeks, nothing can be taken for granted."

It was a silly little gimmick, one that had required a lot of persuasion with a rather rigidly minded pastry chef. But the act of playing with food could provide a primal, childlike thrill, and the gimmick succeeded. Most of the diners eagerly scraped out their crusts and found their numbers. A few others artfully ate their strawberries one by one, until the number was revealed in a purple haze of food dye and fruit jam.

"Uncle Burt, don't." The voice was high and shrill, carrying like a piccolo.

Amy focused on the twelve-year-old girl at table two. She was pulling at the elbow of a thin, tall man in his midfifties, whose pleasant, open face was distorted by a wicked grin. It was a broad, sloppy grin, bulging with strawberries and laced with crumbs. Uncle Burt, it seemed, was in the process of eating not only the filling but the crust.

"It's delicious, Holly. You should taste it." And he held out a forkful to his horrified niece.

"Don't!" The intense young Holly was oblivious to the tease. She grabbed his wrist and wrestled it to the table. The uncle countered smoothly, using his free hand to snatch a dessert fork from another place setting and continue destroying all evidence of his team assignment.

Amy smiled. She had expected someone to pull this stunt and was glad it was a nice guy like Burt. Federal justice Burt Baker, a good-humored, guileless man who'd been crippled years ago in a traffic accident. The rally had been a present to his favorite niece, Holly, by far the youngest member of the tour.

If good humor and an even temper were Baker traits,

then they hadn't hit Holly's side of the family. Her fair, freckled skin turned an exasperated red, which nearly matched the crimson of her gown, a cut-down concoction that left too much room for bosom and shoulders. "Now we won't know what team you're on."

"Then they'll have to put me on yours," Burt declared. "Amy, put me on Holly's team, or I quit."

That was when the twelve-year-old finally got it. "Very funny."

It must be hard, Amy thought, *being born without a sense of humor.*

Most of the guests had been teamed with their travel mates. The exceptions were Georgina Davis and companion, who Amy hadn't even realized were traveling together. Marcus was a number four, a Fidel, while Georgina's purple six had placed her among the Dodos. A flighty, gossipy, oft-divorced heiress. The choice was so perfect that Amy had been a little afraid of giving offense. More than once she had changed Georgina to another team, then had changed her back. It was just so right.

The expected rainstorm never arrived. It had circumvented Monaco, circumvented the entire country, depositing only a sprinkling of drops on the terrace. Now that the evening's dinner theater was over, the maître d' opened the French doors, allowing a tropical breeze to invade the dining room, while his waiters worked the crowd with trays of assorted liquors.

The newly formed teams spent the time getting acquainted and discussing their characters. Above all the hubbub, Amy could hear Marcus's warm, distinctive laugh echoing off the high ceiling. She glanced around and caught sight of him at the center of the Fidels. The limp was nearly gone, she was glad to see.

Amy hadn't spoken to him since their arrival back at the hotel. In the taxi they had agreed not to inform the Monegasque police. There was nothing that could be done other than create needless paperwork, and both of them were anxious not to mar the festivities. Other than that, other than a rock thrown at Marcus's head and her own bumbling behavior, she was gratified by how well the first day had gone. Stifling a yawn, she wended her way toward the lobby and the stairs, which were inviting her up to the oblivion of a crisp, warm bed.

As she stepped from the carpeted dining room onto the black-and-white tile, Amy couldn't help feeling alone and out of place. All her guests were making friends, about to start out on a memorable adventure. And here she was, by herself, a non-player, a self-employed employee dedicated to everyone else's good time.

"Amy, sweetie. Calling it a night?"

She turned to see Georgina Davis behind her in the doorway.

"What a terrific kickoff," Georgina said, her heels clicking on the tile. The light from the dining room chandelier spilled around her, throwing a shadow across the checkered floor and further darkening the already spectral hall. "We Dodos are very excited, you know." The flat, meditative tone was back in her voice.

"Good." Amy tried to keep her eyes averted from the inviting staircase.

"By the way, was it Otto who decided which characters we're playing? No, that's right. You told me. He didn't know."

"It was me." Amy's heart sank. Georgina had taken offense. "There wasn't much rhyme or reason," she tried to explain. "I mean, I tried to match sexes and ages where I could. It's no reflection on anyone." Was she protesting too much?

"Yes, of course. It's all fiction."

"Right. You know, from what I've seen, Dodo Fortunof is a lot smarter than she appears."

"Yes, she is," Georgina agreed and betrayed not a hint of emotion. "And a bit of a mystery aficionado, I think. Our team has very high hopes."

Amy smiled—what else could she do?—then wished Georgina and her team all the luck in the world. Ten minutes later she was asleep, the sheets pulled cozily up over her head.

CHAPTER 4

The second act took place the next morning in the Litcombs' breakfast room, otherwise known as the hotel lounge. A buffet had been set up along the length of an antique credenza, and while the guests hovered and devoured and injected themselves with caffeine, the six remaining actors entered from the hall to continue the drama.

"Daryl must have run off," Stew Rummy offered, looking appropriately hungover. "There's clothes missing from his room and a suitcase. His Porsche is gone from the garage. The idea of foul play is preposterous."

"Why preposterous?" Dodo objected. "And why are you so adamant? No one's suggesting that *you* had anything to do with the foul play."

"Are you suggesting that I had something to do—"

"I just said I wasn't, you alcoholic twit."

Price Litcomb piped up. "I agree with Stew. Dad left on his own. Unless you think the servants waylaid him or that kidnappers somehow broke in."

Dodo wasn't convinced. "Why would he leave in the middle of dinner? What possible reason . . ."

"Shouldn't we call the police?" Dolores asked. Her meek suggestion was met with a silent chorus of disapproving glances.

"No police," Stew said, settling the matter. "Next week there's a new offering of Litcomb Industries stock. If word gets out that Daryl Litcomb is missing—"

"Next week?" Dolores was horrified. "You think he'll be missing a whole week?"

"I hope not," said Stew. "Then we'd have to withdraw the stock offering, and I need . . ." He cleared his throat. "The company needs that influx of cash."

"And don't forget Dad's will," Price reminded his mother. "As of now just about everything goes to that pet charity of his."

A ripple of laughter swept through the room. The players had already been informed that Daryl's pet charity was literally that—the American Animal Rights Federation, rather fancifully known as AARF.

"Dad finally agreed to change it," Price went on. "He was going to put us all back in. I'd like to check with our lawyers before doing anything."

The others all had their own reasons for not calling the police, making it clear to even the densest that no one in the house seemed to have a motive. Daryl's disappearance had been badly timed. Every one of the six suspects had some strong reason to keep Daryl Litcomb alive and in circulation.

"Did you find anything in his room?" Dolores asked her son, confirming last night's hint that the couple occupied separate bedrooms.

"I didn't look," said Price, "other than checking the closet. I thought Fidel . . . That's his job, personal secretary."

Dolores came perilously close to raising her voice. "You mean no one searched his room?"

"I thought you or Price would do it," said Fidel defensively. "After all, it's not my place . . ."

"Damn your place." Stew Rummy was marching out into the hall. "The most crucial room in the house and nobody's given it a thorough inspection."

"Where are you going?" Price yelled as he followed the businessman out.

Within seconds, the characters had evacuated the breakfast room and were all trudging up the marble staircase. As before, Amy led her guests in a round of applause.

"I'm sure you'll all agree that our cast did a splendid job." She was getting used to this speech making. "But now, I'm afraid, the easy part is over. For the next two weeks it will be up to you. Has each team chosen a captain?"

Since last night's dinner, all six teams had spent time together, reviewing the rules and planning strategies. As with most small groups, natural leaders had emerged, making the selection of team captains a rather organic process.

Judge Burt Baker had assumed leadership of the Price Litcombs, while Marcus's competence was obvious enough to get him picked for the Fidels. To no one's surprise, the irrepressible Georgina was elected head Dodo, a title that she herself took perverse pride in.

"All right," Amy said, writing down the last of the captains' names. "Time to begin. Are the Doloreses ready? Let's go search that room."

* * *

Judge Burt Baker and the Prices were the fifth team to get a crack at Daryl Litcomb's bedroom. In honor of the rally's inaugural morning, the jurist had outfitted himself with a plaid deerstalker cap and a magnifying glass, hardly the accessories that young Price Litcomb would have on hand, but festively appropriate. And the magnifying glass was proving to be an asset.

Burt had set aside his crutches and plopped himself in a chair directly in front of a low dresser. He was seated on the edge of the chair, leaning forward, his upper body balanced on the dresser itself, while his legs stretched out behind him as a counterweight. Somehow comfortable in this position, Burt used the magnifying glass to examine the ornamental woodwork directly above the lowest set of drawers. "Daryl kept mentioning this bureau." No one else appeared to be in the room, and to a casual observer, it might have seemed as if he were trying to explain his behavior to the invisible gods of mystery.

"He mentioned it once," said a whiny, disembodied voice.

"No," Burt argued. "At least twice."

"Have it your way. There's nothing under here." Holly, the smallest member of the team, had taken a flashlight and had crawled under the bed for a thorough search. A coughing fit signaled the possible inhalation of a dust bunny.

"Eureka," crowed Burt. "I knew it." He took a second to rebalance himself, then carefully pried a thin decorative panel out of the face of the dresser. The inlaid panel, no more than half an inch tall, formed the front of a shallow drawer, which Burt now slid effortlessly out of the rosewood facade. "I told you the bureau was important. Look. A note." He pushed himself upright in the chair and held up a folded slip of paper that had been slid into the narrow cavity.

From out of the connecting bathroom came Carla Templar, a middle-aged entertainment lawyer with offices in New York and L.A. She and her husband, Rod, always on the lookout for the newest trend in vacations, had been the first people to book the tour. Carla had distinguished herself in Amy's mind by asking for a discount for an early cash payment and, when that didn't happen, paying with a business credit card. Amy was sure this would surface somewhere as a tax deduction.

"What is it?" Carla asked. "Fan mail from some flounder?"

The Bullwinkle allusion was lost on both Burt and his niece, who had just emerged from under the bed. "A secret drawer?" Holly said skeptically. "That's stupid. How would kidnappers know about a secret drawer?"

"It's not from kidnappers. There were no kidnappers." Burt cleared his throat and read the note aloud.

> *I'm okay. Had to get away. I hid this where my pursuer would never think of looking. If you need to contact me, follow these directions:*
>> *Into three parts once divided,*
>> *Now portioned into twenty-two.*
>> *The generic portion holds the key,*
>> *Where Magdalene decided*
>> *To set up house you'll find me, too,*
>> *Beneath the bronze of Calvary.*

"It doesn't rhyme," Holly complained.

"Yes, it does," said Carla, who had never had a child

of her own, had never wanted one, and felt no particular need to be nice to this one.

"There's more," Burt interjected. "Don't call the police. My life depends on it. Love, Daryl."

Holly sneezed into a handkerchief, expelling the last of the dust. "That's dumb. I mean, leaving a poem that doesn't rhyme where anyone can find it."

"Daryl disguised his destination so his killer, pursuer, whatever, couldn't track him down," Burt reasoned.

"Why take all the time to write a poem? Why not send a text to someone he trusts?"

"Holly, dear." Carla feigned a patient tone that was anything but. "If he did that, it wouldn't be a game, would it? We're playing a game. Therefore, we get a rhyme. And yes, it rhymes—ABCABC. We're expected to use our brains to figure it out. Meanwhile, this is all part of a race. Now, I know the real Daryl wouldn't put his friends in a real race. However, this is—"

"Jeez, you're sarcastic."

"Holly!" warned her uncle.

"Holly and I are coming to an understanding," Carla said sweetly. "We're going to stop bickering at every turn and figure out this clue before our time is up and they kick us out of the room. Now, I know the real butler wouldn't kick us out of this room . . ."

"Just solve the damned clue."

"Holly!"

Holly and Carla ignored him. In fact, everyone ignored everyone else as the three crowded around the paper and silently reread the six lines.

"I have no idea," Burt said quietly. At least his admission served to break the ice.

"Into three parts divided," Carla mumbled. "That sounds familiar. Isn't that a Latin expression or something?" She looked to the judge. "You must have had some Latin."

Burt bit his lip. "All Gaul is divided into three parts. It's from Caesar's *Commentaries*. Gaul was the Roman name for France."

"We're right next to France," Holly pointed out.

"So we are," Carla said with just a hint of leftover sarcasm. "So, next line. France was divided into three parts and is now divided into twenty-two. Daryl always was a geography nut. That's why I killed him."

"Provinces," Holly corrected her. "France is divided into provinces."

"You're right," Carla admitted. "Provinces. It may be a good idea to pick up a French map."

Burt was still studying the note. "The generic portion. A generic province. What's a generic province?" He mulled it over for several seconds, then slapped himself on the forehead. "A generic province would simply be called province."

"Provence!" Holly shouted with a little jump in the air. For the first time today, she showed some excitement. "He means Provence!"

Even Carla knew enough to encourage it. "Of course. Well done. Daryl is hiding somewhere in Provence."

Holly had already grabbed the paper. She was out to solve everything now. "Where Magdalene decided . . . You think it's Mary Magdalene, like in Jesus?"

"That's the only Magdalene I know," said Burt.

"Mary Magdalene had a house in Provence?" asked Holly. "I thought she lived in Israel somewhere."

"Maybe she moved," Carla suggested with a glance at her watch. "Where can we buy a Bible?"

Holly smirked. "You think they put her forwarding address in the Bible?"

"Ladies," Burt growled as he stuffed the clue in his pocket, then reached for his crutches. "What we need is a Provence guidebook."

"What we need is Google," Holly countered.

Carla's husband, the fourth member of their team, was not particularly fond of mysteries. Rod Templar had been lured by the game's novelty and by the promise of a few good anecdotes. His contribution this morning had been to pack the luggage into the rented Mercedes, then to stand by, ready to roll, at the front curb.

Amy watched from an upstairs window as the Prices stumbled out the front door and into the waiting car. Burt eased his torso onto the front passenger seat. Holly and Carla each grabbed a leg, tossed it into the foot well, and slammed the door. And all the while, all three continued to argue and point and babble conflicting directions to Rod, their driver. Like a luxury clown car, the Mercedes sprang away from the curb in fits and starts. Halfway down the block it nearly collided with a furniture van.

Amy smiled, then set about placing a new note in the thin secret drawer and slipping it back into place. Team Six, the Dodos, were the next and the last.

So far only one team, the Bitsys, had failed to discover the note. From her second-floor window, Amy had watched as the four women solved their problem by driving off, circling the block, then pulling up around the corner to wait for the next team.

When the Fidels came running out a few minutes later, the Bitsys were ready. Amy saw them ease around the corner and follow the Fidels, staying a discreet distance back, until both cars disappeared from view. And if they were to somehow lose sight of the Fidels? Well, then, Amy supposed, they would be forced to use the desperation phone number.

Otto had set it up. A lost team could call the number and punch in its team code. A recording would then give out the address for that day's final destination, in this case a converted villa in Aix-en-Provence. At the end of each day, Amy would check to see if any code numbers had been used. These teams would be penalized, and they'd lose out on any mystery clues that had been gathered along the way.

The Dodos had been set loose in the bedroom for only two minutes when Amy heard Georgina shrieking with excitement. *Good.*

Amy wandered down the marble stairs to the front desk, thanked the hotel owner once again, then took a narrow set of uncarpeted stairs to the garage. No Mercedes was waiting for her, just a cute little Mini Cooper, all gassed up and ready to head out to the shrine at Sainte-Baume, where she would hide the first packets of clues.

She figured she had half an hour on them, plus the advantage of GPS. By the time the first team found the shrine and the next clue, Amy would be gone. She'd be planting the second group of packets at a nice little café, a perfect spot for everyone to stop for lunch.

Two more sets of clues would lead them to Aix-en-Provence, where Amy would be waiting at the hotel with her trusty stopwatch, recording their times. She estimated the last team's arrival at 6:00 p.m., in plenty of time for a shower and cocktails, followed by a leisurely dinner at what Michelin described as a delightful garden restaurant.

CHAPTER 5

Amy arranged the chair on her balcony to face the western sky, where the evening sun was playing in the trees at the far end of the grounds. Soon it would hit the ivy-covered wall, giving the garden its own premature sunset. Determined to enjoy the last rays of the day, Amy squeezed herself, laboriously squeezed herself, into the wooden chair and reached for her end-of-the-road Campari and soda.

Hers was a ridiculously small single, barely more than a closet. It had been the only accommodation left after she'd reserved the fifteen suites for her guests. The room's one saving grace was that it opened onto the rear garden, with a balcony just large enough to hold a chair, if one took the trouble to move the potted geraniums into the room, which was what she'd done.

The Doloreses, the last of the teams, had checked in five minutes ago, not at all discouraged by their placing. In fact, they'd been flushed with pride at just getting here without having to resort to the phone number.

The one all-male team—the Stew Boys, as they called themselves—had won the first day's leg and was celebrating in a small raised area outside, a *pétanque* court, sandwiched between the garden proper and the western stone wall. The foursome was boisterous as only winners could be as they played their own version of the French bowling game, which was itself a version of the Italian game boccie. From what Amy could see, they had also mixed in elements of shuffleboard. The result seemed to work well enough to keep them happy.

The air was loud with birds and dry, still warm from the lingering sun. It had been an exciting, exhausting day. Amy had managed to stay a few minutes ahead of the teams, hiding the clue packets at one site before driving on to do it again at another.

The last clue was a note from Daryl, saying he would be spending the night in a nearby town. Attached was a custom-made crossword puzzle. Once you filled in the blanks and stared at it long enough, you would realize that nearly all the entries were synonyms for other entries. Only three answers in the finished puzzle didn't have synonymous matches. Old capital, Hugo, and Cézanne. Once this discovery was made, the rest was simple. A check of any tourist guide would show that in the old capital of Aix-en-Provence, there was a small luxury hotel called Hotel Cézanne, located on avenue Victor Hugo.

Amy had arrived to find the desk clerk holding a packet of clues and instructions from Otto Ingo. Tomorrow's itinerary. Amy had read them over, to make sure there weren't any surprises, then had ordered a drink.

As she sipped her Campari, the teams mingled around the bar that had been set up two stories beneath her minuscule perch. Soon enough she would have to play the host and join them. But for right now she was content to sit in the fading sunlight and listen to the birds and the rich, soothing babble of her clients.

The sound of a Harvard-bred honk alerted Amy to the presence of Burt Baker. She readjusted her cramped knees and her red Versaces and peered down through the iron bars to catch a view. "It was Holly who thought to look it up on Wikipedia," Burt was explaining to an audience of middle-aged Bitsys.

"We wound up following the Fidels," the Bitsy captain whispered, then exploded into a giggle. Martha Callas was not the sort of person one would imagine giggling at anything. Martha was tall, as was her hair, tall and silver and firmly lacquered. Like so much about her, the giggles were an affectation. Something about her reminded Amy of Georgina Davis. The two women were worlds apart, of course—a Palm Beach heiress versus a Dallas decorator. But both were dramatic and larger than life, each a shameless promoter of her own version of femininity.

The main difference, Amy felt, was that Martha tried too hard. Georgina's drama was effortless and amiable, the result of a lifetime of privilege. Martha's was forced, the drama of a second-rate actor who doesn't quite believe in the role. Perhaps that had evolved out of the necessity of a freelance living, Amy mused, always having to impress clients with your taste and style.

"Following the Fidels?" Burt gasped. "Ladies, I'm shocked."

The other Bitsys tittered or smiled guiltily. All were either single like Martha or, for some other reason, traveling alone.

"What exactly was that first clue?" asked Martha in a stage whisper. "We never did see it."

Burt recited the clue verbatim, then took great pleasure in explaining. "It seems that after the crucifixion,
Mary Magdalene, her brother Lazarus, and a few assorted others were set adrift in a boat. Somehow they
wound up landing in France."

"It's just a legend," Holly interjected. "It never happened."

"Who knows about legends! Anyway, after arriving
here, the Magdalene went off by herself and set up house
in this cave in the mountains. *Supposedly,*" Burt added to
appease his niece. "For over twelve hundred years
French peasants have been making pilgrimages to the
cave at Sainte-Baume."

"Well, it certainly was a beautiful drive," Martha
drawled.

"If you follow someone else's car, that's cheating,"
said Holly.

"Yes, dear. But you have to realize it was quite in character—following our handsome Fidel, I mean. Oops."
The other Bitsys glared as Martha clamped a hand over
her mouth. "I suppose I shouldn't have said that."

"Well, well. Our haughty TV star has the hots for
Fidel," the judge deduced with a sly grin. "What else has
Bitsy been up to?"

"Don't listen to her, Uncle Burt. She's trying to
throw us off."

Martha slicked a manicured hand back over her hair.
"Yes, dear. I'm just trying to throw you off. Pay no attention to anything I say."

Martha and the Bitsys, their drinks refreshed, wandered away, probably in search of a less critical audience.
Burt and Holly wandered in the opposite direction, replaced at the bar by Georgina and the Dodos. Amy was
surprised by how, for the most part, the teams were

sticking together. She supposed there was a kind of bonding going on, which she supposed was good.

If only Otto could be here to see his game in action. Amy considered violating the rules and putting through a call to New York. The peculiar little man had insisted on not being contacted except in a dire emergency. But Amy was sure that any writer would like to hear a flattering report.

"Third place is certainly respectable," Paul Wickes said hesitantly to his Dodo teammates. The headmaster of a Virginia prep academy, Paul was as prim and contained as Georgina wasn't. "Besides, it's not the daily times that decide the winner. It's solving the mystery."

"We may have an advantage there," Georgina said in an uncharacteristic whisper. She glanced around for possible eavesdroppers but didn't think to glance up. Taking a few steps out of the traffic pattern now placed her and her cohorts directly under Amy's balcony. "I think this mystery is based on a real crime."

"No!" Paul said, letting his mouth hang open. Two stories up, Amy's jaw also dropped.

"It's much too corny to be actually true," a third Dodo observed. "What makes you think . . ."

"Well . . ." Georgina cleared her throat. "The real story didn't take place in the south of France." She raised a hand to her cheek, as if to ward off a blush. "But there was an heiress involved. And she did have a few divorces behind her—none of them totally her fault, mind you."

"No!" Paul repeated. "You're the real Dodo?"

"I think so, yes."

"That's unbelievable," said Paul.

"I can hardly believe it myself."

"The odds against that must be astronomical," the third Dodo objected.

"I don't know about odds," Georgina said. "But I saw the similarities from the beginning. Even the menu, at least I think. It was five years ago at a weekend party. And there was the host getting up halfway through dinner and walking out. And then the disappearance—except we called in private detectives, of course."

"What happened?" Paul demanded, his primness disappearing. "Was he ever found? Was he killed? Who killed him? This is so macabre."

"Hey, Amy!"

The words were shouted and startling. Frank Loyola and his *pétanque*/boccie/shuffleboard-playing teammates had finished their game and were walking down the steps back to the garden. Amy and her third-story balcony lay directly above their line of sight, and it hadn't taken much of an effort for Frank to see her.

The captain of the Stew Boys was a large man with a voice that carried. "You look like some bird in a cage. Why don't you come down and join us?" At least half the crowd had heard Frank's initial greeting. Now the entire tour was glancing up at her postage stamp–size balcony. A scattered few waved.

Amy smiled wanly and looked everywhere but at Georgina. She had to be staring directly up. Was it a friendly stare or a hostile one? Amy didn't dare risk finding out. "I'm coming," she said to everyone but Georgina and reached for her drink.

That evening, all through cocktails and dinner and after-dinner socializing, Amy was desperate to make a call. For someone who'd never been good at hiding emotions, she did well, smiling and pretending nothing was wrong. It was a few minutes after midnight when she was finally able to tear herself away.

The local cell service, she discovered, vacillated between spotty and nonexistent. She was forced instead to use the landline that the owners had someone managed to squeeze into her room. Several calls and several recorded messages later, Amy gave up and dialed a different number, a number she'd first memorized in preschool.

"Mom? Hi," she said, as if they were across town from each other and not across an ocean. "Going great. Look, I'm trying to get in touch with Otto Ingo. His phone seems to be disconnected or dead or . . ."

"Dead," Fanny said. It was dinnertime in New York, and she had just sat down to a warmed-up casserole. "Otto's dead. Not his phone. Him."

"Come again?" Amy had heard fine. She just wanted to give it a second chance.

"Otto's dead. He was murdered Thursday, less than an hour after I wrote the check. Bad luck, huh?"

"Wow!" The air hung heavy on the line as Amy tried to process the information.

"You still there?"

Amy cleared her throat. "Uh, what exactly do you mean, murdered?"

"I mean shot dead with a gun."

"That'll do." Amy was still processing. "What happened? I mean, was he mugged? A family dispute? No, of course. He had no family."

"They don't know who or why. The police were here this morning. They'd found our check in his wallet. I wonder if anyone's going to cash it."

"His estate will, although it's hard to think of Otto with a will and an executor. Have the police contacted Otto's assistant? He should be informed."

"I asked the detective about that. He said he would look through Otto's records for a name, but I think that's pretty low on their list."

"We have to get in touch with his assistant."

"I know. Oh, and his apartment was ransacked."

"Then it was robbery. No. You said he still had his wallet." Amy was surprised at how analytically she was taking all this. Perhaps it was the distance between them, or the fact that she'd played murder games all her life and these were the standard opening gambits. Eliminating the possibility of robbery. Narrowing down the suspects. "Do you think the killer found what he was looking for? The motive couldn't be—"

"Motive? Amy, this isn't one of your little puzzles. Who knows why people kill people in real life?"

"Mom, you don't have to tell me."

Fanny was sobered by the reminder. "I'm sorry, dear. But then, you know better than anyone that some murders are senseless and don't get solved. They're not like your books."

"You're right. This is real," Amy agreed. But unlike Eddie's murder, this one did feel like a book. A man had been killed just hours after selling them a mystery game, a game that no one but an unnamed assistant knew the solution to, a game that might be based on a real-life murder. "Mom, I think we should cancel."

She realized almost as soon as she said it that this was impossible. Too much money had been spent, money that would have to be refunded in full since there was no concrete reason why the rally couldn't continue. Everything was going smoothly, even if she didn't know much more than the players knew. At each hotel along the way, packets were already awaiting her arrival.

To Amy, the idea of blindly following clues left by a dead man was ghoulish at best and probably dangerous. But her pampered guests wouldn't see it that way. Her own mother didn't see it that way, even after she informed her of Georgina's claim.

"So?" Fanny replied, unimpressed. "A lot of fiction is taken from real life. If Otto had based the game on Jack the Ripper, would you still want to cancel?"

"Jack the Ripper is dead."

"And so is Otto," she countered, with logic so arcane that Amy had no idea how to respond.

"Can I at least tell them about Otto's death? Would that be acceptable?"

"Of course. But don't mention the murder."

"Don't they have a right to know?"

Fanny's sigh was almost deafening. "Amy, dear, it would just worry them. And worrying won't do any good. Right? If Otto's assistant really does exist—"

"*If*? What do you mean, if?"

"Don't go off the deep end. But the thought crossed my mind. Otto might have made up the part about an assistant, just to placate us and hike up his fee."

"He exists," Amy insisted. "Why do you have to make things worse? He's following the tour, like Otto said. Maybe he's actually on the tour. That's possible."

"Fine," Fanny said. "Then the two of you can do the worrying for everyone."

"Okay, okay," Amy shot back. "I'm sorry I called. We'll handle it on our own."

CHAPTER 6

In the breakfast room the next morning, she broke the news, being careful not to imply a violent death, merely an unexpected one. Her guests seemed momentarily saddened, the same way they might react to the news of an earthquake in China or the death of an old film star they'd assumed was already dead.

"This was Otto Ingo's very last game," Burt Baker said with gravity and a touch of pride. "We should dedicate it to his memory."

Amy had never understood what dedicating something meant. It wouldn't change the game's outcome or how it was played or even what they were thinking as they played it. People liked to dedicate things. But what did it mean? She was in a cynical mood.

By acclamation, the living detectives dedicated their efforts to the deceased game master, then turned back to their coffee and croissants. Amy was tempted to ask Otto's assistant to identify himself—if he was there, which was by no means a sure thing. But under the circumstances, mere seconds after the announcement of Otto's death, she felt it would be too much like asking if there was a doctor in the house or a licensed pilot on the plane.

The luggage had already been taken care of, transported from the hotel hallways to the covey of waiting cars. Meanwhile, the teams were finishing up their breakfast and wondering where their first clue of the day would come from. When the sound of breaking dishes erupted from the nearby kitchen, they were ready.

The breakfast room fell silent. Into that stillness floated a muffled curse. A woman's voice. Then came another crash, like a dish being thrown against a wall.

Amy was pleased at how well the noisemaker was working. The owners of Hotel Cézanne, an older British couple, wonderfully friendly and cooperative, had placed some broken tiles and pieces of china in a wooden box. It was their own invention. Dropping the box onto the kitchen floor produced a nicely realistic sound. After the second crash of crockery, the dialogue started— raised, angry voices, which everyone in the breakfast room could recognize as belonging to their hosts.

"You mean he didn't give you a credit card?" the wife was heard shouting. "Not even for security?"

"He insisted on paying cash," the husband moaned. A note of authenticity flavored his hen-pecked performance. "We have to accept cash. It's the law."

"But no one pays cash. Only drug dealers and runaway convicts."

A swarm of players were pressing their ears against the swinging door, all convinced that the "he" in question was their runaway friend, Daryl.

The husband tried to explain. "When he checked out, he said he hadn't made any calls. The system must not have updated the computer. So, the fellow cheated us out of one trunk call. Hardly the end of the world."

"Idiot." The crockery box dropped again, eliciting a startled jump from the mass of humanity piled against the door. "You never checked the computer, Nigel. Did you?" A practiced sigh. "All right. Where was the call to? How much was it for?"

"I have it written down right here."

Pens were withdrawn from pockets and purses.

The phone number was barely out of the man's mouth when there was a stampede from the breakfast room. From there they went scurrying in every direction, some to their cell phones, some out to the cars, others racing upstairs to use their room phones. Amy waited in the breakfast room, out of harm's way. She had been up early, driving to Aubagne to plant the first clues, fighting the maddeningly slow farm traffic on one-lane roads, and getting back just in time to make her sad announcement. Now she relaxed over a croissant and a café au lait. By the time she cleaned her plate, the lobby was empty.

"Thanks a mint," she said, walking up to the registration desk. "What a performance."

Nigel Yardley glanced up from the computer, his green eyes twinkling over his half-glasses. "Our pleasure. Marley adores amateur theatricals. It's the one thing we miss, living here." The owner's gaze fell back to the monitor. "I suppose you want to know the damage our little scene caused." He laughed, a thick Yorkshire chortle. "Unlike my fictional counterpart, I'm checking the computer."

"A few calls to the French Foreign Legion headquarters in Aubagne?" Amy guessed.

Nigel's finger scanned down the list. "Four. Room two-seventeen called twice. They must have been skeptical."

"Who can blame them? Daryl is a bit old to be enlisting. Maybe he has something to forget."

"There must be one very confused receptionist at the Foreign Legion." Nigel chuckled. "I hope your people were discreet."

"Me too. Do the French give prison time for crank calls?"

"Hmm." Nigel frowned as he tapped a line of green print. "And one trunk call to the States."

"To the States? That must have been from before."

"No. It's right here with the others. Room two-oh-four. Nine twenty-six a.m. A seven-one-eight city code."

"Area code," Amy corrected him, as she eased her way around the counter. Nigel adjusted the angle of the screen. "You're right. I wonder why someone would take the time."

"Yes," Nigel wondered as well. "They all seemed to be in quite the rush. Hardly the time to call home and chat. The seven-one-eight code is for . . ."

"The New York area. Brooklyn."

Nigel tapped a few more keys. "Two-oh-four is a single. Nice-looking fellow."

"Marcus Alvarez."

"His home is in Brooklyn?"

"Palm Beach, as far as I know. How long was the call?"

"Three minutes and change." Nigel could sense the travel agent's unease. He flourished a pen from his jacket pocket. "Do you wish to jot down the number?"

"No," Amy said without thinking. "No," she added with thinking. She was ashamed of her curiosity. "What do I owe?"

"Are you sure?" Nigel asked, his pen poised over a notepad.

"No," Amy repeated. "How much do I owe?" She was going to ignore it. That was the best way to deal with almost anything.

CHAPTER 7

Vinny Mrozek stroked his bushy mustache and struggled to recall the French he'd been forced to learn all those years ago. "These museums ought to write things in English." Vinny's twin sons stood behind him. They were studying the old, historical print and working on their own interpretation of the plaque beneath it.

Dominick, the more analytical one, pointed to the central figure, a large-breasted woman standing on the top battlements of a seaside fort. She was facing away from the sea, and her hands were behind her back. Despite the yellowing paper and the complex cross-hatching, it seemed obvious that the woman was lifting up the rear section of her dress. "Looks like she's mooning the guys on the ship out there."

Donovan snorted, then stopped. "Hey, that's it. She's mooning them. Outrageous." He pointed, his finger smudging the dusty glass. "Dad, you see this? Dad?"

Their father grunted. "According to this, the woman's name was Caterina, a kind of local Joan of Arc. When Barbarosa and his pirates attacked, Caterina marched up and down the roof of the fort and, uh . . . she lifted up her *jupon,* you know, and, uh, showed the pirates her, uh . . ."

"Her butt," Donovan shouted, his voice echoing down the spiral ramps of the ancient stone keep.

"Hindquarters," Vinny said, using the translation he recalled from his days in cooking school.

"I'll say." Dominick's eyes strayed from the figure and for the first time took in the rest of the print. "This is the same fort, isn't it? This is where she mooned them."

The Naval Museum, an imposing stone fortress overlooking the Nice harbor, had indeed been the site of Caterina's defiance, and for perhaps the only time in their lives, the Mrozek twins felt a connection to history.

"Maybe that's what we're supposed to do next," Donovan suggested. "You know, go up to the roof and . . ." He turned. "Hey, Jolynn," he shouted, his voice echoing down the ramp. "Look at this. You're supposed to wave that little flag and moon the city."

"Augh," screamed Dominick in mock horror. "Show them your butt, Jolynn. Then we win."

"And they lose."

Vinny tried to hush his sons. All through the trip they'd been teasing their new stepmother, egging her on. He hoped she hadn't heard this latest, but who was he kidding? Jolynn could hear insults that hadn't yet been spoken. And this one had been shouted through a nearly empty fort.

"Dom. Don. Enough already."

This vacation had been Jolynn's idea. Vinny had never suspected her of being a mystery fan. When she read at all, it was a magazine or a star biography. But she had somehow latched on to the notion of using this rally to bring her closer to the seventeen-year-old boys, Vinny's boisterous, football-playing baggage from a previous marriage. If it worked, he figured it would be worth the extravagance.

It wasn't working.

Jolynn was nearly twenty years younger than Vinny, late twenties to his late forties. She stood a good six inches below his brawny six feet plus, and the wedding pictures from three months ago showed her posing among the hulking Mrozeks, looking dour and dark and overwhelmed. Her black hair and exotic good looks stood in sharp contrast to the dirty blond homeliness that Vinny had inherited and passed on to his sons. She was their opposite in almost every way, as flinty and hard as Vinny was overstuffed and soft.

The interior of the Naval Museum was little more than a huge spiral ramp five stories high, with display cases and paintings and an occasional cell off to the side, where the larger pieces of ancient weaponry were on display.

Jolynn trudged her way up to the fifth-floor level, pulling herself along the iron rail that jutted from the stone wall. Upon arriving, she proceeded to ignore her stepsons and shove a miniature flag into Vinny's paw. Her lilac perfume seemed strong enough to stir the flag into a flutter. "What the hell are we supposed to do with this?" she demanded.

They had been handed the strange multicolored flag at the museum's entrance by the man from the rental car agency. Against Jolynn's piercing protests, he had insisted on taking back their Mercedes, luggage and all, exchanging it for this flag.

"I'm not sure we were supposed to come in here," Vinny said. "I mean, they take our car, right? Which means there's got to be another mode of transportation. A boat or a train."

"This is supposed to be a road rally." Although not technically a complaint, Jolynn whined it with the same intonation, and the boys registered it as yet another mark against her. "Why would they take away our car?"

"It's a mystery to me," Dominick quipped for the hundredth time. Snatching the flag from his father's hand, the teen wandered up the ramp toward the open battlements. "What country is this from? Does anyone have a clue?"

"I still think Jolynn's supposed to show her butt," Donovan cracked as he joined his brother in the dappled sunlight.

"They're just teasing," Vinny cooed soothingly as they reached the roof of the fort and followed the boys outside. "They know how it gets to you."

"Of course it gets to me. If you had raised them to be a little respectful . . ."

Only the faintest of breezes disturbed the air. The smell of the sea was mixed with a hint of diesel—and Jolynn's lilacs. Vinny had always had a sensitive nose. It was part of what made him a great chef. His initial attraction to Jolynn, he suspected, had been at least partly based on lilacs.

"Damn. Look at this!" Donovan was yelling excitedly from the far side of the roof. "I found it. I found another flag." When Jolynn and Vinny caught up with the twins, they were standing by the battlements, fishing in their jeans for change.

"Anybody got a euro?" Dominick asked. His hand came out of his empty pocket and pointed to a duplicate of their tiny flag. The cheap, colorful cloth was taped to the side of a pair of pay-per-view binoculars.

*   *   *

Amy paced back and forth along the quai Lunel, peering up the streets leading to the Naval Museum, cleaning her glasses every minute, as if it would help. She'd been dreading this kind of situation, but sooner or later it was bound to occur. The first two days had been nearly flawless. The clues had been challenging without being impossible, and her game-loving guests had concluded each day in the glow of their own glory, sitting out on moon-swept terraces, sharing their tales of adventure. Even teams finishing well down the list took pride in their conquest of Otto's diabolical puzzles.

The endless job of dealing with high-paying clients had left Amy with little time to think about her problems. Otto was dead and the game was on autopilot, with the promised, paid-for assistant nowhere in sight. The game was based on a real millionaire's disappearance, and Georgina had been involved. Someone had thrown a rock at Marcus, and Marcus had, in turn, made an inexplicable call to Brooklyn. Amy preferred to ignore all this and sweat the small stuff.

She paced another circuit of the quai and checked her watch. Five of the six teams were on board *L'Albatros*. The impressive silver-white cabin cruiser was supposed to be at this moment ferrying the group from mainland France to the island of Corsica. But where were the Doloreses?

Paul Wickes, the Virginia headmaster, had miraculously recognized the old Corsican flag as soon as the Dodos handed in their car keys. They had arrived at the gangplank nearly two hours ago and were now relaxing on deck with their drinks.

Burt Baker and the Prices had arrived twelve minutes later, having done it purely by logic. It was, after all, a road rally. Giving up their car in a port city could mean only one thing. It was a short walk from the Naval Museum to the harbor, and *L'Albatros* was easy to spot. Among all the pleasure yachts and tourist boats, it was the only vessel flying a full-size version of the antiquated flag.

According to Otto's instructions, if the last team did not arrive within an hour and a half of the first, the boat was required to cast off. The latecomers would be left to telephone the Paris number and find their own way to Corsica, probably by the mid-afternoon ferry. A true gamesman, Otto had operated on the theory that a few harsh consequences would serve to heighten the adventure and make it more real. But then, Otto had never met Jolynn.

Amy could predict the woman's reaction. "We paid for passage on that boat, not on some stinking, smelly ferry." Every tour had a few malcontents. In this case, Jolynn Mrozek had single-handedly taken on the job.

"Any sight of the doleful Doloreses?" Frank Loyola shouted down from the bow. Day three and Jolynn was already a legend. Ten minutes ago the captain had blasted his horn. Twenty of the players were on board and anxious to get moving. "The captain's talking overtime," Frank added. Amy wasn't sure if she was being teased or not.

Reluctantly, she raised a hand toward the bridge, signaling the captain to cast off. The deckhands waited for Amy to reboard, then began to unhinge the gangway. And that was when someone finally spotted the Mrozeks racing down the pier.

"How can you expect anyone to see that flag?" Jolynn said breathlessly as Amy ushered her up the restored gangway. "It's a good thing one of us had a euro." Her eyes fell on the others. "Are people eating already? Is it a buffet? I hate being late at a buffet."

Their opponents greeted them with the kind of good-natured ribbing that Vinny appreciated, the teenage twins endured, and Jolynn resented.

"If I'd known we were going to pay all this money to be laughed at . . . Oh. Box lunches," she observed.

What would have been a six-hour ferry ride was reduced to under four by the power and design of the yacht. It was a perfect length of time to enjoy the cry of the gulls, the Mediterranean's salty spray, the sight of one scenic landmass receding and another one approaching. In between was a leisurely lunch. For those needing more stimulation, there were cards and board games and an Agatha Christie movie playing in the below-deck lounge.

The Mrozeks sat in a sheltered nook of the sundeck. The New Jersey family was at work on their box lunches, layering the cuts of prosciutto and smoked beef and the slices of provolone onto fresh baguettes, then lacing them with sliced tomatoes and red leaf lettuce. Dominick was the first to finish off his sandwich. He ignored the apple and pear and turned to the impressive slice of icebox cake that had been placed in a plastic bubble at the bottom of his box.

"How's the cake?" Burt Baker asked as he hobbled past their corner. Jolynn noticed Burt's sly smile and recalled that this wasn't the first time he'd hobbled past. Others were staring at them, as well, pretending not to.

"Good," Dominick mumbled. He swallowed and prepared for a second bite.

"Why is he asking about the cake?" Jolynn hissed, suspicion rising in her voice. Reaching into her box, she retrieved her own plastic bubble. Right away she could see a design in white and red decorating the chocolate top, a design composed of thin lines of frosting that were not centered on the slice but went straight to the edge, as if part of a larger pattern. "Are we eating some-one's birthday . . . ?" Then her mind flashed back to the inaugural dinner and the strawberry tarts. "Oh, my God. Dominick! Stop. The cake is a clue."

The other Mrozeks froze in mid-bite, sandwiches dangling from their mouths. Blankly, they stared at Do-minick and the half-destroyed field of icing.

"Shit," he mumbled, crumbs dropping from his chin.

"Damn. They don't even let you enjoy lunch." Jolynn gingerly took the piece of cake from her stepson's hands and placed it on the white scarf that they'd thrown over the vent cover to form their makeshift table. "Don't just sit there," she ordered her family. "Get out your cakes. Careful with the frosting."

A small crowd had gathered, keeping a respectful, perhaps fearful distance as Jolynn arranged her slice next to Dom's half-eaten ruin. She was trying to match up the red and white lines.

"Is it a message?" Vinny asked. "Maybe it's a map. We're lucky Jolynn's so observant, aren't we, boys?"

"Shut up, Vinny. We're a laughingstock."

But no one was laughing. Whatever good-natured fun might have been sparked by the situation had been doused by Jolynn's blanket of bile. Vinny and his twins probably would have enjoyed their predicament, all harmless attention and good humor. They probably would have erupted into big, embarrassed grins and re-ceived a hearty round of applause. But not with Jolynn.

"You can still decipher it," Burt offered from a safe twenty feet away. "It's a clue about Napoleon's birth-place. On Corsica." He was rewarded with a punch in the arm from his niece.

"That's cheating."

"Just trying to preserve the peace."

"We don't need your condescending help," snarled Jolynn.

Burt Baker sighed and checked his watch. The four-hour ride suddenly seemed like an eternity.

CHAPTER 8

Corsica would be a two-day stop. The chance to actually unpack had put everyone in a more relaxed mood, and allowed them to focus on things other than Daryl and his incessant travels. At dinner on the first night, Amy promised that nothing game related would occur before 2:00 p.m. tomorrow. No surprises. After that, they could expect the same unexpected chases and red herrings, secure only in the knowledge that whatever happened, they would be spending a second night at the Bellevue Grande Hotel. By the time dessert arrived, everyone had made plans, some for a morning on the beach, some for a relaxed brunch. No one suggested driving along the winding, rugged roads. They would be getting plenty of that when the game resumed tomorrow at two.

"Amy. Yoo-hoo, Amy." The female voice carried well on the evening air.

The sound of someone calling her name had long ago ceased being pleasant. Amy continued down the long wooden stairs from the cantilevered hotel to the beach. She tuned out the voice and concentrated on the soft rush of surf on sand and breathing in the distinctive perfume of Corsica. The sweetly scented mixture of myrtle, lavender, and a host of other wild shrubs was unique to this island, an ever-present fragrance. Napoleon once declared, "I would recognize Corsica with my eyes closed."

"Amy!" It was no longer avoidable. She waited until reaching the sand, then slapped on a welcoming smile and turned.

Georgina Davis, sandals flapping against the wooden steps, was hurrying down to catch her. "I kept calling," she panted. "You were so deep in thought."

Amy began to stroll along the beach. Georgina fell in beside her. Neither one spoke, which gave the moment a strange feeling of importance. For a while they trudged side by side, the dying froth nipping at their feet. Back at the hotel on the cliff, a Portuguese fado played on the speakers, a lament of melody and voice drifting down from the terrace.

"All those Napoleon clues today. And then Corsica?" Georgina wasn't comfortable with too much silence. "Daryl has a Napoleon complex." She paused for a reply that didn't come. "The Dodos think we'll wind up in Elba, the place where he was exiled."

"Are you pumping me?" Amy asked.

"Just making conversation." They were approaching an outcropping of rock that marched out into the Mediterranean and marked the end of the beach. "I guess when we finally do catch up with Daryl, he'll be dead."

"I suppose. This is a murder mystery."

"You suppose? You're the cruise director. You must know how it turns out."

Lying was an effort for Amy, one that she didn't quite

feel up to tonight. "No, I don't. There's a packet waiting for me in Rome with the final scenes in it. We'll find out then. Otto insisted on this kind of secrecy."

Georgina mulled over the revelation. "What a strange man. And you feel comfortable with this?"

"No, of course not." Amy pivoted on her heel and began to retrace their steps in the wet sand. Georgina followed.

"I see." She spoke slowly, her face turned toward the dark sea. "In light of Otto's death, I think there's something you should know." It was almost a whisper. "This mystery of ours really happened."

Amy exhaled with relief. She hadn't even been aware of holding her breath. She'd done her best to forget what Georgina had told her team, to shove it as far back in her mind as it would go. Now she didn't reply, purposely leaving a vacuum, which both nature and Georgina seemed to abhor.

"Five years ago. The man was Fabian Carvel." She said the name as if Amy would recognize it, which she sort of did. "You know. Food Services? They own several chains, including Tico Taco. Tico Taco was the very first Mexican fast food. Fabian invented the concept." The phrases sounded memorized, a testimonial that had been passed on to her and that she passed on in turn.

"We were at his Long Island estate." Georgina continued to fill the pauses. "There were six of us at dinner, just like in the game. Fabian's wife, their son . . . a very similar set of circumstances." She kept at Amy's side, gazing down at the tiny crabs that scurried away from the vibrations of their feet.

"It was somewhere in the second or third course that Fabian left the table. He claimed to be feeling ill. I thought it might be a mood swing. Fabian had them, you know.

Unlike Daryl, our real-life tycoon had been known to walk out on people."

"How did you know Fabian?" It was Amy's first comment since the start of Georgina's confession.

"We met one winter, when he and Doris rented a house near mine in Palm Beach."

"Doris?"

"His wife. Doris? Dolores?" Her eyes never lifted from the sand. "Anyway, after he left the dining room, no one saw him again. And, just like in the game, everyone had some reason not to notify the police."

"What was your reason?"

Georgina tittered, perhaps at the ridiculousness of the question. "Nearly everyone. You know what I mean, the same sort of thing with the inheritance and the stock offering. I tell you, when I heard those actors doing their speeches, you could have knocked me over with a feather."

"So, you didn't go to the police."

"The family put out the story that Fabian was ill, then hired a private detective. It was a secret investigation. There weren't any rhyming clues or other such nonsense. But they were able to trace him through his credit cards. Columbus, Chicago, Salt Lake. I'm making that up. But they were all cities leading west."

"His own little road rally."

"It does lend itself to that format," she conceded. "For about a week, no one heard anything. And then Stu Romney received an e-mail from Fabian himself."

Amy started. Had she heard right? "Stew Rummy?"

"No, no. Stu Romney. Another little play on names. You can't fault Otto for his sense of humor. Now, where was I? Oh, yes, the e-mail. Fabian claimed it had been some business emergency that took him away. He was back in San Diego. That's where he'd founded the company. San Diego. The e-mail told Stu to fly out there right away. Stu was to check in at the Marriott or the Sheraton or the Hyatt—one of those—and wait there for a phone call."

"Was the e-mail really from Fabian?"

Georgina shrugged. "The detective was suspicious. He suggested all six of us go out there together, not just Stu."

"You mean all six of you flew out to San Diego? Why?"

"Well, we were all of us worried and curious, and I had the free time and . . . Oh, I see what you're asking. Why did the detective want all six of us to go?"

"He must have suspected one of you of being involved."

Georgina stopped trudging through the sand and glanced sideways, addressing herself to Amy's sandals. "How do you figure that?"

"He wanted to keep an eye on you. Control your movements."

She began to walk again, eyes returning to her own feet. "I suppose it's possible. We all flew out on a company jet, and we all stayed at the same Sheraton, Marriott, Hyatt. The detective kept us together for several hours, waiting for Fabian to phone. When it got late and he still hadn't called, a few of us went up to our rooms.

"I was getting ready for bed, watching the news, when THIS JUST IN came up on the screen. To this day, I can't see THIS JUST IN without thinking of that night. Fabian Carvel had been found, stabbed to death in a back alley in Old Town, the victim of a mugging—apparently."

Amy recalled it now, vaguely. The New York press had speculated about it for exactly one day. What had a

fast-food magnate been doing at night, alone, walking
down an alley in one of San Diego's more colorful
neighborhoods? Illicit sex was the media's unsubstantiated conclusion, despite Fabian Carvel's age. Something
seedy and perverse and that made a nice headline.
Then, just as suddenly, it was old news.

"Was anyone ever arrested?"

"No one. Once the police discovered the private detective and the e-mail, we were all of us under scrutiny.
It didn't take long before someone squealed and they
found out about the dinner and his disappearance."

"I don't remember reading anything about his disappearance."

"The police were good about keeping that quiet. I
guess money and power are useful, after all."

"Go figure."

"There were rumors, of course. All kinds of nastiness.
I know this barely made a blip on the world's radar. But
in our little world, it didn't die down for years. Darling, if
you thought boarding school was full of rumors and
backbiting, that's nothing compared to . . ." She bit her
lower lip. "I didn't mean boarding school. What do you
call it? You know, before college?"

"We call it high school." There were times when, purposely or not, Georgina made it clear that her world was
not yours.

"Right. High school. Well, this was ten times worse."

They had reached another set of wooden stairs from
the beach up to the hotel. Georgina sat on the third
step. Amy joined her, and together they gazed out in
the general direction of Italy. The Portuguese fado had
faded into ricocheting echoes. The silence between
them grew almost palpable, as if one was afraid of saying too much and the other was afraid of asking it.

Even without music or words, the air was alive with sounds: a pair of evening birds chirping in a thicket, the gentle stroke of the waves—and the approaching sound, followed by the sight, of two pairs of legs slogging through the edge of the surf.

Amy could just make them out in the moonlight. Burt Baker was in a pair of shorts, his crutches maneuvering clumsily forward in the soft sand. Martha Callas was a few steps behind, kicking the foam in an almost natural display of exuberance. Her long, sunburned limbs flung bony and loose from her red, one-piece swimsuit and reminded Amy of a boiled crab struggling to climb out of a pot. As always, her silver hair was piled high in sprayed swirls, adding half a foot to her already substantial height and making her head into an almost surreal interpretation of a human bullet. Even in the forgiving moonlight, she looked ridiculous.

Every thirty seconds or so, a wave would break, threatening to knock the jurist off his crutches. At those moments, Martha would lose her flailing, crab-like demeanor and regard the judge with the wary eye of a lifeguard.

"She's hoping he falls," Georgina hissed.

"You're cruel."

"She wants to rescue him. If there's one thing I know, it's the rites of middle-aged courtship."

Amy thought it over. "I suppose Burt Baker could be considered a catch. Divorced?"

"Widower," Georgina said with assurance. "And too good of a catch for Martha Callas of Dallas."

"She looks stupid," a third voice offered.

Amy and Georgina swiveled their heads and peered up the length of shadowy stairs. Ten steps above them, a small silhouette sat crouched, arms hugging its knees.

"Holly, sweetie. Come join us." Georgina patted the

worn wooden ledge right above her own. "Come on. We were just dishing Martha."

"I wasn't dishing anyone," Amy protested.

The silhouette clumped down the steps, then collapsed right next to Georgina's hand. "She's so pathetic." Holly was in a T-shirt and cutoff jeans and looked miserable.

"She is," Georgina agreed, turning back to refocus on the frolicking duo. "But then, so are you, dear—if you don't mind my saying so."

"Me?"

"This isn't *Wuthering Heights*. You can't just sit in the dark, pitying yourself. That's no way to get anything done."

"I'm not pitying myself."

"You know very well what I mean. It's natural for you to be a little jealous."

"Martha Callas is a pig."

"Well, we prefer a little more style in our dish, but that's a start."

"And I'm not jealous. I'm just . . ."

"Nothing wrong with a little jealousy."

"I'm not jealous."

Georgina sighed. "Yes, dear. And meanwhile . . ."

An unexpectedly large wave nearly succeeded in knocking Burt sideways into the surf. Martha caught him under the arms, and they both whooped, half in fright, half in delight. Holly cringed as a high Texas twang of laughter bounced off the cliffs and vanished into the dark sea.

"And meanwhile . . . ," Georgina purred. "I think the judge would much rather have you playing with him than some old, garish giant. What do you think?"

Holly didn't answer. She sat above them, motionless

for another few seconds, then abruptly jumped to her feet, stumbled down the last few steps, and scampered across the sand. "Hi!" she shouted out to the surf-bound couple. "What are you guys up to?"

Burt and Martha greeted the twelve-year-old with a mixture of surprise and embarrassment. Amy watched, fascinated, as the new configuration played out. Holly, to her credit, got right into the action, attacking the waves with determined glee and outdoing Martha in her spirited cavorting. Burt laughed, enjoying the rare spectacle of his niece enjoying herself. Martha fell in several steps behind them.

"What are you up to?" Amy couldn't see Georgina's face, but she was probably smiling.

"Why, Ms. Abel," she drawled. "Whatever do you mean?"

"You encouraged her to vie for her uncle's affection. That can't be healthy."

"One can't fight fair with a kid," she answered. "A few sets of diabolical stepchildren taught me that."

"Who's fighting with Holly? You?"

"Not at the moment. But I like to plan ahead."

"You're terrible."

"Marcus says the same thing. You two are a lot alike."

"Really?" Amy felt unexpectedly flattered. "How long has Marcus been with you? He seems like a nice guy."

"I don't know much about him, to be honest."

"Really? You seem the type who likes to know everything."

"Not about his personal life. Are you interested?"

"Me?" Amy was taken aback. "I don't know. Is he interested in me?"

"You mean, is he straight? Amy, dear, just because a

man is well groomed and sensitive and doesn't grab at every pair of boobs on the street . . ."

"I know he's straight. I just asked if he was interested."

"No idea, sweetie."

It was past midnight when Amy returned to her room. The combination of sun and long hours on her best behavior had taken their toll.

A breeze from the balcony stirred the light white curtains, billowing them into the room and rustling the thin piles of clue packets, the next two days' worth of clues, all neatly stacked on the desktop. For a moment she thought about her negligence, about keeping the balcony door open. The breeze could have blown away the clues, or someone could have broken in. She told herself to be more careful next time.

The Corsican aromas of myrtle and lavender were blended now with a hint of lilac, making the air more intoxicating than usual. Amy removed her shoes and used them as paperweights, placing the heels on one pile of packets and the soles on the other. Much less negligent now.

Within five minutes of unlocking the door, Amy was undressed, in bed, and asleep. Sleep was always good.

CHAPTER 9

Amy loved the Tuscan hills this time of year, lush with ripe grapes, the vistas almost hypnotic in their rolling beauty. Then, suddenly, around the least likely bend, a gap would open up to reveal not more hills, but a piercing blue sky and a fishing village nestled in the rocks below, the blue-green sea bobbing with brightly painted herring boats and the occasional yacht.

Two days back on the Tuscan mainland, motoring through this ethereal countryside, had brought them to the Piombino docks and the high-speed ferry to the island of Elba. Everyone had more or less assumed they would be heading this way.

The Napoleon subtheme had so far resulted in an excursion to his Corsican birthplace, followed by their first night in Italy, at Villa La Principessa in Lucca, home of Napoleon's sister. As soon as the clues led them back toward the coast, they all congratulated themselves on their brilliance. Before long, they were disembarking at the site of the Emperor's first exile and settling into their rooms at the Hotel Montecristo on the south side of the island.

A tranquil pine grove stood on a bluff a dozen feet above the narrow beach of Marina di Campo. It had a manicured look. Although the trees were not lined up in obsessively exact rows, as in some replanted German forests, the pinecones and needles and twigs had all been raked away. What was left was a sun-dappled carpet of sandy brown earth. This, combined with the tall, elegant trunks and high, wide canopies, gave the place a natural but civilized ambiance.

Very Italian, Amy mused as she strolled among the pines. *Stone pines,* she reminded herself, the trees that had sunk their roots into the forums of Rome centuries before the birth of the first Caesar. Reaching the edge of the rocky bluff, she stopped to listen to the lapping waves and gaze at the outline of the Tuscan mainland six miles away.

It had been a short day, mystery-wise. Barely 2:30 p.m. and no more clues to plant or arrangements to make. Just an idle afternoon on the beach. Then perhaps a relaxing walk into the village and a drink at a dockside trattoria. That sounded good.

She was just starting back toward the hotel when it dawned on her that for the past hour she hadn't seen anyone from the tour. Not that she minded. It was just unusual. There was always someone lurking around the corner to invent a new problem. Amy stretched up her arms and felt the breeze through the cotton of her floral beach tunic, bought for this trip and the dream of a moment like this.

"There you are! Thank God."

She lowered her arms and did her best to paste on a smile. Weaving his way through the shadows of the manicured grove was Marcus, looking fresh and vital in

Bermuda shorts and a white polo. Amy's disappointment was transformed.

"Marcus. Hi!"

"We have a problem." The closer Marcus came, the more his words faded into a guarded hiss. "Someone's been giving out false clues. It's not you, is it?"

Amy was confused. Then suddenly it made sense. "You're Otto's assistant."

"Yes," he confessed with a simplicity that made Amy want to strangle him.

She felt a combination of relief and anger. "Why didn't you tell me?"

"Tell you what? It's supposed to be a secret."

"So, you're not really Georgina's companion?"

"She's just helping me out. Amy—"

"But after Otto's death? How was I supposed to find you? Why didn't you come forward?"

"Look." Marcus took a moment to slow himself down. "I don't know what Otto charged you, but I paid half my own way. Out of my own pocket." Amy was surprised. Even half was a lot. "This was my vacation. I wanted to see how the game played." He spread his arms in a gesture of utter incomprehension. "I can't believe you're upset."

"I'm upset . . ." When Marcus put it that way, it did seem silly. "I'm upset because Otto didn't just die. He was murdered."

"Murdered?" His arms fell to his sides and his voice quavered. "Murdered?"

"Yes. Call me paranoid, but I think it had something to do with this game."

"Oh, my God. Who would want to kill . . . Do they know who did it?"

"Nope."

"Poor Otto. I just assumed it was a heart attack. He took such bad care of himself. Believe me, if I'd known it was murder . . ."

Amy felt a little ashamed of her anger. "You're right. I'm sorry. I should have been more honest in the first place."

"And you think he was killed because of this game? Why, for heaven's sake?" Marcus waved away any answer. "No. Don't tell me. We don't have time for that right now. We have a problem to take care of."

Amy studied his face. Something was wrong. Marcus had adjusted a bit too easily to the news and was too anxious to move on. "You knew about the murder, didn't you?"

"What? I knew?"

"You knew." She thought back to that morning in Aix-en-Provence. "Five minutes after I announced his death, you were on the phone to New York. I saw the bill."

"I have friends in New York."

"You were calling someone about his death."

Marcus shrugged. "Yes, of course. I called Otto's niece, and she told me. What's wrong with that?"

"What's wrong?" It was like arguing with her mother. "Oh, Amy," she mocked, clasping her hands to her chest in faux sincerity. "If I'd known it was murder . . . Well, you *did* know."

"So?" Marcus was amazingly uncontrite. "Can we get back to the matter at hand?"

"I don't know when to believe you and when not to."

"*It doesn't matter,*" Marcus spat. "Look, if you want to hate me, fine. But we currently have six teams running around the island of Montecristo, looking for nonexistent clues."

Amy paused and blinked, befuddled by the revelation. "Montecristo?" She glanced back up toward the resort. "Not as in the hotel? As in the count thereof?"

"Exactly. It's an island a few miles south."

"Yes. I've been there. There's absolutely nothing. A bird sanctuary and the ruins of some old convent. How the hell did they get to Montecristo?"

"That's what I'm trying to tell you. As soon as we checked in, all the team leaders got telegrams from Daryl. It was a clumsy puzzle, not worthy of Otto or even me. But the solution basically said, 'Hire a boat for a few hours and go to Montecristo.'"

"Italy still has telegrams?" It was the first thing to flash through her mind.

"They do. I checked with the office in Portoferraio. They said an Amy Abel sent the messages. I wanted to throw mine away. But all the other teams were running around the lobby, talking about it."

"So why aren't you on Montecristo with your team?"

"I . . . I was thrown." His voice cracked, and for the first time in their acquaintance, he looked helpless. Amy found this appealing, even sexy, and was annoyed with herself. "I knew I had to talk to you. . . . So I pretended to be sick. They went without me."

"Why would someone send them off on a false clue? To sabotage the game?"

"Why would someone want to sabotage the game?"

"Why would someone throw a rock at your head?"

"Oh." Marcus winced. "I'd forgotten that. You think they're connected?"

"I don't know. But there's nothing we can do until they get back."

"True." The stress was starting to leave Marcus's voice. "That's true."

"We haven't really talked since the cactus garden. Your ankle seems better."

Marcus's smile was crooked and sweet. "I'm sorry for the way I yelled."

"No, you were right. I should have chased after him. At least then we might know who we're dealing with, if we're dealing with anyone."

"Just because I'm the confrontational type, I expect everyone to be that way. It probably does more harm than good."

They were walking back through the pine grove, toward the hotel and the two-storied wall of balconies that faced onto the sea. "When they get back, we'll find out what happened on Montecristo. Then we'll find some way of working it into the mystery. With any luck, they'll never know the difference."

"Good idea," Marcus said.

"Good idea? That's the first time I ever heard you say, 'Good idea,' to anyone."

"Oh, I don't know. The words came out so easily. I must have said it at some point in my life."

"Or maybe you just heard other people say it."

The dark, striking man stopped in his tracks, his crooked smile frozen. Had Amy joked too far? She was about to verbally backtrack when she noticed Marcus's eyes focused into the distance.

"What is it?"

The Hotel Montecristo's functional architecture—a main floor topped by two tiers of bland, sea-facing balconies—was being attacked by the bright afternoon sun. Marcus raised an index finger and started counting horizontally from the left. "Three, four. Jolynn and Vinny," he said, sounding vaguely puzzled.

Amy picked out the room, the only one on the lower

level with the drapes closed. The piercing sunlight illuminated a moving silhouette behind the beige barrier. "It's the maid," she said. No sooner were the words out of her mouth than she saw a second silhouette, this one farther back in the room. "Two maids?" Then the legs moved. Two pairs of long, distinct legs. "Two maids wearing pants?"

"Why would maids be in the room at this hour?"

Good point. The rooms had been cleaned before check-in. Any turning down of beds would occur in the evening. And didn't the maids here wear skirted uniforms?

"Why would our practical joker want everyone away from the hotel?" Marcus asked.

Amy suspected it was another rhetorical question, but she answered. "To rob the rooms."

CHAPTER 10

Marcus was already racing across the lawn. He ignored the winding path and cut directly across a rock garden that had probably been placed there to prevent just this type of shortcut.

"What are you doing?" A reluctant Amy began chasing him through the slippery bed of rocks and plants. "Have you thought that far ahead?" Her words floated off in the breeze. Marcus was already up the outdoor staircase and around the pool.

"What's their room number?" Marcus shouted.

The Mrozeks' room was next door to Amy's own. She tried to visualize the hallway. "Two-oh-four."

Marcus was already inside at the reception desk, leaning over, nearly grabbing a startled clerk by the lapels. "Room two-oh-four is being robbed. We need the key to two-oh-four. Amy. Italian."

"Scusi, signore," Amy said. "La camera due-zero-quattro . . ."

By the time the clerk grasped the situation, Marcus had already disappeared up the main staircase. From the next floor came the sound of fists beating on a door.

"Good God. He's going to get shot. Marcus!" Amy turned back to the slow-moving clerk. "Venga subito! Portaci la chiave."

As she tripped her way up the stairs, Amy heard Marcus's voice in front of her. "Olla. Alto. Polizia." Marcus was pounding on the door to 204, pounding and shouting maniacally, with no thought to what might happen next. He paused just long enough to turn her way. "Tell them to open up. We're with the police."

"No," Amy barked back. She was at the next door, her own, unlocking it with her key card. She rushed inside. Her room had been untouched, she noted thankfully as she raced straight through it and slammed open the balcony door.

The two balconies, hers and the Mrozeks, were connected, physically the same balcony. They were divided by a waist-high partition, an angry blue slab of sheet metal welded to the wall and the seaside railing, providing the occupants with minimal privacy from each other.

Even as Amy climbed over the blue metal, just inches from the Mrozeks' sliding glass door, she wondered what the hell she was doing. She would not be making this insanely reckless gesture if Marcus the avenger, the man who had scolded her in Monaco, wasn't right now slamming his fists against the room's only other entrance.

"I know you're in here. Open up." Marcus's voice was loud and forceful.

For a moment Amy stood on the Mrozeks' balcony, facing the glass and curtain, her hand hovering over the handle. The door was probably locked from inside. But what if it wasn't? How would the burglars—two at least, maybe more—react to the sight of an unarmed woman entering from the balcony, from which they were probably hoping to make their escape?

Another moment and her hand still hovered. They would already be unnerved by Marcus's attack on the door. Anyone would be. And at any moment the desk clerk would finally arrive with the key. Then . . . ?

Her hand seemed to hover forever, all of three seconds. And then the glass slid open from inside. The sudden draft forced a cascade of curtains to blow out, embracing Amy in a swirling cocoon. Instinctively, she twisted, trying to free herself from its soft clutches.

She was off balance now, still turning. And that was when the shadows outside the cocoon grew denser and harder, gaining weight and arms and legs and, worst of all, ramming speed.

The force of the burglars' exit was enough to knock a linebacker off his legs. Amy found herself trapped within the twisting, ripping curtains, suspended like a lanky hunk of wrapped taffy.

"*Porco miseria,*" a disembodied voice growled. Two pairs of arms and legs began alternately grabbing the trussed tour leader, then pushing her away in a wild, panicky attempt to keep themselves free of the billowing folds.

It didn't take long for the curtain rod to give way. Pulled from its anchor in the wall above the sliding glass, the left end fell first. One curtain ring slipped, then half a dozen more slid off. The concrete balcony rose up to meet Amy's body with an excruciating impact that knocked the breath out of her lungs and disoriented her even more.

Barely aware of which side was up, she continued to writhe and turn, convinced that she was rolling back toward the room and away from the foot-high gap that she knew existed under the balcony railing.

"Amy, stop." More hands grabbed at her, and she fought back, hearing the words but not connecting them to any meaning. "It's Marcus. Stop. Stop moving."

Like a dog obeying an unwelcome command, she snorted and fell limp, giving up any attempt at control.

The hands returned—helpful hands this time—and within a minute, she was being pulled from the ripped strands of beige curtain, like a floral butterfly emerging from a chrysalis. "Pig misery," she moaned as her eyes focused on Marcus's face.

"Pig what?"

"Just quoting someone," Amy said, now finally able to help free herself. "Did you see them? I think there were two."

Marcus rose from his knees and stumbled over the curtains to the balcony railing. "What the hell were you doing?" He continued to stare out over the rock garden and the pine-sheltered bluff beyond. "You could have been killed."

"At least I slowed them down."

Marcus turned back. "You were an inch away from rolling off the balcony." His voice was angry, but his eyes looked frightened. Amy stared into those eyes and for a few seconds forgot the pain from the pummeling and the twisted ankle and . . . Damn, her new beach tunic had a split at the seam.

The desk clerk had joined them, key in hand, eyes focused on a white poplin object among all the heavy beige. "Ecco, guarda," he said, pointing to the bulging pillowcase.

"They dropped their stash." Amy said it brightly, hoping to call a truce with Marcus. "We did good." But he wasn't listening. He was bending down by the railing, pulling a sliver of paper from where it had been caught between two points of decorative ironwork.

"What?" Amy asked as she wriggled her way free of the curtains. Her new Fendis sat twisted on her nose, perhaps permanently twisted.

"A list of numbers. Two-oh-four, two-oh-six, two-oh-eight . . ."

"Room numbers." Amy joined him, twisting her glasses to look at the handwritten note. "Our rooms," she said. "Mrozek, Callas, Davis. The whole tour."

"Not quite." Marcus reviewed the list again. "Two rooms are missing. Yours and mine."

For just a second she was flattered that Marcus knew her room number. Then the oddity of the note sank in. "What does it mean?"

Marcus turned the note over and back and thought out loud. "The burglars—probably locals—had a list of everyone who'd been lured away to Montecristo." He looked up. "What's in the pillowcase?"

Back in the room, the desk clerk had already dumped the contents out on the bed. "Purse," Amy said, pointing out the scattered items. "Man's watch and wallet. A few rings and a necklace. Cuff links. Two passports. This must be the first room they hit." She crossed back to Marcus and lowered her voice. "So? What now?"

"Go yell at the manager. Enough to make him cooperate. We have a lot to do before our people return from Montecristo."

"Right." Amy sighed. "If only it hadn't been the Mrozeks."

* * *

They began arriving back at seven, a convoy of four tiny tour boats, plus two rusty trawlers that had been hired by the slower teams. Amy was at the docks to greet them, relieved to discover that her players weren't nearly as cranky as she'd expected. More shamefaced than cranky.

"Well, Otto finally fooled us," Burt Baker said, reflecting the general sentiment.

The moment the first boat landed, the hotel inaugurated a program of pampering. Nothing that smacked too much of an apology. But there was a full staff of waiters on the terraces and in the lounge, ready to jump at the merest hint of a drink order. A special dinner was on time, on the best linen, and accompanied by champagne, compliments of the management.

The manager, unable to hide the fact that someone had ripped down their curtains, took Vinny and his wife aside and confessed a version of the truth. Two thieves had broken into their room. But an alert employee had intervened before anything was stolen.

"There's nothing missing," Vinny exulted with his usual positive attitude.

"I guess it's all here." Jolynn sounded disappointed.

"Of course it is." Vinny was opening his wallet. "Now, where is that guy who risked his life for us? I'd like to give him a little something."

"That won't be necessary," the manager said. "It was his job."

"Nonsense. He deserves a reward."

"Is everything all right?" Amy asked, appearing in the doorway. She and Marcus had been next door, in her room, listening through the wall. Now that the Mrozeks seemed to be taking it so well, they felt emboldened to drop by.

"Abel. Marcus. Come in." Vinny was reluctantly putting his wallet back in his pocket. "I guess you heard about our good luck."

"Nothing was taken?" On Amy's first step into the room, her right ankle twisted, sending a spasm of pain up her injured body, intensifying the throbbings in her left elbow and right side.

"Nothing at all. Are you all right? Looks like you hurt yourself."

"Oh, just banged myself up in the pool. Acting stupid."

"I'll bet the pool was nice," Jolynn said. "Was it nice?" The short, hard woman was smiling at Marcus, who had just entered the room. "You were so clever not to come along. How on earth did you know it would be a wild-goose chase?"

"I didn't." Marcus shrugged uncomfortably. "I should have gone. A once-in-a-lifetime chance to see Montecristo."

"You didn't miss a thing." Vinny laughed. "I never knew how boring ruins could be until we examined every inch of that godforsaken island."

Jolynn's steely gaze switched from Marcus to Amy. "I assume our boat costs will be reimbursed." It was a statement, not a question.

"Absolutely," said Amy.

"Unless this little excursion was some sort of mistake."

"I sent the telegrams myself. How could it be a mistake?"

"But there weren't any packets of clues, were there?

You didn't have time to sail out there and plant clues. Yes?"

"No . . . I mean, not exactly." She breathed deeply, trying to regain her composure. "Jolynn. If you missed a clue or you didn't, you certainly can't expect me to tell. Daryl asked you to go to Montecristo. He must have had a reason."

It was a rebuttal that was, for the moment, unassailable.

CHAPTER 11

Amy lay wide awake in the dark, wondering why exactly she was awake. She so rarely had trouble in this department. Was it the soreness? she wondered. The trauma and punches she'd endured in the curtain cocoon? Perhaps. Although a few aspirins had helped to ease the aches and she'd certainly slept through worse.

It wasn't her personal life keeping her awake. What personal life? And as far as she could tell, she wasn't obsessing about the tour. But, of course, the fact that she was thinking about not obsessing probably meant she was. She had just checked the bedside clock—4:58 a.m.—when there was a light knock at the door, a soft but insistent rapping of knuckle against wood. She got up, grabbed a hotel bathrobe and her nearest pair of glasses.

"Did I wake you?"

Marcus was standing in the hall. For a second, her heart beat a little faster. But the man was fully dressed, with a light jacket and a leather portfolio under his arm.

"Do you know what time it is?"

"Five o'clock," he answered without bothering to check his watch. "I've been trying to figure out how to fix the Montecristo thing. Get dressed. I've got a boat."

"What the hell are you up to?" Given the time, Amy felt she was being more than civil.

"Bring a jacket, waterproof if you have it. How are your bruises?"

"Sleepy. Thanks for asking."

It was wet and chilly on the motor launch, as predicted. At some juncture, while Alberto, the youngest of the local fishermen, skidded his boat across a black glass sea, Marcus shouted out an apology and even thanked her for coming. It was timed to seem offhand and inconsequential, delivered over an eighty-decibel background.

"What you said about Daryl having a reason for sending them to Montecristo . . ." Marcus's mouth was an inch from her ear. "It made me think." The boatman cut the engine to half as they eased into the bay, and conversation became easier. "We have to find the right clues—hard but not impossible. The ruins, of course, are the island's most distinct features. The number of intact arches. The color of the marble or brick."

Amy caught on. "You're making it a memory game. That's good." For the tenth time this morning, she wiped the spray off her tortoiseshell Lafonts.

The sky had turned pearl gray in the east. Alberto tilted the outboard out of the water and let the launch gently beach itself on the island's pebbly shore. Amy asked him to wait, then raced to catch up with Marcus, who was scaling a boulder in order to get a quick lay of the land.

When the dawn finally came, they were sitting on a fourteenth-century foundation stone, munching on the bananas and apples they had providently thought to grab from the lobby's fruit bowl. Amy shielded her eyes from a cold sun that threw long, cloudless shadows, brightening the roofless peaks and solitary doorways.

The remains of the old convent were a gold mine of memorable images, and Marcus was even now putting the best ones into a rough draft. "We can make it like a treasure map. 'Turn right. Pace out four times the number of stars in the stone crest.' "

"They'll remember details like that?"

"My Fidels took pictures. I'm sure the others did." He flipped shut his notebook. "When they wake up tomorrow, we'll have this puzzle waiting for them."

Amy thought forward to the next stop. Siena. "How is that going to work?"

"Tomorrow morning, when they're having breakfast, they're supposed to find a clue in the personal ads of the local English language paper. That's a cool way to get a clue, and I don't want to lose it. You and I will hide those six newspapers in various spots around the hotel garden."

Amy grimaced. "Management's going to love that. Won't the papers get muddy?"

"Plastic bags." He had an answer for everything, and for once, she appreciated it. "At breakfast tomorrow, instead of finding the papers at their table, each team will find a different treasure puzzle, based on their memories of Montecristo."

"Pace out four times the number of whatever."

"Right. They'll follow those clues, find the newspapers, and we'll be back on track. I can't wait to see Jolynn's face."

Amy peeled her second banana and took a bite. "Tonight in Siena we'll write the puzzles, then go hide the papers."

"Oh, boy. A second date."

"A date." Well, there it was. She let the moment linger, then stole a sideways glance.

Marcus caught her eye. "We could call it a work session."

"No, a date's fine."

"For all I know, you're married without a ring or happily attached."

"Hardly." She shrugged. "Not anymore." It was her turn to keep things going. "So, what's a nice guy like you doing on a desert island?"

He smiled his killer smile. "It's a living. I worked for a bank until I was forced to reconsider my career path. A friend of a friend of mine knew Otto, so . . . I guess I'm out of a job again."

"Well, I appreciate all your help."

"You paid for it. What about you? What's your story?"

And so Amy told him—about her career as a copywriter for a Madison Avenue ad agency, about Eddie's murder, about her own breakdown, or time off, or whatever you want to call it. Marcus listened patiently and laughed out loud when she got to Fanny and her antics.

"I'd love to meet her," he said, reaching into the bag for an apple.

"I'm sure you will." Amy watched as he polished the apple on his jacket sleeve. "Those two robbers . . ."

Marcus moaned. "Just when I started to relax."

"What were they doing with a list of rooms?"

Marcus crunched into his apple, chewed thoroughly, and swallowed. "Someone gave it to them, someone who knew which rooms would be empty."

"A hotel employee? He sees everyone running off and chartering boats, meaning they'll be away for a few hours."

Marcus shook his head. "Don't forget the telegrams. This had to be someone who knew the game."

"Right. Someone from the tour?"

"Who else? People guessed we were coming to Elba. If our joker already knew someone here, someone who could arrange a robbery, he could have phoned ahead." Marcus shivered in the morning chill and took another bite. "Would you have canceled the tour?"

"If the rooms had been robbed? Money and passports? Some people might have gone home. Rich people take that sort of thing seriously. They have this heightened sense of property, although I shouldn't generalize."

"It would certainly have ruined the rally."

Amy was at a loss. Otto's murder, the rock in Monte Carlo, and now the fake telegrams and the robbery. She didn't want to think about how these dots might be connected. And, for the same reason, she didn't want to bring up Fabian Carvel and the real-life case.

Being Otto's assistant, Marcus must know something about the Carvel case. So why didn't she ask? Was it because she didn't trust him? Maybe. The man lied with such incredible ease. "We should get moving." Amy pushed herself up from the damp foundation stone and brushed off the seat of her skinny black jeans.

Marcus stood up and stretched. "It's a puzzlement," he said, gazing back over the ruined wall to the pebbly beach where Alberto sat on the bow of his boat, smoking a pipe.

Alberto saw them. He stood up, too, knocking the bowl of his pipe against his heel.

"Kind of makes you want to take up the simple life," Marcus said. "No mysteries. No worries."

"He's probably thinking the same about us."

"We should go. If memory serves, this is muffin morning."

"Muffin morning," Amy confirmed with a nod.

Marcus tossed the apple into a rocky field. He wiped both hands on his tan slacks, then held out his right. "Peace? You still mad at me for not telling you about my job?"

It was an awkward gesture, too formal for their current relationship. Amy took his hand. "Peace. By the way, how did you get Georgina to pretend you were together?"

"She's a sweetheart. We met at JFK on our way here. I was in the boarding area, reading an old Dorothy Sayers, the mark of a mystery junkie. I mean, you can catch anyone reading a mystery best seller. Even an old Agatha Christie will lure in the casual fan, don't you know. But Dorothy L. Sayers? My dear, I knew in a trice. Half a trice, if that doesn't sound like bragging." He had eased into a Georgina impression so perfect that Amy could almost see the cleft in his chin.

"Bravo!"

Marcus laughed. "That's how she introduced herself. It seemed like such a perfect opportunity to disguise my presence. Mystery fans are always the first to volunteer for any little deception."

"I'll have to remember that. Muffin morning," Amy added, reminding them both of the need to hurry.

Neither said a word during the long ride back. The water was choppier now. At one point their bow hit a wave directly. Amy didn't see it coming and was thrown back, nearly teetering off the bench. Marcus was right there, catching her by both shoulders and steadying her. His hands stayed on her shoulders, firm and steady. Amy wondered if this might turn into a kiss. Did she want it to turn into a kiss? But it didn't. Just a warm smile and then it was over.

It was a welcome sight, the gray docks of Marino di Campo growing solid and larger. Also growing solid and larger, but definitely less welcome, were the three anxious figures milling about the length of a pier.

Harry Greenbaum was there to grab the towrope. "Georgina told us you might be off together," he said with a glare that began on Marcus, then moved on to Amy. The other Fidels remained icily silent. "Everyone else is halfway through the clue."

"No!" Marcus said. "You should have started without me. Where's the clue?" With a nimble leap he was out of the boat. "What does it say?"

"We don't know," Harry moaned. "It was in the middle of a muffin."

"In the team captain's muffin," Harry's sister added.

The three Fidels were hurriedly escorting their captain along the docks, back in the direction of the hotel. "The waiter put a muffin at your place setting," said Harry. "But by the time we figured out what was happening, he'd already taken it away."

"Well, ask for it back. Just go to the kitchen and ask the waiter—"

"Don't you think we tried?" said Harry. "Three times I used my Italian on that stupid waiter. And every time he brought us a new muffin."

Amy couldn't suppress a laugh but managed to turn it into a cough.

"Finally, he said if we were just going to tear the muffins apart without eating them, we couldn't have any more. That's what I think he said."

Marcus glowered over his shoulder, straight at Amy. "You told me we'd be back by breakfast. You said—"

"Oh, it's not her fault," said Harry's sister. "But since Amy speaks such good Italian, maybe she can help. . . ."

"We'll do it ourselves," Marcus snapped. "We'll tear that kitchen apart if we have to." And he redoubled his pace, the warrior king leading his faithful Fidels into battle.

Amy stumbled to a halt and watched as they marched their way toward the Montecristo. Not for a second, not in a single word or glance, had Marcus given away the truth, to the extent that Amy herself was half convinced that their morning excursion had been all her doing and that she owed them all an abject apology.

CHAPTER 12

The muffin clue led them from Elba back to the Tuscan mainland. Then came Siena and the Montecristo memory game. Not all the teams remembered the clues perfectly, not on the first guess, so there wound up being more than six holes dug among the hotel's lush flower beds. Fourteen holes to be specific—plus a hundred-euro tip to the gardener. But they all solved it, and they all went on to decode the personal ad in the newspaper.

After Siena came Assisi, their last stop before Rome. The end was in sight.

Amy's clients were looking forward to the Eternal City and the prospect of their last hotel. Other emotions were also in play. There was anxiety and excitement about the murder they all assumed was coming, about solving it. And in a few days reality would once again force them—some gladly, some not—back into the world. *Bittersweet* was the word Martha Callas kept repeating wisely, as if she'd just invented it.

The intensity of the rally had forged a bond among the captains. They were in general the most vocal and competitive of the players and had often been placed in conflict over rules and procedures, not to mention bragging and taunting and making excuses—integral parts of any good game.

A captains' dinner suddenly seemed appropriate, something off the itinerary, off the premises, and before the final barrage of competition that was to come in Rome. Amy arranged it with a minimum of fuss.

"Aren't you joining us?" asked Georgina as the six of them were about to hop into a pair of taxis. "You must."

"It's for the captains," Amy demurred. In truth, she was looking forward to a rare night alone, snuggling in bed with that novel she'd been neglecting.

"Nonsense," Georgina insisted. "You're coming. A small thank-you for all your hard work. Our treat."

"Our treat?" Jolynn asked. But the others took up the cause, and Amy had no choice.

La Taverna dell'Arco was the pride of Assisi, a cavernous underground dining establishment full of stone-vaulted atmosphere. In its early life, the tavern had been a monastery, home to those first modest followers of Saint Francis. Nowadays, waiters took the place of monks, flitting among the shadows, serving tourists instead of God and seeking tips instead of alms.

"Now be honest." The second courses had just arrived, and Frank Loyola was waiting patiently, fork in hand. He always waited for the ladies, as he called them, to start, even when they told him to go ahead. "Did anybody actually get the clue about the patron saint of television? Us Stew Boys, we thought it was just one of Daryl's jokes."

"Saint Clara." Burt nodded. "My niece picked up this little book on the saints. It's got this marvelous index that tells you which saint goes with what."

"You mean, which saint goes with what wine?" Georgina teased. "Offhand, I'd say red for the martyrs."

"No, you heretic. Which saint goes with which cause."

"You mean she really is the patron saint of TV?" Georgina slipped her hand lightly onto Burt's forearm in what would have seemed like a natural gesture had she not already performed it once during cocktails and once during the first course.

"She is."

"Are you sure you don't mean Santa Cable?"

Burt chuckled and patted her hand, a casual action that went unnoticed by everyone but Martha Callas. "Do you want to hear the story?"

"I'm on tenterhooks."

Burt pivoted his body to once again face the heiress. "It seems that one year, on Christmas Eve . . . I guess this was about seven hundred years ago. Anyway, Saint Clara was a devout nun, and she desperately wanted to go to the midnight mass. But on this particular night, Christmas Eve, Clara was sick in bed, unable to move. So she prayed, of course—and, of course, a miracle happened. The wall of her little cell lit up like a TV screen."

"No! And this was years before satellite."

"Several years. So, Clara sat in bed that night, watching the wall. And there it was, the mass that was being said in the basilica across the street. On her wall. In color, I assume."

Georgina released Burt's forearm and clapped her hands. "No wonder they made her a saint."

Frank Loyola, for all his boisterous swagger, for all his practical jokes and backslapping friendliness, was now pursing his lips like a maiden aunt. "You shouldn't joke about other people's religions. You're in Italy, for

Pete's sake." And with that, the most vehement curse in his vocabulary, Frank returned to his small roasted bird arranged on a bed of fried polenta. No one else moved or spoke as he sullenly attacked his main course.

"I'm sorry," Georgina apologized in the hush.

This wasn't the first time that Frank had called them to task. He was the only Catholic on board to defend vocally the Roman church and, at one point or another, had been a sanctimonious thorn in the side of nearly everyone.

As a captain, Frank had not been the best choice, either for his team or for the game at large. A man of nearly forty, he was a reluctant bachelor, respectful and ill at ease with women, and constantly on the lookout for "Miss Right," as he was fond of saying. "He's holding out for a fellow virgin," Georgina once quipped within his earshot, and he hadn't denied it or seemed embarrassed.

Frank had made his career as a police officer, and if there was a typical look, he had it—large and thick and stalwart. He was undoubtedly the least affluent member of the tour, perhaps the least educated. He was also one of the few members of New York's Finest, at least in Amy's experience, never to use profanity.

During a week and a half of late-night beers and small talk more plentiful than bar pretzels, Amy had pieced together a fairly complete portrait. Born and bred in the Bronx, Frank continued to live there, in the house he bought from his father. Francis Sr., also a cop, was retired now, a man just as religious and rigid as his son. But in the more amenable world of forty years ago, Big Frank at least had managed to find a compatible mate.

For this year's vacation, Frank had been planning to

do another Knights of Columbus retreat when he saw the tour's Web site and impulsively dipped into his retirement fund. His one vice, so he piously claimed, was a lust for murder mysteries, not a common pastime in a profession that saw its share of the real thing. But here, too, breeding showed, and his taste was strictly limited to cozies, the Agatha Christie format. Murders were never graphically described, the motives never too sordid, and the action usually kept to a series of gentle interrogations.

The patrolman had been ill prepared for the irreverence of the other players and for Otto's sometimes ribald sense of humor. But his worst failing as a player was his reluctance to play his assigned role.

His character, Stew Rummy, according to his team's secret packet, wasn't a drinker at all but used this ruse to disguise his real vice, sexual addiction. Every woman Stew met became the object of his unbridled lust. Unfortunately, none of this had even been hinted at during the game, thanks to Frank's inhibited, moralistic role-playing. One of the teams was even toying with the theory that Stew was in reality a Jesuit priest who, at the time of Daryl's disappearance, had been in the process of converting the tycoon to a life of the cloth.

Frank had already forgotten his outburst and was concentrating on his meal. "Delicious," he mumbled and slurped, his mouth half filled with bits of breast meat. "Why can't they make this back home? I'm sure you can get this kind of bird, whatever it is."

"I'm sure you can," Jolynn Mrozek volunteered. The restaurant owner's wife was barely able to restrain her mirth. "In fact they're quite common." Amy knew what she was about to say, and wished she wouldn't. "You ordered *piccione?*"

"Jolynn," Amy warned. Ever since Montecristo, Jolynn had been relatively subdued, her supply of bile left to bubble and build like puss under the skin.

"That's a pigeon," Jolynn chuckled. "You know, a flying rat. Why do you think no one else ordered it?"

"Oh." Frank gulped, accidentally swallowing the last bit of his last mouthful. Everyone watched as the patrolman squinted, in some kind of pain. His fork clattered to his plate. "People actually go out in the street and catch those filthy, disease-ridden—"

"They're not the same," Amy said. She tried to explain that cooking pigeons were specially raised on farms, not streets, but Frank's eyes refused to unsquint. "In most of the world, pigeon is a very common dish."

Frank shook himself free of whatever images had been playing in his head. "Yeah, well, I guess I'm not as sophisticated as you guys. A little out of my depth, huh?"

"That's not true," Marcus protested softly.

But it was. And it was this, and not the taste of pigeon, that seemed to linger so bitterly. This wasn't the first time that Frank had been made to feel out of place. But this time he was isolated, without the protection of his backslapping, all-male team. The rest of the table was grateful when Judge Baker cleared his throat and plowed into a new topic.

"You know, I'll lay you better than even odds that our killer . . . I know we don't even have a victim yet, but humor me. If this game is anything true to life, I'll wager the killer is a member of Daryl's family. I mean, in the real world the family is where most murders occur. I've worked in the court system long enough. Jealousy. Revenge. Money. It's all there. Especially money. It doesn't have to be a lot."

"Yes." Amy jumped in, happy to keep the topic going. "But this isn't real life."

"Well, maybe that's Otto's twist. I know this doesn't follow the formula of 'least likely suspect,' Georgie?" He turned to the woman on his right. "You're a dedicated true crime fan. What do you think?"

The woman who all evening long had been devoted to the judge's every move now seemed to be ignoring him. Georgina stared blankly ahead, wearing an expression not unlike Frank's, except that her forehead, which had undergone such massive medical efforts to remain wrinkle free, was furrowed into a deep, unflattering pucker.

"Of course," Georgina mumbled to no one. "That's what it was. That's why he . . . I should have remembered."

"Should have remembered what?" Martha pounced from across the table. And then she gasped. "You know who the killer is!"

Georgina had a second to deny it but didn't.

"Damn," Martha growled. "I hate it when people have breakthroughs. It makes me feel stupid."

"What did you figure out?" asked Burt. "Was it something I said?" His lips moved as he tried to recall his own words. Two other team captains had already taken out pencils and were jotting down notes.

Georgina blinked and refocused, back at last from her reverie. "It's no big thing," she apologized, for once uncomfortable being the center of attention. "It probably has nothing to do with the murder. You know how it is when a notion suddenly strikes you. It's the most brilliant revelation, until you start thinking about it. Then it winds up being nothing."

"What is this revelation?" Marcus asked. "If it's so nothing, you should let us in on it."

Georgina turned on her "companion" with a trembling, thin grin. "Marcus, you've had exactly the same opportunity as I to figure it out. Exactly. That's all I have to say."

"She knows," said Martha. "The murder hasn't even happened, and she knows."

The party never quite recovered. At the end of the evening, the check was delivered by a noiseless waiter and snatched up by Jolynn Mrozek. For the next minute, all that could be heard was the scratching of a pen on the paper tablecloth as the chef's wife skillfully divided the tab, assigning each drink and appetizer and bottle of wine to its appropriate consumer. The menu had left it unclear if a service charge was included. But Jolynn assumed that it was, and didn't add a tip.

"Is everyone ready to hear the damage?"

CHAPTER 13

The teams began arriving in Rome late the next afternoon. Amy was waiting at the grand double doors of the hotel, the Albergo Marcello, stopwatch at the ready. At the previous stops, she had done her best to make the event smooth and welcoming. But this was Rome and the grand finale. It had to be a little more.

With the hotel's grudging consent, she'd hung a banner above the entrance. MONTE CARLO TO ROME RALLY was printed in gold on a swath of red satin. It obscured the fifteenth-century pediment that had been the building's pride and joy ever since its days as the home of Pope Julius II, before Julius moved to the big house on the far side of the river.

"It's like the end of a race," Amy had explained to the sleek concierge and the even sleeker, more dubious manager. "They're going to expect a finish line."

"Finish line?" The manager had choked with such disgust that for a second Amy thought she had made a mistake with her Italian and had accidentally said something like dung heap. "They're going to be expecting a dung heap."

"Finish line?" he repeated. "You intend to put one of those cheap little ribbons across the door like for some footrace?"

"No, no." Amy stopped herself. "Actually, that's a good idea."

"No. I will not allow it. The banner is bad enough. Thank God it's not in Italian."

"A ribbon." Amy had to have it. "It will be for only a minute. When the first Mercedes pulls up, I can stretch it across the doorway. Signore Piroli." She lowered her voice. "We are filling your hotel for the next three nights, plus the banquet. A little cooperation . . ."

For once she got her way, without so much as a "haricots verts" compromise to sour her victory. The concierge disappeared inside, returning a minute later with a red crepe paper ribbon left over from a six-year-old viscount's birthday party.

The finish was as exciting as Amy could have wished. Even though first place meant no more today than it had for any of the earlier stops, the teams had begun the day by challenging each other. Being the first to complete the two-week rally took on an exaggerated importance. All six teams had burst out of their peaceful Assisi hotel that morning, their boat shoes nearly burning rubber across the cobbled drive.

Via Sant'Angelo was lined on both sides with Rome's typical ocher facades, severe and respectable. Just one block long, the street was nestled in the tight triangle between the Capitoline Hill and the Tiber, a quiet upperclass neighborhood that slept in the late afternoon sun like a cat on a sill.

The tranquility was broken at 4:32 p.m., when the first Mercedes squealed around the corner, followed seconds later by another. The man from the rental car agency was standing in the doorway with Amy and turned white when he realized that these dusty, maniac-driven vehicles were his.

"Get out of their way," Amy shouted in Italian. "Help me with the ribbon."

From their vantage point at the top of the steps, they watched as the Stew Boys barreled down the single lane between the two curbs of parked cars. Frank Loyola was in the front passenger seat, his head bobbing out the window as he studied the buildings.

In addition to obscuring the pediment, Amy's banner succeeded in covering up the hotel's street number. By the time Frank realized what the banner said, they had gone too far. He called frantically to his teammates, and the Stewmobile jerked to a halt.

The driver, an Atlanta gem dealer, was just about to throw it into reverse when he saw the second car in his rearview mirror. "I can't back up. Make a run for it."

Meanwhile, in the second Mercedes, Vinny Mrozek was forced to stop directly in front of the Albergo Marcello. "Damn, we're blocked. What's the number?"

"There it is!" Dominick yelled from the backseat. "The house with the red. Go!"

In a flash, the front passenger door flew open and his twin, Donovan, was leaping over the bumpers of the tightly parked cars. He hit the sidewalk a split second in front of Frank.

As they raced up to the stoop, the grunting patrolman tried to pass. But the teenager thrust out his arm in a horizontal block. With the same hand, he grabbed the top of a five-century-old lion-headed post and used it to catapult himself up the stairs. His jutting chin broke through the crepe.

By this time, a third Mercedes had pulled up behind

the second. Martha Callas and her Bitsys sat in the Mercedes traffic jam, transfixed by the athletic event unfolding on the street. The ladies celebrated Donovan's win with a burst of applause, honking their horn and waving.

Amy celebrated with a little cheer of her own. The Mrozek team had been the only ones never to win a single day's competition. Having them break the finish line would go a long way toward giving Jolynn's husband and stepsons a fond memory of the tour.

The broken ribbon dangled from Amy's right hand. She glanced past the rental car representative, past the two laughing, panting men bent over in the pink marble lobby. Reluctantly, she caught the eye of the manager, a man who was decidedly less tanned and sleek than he'd been just a minute before. "The worst is over," she said in soothing Italian. "They're really quite civilized people. Trust me."

Within an hour, all six teams were lifting champagne flutes in the lounge. The Doloreses were in their glory, while the slower teams shared stories of bad luck and wrong turns and horrible traffic, traditional topics among the late arrivals.

"Amy? Can I have a word?"

Her back was turned, but she recognized the syrupy drawl and mentally swatted it away like a sand fly. Like a sand fly, it returned, ever more insistent. "It's nice being tall, isn't it? People can always pick you out in a crowd."

She turned and forced a grin. "Martha."

Martha Callas grinned back, closemouthed and mirthless. The parts of her sunburn that hadn't peeled were fading now into a blotchy tan. The nose was particularly striking, since it had been the victim of two distinct peelings and was teetering on the brink of sun poisoning. A layer of lotion glistened on the tip. "Last night I was on the phone to my sister."

"Can this wait until cocktail hour?" That was always the best time to deal with Martha, when they both had drinks in their hands.

"Her husband is a homicide lieutenant in San Diego." Martha said it in a near whisper. "My sister knows I have this passion for mysteries. Of course she knows. She's my sister. Often she'll tell me about Arnie's old cases."

"San Diego?" Amy said in a true whisper. "Oh. Let's discuss this somewhere private."

The dining room was decorated in the classic Roman style, with aged red velvet on the walls. Matching floor-length curtains framed the tall windows. Gathering dust on the high eggshell ceiling were elaborate plaster moldings—cherubs and clouds. The room was laid out as a dramatic oval, impressively large for a small hotel but probably just the right size for Pope Julius II. At the moment it was empty except for Amy and Martha and a lone waiter setting up tables in the oval's far end.

"What exactly do you know?" Amy asked. The late sun had just passed the corner building, and streams of light illuminated the suspended motes of dust like pale spotlights. Silently they faced each other until the waiter made his exit.

"Let's cut to the chase," Martha suggested. "This game is based on the Carvel murder. From your reaction, I assume this is something you don't want to become general knowledge."

Amy shrugged. "Other members of the tour know."

"Georgina Davis, of course. And Marcus Alvarez."

"You know about Marcus being the assistant?"

"Assistant, secretary. Whatever you want to call it."

The Dallas decorator fingered a water glass, a manicured nail scraping around the rim. "So . . . how much of this game is based on Carvel?"

"Very little," Amy lied emphatically. "None of the Carvel guests were ever suspects. And Otto didn't uncover anything new."

Martha returned her stare, backing down just a little. "Sweetie, look. I don't want my Bitsys left out. We've invested a lot of time and ego in this. It would be a shame if someone had an unfair advantage."

"No one has an advantage."

"You have to admit it's quite a coincidence, people involved in the real crime who are now playing this game."

"What do you mean, people?"

"People, dear. Homo sapiens. Georgina, otherwise known as Dodo Fortunof, and Marcus, otherwise known as Fidel, the private secretary."

"Secretary?" Amy swallowed hard. "You mean Fabian Carvel's secretary?"

"Secretary, assistant, whatever."

"Marcus was the real Fidel." Amy tried not to make it sound like a question.

"Isn't that what we're talking about? Amy, if I have your absolute word that they don't have any inside knowledge, then I'll keep quiet. But I'm going to be very suspicious if either of them wins the whole thing. Do you understand what I'm saying? Look at me, dear. Let me know you're paying attention."

Amy didn't want company. Marcus should have been able to understand. On other nights in other towns, she had gone off by herself after dinner, and no one had objected, at least not too much. Everyone seemed to respect her need for some alone time. But not tonight. At the very moment when Amy felt she needed some time to think about Marcus, there he was, strolling by her side, determined to keep her company.

Isola Tiberina was a short walk from the hotel. The island had once been a sacred, mysterious place, shaped like a ship floating in the middle of the Tiber. Now it was little more than the midsection of a busy bridge connecting the two halves of Rome. But there was still a part of the island, behind the old basilica and several blocks from the traffic, where the rush of a little waterfall obscured the sounds of the city and you could imagine yourself far away from all your troubles. Unless they were walking right beside you.

"Penny for your thoughts," he said.

"Do you think Otto was killed because of the game?"

"You said that once before. Why?" Their eyes met. His reply seemed so innocent, not overplayed or underplayed. *Hazel,* she noted, not for the first time.

"It's just . . . I don't know. So many weird things. He sells us the game and gets killed. Someone throws a rock. Someone messes with the game and robs the rooms. Georgina winds up on this tour. . . ." She hadn't meant to add that part.

"Georgina? Why is that weird?"

Oh, well. In for a penny . . . "Because she was involved in the Carvel murder, and this game is based on the Carvel murder." *There.*

"Wow." Marcus cleared his throat. "I'm really getting my penny's worth."

"Half the damned tour knows. Well, the Dodos and

Martha Callas." Amy shut her mouth. She had a tendency to ramble on, single-handedly filling the awkward silences. This time she wanted Marcus to fill them.

"All right." His words became measured and exact. "It was Otto's little joke, something he didn't expect anyone to catch. He had no way of knowing Georgina Davis would be signing up. He would have loved the irony, I'm sure."

"How much research did you do on the Carvel case?"

"Quite a bit. The real characters included Fabian's wife, their son, Georgina, Fabian's finance guy, a TV soap star . . . How many is that?"

"Five. How about the personal secretary?"

"Yes, the secretary. I forgot."

"Was that a man or a woman?" Amy asked with no special inflection.

"A man."

"And, as far as you know, Georgina is the only one of Carvel's dinner guests on this tour? I assume you did enough interviews and research to know what they all look like. I mean, let's say this secretary guy happened to be traveling under a different name. . . ."

"I would have recognized him, yes."

"Are you sure? What was his name, by the way, Fabian's secretary?"

Marcus tilted his head. "Are you sure everything's all right?"

"Perfect."

Amy had intended to confront him but now changed her mind. Knowledge is power. What would be the point of letting Marcus know what she knew? So he could lie again? She'd seen Marcus lie; he was good. He might easily admit to being Carvel's secretary and then explain it away, another detail he'd promised a dead man he wouldn't reveal. *No,* Amy decided. *Knowing what your enemy doesn't know you know . . .*

Her enemy? That was too dramatic. But what was he? Not a partner anymore. Not someone to trust. Maybe that was the cause of her strange look, the realization that she was alone, responsible for twenty-four lives, and no longer able to trust anyone.

Later, when she walked back into her room, a red light was throbbing on the nightstand. A call from home had never seemed so welcome, which made her feel embarrassed and resentful and grateful all at once. Only it wasn't a call from home. From New York, yes, but not from home. Amy listened to the message, then did the six-hour subtraction. Sergeant Rawlings might still be in his office.

"Ms. Abel. Thanks for returning my call. I know this is on your dime, so I'll keep it short. I assume your mother has informed you of Otto Ingo's murder?"

"Yes, she has. Do you have any leads?" Did the police really use that term?

"Not yet, I'm afraid. No one in the neighborhood knew him. No known intimates. I think it would help if we could talk to the assistant he was working with."

"You don't know . . . I mean, you haven't been able to identify him . . . or her?"

"Mr. Ingo never mentioned his name. We checked with the bank. He—or she, as you say—must have been paid in cash. I take it that he hasn't been in touch."

"Not yet. He or she was supposed to contact me only in case of an emergency. Everything's been going so smoothly. . . ."

"That's good to hear. The wife and I always wanted to get to Europe. Maybe when the girls are a little older."

"This person may not even exist, Sergeant. I mean, I

wouldn't put it past Otto to invent some imaginary assistant, just to jack up the price."

"A possibility." He sounded unconvinced. "If he does get in touch, will you call me right away? It's important."

"Uh, yes, of course."

Rawlings gave Amy his home number, thanked her again, and wished her a happy conclusion to her tour.

For a full minute after hanging up, Amy sat and stared at the phone number. Why hadn't she said anything? Was she protecting Marcus? Protecting Marcus from what? Or was this just another example of Amy's penchant for ignoring unpleasant facts?

"One day at a time," she told herself. "The game is over tomorrow. The tour ends the day after. Whoever said you can't run away from your problems just didn't run fast enough."

Two more days. Then Otto and Marcus and this whole mess would be someone else's problem.

CHAPTER 14

"It must be hard for you, being back in Rome and all." Holly Baker sat on a limestone step, hugging her legs. She was staring up at her uncle's profile, bathing him in the kind of profound, motherly concern that Burt Baker had grown very used to.

"Eat your *marroni*," he said, holding out the waxed-paper cone of roasted chestnuts. "The clue told us to eat them."

Holly made a face and pushed them away. "What difference does it make, eating them or not?"

The judge finished chewing his current piece of nut meat, then picked out another. "I don't know."

They sat near the top of the Spanish Steps, just out of the flow of pedestrian traffic. The judge's legs were splayed out stiffly in front, and he gazed past them, down the river of steps to the Piazza di Spagna below. At the piazza's center stood the famous whimsical fountain, shaped like a sinking boat. Beyond it, alleys of stylish shops radiated from the expanse of sand-colored paving stones like the spokes of a half wheel. The piazza itself was dotted with postcard stalls and thronged with tourists taking pictures of one another to prove to themselves that they were here.

"Alice loved Rome," Burt said softly.

"I like Paris," Holly countered. They had stopped in Paris for a few days on their way to Monte Carlo, making Holly something of a world traveler.

Burt nodded. "Rome isn't easy. Paris has all that eye-catching architecture and those leafy, romantic parks. Rome is full of monuments and squares. And monolithic buildings that thrust out right to the sidewalk and reflect the heat."

"It is kind of hot."

"But behind those stone walls, that's what Alice loved." He glanced up at the hazy blue sky. "You should see Rome from the air. All the roof gardens. And inside those monoliths, the hidden courtyards with their fountains, and maybe in a corner some two-thousand-year-old pillar stolen from the Forum by some medieval farmer and now holding up a wall. All the layers of art and history hidden from public view. Rome takes a bit of knowing to love." He smiled. "Like me."

"Everyone loves you, Uncle Burt. Too many people."

Burt Baker thought carefully. "No one can take your aunt Alice's place. But sometimes I get lonely, pumpkin."

"I know. You like that woman with the big chin and all the money."

"Holly, you're being cruel."

"Judge! Don't throw out your paper!" Their teammates, Carla and Rod Templar, were clambering up through the tide of tourists, waving an unfolded cone of waxed paper. "There's a message from Daryl on our sheet," shouted Rod as he came closer. "It's in some kind of gibberish code."

"I thought the street vendor might be a plant." Burt shook his head in admiration. "Holly, take this." A second later he dumped the remaining chestnuts into his niece's hands. "This is why we were told to eat."

"Right," said Holly and let the chestnuts escape. They fell like soft marbles down the long steps.

Burt unfolded his own cone and held it up to the light. There were deliberate lines and loops, half-formed letters visible where the wax had been scratched away with a sharp point. "You're right. It's some sort of gibberish."

"Put them together." Holly was peering over her uncle's shoulder. "Put the papers one behind the other."

"What?" Carla didn't understand.

"They're part of the same clue." Holly rolled her eyes in exaggerated annoyance, grabbed both sheets of waxed paper, and held them up to the light. Slowly she rotated them, one against the other, until the lines and loops on the one began to line up with those on the other. "We're on the same team, right?" She spoke almost tauntingly. "But they tell us to split up and get two different things of chestnuts. Why?"

"I'm sure you'll tell us," said Carla.

"We're supposed to put them together. Sheesh. It's like we're back in grade school."

"Holly!" Burt would have tried being firmer, but she seemed to be right.

The twelve-year-old squeezed the sheets together, visually combining the lines and loops on the two unfolded cones. Soon she was picking out letters, then combining them to form words. "Meet me."

Rod was surprised. "Meet? We're actually catching up with Daryl?"

Holly continued. "Immaculate Conception. Capu—Capuchin Church.' Anyone know where that is?"

"Yes." Uncle Burt shuddered. "Just a few blocks away. But I'm not sure it's the sort of place to take Holly."

"That I'd like to see," said Carla.

Rod looked at the long, flowing staircase spread out below them. "I hope we can get there from the top." His gaze fell on Burt's crutches, then moved somewhat guiltily up to his face. "Can we?"

"Yes. It's closer to the top." The judge grunted in anticipation, then braced himself against the marble rail and pushed himself up. "I think this is the end. This is where we find Daryl's body."

"How can you know that?" Holly asked.

"You'll see." He was already propelling himself upward, toward the smaller piazza. "It's on Via Veneto. Maybe four blocks away."

They were still over a block from their destination when Holly tugged on her uncle's sleeve and nearly sent him sprawling. "Those damned Bitsys." She had stopped and turned and was now pointing across the street and back twenty yards. "They're following us. Cheaters!"

Burt and the Templars saw the bevy of middle-aged women scurrying up on the other side of Via della Purificazione. "They're going to pass us," Rod said, keeping his eyes averted from the judge and his crutches.

Martha Callas was at the front of the pack, consulting a small street map. Now she saw them and waved. "Hello!" She quickened her pace, and the other three Bitsys strode to catch up. "Looks like we're heading the same direction. Care to call it a tie?"

"No," insisted Holly. "They're just following us."

"Absolutely," Rod called out. The striding, sweating

women were even now crossing the street to meet them. "That's very generous of you."

"Well, you are in the lead," Martha cooed breathlessly. "And racing you in this heat wouldn't be civilized. After all, this is a vacation." Gently, expertly, she wedged Holly out of the way and fell in beside the judge, threading her hand through the crook between his arm and the crutch.

They arrived at the Capuchin Church of the Immaculate Conception just in time to sight a third group making their way around the church's long main staircase to an unassuming entrance on the street level.

"Georgina," called out Burt. He quickened his pace, inadvertently pulling himself free of Martha's velvet grip. "Shall we call it a three-way tie?"

"Not on your life. Even if we weren't in the lead, which we are, we could still kick out your crutches. We Dodos are ornery, and we need a win. Hello, Amy." Georgina had turned to face their tour leader, who was waiting for them at the door. "Has our Daryl joined the Capuchin monks? I adore their coffee."

"I'll tell them." In deference to the location, Amy had changed into a gray silk dress, sleeved and waisted, with a conservative neckline, but still a few inches above the knee. "I take it the Dodos are claiming first?"

"The Bitsys and Prices have agreed on a tie," Martha said. "For second."

Amy noted the time, then adopted her serious face. "Only one team at a time. And please, it's a religious site. You should behave accordingly."

The Dodos were ushered in while the others waited. According to a sign, the museum and the crypts were officially closed between the hours of noon and three.

"We must have made a generous contribution," guessed Georgina.

"A contribution," Amy confirmed and led them past the first room, the museum, up to a dark-paneled door. A brown-robed monk opened it solemnly and motioned them into the next room.

"Oh, my God." Georgina couldn't help herself.

This lower level of the Capuchin Church was in reality five crypts, lined up one behind the other. The vaulted rooms had a rectangular floor plan, and each was about the length of a limousine. All four walls were roped off, leaving only a walkway down the middle, which led the visitors from one chapel into the next. Even if the public were allowed near enough to touch anything, it was doubtful that many would, since the rooms were decorated almost entirely in human bones.

"I've heard of this place," Paul Wickes whispered. "These are the bones of the monks themselves."

Georgina was staring at several full skeletons dressed in brown robes, one of whom bore a disturbing resemblance to the man at the door. As she walked from room to room and grew accustomed to the theme, the gruesome ingenuity of the place became apparent.

Few of the skeletons were complete sets of bones, the demands of design having clearly won out over mundane anatomy. One chapel was laid out in a head motif. Three of its walls were decorated in jawless skulls. Some were stacked in simple, mind-numbing piles; others arranged in fanciful designs, the skulls alternating playfully with collarbones and femurs. Everywhere, hundreds of empty, dusty eye sockets stared out.

In the next room, what had originally looked like a rococo ceiling turned out to be a rather graceful combination of finger and foot bones. Along one wall, a

clock face of bones—nonfunctioning, thank heaven—
was surrounded by dainty rosettes and topped by the
needless but still chilling axiom "Tempus fugit." All in
bones.

"There must be thousands." Georgina spoke in awe
as she passed under an archway lined with short leg
bones. Or were they arms? She forced her gaze to the
floor. "I never knew you could do so much with bones.
Well, I never gave it much thought. Can you imagine
being a priest around here?"

"I'll bet their benefits include a funeral package,"
Paul said. It was funny enough, but no one laughed.

At the end of the fifth chapel, an open door beck-
oned them into a shadowy, lightless chamber.

"I'm not going in there," Paul declared. "I don't
care. . . ."

Then a switch was flipped by an unseen hand. Inside,
a single naked bulb dangled from the ceiling and revealed what was probably a storage room, now converted into the setting for the mystery's climax.

"Oh, good," Georgina sighed. "It's just Daryl."

On the floor in the middle of the vaulted room was
the actor they all recognized from Monte Carlo. He was
lying in a pool of fake blood, the handle of a knife pro-
truding from a latex gash in his chest. After the last five
rooms, this bloody crime scene was almost a relief.

Without exchanging a word, the Dodos began to
search for clues, poking around the pretend corpse with a
reverence for life, which they probably wouldn't have felt
had they not just been forced to confront so much death.

"Take out your notebook," Georgina instructed her
second in command. "Poor Daryl. He deserves our best."

CHAPTER 15

The interrogation took place on the roof garden, offering a spectacular view of the Capitoline Hill on one side and the Tiber on the other. The hotel staff had spaced six tables evenly around the garden, then had set up an open bar in the middle. This would be the teams' only chance to grill each other. And while they might not be assured of complete and honest answers, at least they wouldn't be lied to.

For today only, outright lies were forbidden. Teams could even ask, "Are you the killer?" although it wouldn't do much good. No one knew that answer, not even the killer, who, if he wanted to win the game, would be put in the awkward position of having to accuse himself.

At Amy's urging, the captains pulled together their own costumes and did their best to inhabit their characters. Martha, as the daytime drama queen, had constructed a tacky Hollywood outfit that featured various bits of lingerie. This she wore gamely, despite her size and the autumn chill, which was producing expansive fields of purplish goose bumps. A dark suit and bow tie made Marcus resemble a butler more than a private secretary, while Georgina autocratically refused to change a thread or a gesture—which made her an absolutely perfect Dodo.

A captain presided at each table, and in round-robin fashion, the three non-captains from each of the other teams sat down and posed their questions, trying to piece together the hidden, secret motives they all so jealously guarded. "Were you and Daryl having an affair?" "How much of the company do you own?" The captains were forced to give answers that could turn out to be either misleading or revealing, depending on their skill. Amy spent her time settling small disputes.

She had just finished clarifying a point between the captain of the Dodos and the Doloreses, calling it in Dodo's favor. The Doloreses, Vinny and his twins, were enthusiastic rally players but indifferent detectives. They accepted Amy's decision and didn't even rephrase their query.

"If you'll excuse us . . ." Vinny glanced over at his wife's table. Jolynn was facing down an inquisition from the Fidels. "I think the boys and I might pay a call on the refreshments."

"You still have about three minutes," Amy said, checking her watch.

"I know." The twins were already on the way to the hors d'oeuvres. "You won't tell Jolynn about this. She'll have my hide."

"Not me," Georgina vowed. "The fewer questions, the better."

Amy watched as Vinny tiptoed around to the far side. All the other interrogations seemed to be going smoothly. "So, you have it all figured out?" she asked.

Georgina guffawed. "Darling, we haven't got a clue."

"I thought the other day in Assisi . . ." Amy frowned.

"I mean, when you had that brainstorm . . ." Okay. She might as well just say it. "It was about Fabian Carvel, wasn't it? You remembered something about his murder, not Daryl's." As her words hit the air, she realized they sounded like an accusation.

"Fabian's . . . you think . . ." Was her smile trembling just a bit? "Really, dear. I can barely remember what I did yesterday. And you think something that happened five years ago—"

"Someone said or did something that reminded you."

"No. It wasn't anything." She lowered her voice. "It was a little inconsistency, that's all."

"You know why he ran away." Amy's guess was answered with a helpless roll of the eyes. "You do! Oh, my God! Georgina, this is serious. What made him leave the dinner table? Was it a guest? A family member?"

"No one, dear. That's the problem."

"No one? What do you mean? Was it Marcus Alvarez?"

Georgina was taken aback. "So, you know about Marcus."

"He was the real Fidel."

"I didn't think he'd tell you. He made me promise not to."

"Marcus is not your companion. And don't tell me the two of you met at JFK."

"Yes, we did. Why are you so hard on me?" She glanced around at the other tables. "Shouldn't you be blowing your little whistle and sending in the next pack?"

"This is more important. You knew Marcus from five years ago."

"Yes, yes, yes. But not well." She reached across the table, grabbed Amy's glass of club soda, took a sip, then used a napkin to wipe her lipstick off the rim. "Marcus was always around the Long Island house, doing correspondence for Doris or keeping Fabian on his schedule. He hadn't been with them very long when it happened. After the San Diego trip and Fabian's funeral . . . we lost touch."

"When did you restore touch?"

Georgina squirmed. Was this like the other interrogations? Amy wondered. Did the same rules apply? Evasions but no lies?

"I was in New York for Fashion Week. Well over six months ago. Marcus saw a photo of me on Page Six and called me at the Waldorf. We had drinks. He was very upfront about working for Otto. According to him, Otto was brilliant and underappreciated and just needed good management."

"Did you know they were making it into a game?"

She shook her head. "Marcus told me they were working on a mystery rally. But I had no idea it was based on Fabian. He made it sound wonderful."

"That's how you found out about the tour?"

"Uh-huh. By the way, your publicity was dreadful. My travel agent had the hardest time figuring out what I was talking about."

"I'm a small operation."

"Forgiven. I don't think Marcus even knew I'd signed up, not until we ran into each other at JFK."

Amy rechecked her watch. Some of the teams had taken breaks and were standing with Vinny and his sons at the hors d'oeuvres table. "That day at the Waldorf, did you talk about Fabian and the case?"

"We did. In retrospect, I suppose he was grilling me." Georgina raised her shoulders and grinned sheepishly. "You know how it is when you share a traumatic experience. It's always the topic of conversation, every time you meet. It was only natural that we gossip and speculate. Really, Amy, I still have the Stew Boys coming up. If we keep talking about the real crime, I'm going to get so confused. It hasn't been easy keeping things straight."

"I sympathize. What did you tell Marcus about the murder?"

"Ask him yourself. Now it's really time for you to blow that whistle. Time to move on."

CHAPTER 16

The laughter in the dining room was friendly, harmless and, at least to the Price team, annoying. Burt did his best to be a good sport. He was certainly taking it better than Holly, who was back at the team table, shrinking sullenly into her chair.

"No, no," he stammered into the microphone, straining to be heard. "Think about it. The actor who played Fidel in Monte Carlo had a bit of that androgynous look. Kind of a slight build and wide hips . . . Damn, I just know I'm going to say something derogatory about women or the transgendered and my career is going to be shot to hell." The judge tried to cover his embarrassment by leaning over the podium to retrieve his water glass.

"Are you saying that actor was a woman?" Frank Loyola shouted from one of the tables of four.

Burt was talking into the glass. "Well, maybe. Or maybe he was just hired to give the illusion that he was a woman playing the role of a man."

"Is this a comment on me?" The captain of the Fidels

stood and posed, his fists pumped playfully into his hips.

"No, no," Burt shouted above the laughs. "Marcus, please."

Burt had donned his deerstalker cap in honor of his team's official solution. Now he removed it, setting it on the podium's upper shelf. "I am required to give my team's theory, whether I agree with it or not. And if you quote me, I'll deny it."

There had been a certain amount of heckling all evening, and the others were now almost euphoric to see the last team presenting such a far-fetched solution.

"Anyway . . ." It was only a game, as he'd told Holly so often. "It is our opinion that Daryl's very private secretary, Fidel, is a woman in disguise."

Applause and whoops greeted this official declaration.

"Let Burt have his say." Amy was seated next to the podium. "After all," she added, "after all, transsexual disguises are a tried-and-true convention in the mystery field."

"Burt has a perfect right to hang himself," yelled Georgina.

The finale had convened at seven o'clock in the red baroque dining room. For much of the actual meal, the tables of four whispered and argued in private as they worked out the fine points. And then, during dessert, the captains, fortified with various amounts of wine, one by one rose and came forward to become the somewhat willing targets of abuse. Each outlined his or her team's theory—the murderer, the method, and the motive, including such details as why Daryl left the table and what had prompted him to flee all the way to Rome.

The judge continued with a smile, determined to enjoy this as much as anyone. "Fidel—or Fidelia, as we've dubbed her—disguised herself as a man so that she and Daryl could carry on an affair right under his wife's nose."

"Weak," shouted Frank Loyola.

Burt ignored the critique. "Price found out about the affair. Not knowing Fidel's real sex, Price assumed his father was a latent homosexual. Not latent. Closeted." Burt looked up from his notes. "This is merely our interpretation of the evidence. Anyway . . ."

Burt soldiered on, managing to make a certain amount of sense, but only a certain amount. The audience was on his side now. They admired his tenacity and imagination and greeted the conclusion of his painfully bizarre explanation with a hearty round of applause.

"Thank you, Burt," Amy said, taking over the microphone. "Now if I can have all the captains come up to the table . . ." From her briefcase, she brought out seven scripts, six for them and one for herself. "Everyone please take a script and a chair."

Amy had hoped for a round table. A round table would have been more reminiscent of the original scene in Daryl's mansion. Instead, she had settled for a thin rectangular model. It was in front of the podium, set with chargers and silverware and glasses for dessert wine. During the entire six-course meal it had stood conspicuously empty.

The captains all took their scripts and their seats. Instinctively, the dominant males, Price and Stew, or rather the captains representing them, gravitated to the two edges of the table facing the audience. Dolores, as matriarch, was granted the spot in between. On the op-

posite side, Bitsy Stormfield and the sexually confused
Fidel took the edges, leaving the center position for
Dodo Fortunof.

"Ladies and gentlemen, thank you for coming." Amy
had retrieved Burt's deerstalker and had borrowed
Vinny Mrozek's unlit pipe. "My name is Inspector Abel of
Interpol." Her transformation was greeted with appreciative chuckles.

From her true-crime reading, Amy knew that Interpol was just an international fact-gathering system, little
more than a building full of files and computers, and
had no official jurisdiction. But the "Interpol inspector"
had served fiction well throughout the years, and Amy
saw no reason to second-guess Otto's script.

"What does this have to do with Interpol?" Jolynn
Mrozek read from her script. Her sour tone was just
right for the freshly widowed Dolores. "We, my family
and a few friends, came down to Rome for a vacation.
Daryl went off by himself for a walk. His senseless murder in that chapel today . . ." Pause.

Amy jumped in a second late. "You are not here on
vacation, madam, and your husband did not go out for a
walk. He has been missing for two weeks. This is an international matter." She turned a page. "I have been following this case from Monte Carlo, and I am prepared to
make an arrest. Daryl Litcomb was murdered by someone at this very table."

"One of us?" Frank Loyola read the line as a threat.
"Explain yourself, sir."

And so Amy explained.

As the twenty-four players listened, she circled the
table, head bent over her script, outlining the entire plot,
detailing each one of their secret relationships to the victim and their possible motives. Gently mocking snickers

bubbled up as it grew apparent that Fidel was indeed a man and had always been one.

"I told you," Holly hissed into Carla Templar's ear. "Why didn't you listen?"

At this point, the Fidel character had several lines of dialogue, and Marcus made the most of them. He rose from the table, borrowed Amy's borrowed pipe, and swaggered straight up to Burt Baker. In place of the obsequious whine he normally used for Fidel, Marcus adopted a broad, macho accent with origins somewhere between Brooklyn and South Boston.

"Yo, Inspector." He pointed the pipe into Burt's face, and even though the lines were written to be delivered to Amy, they worked beautifully. "I hope you realize that youse is running my good name tru da mud. Dese allegations is slanderous. My relationship with Mr. Litcomb was strictly on the up-and-up. And, may I remind you, you cannot prove a ting." Marcus grabbed his crotch and snorted. "Not a ting. I am gonna have to demand a public apology."

Judge Baker joined in the fun. "I apologize, sir, from the bottom of my heart." He pushed himself to his feet. "I don't know what I could have been thinking." And before Marcus could prepare himself, the crippled man took his face in both hands and planted a long, exaggerated kiss on his lips. The crowd went wild.

Except for Holly, of course.

It was well after ten when Amy announced the solution and placed Georgina in handcuffs. Then she explained how and why Dodo had murdered Daryl, the man who had bankrupted her family through a labyrinth of fiscal skulduggery.

"You are completely broke, Miss Fortunof. I found that out in Assisi." She was referring to a clue they'd all unearthed at that particular stop. "You came to Monte Carlo to beg for a loan, but Daryl just sneered at you—you, the woman who had given him his start in business."

It was nearly eleven when Amy handed out the trophies to Frank and the Stew Boys, a surprise win that had been achieved by a combination of good guessing, respectable times, and their own limited imagination, which, unlike the Prices' imagination, never went too far.

Holly was nearly asleep in her chair. The adults all looked pleasantly full and ready to call it a night. That was when Marcus rose from the narrow table.

"I offer you the warmest congratulations of Otto Ingo." Their sleepy smiles faded, as did the warm, soft buzz. "I know how proud he would have been. There was nothing Otto enjoyed more than creating mysteries and seeing people solve them." Marcus caught the maître d'hôtel's eye and signaled him with a raised finger. "I was honored to have been Mr. Ingo's assistant, working at his side while he created some of his most intriguing games. Including this one."

"He's a ringer," Jolynn muttered.

Confused glances darted around the red oval room. Nowhere was the confusion more pronounced than at the Fidel table, where Marcus's partners were wondering if his presence on their team had been an advantage or a disadvantage. It certainly had to be something.

"You wrote this game?" asked Martha.

"No, no. Otto sent me here for an education, to see how his games worked in real life. He kept me in the dark, made me play it for real."

This time, Amy was grateful for the lie. She could feel the tension ease.

Marcus went on. "I didn't know anything more than

you. Sorry, Harry, Rosemary, June. I did my best. I do, however, have one official duty to perform."

The maître d' was approaching with a tray. On it were a small wine bottle and a glass, the freshly removed cork lying between them.

"Before I left New York, Otto asked me to share this dessert wine with you. It was presented to him two years ago by the king of Sweden." He accepted the bottle and made a pretense of examining the label. "There is only enough for the team captains, unfortunately. Or fortunately. After all, it's a Swedish wine." The ripple of laughter from the lower six tables was tinged with disappointment.

Once again, Amy was surprised by the facility with which Marcus could spin a yarn. She had seen him buy this bottle yesterday in a wine shop on Via Goito.

Marcus circled the long table, pouring the pale liquid into the six glasses. Like an experienced waiter, he stopped at each captain's left, reached over with the bottle, and single-handedly measured the right amount. He was at the middle of the table, leaning over to pour for Georgina, when the bottle's mouth clinked against her glass. Marcus had to grab the glass with his free hand to keep it from tipping over.

He finished the round in front of his own chair. Several of the captains had already picked up their glasses and were sniffing them curiously.

"And I had to leave a taste for our wonderful leader," added Marcus, taking the lone glass from the tray. It was spoken as an applause line, though the audience needed little prompting. Amy stood to accept their noisy, heartfelt tribute.

"Good job." Marcus's hand brushed against hers as he handed her the wine. Amy's pulse quickened. She took a deep breath and tried to deny the feeling, tried to pass it off as a reaction to the whoops of appreciation coming from the other twenty-three.

"To Otto." Marcus raised his glass and was respectfully mimicked by his fellow captains. About half the non-captains joined in on the toast, honoring Otto with everything from after-dinner port to Pepsi to one hastily prepared dose of Alka-Seltzer.

"To Otto," Georgina echoed with the others. Not being all that fond of sweet wine, she was a little slow in picking up her glass, the last on the table. She toasted and sipped. It was even worse than expected. How could they drink this swill?

Jolynn smiled at her from across the table and executed a mini-toast.

Georgina felt obligated to take another sip. What was that taste? Under the tannin and the sweetness was a slight fragrance of amaretto, she decided and followed this observation with another, more curious sip. Not a natural amaretto, either. There was something metallic to it.

Lowering her nose to the rim, she sniffed. Again and again she sniffed, forcefully, in and out, not so much to identify the sweet-sour bouquet anymore. No, that was no longer a priority. Her mouth exploded open. She was just trying to breathe.

With her mouth gaping wide, Georgina began to gulp. Air. She needed air. But the more effort she put into breathing, the less oxygen she took in. Shallow, fast breaths now. Terrified breaths. And before she knew it, she was choking.

Amy was not the first to hear the gasps.

Martha Callas, to Georgina's left, wrinkled her nose, quick to show disgust at what sounded like the throaty gurgle. A few seconds later and Martha knew something was wrong. She stretched an arm to the other woman's shoulder. "Something go down the wrong way?"

Georgina responded by collapsing, dropping her head onto the empty charger that marked her place setting.

Frank Loyola threw back his seat and rushed to her side. Meanwhile, Burt pushed himself to his feet and began propelling his crutches around the table. He looked down helplessly as the Bronx patrolman stooped over Georgina, grabbed her around the rib cage, pulled her to her feet, and pulled sharply upward. Then he did it again.

The rest of the room looked on as Frank lowered Georgina into her chair, turned her head sideways, and pried open her mouth. As he worked on clearing an already unobstructed air passage, Amy's eyes fell on Georgina's wine.

She felt self-conscious doing it but did it anyway, picked up the glass and sniffed inside the rim. Having just tasted the wine, Amy knew what to expect. This wasn't it, not quite. "Does anyone have any heart medicine?" She asked the question without really thinking.

"She's not choking," Frank said, his fingers coming out of Georgina's mouth. "You think a heart attack?"

Amy sniffed the glass again. "Anyone with amyl nitrite? It's an emergency."

"A heart attack?" Burt asked, looking completely helpless.

"No." Amy was thinking back to that mystery seminar she'd attended last year up in Boston and the lecture entitled "Scents of Crime." At the door, they'd passed out "scratch and sniff" cards. All very cute and harmless. "Amyl nitrite. You know, the little things you break open for heart patients. Or sodium something. Sodium nitrite. Where the hell do you get sodium nitrite?" She was starting to panic now, babbling on as Georgina's face lost its color, then quickly gained a bluish tinge.

Everyone just looked on, stunned.

"My God. Call a doctor!" Amy screamed. "Why are you just standing there? Don't you idiots know cyanide poisoning when you see it?"

CHAPTER 17

Rain clouds drifted over the broken vaults and arches. The dirty cotton balls floated among patches of blue, bringing drifts of light showers that alternated with long streaks of morning light. First one side of the Colosseum, then the other would be bathed in bright sun, followed by shadows and rain, followed by sun. It was a darkly dappled September sky, the kind of unsettled weather pattern most conducive to rainbows, although Amy wasn't in the mood to look for rainbows.

She was sitting on cold limestone in the stands, just a few arches in from the street and the traffic. Sheltered from the current spattering of rain, she poured another cup of strong black coffee from a thermos on loan from the hotel. The concierge had proved to be most understanding, more understanding about the murder, in fact, than he'd been about the finish line.

Amy blamed herself for things getting so out of hand. Not that she could have prevented Georgina's death. No one could have except the killer. But she should have done more to take charge. Perhaps if she had made people stay in their seats until the police arrived . . . Then again, they might not have listened. Calling them idiots hadn't won her a lot of points.

By the time she did try to assert control, it was too late. Twenty-three mystery fanatics were already running amuck. The effect of Georgina's death, once the initial shock had passed, had been like throwing raw meat into a pack of wolves. Even Frank, a police officer who should have known better, had joined in the frenzy.

A dozen evening bags had flown open, and two dozen hands had foraged for empty plastic bags. *Why,* Amy wondered, *do women always carry plastic bags in their purses? For moments just like this, obviously.*

Amy had never been able to figure out the difference between the two Italian police agencies, the *polizia* and the *carabinieri*. For what it was worth, the *polizia* seemed to be in charge of murders. They were the ones who had shown up, looking bewildered as they were greeted by a horde of chattering Americans, who shoved approximately four dozen plastic bags into their faces. The bags were filled with potential clues, they were told, everything from the wineglass to the cork to a lone breath mint extracted with tweezers from Georgina's evening bag. Even Georgina's own plastic bags had been preserved inside other plastic bags.

"Tell them the bags are hermetically sealed," Holly Baker insisted.

Each professional detective was surrounded by a small pride of amateurs, who pointed and grabbed and spoke in torrents of English. The few of Amy's guests who did know bits of Italian didn't seem to know the right words, which only added to the confusion.

"They call this a phrase book?" Jolynn growled as she threw her thin red dictionary against the red brocade wall. "It doesn't even have the basics. *Fingerprint. Witness.* How are we supposed to carry on a conversation?"

Amy finally pinpointed the captain in charge, an increasingly agitated man by the name of Boido. When Amy approached him, speaking passable Italian, the man's face lit up.

"Finally. Someone who can make sense. That woman . . ." He was pointing to Martha Callas. "My English is so bad. I thought she told me this murder was a game."

"Not really," Amy said with a sheepish grin.

"What? You mean to say it *was* a game?"

"No. I mean, we were playing a game when it happened. But the murder is very real, very serious."

"I know."

"No one thinks it's a game."

"Then why do they hand me little bags of clues?" Captain Boido shook his head in the direction of the melee. Holly Baker was on her hands and knees, trying to get a uniformed officer to inspect a stain under the table. "It has been my experience that most people are sad and quiet at a murder scene."

"Yes, well . . . they're just trying to help."

"Amy," Burt called out from the other side of the oval room. "I'm having one person from each table write out a deposition—while it's still fresh in their minds."

"Judge, I think the police would prefer . . ."

"I'm a notary," piped in Bill, the Atlanta gem dealer. "Should I notarize their statements?"

"Absolutely." She was speaking perhaps a bit too loudly. "Notarize everything."

A light breeze scooped a few sprinkles of rain up under Amy's arch and brought her back to the present.

For the third time she removed her glasses to wipe them and this time decided to keep them off. It had been a long, unpleasant night with very little sleep.

The one bright spot had been the way her clients had accepted the death. As opposed to the members of most tours, who might be resentful of police questions and frightened by a death in their midst, her people were treating it like part of their schedule. "Finale banquet to be followed by murder of tour member. Gratuities included."

She sipped her coffee, hot and good, then listened to the faint sounds of morning traffic. The Colosseum was her favorite place in Rome. In the days of her first tour with Eddie, it had always been open—free, tranquil, and ancient. A world-famous marvel you could slip into at any hour of the day or night. She recalled standing under an arch at midnight on Eddie's birthday, the two of them sharing a kiss. Then he'd pulled a bottle of champagne from his knapsack and popped the cork. They'd drunk from the bottle, giddy with the moment.

It had been too good to last, of course. The Colosseum had hours now, like any other tourist attraction— hours and gates, audio guides and admission fees. At least it wasn't too crowded this morning. And it was quieter than she remembered. No more blaring horns. Rome, like Amy's hometown, had instituted an ordinance against honking, except for danger. Here in Rome the law seemed to be generally respected, whereas in New York, it was regarded as little more than a cute throwback to a gentler day, like the law prohibiting you from hitching your horse to a public lamppost.

Amy checked her watch. Soon she would have to leave this sanctuary and return to the messy unpleasantries. The American embassy. The airline, for shipping the body. The police, who would undoubtedly want an autopsy. Contacting Georgina's relatives in the U.S.

And then there were her clients. Today was their final full day. It had been set aside for sightseeing and relaxation, although seven of them had planned to leave early. Would they be allowed to go?

"I like you better with your glasses on."

Amy didn't look up but continued to sip her coffee, hunched over and pensive.

"The concierge said you might be here." Marcus brushed the area beside Amy clear of raindrops. "It's nice," he said but couldn't mask the shiver as he settled onto the cold, wet limestone.

Amy didn't reply but refilled her cup from the thermos and passed it over. Marcus accepted it, warming his hands on the plastic. "Today will probably be worse than last night, now that the excitement has worn off. If there's anything I can do . . . There must be a lot of details." Amy looked at him for the first time. He was wearing jeans and a light jacket and looked tired.

"Did you come here to coordinate our lies?" she asked coldly. "Get our stories straight for the police?"

"Stories straight? What stories?"

"Well, for one, our friend, the king of Sweden. The guy who hands out bottles of poisoned wine."

Marcus shrugged. "I wanted it to be special. What's the harm in letting people think it came from Otto? We all do that—like writing a thank-you note and adding your husband's name at the bottom."

"My thank-you notes don't contain cyanide."

"Neither did the wine. The poison was in the glass." Marcus paused. "You're not going to tell the police about the wine?"

"I won't have to. The EEC requires all foreign wines

to have the importer's name on the label—an Italian firm in this case. So, unless the king of Sweden buys his wine in Italy . . ."

Marcus whistled. "Thank you. Really. You saved me from an embarrassing little fib."

"I saved you from nothing. They have a dozen notarized depositions featuring your lie about the king of Sweden."

"I'll just tell them what I told you. They'll understand."

"Understand?" She was on her feet, her voice echoing throughout the cavernous arena. Nearby, a bevy of teenage girls looked up from their audio guides. "You still don't get it." Amy grabbed the plastic cup, tossing the leftover coffee out into the rain, which this time was refusing to stop. "They know you lied about the wine. They know you were Otto's assistant." With a jerk, she screwed the cup back on the thermos. "One phone call and they'll find out Otto was murdered, too."

"So what? I didn't kill . . ." His eyes widened. "Is that what this is about? You think I'm a killer?"

"No." Amy tried it again with more sincerity. "No. You couldn't have thrown the rock at yourself or robbed the rooms. Even you couldn't do that."

"I didn't do anything."

"Look at it from their point of view. You worked for Otto. You poured the wine that killed Georgina. You worked for Fabian Carvel. How long before they find out about that?"

"Oh," Marcus muttered, the last vestige of spirit draining from his voice. "How long have you known?"

"Long enough. Why did you lie about being the real Fidel?"

"I didn't lie—exactly."

"The hell you didn't. Was it your idea, basing the game on the Carvel murder?"

"No." He sounded sincere, but then he always did. "As soon as Otto found out I was involved, he began asking questions. It fascinated him."

Amy nodded. "And so what do we have? Three unsolved murders, all connected by a single thread. You. The cops love this. They call it circumstantial evidence."

"I didn't kill anyone."

"And I believe you. Being a liar doesn't automatically make you a killer."

She was doing her best to stay indignant, but it wasn't easy, not in the face of such helplessness. She smiled, hoping to take the sting out of her words. But Marcus was somewhere else now, staring at the hands in his lap, arranged as if they were still holding the warm plastic cup.

"Is there anyone else on the tour, perhaps another team captain, who knew the Carvels? Someone Fabian knew? Had business dealings with?"

Marcus shrugged. "I wasn't with him all that long."

"Well, someone was pulling those stunts. It wasn't you, and it wasn't Georgina."

"Poor Georgina. Dying in a strange country, surrounded by strangers. No one's even mourning, not really." Marcus glanced up from his hands. For the first time that morning their eyes met—and held. "Jeez, don't look at me that way."

"What way?"

"That way. That sentimental wince, like you just drove by a cute little rabbit roadkill."

"You may be arrested, you know. Just so you'll be prepared."

"I know."

They both stood, facing each other. Then Marcus gently took the glasses from her hand, wiped the lenses with the tail of his shirt, and placed the frames on her face. "Better."

Wordlessly, they made their way through the canyon of shadowy arches that led out to the cobblestone piazza. In the street beyond, a busload of Italian schoolchildren was just filing toward the entrance gate. A similar load of Japanese tourists was also climbing down from their motorized chariot, gaping and chattering and taking pictures as they prepared to enter the pagan amphitheater.

Directly overhead, the stubborn, unmoving cloud had nothing more in it than spray, tiny droplets that evaporated almost as soon as they touched the skin. "You want to walk, or you want to cab it?"

"Let's walk," Marcus said. "It may be a while before I get any more exercise."

They fell in side by side, hands almost touching. At a street corner Marcus reached out an arm to bar her from stepping out into a bustling herd of motorbikes. She let his arm stay there until the crosswalk was clear.

CHAPTER 18

During Amy's absence, the *polizia* had returned to the hotel, collected passports, and advised everyone not to leave town. Under the circumstances, with another night of lodging still paid for and an unsolved murder in their midst, Amy wasn't surprised by the cooperation her people were showing. She figured she had twelve more hours before the complaints began.

The concierge had arranged taxis, which showed up just as they were finishing a buffet lunch in the red brocade crime scene. For three hours that afternoon, Amy led her troops around the Forum and the Palatine Hill, perched above it. Marcus stuck by her side at the head of the procession, as if hesitant to mingle in the trailing pack. This was understandable. The tour members seemed to spend even more time than usual whispering among themselves.

"You shouldn't have come," Amy said as she checked his map and turned left up the Via Sacra.

"It beats sitting in my room. And I'm giving them so much pleasure."

Marcus was still at Amy's side when the two officers saw them entering through the hotel's mahogany doors. Almost simultaneously, the men rose from the lobby's satin upholstered chairs. Both were young and deferential and, like a surprising number of their compatriots, impeccably dressed. The tour stayed back, behind an invisible rope, as the taller officer spoke in Italian. He addressed himself to the air between Amy and Marcus, as if knowing that a translation would be provided.

Amy's voice quavered as she interpreted the single sentence. "Marcus Alvarez, in the name of the Republic of Italy, I arrest you for the murder of Georgina Davis."

"Very good," the shorter man said in English. "You are welcome to escort Mr. Alvarez to our station, although a representative from your embassy will be there."

"I would very much like to," Amy answered in Italian.

True to the officer's word, an embassy staffer, a cheerful, helpful middle-aged woman, was waiting at the Prefettura di Roma, located at the foot of Via dei Fori Imperiali, about halfway between the hotel and the Colosseum. They had walked right past the imposing building that morning in the misty rain without realizing it.

The staffer followed them into the booking room, her good cheer startlingly out of place. It was apparent that she had been only briefly briefed. This was undoubtedly a misunderstanding, she said blithely. The embassy dealt with this kind of thing all the time. Not to worry. And although both Amy and Marcus knew this was nonsense, still they took a measure of comfort in her self-assured ignorance.

A face still familiar from last night passed by in the hall. Amy excused herself from Marcus and the fingerprinting officer and the embassy staffer, who had just finished reading the arrest warrant and was no longer smiling.

"Capitano Boido," Amy called out, chasing the man down the long green corridor.

Boido was a thin, angular gentleman, probably not far from retirement, a polite, worldly man whose rear bald spot had years ago merged with his front bald spot, leaving him with a thin laurel wreath of gray, well-manicured hair. As Amy spoke, the captain patiently adjusted his pocket handkerchief.

"Exactly, Signorina Abel." His tone was soothing. "You wish to know the position of our case against your friend. That is reasonable. Please come to my office."

For all of Boido's slow charm, the ensuing interview was surprisingly short. Amy barely had time to settle uncomfortably into a tall, straight-backed chair, the only provision in Boido's office for visitors.

The cyanide had been found in the wineglass, the captain explained, not in the bottle or in the food, not even in the single breath mint. Boido seemed perfectly at home in the neat, almost prim office. "According to many depositions drawn up by many expert witnesses . . . ," he said, a note of irony creeping into his voice, "no one but the victim and the accused touched the wineglass. Our case is very simple."

"He was keeping the glass from falling. Look, what possible motive could he have for killing her?"

"Who knows how the human mind works?" Boido said philosophically. "Have you another theory?"

"No," she had to admit.

"You, too, would sign an affidavit saying that no one else touched the glass?"

Amy grunted. "Yes."

"Just so. Signore Alvarez bought the wine on this

same day, obviously with this purpose in mind. A cyanide pill is very small. A stumble and a little sleight of hand and in it goes."

"If a cyanide pill is so small, then maybe someone just tossed it in."

"And no one saw this person take aim or noticed a splash? Yes, I will keep your theory in mind."

Amy returned to the booking room to find that Marcus and the staffer had been shoved on to yet another room, to be put through more of the endless paperwork that had helped make Italian bureaucracy world famous.

She borrowed a piece of paper from the fingerprinting officer and wrote. Her assumption that this note would be misplaced within minutes of its completion made her more honest that she might otherwise have been.

Don't lose hope. You are not alone. Love, Amy.

The Marcello's lobby was filled with stacks of familiar-looking suitcases, islands of black and brown dotting the pink marble floor. Amy wended her way through them. Not far away, some of her people stood in a cluster, waiting for their airport taxis. The passports, it seemed, had been released, and the seven early departures were trying to make their planes. There were last-minute hugs now and the checking of tickets, as if the events of yesterday and today were part of some half-forgotten movie. *And why not?* Amy mused as she ventured into the shadows of the dining room. *Life goes on.*

"Amy. How is he? Does he have a lawyer?" Judge Baker was seated at one of the small round tables, a cocktail lamp illuminating his notepad. Beside him, Martha Callas sat poised over a similar notepad, her silver bullet reflecting the glow of a mauve lampshade. "Martha and I are staying a few extra days. How's he holding up?"

"He didn't kill Georgina."

"Of course not," Martha snorted, as if this was the most ludicrous thing she'd ever heard. "Our first goal, as we see it, will be to get him out of jail. Burt here . . ."

"I made a call to the Italian Bar Association," Burt said. "They're contacting one of their top criminal lawyers and trying to persuade him to help out."

"Great. But I can't speak for Marcus. I don't know if he'll be able to afford—"

"Don't worry. The captains all contributed." Martha waved a small sheaf of checks. "And most of the others."

"We had to use a bit of coercion on Jolynn. You know Jolynn."

"Hold on. You think he's innocent?" Amy felt she must be missing something. "Look, either Marcus introduced the cyanide or it was one of the other captains. One of you. No one else even came near the table. You understand . . ."

"Naturally. How do you think we coerced Jolynn?" Martha performed her dramatic laugh with a gesture to match. "I said to her, 'Jolynn, if you don't contribute, everyone will just assume that you're guilty, including the papers. Amy's already had a phone call from the New York Times.' That was a bluff, of course."

Burt nodded. "One of us must have slipped the poison into her glass during Marcus's speech, although I really don't see how. Not yet."

Amy was both pleased and perplexed. "Um, just to play devil's advocate . . ." She cleared her throat, then settled into the table's one remaining chair. "I believe in Marcus, too. But wouldn't it be logical to assume that the one person who could have committed the murder actually did?"

Martha's smirk was full of pity. "Amy, Amy. Some of the best mystery players on earth have spent the past two weeks picking apart clues, constantly thinking about murder. Marcus would not do anything so obvious. Right under our noses? It has to be a setup."

"The Rome police don't see it that way."

The judge placed a hand, large and gnarled, on the table, enfolding Amy's two folded hands. "This is not a joke with us. As you know, I admired Georgina a great deal. She didn't deserve to die."

"Her murder casts a shadow over everyone," Martha added. "It's our duty to bring the killer to justice."

"Bring the killer . . . ?" Amy swallowed hard. "You don't actually mean that. You mean pay a private eye, that sort of thing." She nodded, hoping they would nod back. They didn't. "You're not saying you want to conduct your own murder investigation. Please say that's not what you're saying."

Burt broke into an eager smile. "Ninety-nine times out of a hundred, the police are the best at doing their jobs. They have the manpower and the experience."

"Not to mention legal authority."

"But they're not infallible. Believe me, I've seen it. And in this case, the killer isn't some wild kid or jealous spouse. It's one of us, someone who loves mysteries and knows how to misdirect our attention. How can the police solve that? We were witnesses. They weren't. No matter what they think, and I'm sure we made a lousy first impression . . ."

"You did."

"But we have a skill set. Granted, it's probably good only when pitted against a killer with a similar skill set.

But that's exactly the situation we're faced with. We're after a murder-mystery murderer. We owe it to Marcus and Otto and especially Georgina not to let this go unsolved."

"That's pretty much the oration he used on the rest of us," Martha said with chiding affection. "No one applauded, but no one objected."

"Officer Frank went along with this? He should know better."

Martha nodded. "Frank was one of the more enthusiastic ones. Just between us chickens, I think he has dreams of making the homicide squad."

"There is a realistic limit to what we can do," Burt warned. "Besides the money. I can arrange a lawyer. Martha can influence the embassy when required."

"Texas connections," Martha explained. "We're everywhere."

"Frank can use his police contacts in New York to get information. We were hoping that you could help, too."

"Of course." Amy felt herself getting defensive. "I wasn't going to abandon him."

Martha clasped her hands to her breast. "I knew it. I told you Amy would do it."

"Do it?"

"We were hoping you could take charge," Martha said demurely, more Southern and helpless than ever.

"What?"

"Everyone agreed," she continued. "After all, you're so organized and bright and full of energy and . . . Well, you and Marcus do seem to like each other, not in a romantic way perhaps."

"He's not gay," Amy blurted.

"I never said he was."

"You can count on us to back you up." Burt handed

Amy the sheaf of checks. "We made them out to you. We figured Marcus might not be able to do much banking."

It was only after Amy accepted the checks that the full implication dawned on her. She—Amy, "the Indecisive"—was in charge of an investigation, one unsanctioned by the police departments of two continents, aided by a handful of mystery fanatics, one of whom wouldn't be any help at all.

"I don't mean to harp on this, but you do realize that one of you is a killer? I mean, for real. Not fiction. One of my loyal assistants."

"There's nothing we can do about that," said Burt.

"We can't let that stop us," Martha added. "The killer will just have to take his chances."

"And so will I," Amy added.

"Does that bother you?" asked Burt. "I mean, you were planning to help. You weren't just going to abandon him?"

"You're right." It was amazing how one well-phrased question could make it all simple again. "Yes, all right."

"Good," Martha chirped. "So, where do we start?"

Amy sighed. "Well, if we're working together, I suppose you ought to know what I know. The police are going to find out soon enough."

"This is all tied in to San Diego, isn't it?" Martha dug Burt in the ribs. "I told you it went back to San Diego. This is all so Perry Mason."

"No, it's not Perry Mason. It's real life. Please remember that. I don't want my head crashed in by another falling rock, okay?"

"What falling rock?" Burt turned a page in his notepad and unscrewed the cap to his fountain pen. "Tell us everything."

"Okay." Amy took a deep breath. In retrospect, she would see this as the moment, her crossing of the Rubicon. After this there would be no turning back. "I don't know what any of this means." A wimpy start, but a start.

"We're waiting," said Martha.

"Here goes," said Amy. "It all began five years ago on a country estate on Long Island. . . ."

PART TWO

HOME GAME

CHAPTER 19

Home for Amy was a tree-lined block of Barrow Street. The narrow, unassuming lane was all but ignored by the hordes of revelers that invaded the local bars and cafés after their own towns and boroughs had closed up for the night. About half the brownstones on the block were single-family homes, owned by the same middle-class clans for decades before the excess of demand turned them into multimillion-dollar properties. It was a stubborn slice of old Greenwich Village. Conservative Italian householders and aging socialists lived in harmony with the occasional gay or lesbian family. And all of them barely tolerated the few lawyers and brokers who had managed to buy their way into the enclave.

It was the last Monday in September, a bright, warm morning that prompted Fanny Abel to open up the rear French doors to the patio. She brushed the debris from the wrought-iron table and set up an alfresco breakfast, arranging the two place settings so that they faced the communal garden, one of the few left in New York.

Beyond the tiny patio that lay nestled up against the rear of each brownstone was this common area, the local pride and joy, a garden carved out of the block's interior and accessible only through the houses themselves. It was maintained by common fees and was the force that preserved the block as a true neighborhood.

A communal garden gave you the right—nay, the duty—to mind everyone else's business. And that, according to Amy's thinking, was the defining characteristic of a neighborhood. The garden was part of their backyard, and every new dog or window box or live-in boyfriend became the subject of endless discussion, a kind of informal disapproval process. Some of Amy's earliest memories were of her mother shaking rugs off a balcony as she carried on conversations with both adjoining balconies and simultaneously eavesdropped on a domestic squabble. When people complained about the isolation of the big city, Amy knew what they meant in theory. But not really.

Amy emerged through the French doors, testing the brisk air and the temperature of the day's first cup of coffee.

"We'll open the office a little late," Fanny said as she motioned her daughter to an inviting array of bagels and butter and jam. "You never finished telling me about the tour. Do you think they had a good time?"

Amy nearly choked. "Mom, there was a murder."

Fanny made a face. "Don't be condescending. We put a lot of effort into this. I'd like to know if it was a success. Is that too much to ask?"

Amy sat on a cushioned wrought-iron chair and gazed out at the stone fountain bubbling in the garden's epicenter. "As ghoulish as it sounds, I think they had a great time. We could fill a tour like this every month if we could guarantee a real murder."

Fanny appeared to give the idea serious thought as she lit her second cigarette of the day—although if Amy asked, it would be her first. "And what about this Marcus Alvarez?" she asked with purposeful nonchalance. "Is he a nice boy?" During their few long distance conferences, Amy had mentioned Marcus.

"Very nice, yes. And in jail."

"You shouldn't hold his lying against him. People lie."

"Look, Mom. Anything in that department is on hold. Did I neglect to mention—"

"In jail. Yes, I know. There's always some excuse."

Amy looked up. "What do you mean by that?"

"Nothing." Fanny pursed her lips and fell silent, but not for long. Never for long. "Rita Crenshaw across the garden has been asking about you again."

"Mrs. Crenshaw." Amy smiled. "How is she?"

"People like her don't change until they die." Fanny inhaled, creating a new half inch of ash, then exhaled a ribbon of smoke. "She asked if you were dating. I would have mentioned Marcus just to shut her up, but I don't know much about him."

"Good."

"So I told her you were confused."

Amy selected a sesame bagel from the tray. "Confused?" She had no idea where this was going. "About what?"

"Well, it's not normal for a young person to cut herself off for so long. I told her the trauma of Eddie's death might have turned you into a lesbian."

"I see." Amy was mentally prepared. This was par for the course. "How'd she take the news?"

"Pretty well. I did not take it well. I want grandchildren."

"Lesbians can give you grandchildren."

"You're not a lesbian, dear. But you have to admit, it's a better explanation than saying you're not interested anymore. It makes you sound like an old maid."

Amy laid the odds at fifty-fifty that the Crenshaw conversation had never taken place, though you could never tell with Fanny. "Would you rather I be an old maid or be in love with a murderer? Not that I'm giving you a choice."

"He's not a murderer, for heaven's sake. Murderer? Killer? Which title do you think they prefer as a rule?"

"I don't know. I'll ask him."

"This will get straightened out in a few days. Does Marcus live in Manhattan?"

"I'm not so sure . . . about the few days. The evidence against him . . ."

Fanny dismissed it with a wave of the hand. "What evidence? From what you've said, all this goes back to that dinner party. That's the reason you came home, isn't it? Instead of staying in Italy? The real investigation is here."

"I know that. I just don't know where to begin."

"Don't be such a baby." Fanny mulled over the possibilities as she warmed up her daughter's coffee from the carafe. "Otto and Marcus did research. You'll take a look at their notes."

"No notes were found in Otto's apartment. That's what the cops said. The place was ransacked. If there was something there, Otto's killer removed it."

"What about Marcus? Maybe he kept notes. You know, gratitude is a very strong emotion."

"Are you this desperate to get me a boyfriend?"

"I'm trying to help an innocent man."

"Maybe you should take a road trip to Sing Sing. Line me up a few dates."

"Even if nothing happens romantically, you still want to help him. That's what you said."

"Of course I want to help."

"Then what's the problem? I've never understood people who just whine and worry. If you want to do something, do it!"

And, as if to illustrate her point, she grabbed the bagel out of her daughter's hand and boldly sliced it in half. Amy had often wondered where she had gotten her indecisive nature. Not from Fanny.

The superintendent of 640 Eighth Avenue unlocked the door to apartment 5C, flipped the light switch, and motioned for the prospective tenant to make herself at home. "The place is move-in ready," he said in fast, fluent English tinged with a Spanish accent.

The woman stood on the threshold and peered inside. "Move-in ready?" she said, wrinkling her nose. "It's a mess."

"Well, the last guy here . . . His niece was supposed to clear out his stuff. If you need to move in right away, we can junk the stuff, you know. It's junky anyhow, huh?" And he laughed.

This lady made him nervous. She was short and well fed, with clipped, old-fashioned henna-red hair that had probably been stylish when she was a young *chica* maybe forty years ago. Dolled up in a tweed dress and short white gloves, she looked like she belonged in the suburbs, not in a one-bedroom roach trap a few blocks off Times Square. He had tried to talk her out of even looking at the apartment, but what the hell. It was a changing neighborhood, even if this particular slum hadn't seen a fresh coat of paint in twenty years.

"You know these people. They say they gonna come and move stuff out, even give you a time. Waste your time is all. I wanna get tough with 'em, but . . . you know how it is. You gotta be sympathetic."

"The man who lived here died?" the woman asked as she glanced around the dingy living room. "He died here?"

"No, no." The super laughed, his eyes perusing the floor for any trace of the bloodstain. "In the hospital, you know. Heart attack."

She took a few steps into the dust-covered clutter. "Do you mind if I spend a few minutes looking around? It's so hard to visualize. I won't touch a thing." She shuddered, as if to say that touching was the last thing she wanted to do.

"Visualize," he said, already halfway back into the hall. "You visualize. Knock yourself out. I be downstairs. You come ring my bell. Ring hard on account of the TV. Okay?"

Fanny waited until she heard his footsteps negotiating the second set of stairs and the landing below that. Only then did she ease the door shut, straighten her gloves, and set about her mission.

Otto's living room was a shambles, although it was hard to say how much of that was from his slovenly habits and how much was from the murder, or from the searches. There had been at least two, she theorized. One by the killer—what had he been looking for?—and one by that nice Sergeant Rawlings and his men.

Fanny knew her chances were minimal. But she had always trusted in her own superior luck. Stan had been regularly infuriated by her insistence on looking under the hood herself or grabbing the pickle jar from him and trying the lid. "What makes you think you can do better?" he would ask. But then with maddening frequency, at her magic touch the car would start or the jar would nudge open. Although . . . although in this case . . . She tiptoed around the squalid room and honestly couldn't see much reason for optimism.

A plywood bookcase lay sideways on the beige shag area rug. The hundreds of books that had once rested on its shelves were now in scattered heaps on the floor, just neat enough to show they'd been inspected.

Undaunted, Fanny spread her handkerchief on the floor and sat down by the first pile. These were assorted reference works: *The Handbook of Poison; Crime Scene Investigation; Codes, Ciphers and Secret Writing. Secret writing?* She prayed that Otto hadn't disguised his notes in some sort of code. Even her luck wouldn't help out there.

The books in pile two, although of varying thickness, were all about the height and width of college yearbooks and were identically bound in red leather. Custombound, she saw at a glance, like the prized original scripts that her brother-in-law, the producer, preserved along the walls of his Broadway office.

Fanny examined the top volume. *Mohonk Mystery Weekend, 1992* was emblazoned in gold leaf along the spine. Flipping through the pages, she saw that, true to its spine, the book held a printed copy of the game Otto had constructed for that long-ago event, the dialogue and plot and instructions, even research notes, all mapped out and ready to use. Dozens of other parties, weekends, and assorted contests were similarly preserved in red leather, the shorter ones often squeezed two to a volume.

One by one, Fanny leafed through the books, restacking them into a new pile. She'd never been one for much introspection, unlike her husband or daughter. But this exercise was turning her just a bit melancholy. Here, within the span of her arms, was the whole of a man's life. His obsession and pride. The sum total of it, here on this ugly beige shag. In all probability, no other record of his work existed, except perhaps in someone's dusty scrapbook or dustier memory. Fanny tried to think of other things.

There was no *Monte Carlo to Rome Mystery Road Rally*, she noted, hardly surprised. If such a book had ever existed, it was now long gone, the spoils of murder.

She set aside the very last one, laying it unevenly on top of the others. The book teetered. Then it lost its balance and toppled, sending the red leather tower into an avalanche. Mortified by her sacrilege, Fanny scrambled to retrieve the splayed volumes and saw that one of them had suffered a tear on the rear flyleaf.

"Sorry, Otto," she whispered.

That was when she noticed. The words were printed small and modest at the bottom of the torn page. She checked several other volumes and found them identical. The rear flyleaves all carried the same declaration. "Stage Duplicating and Binding, 426 West 44th Street, NYC."

It was hardly a revelation. Otto wasn't a bookbinder. He would naturally go to a service like this to preserve his treasures. But the label's implication was enough to make Fanny scratch the fringe of her pageboy and smile. Her luck just might be infallible, after all. The motor was starting to turn over; the jar lid starting to budge.

CHAPTER 20

Amy took a break from cleaning the squid to check on the cake in the oven. She didn't cook much. It was easy to survive without it, thanks to telephones and take-out menus. But after work today she'd gone on a little errand, which had left her in a good mood and in the vicinity of the Morton Williams on Bleecker Street. A display of fresh squid on ice had reminded her of the one dish she made that Fanny actually liked. It might be nice, she'd thought, to repay her for last night's welcome-home dinner.

Hers was a new kitchen, installed a year ago, when she'd moved back in and they'd divided the brownstone into separate living quarters. Fanny kept the lower two floors, while Amy claimed the upper two, turning a small bedroom into a kitchen, as well as throwing up a few well-placed walls and doors.

Before that, she'd lived in a one-bedroom co-op in the heart of the Village, a few blocks away. She and Eddie had found it together, scrimped to make the down payment, and compromised over furnishings and decor. Everything there held a memory. After his death she'd refused to use the bed and had slept on a pullout sofa in the living room. It was Fanny who finally called the real estate agent and the kitchen renovation people and forced the issue.

There was a certain comfort to returning home, she had to admit. And the accommodations couldn't be beat. A roomy one-bedroom with two baths, dining room, sunroom, and a terrace overlooking the garden.

"No smoking in my kitchen!"

Even over the smell of cake and raw mollusks, she could tell that Fanny had invaded her living room and was heading her way. For the first few months, Amy had tried training her to call ahead, or at least to knock. She'd even resorted to locking her door, which had resulted in alternating bouts of pouting and suspicion. So she had learned to remain dressed at all times and to accept the intrusions philosophically.

"You left work early," she observed.

"You, too." Fanny appeared in the doorway, stubbing out a cigarette in an ashtray that she'd appropriated from the Showboat Hotel in Atlantic City. "I called the shop at four thirty, but you'd already closed."

"I was running an errand." Amy could barely repress a grin.

"Me, too. Good lord, you're cooking. Squid, I hope."

"No. Calamari. If you have the evening free, milady, please do me the honor of joining me."

"Hmm. You're feeling no pain."

"I think I know where the master script is. Otto's script with all his notes from the Carvel case."

"Really?" Fanny sounded impressed, though a little subdued. "How did you track it down?"

"Well, I spent the morning trying to get in touch with Marcus, but between the Italian bureaucracy and

the Italian phone system . . . So I changed tactics." Amy
had rehearsed all this, a concise explanation of how
she'd been so brilliant. "In my records I have Marcus's
address and home phone. I called the number, to see if
maybe he has a roommate, but it went to voice mail. So
I just walked over there. It's only eight blocks, over by
Morton Williams."

"Did you pick up any of those South American snow
peas I like?"

"Mom, I'm telling a story. Yes, as a matter of fact."

"Good. Steam them with a little lime juice."

"Are you listening?"

"Yes. Marcus's apartment. I assume he has a roommate and the roommate was at home. Otherwise, this
story would be pointless. Male or female?"

"Male. He was there. And before you ask, his name's
Terry and he is not Marcus's boyfriend." Amy was trying
hard to maintain her enthusiasm. "If I may continue . . ."

"Sorry."

"Marcus had mentioned my name, so Terry knew."

Fanny seemed impressed. "So . . . Marcus mentioned
you."

"Mother, stop it. You can clean the squid."

Fanny put her ashtray on the kitchen table, reached
for an apron, and didn't say another word.

As they stood side by side at the double sink, Amy
outlined her conversation with Terry. Marcus had told
Terry plenty of anecdotes about the eccentric game
maker. "For every one of his mysteries, Otto put together
a master script, complete with all the research material.
In our game there was a lot of research, all the documents from the Carvel case, the police reports, interviews."

Fanny took another handful of squid from the plastic bag, threw them into the colander, and rinsed them. "All this is in the master script?"

"All in one neat package. Otto had each script professionally bound and on display in his apartment."

"The Road Rally script is probably gone," Fanny said. "I mean, either the killer or the police—"

"I know. But Otto was killed so soon after finishing the game." Amy paused dramatically. "What if the script is still at the printer's?"

"Oh, my." Fanny stopped cutting and peeling. "That's brilliant!"

"There can't be many services that still do it. Uncle Joe has his Broadway shows printed and bound, right?"

"I believe so. Why don't I check it out for you?"

"You?" Amy looked skeptical. "I'm not sure I want you involved in this."

"Nonsense. I'll call Joe, get a list of printers, and track it down. Otto Ingo. Road Rally. Red leather. It shouldn't be hard."

"Red leather?"

"That's what you said, isn't it? Otto had them bound in red leather."

"Actually, no. I didn't say that."

"Oh, I'm sure you did."

"I couldn't have. I have no idea what color they are, or even if they're leather."

"My mistake, then. Maybe it's Joe . . ."

"Uncle Joe's scripts are black leather." Amy turned off the water, removed her oval Anne Kleins, and squinted quizzically.

To Fanny's credit, she didn't flinch. "What?"

"What aren't you telling me?" Her mind raced over the possibilities. "Have you been talking to Marcus? No.

Did you break into Otto's apartment? Is that how you know what color his scripts are?"

"I didn't break in."

"Good lord, you did."

"I didn't. The super . . . oops."

"What? The super let you in?"

"In a way. I was thinking of renting it."

Amy was almost hyperventilating. "I can't believe it. That's what you were doing this afternoon. Breaking and entering. What do you think? You can just run around being a detective?"

Fanny had had about enough. "Yes. That's exactly what I did. I got into Otto's apartment. Perfectly legally. And I came to the same conclusion you did." She slapped the paring knife down on the cutting board. "And what on earth is wrong with that—besides the fact that I beat you to it?"

"So, you know where the master script is?'

"It's in my bedroom."

"You have it? When were you going to tell me?"

"As soon as I could figure out how. You don't make it easy."

"So, you were just listening to me ramble on about how clever I am."

"That's a mother's job."

Amy was speechless, which was Fanny's cue to keep talking. "Harold, the man at Stage Duplicating, is very sweet, a courtly sort. He's been doing Otto's binding work for years, and they long ago stopped fooling around with claim checks. If there'd been a claim check, someone would have figured this out weeks ago."

"And he just let you take it?"

"Well, I had to pay for it. Not cheap. Harold knew

about Otto's death. He'd been expecting a member of the family to drop by. I told him I was Otto's sister, and he saw the resemblance, which I resent."

"Mother!"

"You're not the only Abel with some imagination."

"We have to turn it over to the police—after reading it." Amy ran a hand through her hair. "How do we tell them we got it? We can't let them know we've been sniffing around. They don't like that."

"Well . . ." Fanny thought. "The script was a gift. Just arrived. Otto mailed it to us before his death, and the post office screwed up delivery."

"That's good," Amy had to admit. "But no more detective work."

Fanny looked genuinely hurt. "Why not? We make a great team. Me to do the thinking and the legwork, and you, well . . ."

"No more detective work. Do you hear me? You're fearless and impulsive and old. You could get yourself hurt."

"Old?"

"I appreciate you finding the master script. That was great. But no more."

"Old?"

"You could get yourself killed."

"So could you if you keep calling me old. You're just afraid I'll steal all the glory."

"Glory? Ha!"

"It's the truth."

"You want the truth? Okay, I am afraid. I'm afraid you'll be a loose cannon, running around and getting us killed. What am I saying? A loose cannon would be safer."

"Your own mother! Fine." Fanny tore off the apron

and threw it on the floor. "Reimburse me for the script and we'll forget it. You try to help your kids and what do they do? I wash my hands. That's it. I wash my hands."

And, setting action to her words, Fanny tossed the knife into the sink, rinsed off her hands, and stormed out. "Let me know when dinner's ready."

It was about six months ago, shortly after opening the agency, that Amy started using the fourth-floor sunroom as a home office. Inside the rectangle of steel and glass she'd placed an old oak desk facing a wall of windows that looked out onto a narrow balcony and the communal garden beyond.

Amy sat at the desk, oblivious to the smattering of bedroom lights peering out from the rear of the brownstones across the way. Her stomach, probably her whole body, was attempting to digest the squid, a meal that had not been eaten under the most congenial of conditions.

In front of her lay open the red bound script. She was trying her best to concentrate, but the bangs and clatters drifting up from the third floor weren't helping. Fanny was doing the dinner dishes by hand. The dishwasher wouldn't make enough noise, Amy surmised. She got up to close the door—it barely helped—then returned to the desk and her view of the shadowy garden below.

Deep down she knew why she'd been so upset. Her mother didn't even know Marcus, had no connection to poor Georgina. And yet she had leapt into the fray, conning her way into Otto's apartment and charming a vital clue out of the printer's hands—things that Amy herself might have done.

She had always thought of herself as levelheaded and rational, much like her father. But there was another side to being rational. Was she, at the end of the day and of all her rationalizing, just a coward? She winced at the word. So melodramatic. And should it even apply to women? Weren't those manly terms, *hero* and *coward*? Despite all the progress between the sexes, this seemed to be the final, entrenched vestige of inequality. Women were allowed their natural cowardice.

Still it bothered her. The contrast between her lame investigation and Fanny's fearlessness. Then there was the incident with Marcus and the rock. And, of course, two years ago with Eddie.

It had been a warm November night, a Saturday, after a party at a friend's place. On the way home, they'd got into an argument. At 1:00 a.m., they were back in their claustrophobic apartment, still fighting, trying to keep their voices down. And then Eddie stormed out, slamming the door.

Amy caught up with him blocks away on Minetta Lane, at the spot where the narrow street bent out of sight from a Sixth Avenue still busy with traffic. She grabbed Eddie's arm and offered a halfhearted apology. Amy recalled that distinctly, even though she'd forgotten the reason for the fight.

But the fight only got worse. Accusations, name-calling, and all in public view. Street theater of the worst sort, something they had seen hundreds of times in New York but had never before taken part in, too civilized and controlled for that, until now.

"You always say that, but you never mean it." Those were the last words he ever said to her. She recalled them so perfectly, the biting intonation, the expression in his eyes. But again, the context was gone. What did she always say but never mean? And then he disappeared, striding away down a narrow brick alley.

Amy had just stood there, staring at her feet, too ashamed and angry to look up. And then she was suddenly following him down the alley, with something new to shout out. Something hurtful but half true, whatever it was.

When she saw Eddie next, maybe twenty seconds later, he was being mugged. They had discussed what to do if they were ever mugged. "Give them what they want," Eddie had instructed. "Don't make eye contact. Don't get emotional." But now, with his anger overpowering his common sense, Eddie disobeyed his own rules.

The gang of three must have come in from the other side, from Carmine Street. They were young, Amy later told the police, probably teenagers. She had always assumed it was a mugging, but maybe they were just trying to push past Eddie in the alley. Maybe someone bumped someone and words began flying, an outburst of his Irish temper meant for her, left over from just a minute before.

Should she have spoken up? she often asked herself. Shown her presence and broken the cycle? A woman, a witness? She hadn't even thought of it but had stood transfixed, even after the gun came out. Why? Why hadn't she . . . ?

The police would say he died before hitting the ground. That was meant to be comforting, and it was, to a degree. Her last little pause before dialing 911 meant nothing. The slow arrival of the ambulance meant nothing. She was probably smart not to have drawn attention to herself. And yet she had let Eddie down. She had made him fighting mad and had let him run off down an alley and then had just watched.

The wind was picking up now, rattling the wall of double-paned windows. The seasons were changing, summer and winter slugging it out in the wild battleground of autumn. Tomorrow would be a major skirmish, Amy predicted as she switched off the desk lamp and headed sleepily for her bedroom. The bangs and clatters from below had finally stopped.

CHAPTER 21

"So, you're a friend of Marcus's."

"Yes," said Amy and left it at that. Going out to view the scene of the crime had been Fanny's idea, but still a good one. "We spent time together," Amy explained. "You know, being about the same age. As the tour operator, I feel somewhat responsible. I mean, a client getting arrested?"

"I should hope so," Doris Carvel said with a shudder.

"Well, it was hardly my fault. There was a murder."

"Of course. Poor Georgina. And Marcus." It definitely seemed to be Amy's fault.

"When was the last time you saw him?"

Mrs. Carvel rearranged the shawl around her shoulders. "It must have been the spring. I don't get many visitors. We had a nice chat about the old days. About Fabian." The widow, Amy decided, was probably pushing eighty.

Doris turned her face toward one of the solarium windows and watched as the rain played with the oaks and maples, changing directions with each fresh gust, tearing off the first golden leaves of fall and sending them racing down the lawn to the Long Island Sound. "I miss the summer already," she murmured and pulled the shawl tight. This, too, might have been Amy's fault, from the tone.

Tall, Amy thought, *despite the stooped posture, with piercing gray eyes and fine-boned features*. Her hair was also gray—long, surprisingly thick, and flowing loosely. It was well conditioned, too. How did she do it? Amy was not looking forward to dealing with her own "old lady hair," should she be lucky enough to last that long. Doris had undoubtedly been the model for Dolores, a meek woman who lived for others, asked for nothing, and always managed to get her own way. Passive-aggressive was the label—as opposed to Fanny, who tended more toward the aggressive-aggressive.

Amy had been surprised to get an appointment, a stranger calling out of the blue. In retrospect, she saw how easy it had been. An old friend murdered, an ex-employee arrested. And Amy had been there. The lure was irresistible enough to get Amy ushered into an overheated solarium, where Doris Carvel sat bundled up against a nonexistent draft, watching the rain.

"You knew Georgina, too?"

"We also met on the tour." Amy hadn't told her about the rally aspect. God knows what she would think of two dozen people playing a game based on her husband's death. Thanks to the discretion of the Italian police, this had not been featured in any of the media accounts. For now, she wanted Doris to assume it had been just an ordinary tour—with a murder.

"It's ridiculous. Marcus couldn't kill anyone. He and Georgina barely knew each other."

"Ridiculous," Amy echoed.

"The police must have some sort of motive," Doris said, her inflection rising.

"The only thing they have is the fact that he poured the wine. Opportunity, not motive. They may think the motive dates back to when Marcus worked for Mr. Carvel. That's when he and Georgina had the most contact with each other."

"Motive?" Doris said, as if the word were new to her.

"The police are grasping at straws." Amy had given this a lot of thought. "Perhaps they think Marcus killed your husband and that Georgina knew something about it."

"Marcus kill Fabian? That's preposterous. Marcus didn't kill Fabian or Georgina, certainly not both."

"Neither one."

"That's what I said."

It wasn't, but she let it pass. "Marcus didn't inherit anything from Mr. Carvel." Amy waited. "Did he?"

"Barely anything. A few months' wages."

"And there is no other reason, a business reason perhaps, that Marcus might have to kill your husband?"

"What business reason? You sound as though you think he's guilty."

"No," Amy apologized. "I'm just trying to figure out what the police might be thinking."

"Marcus was a personal secretary. He didn't deal with the business. He worked here. Appointments and charities and personal correspondence. My husband was toying with writing his memoirs. I believe Marcus did some work for him on that front."

"You mean organizing old company documents, old diaries, old letters? That sort of thing?"

"I suppose. His life would make a good book, you know."

"I'd read it," said Amy. The memoirs of Fabian Carvel were exactly what she needed right now.

"He was a fascinating man." Doris's voice turned softer, and for the first time she spoke without hesitation. "He was self-made. My family objected, as they would have with any man of his background. But there was something so powerful about Fabian, as if he could get anything he wanted. I suppose that included me." She smiled shyly, a love-struck girl hiding in a frail, wrinkled shell. "Fabian practically invented Mexican food," she said. "You probably know that."

Amy could think of at least one entire nation that might be unaware of that. "Your husband made it popular in America."

"That's what I meant. Mexican food didn't become what it is today without a lot of innovation." She clucked her tongue, just like Miss Lambert back in kindergarten. "When Fabian was right out of school, struggling to start up a food company, he invented the taco shell." She paused, as if waiting for applause.

Amy was dubious. "He invented the taco?"

"The prefolded corn taco. You know, the hard shells you see in grocery stores."

Amy scoured her memory. Perhaps this was right. She had certainly never seen those folded corn shells in a real Mexican restaurant. "That's an American invention?"

"As American as chop suey." Her shoulders straightened, and the shawl fell away. "The very first inroad of Mexican food in this country was the hard taco shell. As a child, you must have seen Tico Taco shells in the grocery store. Do you remember seeing Mexican food before that? No, you don't. It was too different and too spicy. This was in the sixties, you have to remember, when

American tastes rebelled at anything even remotely exotic. But Fabian gave them ground chuck, lettuce, tomato, and American cheese in a ready-to-eat corn bun. It was just novel enough to succeed."

Amy chuckled, genuinely amused by the revelation. "It's one of those things you never think about."

Doris chuckled back. If there were enough blood to flow to her cheeks, she might have blushed. "I don't mean to go on. But it's been my bread and butter for fifty years."

"When did the Tico Taco restaurants start?"

"A few years later. Fabian saw all these hamburger places, and he wanted in—'in on the action,' as he liked to say. He began with one shop. Not any messier than a hamburger. But he needed more than tacos. That's when he came up with sour cream."

"He invented sour cream?" Amy was almost ready to believe it.

"No. But stop and think. Where does sour cream come from?"

"You mean, other than cows?"

"Yes, dear. What part of the world?"

"The origins of sour cream." Amy hemmed and hawed and wound up free-associating. "Um. Borscht. Blintzes. Stroganoff. I'm guessing that cattle milk products are more of a staple in colder climates. So . . . um . . . Slavic?"

"Well done."

Amy felt like a grade-schooler.

"Now, how do you think sour cream found its way into your enchilada?"

This question was easier. "Fabian Carvel."

"Yes." The matron clapped her hands. "No one thinks about it, but sour cream isn't Mexican. Mole, guacamole, yes. And yet, for millions of Americans, sour cream is the ingredient that cools off the spices and complements them." She was sitting erect, her voice ringing with pride. "My Fabian was the first to add sour cream to the enchilada."

When Amy would tell the story to Fanny that evening, both of them would laugh and marvel at the small, odd turns that created fortunes and changed national eating habits. "The first man in history . . ." And they would laugh again. But here and now, as she sat in this old-money mansion and faced the aristocratic profile of Doris Carvel, it all made perfect, sober sense.

Doris seemed to appreciate Amy's appreciation. "I know how silly this sounds. Prefolded taco shells and sour cream. Tico Taco makes up less than a third of F.S.C.'s business today. But it's the root from which everything else sprang. Managers can grow a company. There was no big trick to that, especially during the sixties. But it was those early innovations that Fabian was the most proud of." Doris's entire speech seemed straight from Fabian Carvel himself. How many times, Amy wondered, had she sat at dinner parties, listening to her husband make these same heroic claims?

"Food Services is a publicly held company?" It sounded like such a non sequitur, but not really. "If I wanted to buy stock in Food Services Corporation . . ."

"We went public in nineteen ninety-eight, although Fabian did maintain a fair number of shares."

"That's right. Marcus told me. Your husband planned to leave his stock to charity. And then he changed his mind." Amy knew this was wrong. She was trying to prime the pump.

"No," Doris corrected her, right on cue. "Most of it did go to charity. The Long Island Conservancy. They build parks and wetlands," she continued. Her eyes rose to meet Amy's. "Don't waste your pity. Fabian left us well cared for. Our son, Daniel, and I received gifts of stock and property all throughout his lifetime. Neither one of us is going hungry."

"Marcus told me about a will change. . . ."

"Will change?" Doris looked puzzled. "There was no change to his will."

"Sorry. I must have misunderstood."

"There was a gift, a proposed gift, but no change in the will."

Amy stayed quiet, doing her best to look relaxed and receptive.

"Fabian was a generous man," Doris continued. "No one objected to this. But then Daniel discovered that his father was planning to give millions of dollars' worth of stock to . . . Well, never mind to whom. It was going to be an outright gift, not part of the will. My husband offered no explanation. It was his stock, and he would do what he wanted. Well, Daniel got upset. Stu Romney got upset."

"He worked for your husband?" Amy ventured. "Stew Rummy."

"What? Rummy?" A lilting laugh. "No, no. Stuart Romney. The company's CFO. Anyway . . . Rummy. That's funny. I'll have to tell Stu. . . ." Her voice trailed off. When she spoke again, it was hesitantly, perhaps not sure how much more she should confide. Only the fear of being rude seemed to make her go on. "It caused a rift. Fabian remained determined to make this huge, ridiculous gift, and the resentment grew. On both sides. You know how these things are."

"You eventually talked him out of the gift."

"Not me." Doris seemed horrified at the idea. "Our son, Daniel." *Price Litcomb,* Amy translated mentally.

"You know how children are. For weeks Daniel wouldn't speak to him. Fabian was ignoring his family, he said, so . . ." She looked up from her hands and gasped, as if surprised to find Amy still in the room. "You don't want to hear this."

"You haven't talked about it in a long time," Amy observed.

Doris took her soft words as encouragement. "You're very kind to listen. All of this has taken on such an exaggerated importance in my mind. I sit here and think. . . . This took place only a short time before he disappeared. I mean, before he died." She looked flustered. "We were visiting San Diego, the whole family . . ."

"Marcus told me the real story," Amy confessed. "The dinner party here. Your husband's disappearance."

"He told . . ." For a second it seemed as if she might try to keep up the charade. Then she relented. "Yes, of course. What does it matter now? Of course he'd tell you. The gist, I suppose . . . and it's a long way to answer a simple question . . ."

Amy forced herself to stay expectantly silent.

"Fabian and Daniel made up. He didn't give anything to that woman. And he transferred some more stock into Daniel's name. What was your question? Did Fabian's estate go to charity? Yes, most of it did. We never contested the will. It's a worthy cause."

"Uh, yes. That's too bad. Too bad." Amy was barely aware of what she was saying. Her mind was still on "that woman."

CHAPTER 22

Two simple words. *That woman.* But what woman? A mistress? Georgina perhaps? That was all Amy could think of. Some woman had come within a hair's breadth of getting millions in F.S.C. stock.

"No, it's not bad," Doris said, responding to something Amy must have muttered. "Daniel has his own life. And the conservancy put me on the board. It gives me something to do." She poked a hand out of her shawl to retrieve the cup of jasmine tea that had been cooling on an end table. They were back in safe territory. For the moment at least she had lanced the festering memory. "It's been good of you to visit. I was so shocked to hear about Georgina. And then to hear about Marcus . . . such a nice boy."

"I'm sure he had nothing to do with it."

"If there's anything I can do to help . . ." Her gray eyes focused on Amy's brown eyes. "I'm serious. If you need money for bail or someone to make a phone call. Fabian's name still carries some weight."

"Thank you. That's very kind."

"I'm sure my son would love to help, as well. Unfortunately, he's overseas."

"Overseas?" Amy asked, perhaps too eagerly. Did her eyebrows rise? She had to learn to control that. "Where exactly overseas? Italy maybe?"

"No. Daniel is spending the fall—I guess the spring, really—in Sydney. His wife's family lives there."

"Ah." One good suspect down the drain.

As they were saying good-bye, the awkward good-bye of strangers who might never see each other again, a butler appeared. Either this was a man with incredible instincts or he'd been summoned, perhaps by a buzzer hidden in the arm of the wing chair. Kevin, as she called him, led Amy out through the same configuration of rooms that she'd seen on her way into the solarium, an incongruous addition tacked onto the rear of the brick mansion and built to take advantage of the view.

This is the house, she thought as they passed into the main hall. *That's the dining room off to the right. That's the staircase that Fabian used to make his escape from dinner. Like the game, only real. A mystery puzzle come to life.*

"How is Marcus?" the butler asked as they stood at the open front door. The rain had stopped, but the wind was still substantial. It whipped through the hall, rattling the hunting prints that hung by velvet ribbons from the ivory-colored walls. He was only slightly older than Amy, and not fussy or overly proper. An efficient and friendly man, large but not fat, he had the freckle-faced good looks of an Irish charmer and more than a trace of a warm Boston accent. His red hair was short and straight, spiky and gelled.

"I'm sure he'll be home in a week."

"Good," said Kevin. The concern in his voice sounded genuine. "Marcus is a good guy, a lot of fun."

"You worked with Marcus?"

"Yeah. I've been here forever." Kevin touched Amy lightly on the back, then eased her out the door. "Give him my best."

Amy's key had barely turned in the lock when a voice accosted her through the door. "How did it go?"

"Fine."

As usual, the door between Fanny's rooms and the common stairwell was open, her way of refusing to acknowledge that the house was now separated in two. "Hope you haven't eaten." Amy could tell from her tone and from the brown smell of brisket that all was forgiven, if not forgotten. She wandered into the first-floor kitchen, unchanged from her childhood, right down to the decades-old pot holders on the refrigerator. Instinctively, she gravitated to a sinkful of green beans and began to snap and rinse.

Fanny stood at the stove, basting and listening to her daughter, treating the moment as if it were perfectly ordinary instead of a cease-fire. Her peace offering was the brisket, and Amy's acceptance was her candor, sharing the first tentative steps of her detective work.

They laughed together about the genius of prefolded tacos and sour cream. Then Fanny listened patiently to her analysis, interrupting only once for a point of clarification. She didn't want to get into a repeat of last night and so was careful to give Amy the proper time and appreciation before delivering her own news.

"You got a call at the office today." She was sliding the brisket into the oven. "An Officer Francis Loyola."

"I wonder what he wants. Frank was on the tour."

"Really?" Fanny knew exactly who Frank was, having spent over an hour talking to him. She had a talent for conversation, even on the phone, when people were leaving messages or had dialed the wrong number. "He says you should call him at home."

"Right after dinner," Amy said with a yawn. She finished rinsing the beans and, leaning back against a row of cupboards, proceeded to outline her next step. "I told you about Mrs. Carvel's slip of the tongue—about 'that woman.' "

"Yes, dear. Very perceptive."

"That may be the key. I mean, losing out on millions of dollars in stock could make anyone homicidal. Tomorrow I think I'll track down Betsy Caulfield. She's the daytime television actress."

"The model for Bitsy Stormfield."

"Exactly. If she's not 'that woman,' maybe she knows who is."

"She shouldn't be hard to find. Her soap is filmed here in New York?"

"*The Roads We Choose*," Amy said with a nod. "Do you mind if I take off tomorrow afternoon?"

"You can take off all day." Fanny knew that Amy already had a tentative morning appointment with Frank Loyola. But Amy would find this out soon enough. "Don't forget to call Frank."

"I'll call right now," Amy said as she bounded out of the kitchen and toward the stairs. "This woman theory is the right direction. I can feel it."

"Plenty of time before dinner."

Fanny didn't know what she felt. All she knew was that Frank—a nice, polite man, to judge by his voice—

had sounded worried. He wouldn't say why, not even to Fanny, his new best friend. Whatever it was, Amy would have to find out for herself. Fanny was through meddling.

Well . . . maybe she'd just pace herself more carefully.

CHAPTER 23

The Cindilu Dairy was a Greenwich Village institution, a one-story, shingled structure that had the well-weathered look of a country general store plopped down on a New York street corner. Local legend stated that this had been the favorite tobacco shop of Edgar Allan Poe when he lived on one of the neighboring streets. In fact, the decor seemed little changed from Poe's heyday, which was how the current owners liked it. Lou and Cindy Halpern presided over the dusty shelves and the lunch counter and the cats that lounged like furry mannequins in the storefront windows.

The Halperns were twins, both single, probably in their late forties; that was Amy's guess. Their parents had been television writers during the Red Scare, when Joseph McCarthy was engaged in rooting out subversives from the ranks of the artistically employed. The Halperns became late victims of the blacklist, forced to retire their typewriters and take their socialist views into the grocery/delicatessen trade, where they named the store after their twins and left it to them, along with their deeply rooted views.

All through her childhood, this had been Amy's hangout, the sanctuary where she and her friends would try on lipstick and talk endlessly about boys. On rainy Saturdays she would come in alone for hot cocoa. Cindy would sneak her a few leftist comic books featuring such superheroes as Samuel Gompers and Emma Goldman. For hours she would sit contentedly, sipping and reading, while the grown-ups lounged in the windows, like the cats, and complained about the weather or the government.

Amy pushed open the screen door and immediately spotted Frank in the remotest of the high-backed wooden booths. She signaled Lou for coffee, then joined the patrolman, scooting Alhambra off the cushioned seat and back to her spot in the sunlight.

"They have good muffins here. You want a muffin?"

Frank nodded.

"Lou, two of your best blueberries."

"Nice place," Frank said, crimping his face into a smirk.

Amy turned her head, following Frank's line of sight. "Which one?" he asked.

Amy looked up to see the sign on the wall above her own head. A familiar bumper sticker was hanging in a frame: IMPEACH THE PRESIDENT.

"Any. Lou doesn't play favorites." She settled into the prewarmed seat. "So, what's the deal? You sounded so mysterious on the phone."

"You got the rest of the morning free?"

"I told you that last night. Yes."

Frank sighed. "Okay. We got a meeting this morning with Sergeant Rawlings of Manhattan South Homicide Division."

"Rawlings?"

"We gotta handle this right." Frank seemed edgy, and Amy was beginning to share the feeling. "Manhattan homicide is not my beat. You know, protocol and all that. They have this status thing, more like an attitude. Too smart and tough for the rest of us. So here I am, you know? A Bronx patrolman sticking my nose into a Midtown murder?"

"Midtown murder?" Amy choked on the words.

"That's what I wanted to warn you about." Frank leaned across the table and lowered his voice. "Martha Callas called me from Rome and asked me to do a little checking."

Amy's heart sank. "She told you about the Otto connection. And you went to Rawlings."

"We're all on the same team, right?" He paused and leaned back into his booth as Lou delivered their mutant, blue-speckled muffins and two cups of much-needed coffee.

"You in trouble with the pigs?" Lou's tone was at once aggressive and protective. The fact that Frank was out of uniform didn't fool him for a minute.

"It's all right," Amy said, shooing Lou away. "Frank is a friend."

Frank took his muffin and began to pick at the paper baking cup, waiting until Lou was out of range. "Strange bird."

"Look, Frank, I don't want to seem ungrateful. . . ."

"I can help, you know. Rawlings is gonna extend me some courtesy. Hey, I had to tell him. I'm an officer, for Pete's sake."

"There's no proof the murders are connected." Amy sighed. She had been hoping to keep the two halves of the case separated, without having to deal with the NYPD. "I'm sorry. Maybe you're right."

"I'm right. We can't solve this on our own. Of course we gotta be careful. I mean, with New York and Rome both investigating, it could get complicated."

"So we're going to Rawlings's office."

"Don't underestimate him," warned Frank. "Okay? It's not like on TV, where the cops are gruff and dumb and can't put two and two together. These guys are smart. Rawlings wants to know what you know. You act like a harmless, curious female, and maybe he'll give you something in return. You were in Monte Carlo at the time of Otto's murder, so there's no chance of you being a suspect."

"God, I hope not."

Frank flinched at the profanity. Amy wondered how the man survived day to day in a Bronx precinct house. "Just stay calm and honest. If you're unsure about something, shut up and let me do the talking."

Amy nodded. She would have felt more reassured if all throughout his words of comfort, Frank hadn't been unconsciously tearing off bits of the muffin baking cup and scattering them over the tabletop. The spot in the wood where Amy's first boyfriend had carved their initials was already covered up with the blueberry-stained litter.

"Is there something you're not telling me, Frank?"

"Not telling you? The reason we're here is for me to tell you. What ain't I telling you?"

"I don't know."

Amy watched as the table's oak surface became a mess of paper and crumbs.

CHAPTER 24

A detective squad room wasn't like TV, either, Amy discovered. She had been looking forward—well, not looking forward; expecting— a large, open floor chock-full of camaraderie, with action and flying wisecracks, with swaggering perps sitting across from gruff detectives who banged away on triplicates stuffed into their Remington Rands. Okay, maybe computers. This wasn't TV Land.

Instead, the homicide squad room was a warren of quiet cubicles, essentially small, depressing, sound-insulated booths. Each cubicle had walls about seven feet high and was outfitted with a desk, three chairs, a computer terminal, and the few touches of home that office workers everywhere bring in to humanize their little corners. In Sergeant Rawlings's case, this included a triptych silver frame encasing the smiling faces of his blandly attractive wife and two young daughters.

As she sat in the chair opposite the desk, Amy proceeded to notice other unexpected touches. Rawlings was apparently without a partner, a television no-no, and had the wrong appearance and style for the job. To start with, he was too friendly. With his sandy hair cut stylishly short, his open Midwestern face, and a white, tapered shirt, tie, but no jacket, the homicide detective had the amiable look of an actor/waiter about to introduce himself and take your drink order.

He seemed about the right age for an actor/waiter, in his early thirties, with an ingratiating enthusiasm just right for selling the daily specials. His eyes were a sincere gray blue, with pale, almost invisible eyebrows that served only to increase his look of wide-eyed wonder. Amy recalled Frank's warning and reminded herself not to underestimate him. The last thing she wanted was to spend her next few breakfasts picking apart muffin cups.

"When we talked on the phone . . . What was it? Two weeks ago . . . ? You didn't tell me you had a city police officer on the tour. Trying not to ruin Frank's vacation, huh?" The tone was gently chiding.

"I didn't even think about it."

"You can imagine my surprise when Patrolman Loyola called me Sunday night and told me about your situation in Rome. Sounds like you had your hands full."

Amy threw a sideways glance at Frank. *Sunday night?* Frank must have squealed the second after hanging up from Martha. Would it do any good to change the subject? "By the way, my mother . . . You made quite an impression."

Rawlings stretched his thin lips into a smile. "Yes," he drawled. "Fanny. Be sure to give her my best. Now, Amy . . ." He leaned across the desk. "I spent some time on the phone to Captain Boido in Rome. He speaks excellent English. And Lieutenant Jorgenson in San Diego. His English is even better. At one point we had this conference call going. New York, Rome, San Diego."

"San Diego," Amy repeated. This didn't bode well.

"Yes. A murder there five years ago. But this is stuff you already know. I'm still getting up to speed."

The sergeant took a file folder from his top center drawer and opened it, covering up the faint water rings on his desktop. "I'm hoping you might be able to confirm a few facts. We're in the early stages, so I'd appreciate it if you didn't repeat any of this. We don't want to go upsetting people."

"I understand," Amy lied.

"Good. First off, I guess you should know we're starting to build a case against Marcus Alvarez."

"But isn't that Italian jurisdiction? Georgina was killed there." Amy frowned. It took her several seconds to fit the pieces together. "Oh, you're talking your case." She swallowed hard. "You're accusing him of killing Otto Ingo?"

"We're not accusing anyone of anything. But . . ." He referred to the open folder, half reading from a report. "People in Otto's building remember seeing him enter Otto's apartment quite a few times. Boido faxed us his prints, which match prints lifted from the deceased's living room. There was no forced entry, no wounds to indicate a struggle, which leads us to suspect a friend or associate. Mr. Ingo had precious few of either. And finally, we have a definite sighting of Marcus there on the morning of the murder. He didn't fly off to Monte Carlo until late afternoon." Rawlings looked up with a satisfied grin, as if he'd just rattled off all the chef's specials. "It's a good start."

Amy was stunned. "Marcus worked for Otto. Naturally

he'd visit. Naturally his prints would be in the apartment. What possible motive could he have for killing him?"

"Motive indeed. We're looking into the possibility that Marcus was hired by the Carvel family to assassinate Ms. Davis."

"Assassinate?" Amy was doing her best to keep up. "What are you talking about?" In seconds they'd gone from one murder to two, from shreds of circumstantial evidence to a theory of Marcus Alvarez as a hired hit man.

"I'm sorry. Let me start at the top." The sergeant leaned across his desk, smiling. He seemed to enjoy Amy's confusion. "Lieutenant Jorgenson faxed us the file from five years ago."

"San Diego."

"Correct." Rawlings reached into his top drawer and pulled out a file folder. "No arrest was made in the Carvel case, but they did have a prime suspect."

"Marcus, yes. Why not?" Amy said, impatient with this absurdity.

"No. Georgina Davis."

"Oh."

"I'm not going to go into the evidence," he said, tapping the file. "Jorgenson wanted to pursue an arrest, but the district attorney refused. The evidence against Ms. Davis was circumstantial at best, and she'd hired some impressive legal talent. Budgets were being slashed at the time. A lot of California DAs were getting gun-shy of these expensive, high-profile cases."

"Georgina killed Fabian Carvel?"

"The police theory." His eyes crinkled at the corners. The detective/waiter was definitely enjoying this. *I'm sorry, ma'am, we're all out of the special salmon. Might I recommend the liver?*

"Georgina? That's ridiculous." She turned to Frank for help, but the patrolman was staring at his feet, refusing to speak or look up. "Why would she kill Carvel?"

"That's not important," Rawlings said with a dismissive wave.

"It was to her."

Rawlings slipped the file back into the drawer. "So, five years go by, and Otto Ingo starts looking into the Carvel murder. Maybe Marcus Alvarez talked him into it. Maybe not. That's not important."

"It was to him," Amy said. Well, it sounded good.

"In creating their game, Otto and his employee uncovered new evidence. Very possible. After all, Otto was a mystery expert, and this employee was intimately connected to the case." The sergeant looked up from his hands and into Amy's eyes. "In your game, who wound up being the killer?"

Amy hesitated. "Dodo Fortunof."

"The Georgina Davis character."

"Correct."

"And so, if Jorgenson is right . . . You can see why Ms. Davis signed up. Someone was making a game based on a murder she thought she'd gotten away with." He let the sentence hang.

Amy nodded absently, her thoughts flying back to the tour. Could it have been Georgina all along? Ditzy, harmless Georgina, following them to the garden and throwing the rock. Arranging the robberies. She wasn't about to tell Rawlings any of these details. He was doing fine on his own.

"Marcus Alvarez visited the victim's widow," the detective continued. "His phone records show several calls to the Long Island house. And, most persuasive, there was a deposit made in his account two days before the tour began. Twenty thousand dollars. We're trying to subpoena Mrs. Carvel's bank records."

"You think Marcus told Mrs. Carvel about the evidence," Amy mumbled.

"Or her son, Daniel."

"And they paid him to kill Georgina."

"We should know more in a day or so."

"But before killing Georgina, he had to kill Otto Ingo."

Rawlings nodded. "Doesn't that make sense?"

Unfortunately, it did. Otto had to have recognized the evidence, whatever it was. He himself had picked Dodo as the fictional killer. If the real Dodo was murdered during the game, the game master would undoubtedly take it personally. He would go to the police. So he had to die as well.

"It makes perfect sense." This was Frank's first contribution to the debate, and Amy was taken aback by the adversarial tone.

Rawlings ignored him. "We need to find whatever evidence Mr. Ingo might have uncovered. But we haven't been able to locate his research. We searched his apartment. He's got master scripts to all his previous games, but not to this one."

Amy felt a little weak in the knees and was glad she was sitting down. "Maybe his killer took it."

"We considered that." Rawlings's focus shifted to a moving object: Amy's knee, bobbing up and down, up and down. She couldn't help it. Amy followed the sergeant's gaze and did her best to stop. "You don't know anything about that, do you, Ms. Abel? Mr. Ingo's master script?"

"How could I?" Amy placed her heel flat on the floor and concentrated on not moving it. "Otto never gave us a full script. That's not to say that he might not have sent us a copy right before he died—you know, as a memento, maybe. But we haven't yet received one, if he sent it. Of course, you know the post office, always screwing things up. If we ever do get a copy in the mail, we'll be sure to give it to you. Right away." She couldn't stop herself from babbling. "We won't even look at it."

Rawlings's face was unreadable, but Frank was thoroughly confused. "What are you saying? Otto mailed you a copy of his script?"

"No! But he might have, right before he died."

"But that was weeks ago. You would have gotten it."

"You're probably right."

"Did Otto say he was sending you a script?"

"No. Forget I mentioned it."

Frank didn't. "Maybe he put on insufficient postage, and they returned it to sender. Then let's say his super was a nice guy and put on a few extra stamps and sent it back. That could take weeks."

"Forget it!"

"You're the one who brought it up," Frank said.

And you're an idiot. It felt good just thinking it.

"Excuse me." Rawlings raised a finger, as if warning the kids in the backseat to stop fighting. "We're straying from the point."

"The point is you think Marcus is a hired hit man." Amy was raising her voice and regretting it even as she did. "There is nothing—absolutely nothing—in his background to indicate that. Am I right?"

"How do you know about his background?" Frank demanded. "Just because you played hanky-panky with the guy doesn't make him innocent."

"Hanky-panky? What are you talking about?"

"Had sex with him."

"I know what *hanky-panky* means."

"Everyone on the tour was talking about it."

"What? We did not hanky-panky—which is none of your business, anyway." Amy glanced to the cubicle walls. Maybe she should lower her voice. "Does he have a criminal record? Anything that would point to him being . . ." She gritted her teeth. "What makes you think we slept together?"

"Oh, come on," Frank said with a snigger.

"No, *you* come on."

"People!" It was no longer "Excuse me." "You're right. He doesn't have a sheet," Rawlings said, his tone so calm it was almost eerie. "But you'd be surprised how many murders are committed by first timers. As for the term *hit man* . . . what we're suggesting is that Marcus went to Mrs. Carvel. That's been established."

"To do research."

"Shut up," Frank ordered.

"You shut up."

"Guys!" It was no longer "People." "Mrs. Carvel might have been distressed to hear Georgina Davis named as her husband's killer. Her son, Daniel, might have been present. At some point, the subject of retribution might have come up. We'll know more when we find out where Marcus's twenty thousand came from."

"Why are you telling me this?" Amy asked.

"What do you mean?" Rawlings asked.

"Do you usually call people in and tell them your unsubstantiated theories?"

"Ms. Abel." Rawlings seemed to measure his words. "You worked closely with Marcus Alvarez on this tour. Correct?"

"We didn't sleep together," Amy shouted.

"Good for you," barked a voice from the next cubicle.

"Smathers, butt out," Rawlings said and slammed an open hand against the particleboard partition.

"Yes, sir." Smathers sounded unrepentant.

"What I'm saying"—Rawlings lowered his voice—"is that you want to help your friend. Understandable. But you have to realize we are pursuing a case against him. Any cooperation will be appreciated. Any interference or withholding of evidence will not be appreciated."

"You're trying to intimidate me."

Rawlings lowered his voice even further. "How am I doing?"

Frank chuckled through a nasty grin. Amy didn't know why she was letting Frank get under her skin. Maybe it was just the shock of being betrayed by a man who was supposed to be helping.

"Some friend you turned out to be."

Frank bristled. "Hey. No one believed in Marcus more than me. But that was before I knew the facts."

"What facts? There are no facts. If you stopped to think—"

"Shut up." Frank's thick hands flew to his armrests, tensing, about to push the rest of his body to its feet. "You and your sophisticated, know-it-all friends. The whole trip long making fun of me. Don't think I didn't know. Well, for your information, you don't know squat about real homicide. Not squat."

"Neither do you."

"What're you talking about?"

"Officer Loyola." Rawlings had had enough.

Frank slumped back into his chair. So did Amy. Like prizefighters resting between rounds.

The sergeant stood up. "Thanks for coming in. I just wanted to apprise you of our current thinking." He turned to face the cubicle wall. "Keep in mind what I said about withholding evidence."

Amy had been about to get up. Now she found herself glued to the spot. "Withholding . . . ?"

"Yes." Rawlings continued to speak to the wall. "I suspect you do have a copy of Ingo's script. Whether you received it through the notoriously unreliable postal service or you acquired it some other way, I don't care. But I would appreciate if you turned it over. Evidence, you know."

"I don't have . . ." Amy was sputtering. "What makes you think . . ."

"One of my theories. We cops aren't very good at reading people. That's why we get so many ridiculous theories."

Frank held the door for her, which felt awkward, given his antagonism, but Amy accepted his chivalry and walked through. She felt him following her, a few steps behind, through the maze of squad-room cubicles, past the holding cells and booking rooms and finally the central command desk that dominated the lobby. Once out the main double doors, she paused and watched Frank veer off to the left. Amy turned to the right.

"Thanks, Loyola," she said as she walked. "I'll tell everyone how you sold us out."

"Hey!"

Amy didn't turn around but walked a little faster.

"Hey!"

She was vaguely aware of steps behind her and then a hand on her left shoulder. A second later and she was being spun around and thrown back against a brick wall.

Amy might have been expecting some sort of confrontation, but not this, not a physical assault.

"Who the huey you think you are?" The patrolman had a hand on each shoulder; then, as if suddenly realizing what he'd done, he backed away.

"Huey?" She was about to make a crack about his choice of cusswords but changed her mind. "Frank, come on. Hitting a woman?"

"I didn't hit you." They were on the far side of a bike stand, out of the flow of foot traffic but still within view of the trickle of humanity going in and out of the station. "Don't think I wouldn't." And with that he lunged an inch forward.

Reflexively, Amy snapped her head back, smacking it bluntly against the brick. It hurt like hell and her head spun, but she managed not to cry out.

A single snort of a chuckle escaped his lips; then he turned serious. "You shamed me in front of a detective."

Amy was within an inch, one deep breath, of throwing up. "You'll never make Homicide, Frank," she heard herself say. "Never."

He lunged forward again, and again her head snapped back against the brick, not as hard this time, but more embarrassing. The nausea in her stomach grew, but she pushed it down, along with a growing sense of panic.

"I guess you're a girl, after all." It was like he was reading her mind. "Good. A healthy fear is the best deterrent."

"Deterrent to what?" she gasped. "I assume you're no longer an active member of the Marcus Alvarez defense fund."

"I tell you what's gonna happen." Frank wouldn't move. His foul breath and menacing, hovering presence kept her head spinning. She glanced sideways, desperate, thinking someone going in or out had to be watching, but no one was.

A thick finger under her chin turned her face back to his. Again, the breath and the hovering, and the finger stayed in place. "I'm gonna be Rawlings's right-hand man on this case. Paperwork already went through."

"You're working homicide?"

"Why not? I was there. I know the people." Frank was almost licking his lips. "We're gonna snag him, me and Rawlings. One way or the other. And it's gonna be my ticket to a gold shield."

Amy opened her mouth, lifting the rest of her head from Frank's supporting finger.

"You understand me?" he hissed.

Amy's reply was earthy but eloquent. And a little tilt of the chin made sure the blueberries hit Frank's shoes instead of her own.

CHAPTER 25

"I assumed that information was for all the captains. Amy, I'm sorry. Again." It was the fourth time Martha had used the phrase, and she was tired of it.

"You don't have to be sorry," came the transatlantic reply. "I'm just telling you what happened."

"He actually threatened you? Pious, polite Frankie?"

"Yes, but I got even."

"You pressed charges?"

"Not exactly. Martha, I'm not blaming you. But whatever you and Burt come up with, I'd appreciate it if you didn't spread the news. That includes Frank and Jolynn and Holly."

"Holly flew home days ago."

"You know what I mean. I'm the only one you should trust."

"Okay." Martha was growing a bit miffed. "You're really getting into this."

"No," Amy shot back. "We just have to stay focused."

"Fine. So that's it? No other progress?" They had last seen each other Monday. It was now Friday, early morning in New York, around noon in Italy. Amy was glad she had caught Martha with her cell phone turned on.

"I think I covered everything," said Amy. "I've been meaning to check up on Betsy Caulfield, but things have gotten too busy. How about you? What's happening in Rome?"

Martha wasn't calling from Rome, but she was just angry enough not to mention it. "Good things," she reported. "Our Signore Guziano is optimistic about the case. It seems the twenty-three of us did an admirable job of tainting the evidence."

"You're referring to the plastic bags?"

"Things got all mislabeled and misplaced. Other pieces of evidence had smudged fingerprints, multiple fingerprints. I guess we got too excited. Even our notarized statements contain enough discrepancies to confuse a jury. Captain Boido is reportedly tearing out his neat little semicircle of hair."

"That's fantastic."

"Guziano is working on a dismissal. My Texas connection at the embassy is pressuring the Italian government. Any day now he'll be released."

A moment of dead air, followed by "Oh."

"What do you mean, oh? I would think that deserves another 'Fantastic.'"

"It does. Sorry. But as soon as Marcus is released . . . he may be facing a murder charge here. They're saying he killed Otto Ingo."

"Otto? Well, that's plain stupid."

"I know. They're grasping at straws."

"Out of the frying pan . . . Well, we've done our part, dear. You'll have to get busy and taint your own evidence."

"That's one approach."

"Oh, Burt just walked in. Hold on."

Martha cupped a hand over the phone and waited until Burt Baker had maneuvered his crutches across to the bedside phone. "It's Amy," she whispered. "Don't tell her where we are."

The judge nodded.

"Amy, girl. How are you?"

Amy repeated her update. Burt was even more outraged by Frank's behavior than Martha.

"Don't worry about the script. They may think you have it, but they can't possibly get a search warrant. Oh, by the way, Martha and I are following up a lead." He glanced up with a smile, only to see his partner mouthing "No" and sawing the air like a railroad crossing signal. "Uh. She doesn't want me to tell you."

"What do you mean, she doesn't . . . You guys aren't doing anything dangerous, are you? Promise me."

"Dangerous? We've done nothing more than make a few calls and meet a few people."

"What are you up to? Are you still in Rome?"

"Look, if anything comes of it, you'll be the first to know. The only one. That's a promise." Burt spent another minute reassuring her, then hung up and turned to Martha. "You're full of secrets."

She shrugged. "I don't want her worrying about us or telling us no. She's gotten so terribly bossy."

"We did sort of put her in charge."

Her second shrug was a repeat of the first. "Were the local cops cooperative?"

Burt brightened. "I showed them the papers from Billy at the embassy and tried to make it sound official. They're going to help. Do you want to come along?"

"Wild horses couldn't stop me."

Martha waited until Burt was out the door. She caught up with him in the hall, fell in beside him, then skillfully, casually looped a hand between his right brace and right hip, letting it rest gently on his forearm. She was getting good at this.

They had arrived in Elba yesterday, booking themselves into the Montecristo, one room. The manager had readily recalled them from their earlier visit and had greeted them like old friends. "Welcome back," he'd said, his arms spread wide.

This morning Burt had taken the hotel manager with him to see the Portoferraio police, to substantiate his story about the break-in and attempted robbery. As a judge, he knew the importance of making things look legal and proper, even if they weren't.

"The police understood what you wanted?" They were in the rental car, whirling past the autumn purple of the vineyards, the silvery olive groves, and the occasional dusty donkey cart. Martha drove, fast and decisively.

Burt checked the directions the police chief had written out, half in Italian, half in English. "I told him the U.S. government is looking into the robbery, taking it very seriously."

"There's a fork coming up."

"Left. I told him, 'We suspect someone on our tour of hiring a pair of local men to break into our rooms. Do you know of any local men who might do this? Men who might have a reputation for this sort of work?'"

"Good." The car swung onto an unpaved road, and a bucket's worth of gravel leaped up to attack them. Martha shifted into a lower gear as they bounced from rock to gully. "If Amy is right and the robbery was arranged, then it's our best shot—our only shot. These guys must have had direct contact with the killer. I mean, would you agree to do such a thing without at least meeting the guy who put you up to it?"

A red Fiat was parked beside a low stone wall that had probably been in the same state of collapse for the last hundred years. The Portoferraio police chief stood propped against the Fiat's dusty flank, frowning, arms folded across his preternaturally large gut, the image of reluctant cooperation.

Burt saw Martha's expression and laughed. "You should have seen him before I showed the letter."

The chief didn't move but waited for them to get out of the car and approach. He inclined his head toward a small cottage, the only building in sight. "The brothers Grigio, they live here with their auntie since their papa and mama they die." His English was basic but sturdy.

Burt introduced Martha. The chief made no acknowledgment but turned and led the way toward the cottage. It was a stone dwelling with a roof of broken red crockery. *Too small,* mused Burt, *to comfortably house a bachelor, much less two men and their auntie.*

"The family Grigio do many things. All of Elba, we know them for these things. But to do it for strangers? No one does anything for strangers."

"Look, it won't hurt to talk," said Burt.

The cottage was divided into two rooms, each with an oak-plank door to the outside. The chief led the way through the door on the right. This seemed to be an all-purpose room with five or six pieces of humble, mismatched furniture. A thin, sullen-looking man in his early twenties sat on a stool in the room's far left corner. He was repairing a tackle block, knotting a length of twine around the cracked wooden mechanism. His work space was illuminated by a hole in the crockery roof, and the room was strong with the smell of horse glue.

"Il fratello. Dov'e?" the chief asked. "Your brother. Where is he?"

If the man was surprised to suddenly find the chief, a crippled American, and a woman with a silver bullet hairdo standing in his cottage, he showed no sign of it. "Fuori," he answered. Then, turning his head to a shuttered window, the young man called out, "Sebastiano!"

Martha used a handkerchief to wipe a layer of dust from the seat of a high-backed chair, then settled gingerly onto the cracked wood. Burt lit on the chair next to hers. Together they waited, listening to Sebastiano's heavy footsteps as he made his way from the stone pasture, over the low stone wall, and into the stone cottage.

Less than an hour later Burt and the police chief were sitting in a seaside taverna not far from the string of resort hotels that dotted the scenic Gulf of Procchio. Martha wasn't with them. She had driven back to the hotel with a severe headache, and though Burt had been desperate to join her, he'd felt obligated to treat the chief to a glass of grappa.

"I told you," the chief said yet again. He was in a better mood now that he'd been proven right. "We do not trust easily."

"But we told them they were in no danger. We offered them money." Burt stared at the pictures spread out on the old pub table, the smiling snapshots taken on the last day of the race, their edges now decorated with the brothers' grimy prints.

The conversation in the Grigio cottage had turned

out to be rather one-sided. The police chief had duti-
fully translated Burt's and Martha's questions and as-
surances and offers of cash, though his attitude had
bordered on the apologetic. *These crazy Americans want me
to ask you this,* his eyes and shoulders and hands seemed
to say. *What can I do? It's my job.*

The Grigios' responses had been terse. No, they had
not done a job for any American. No, they had never
robbed anyone. Ever. This last statement had provided
the afternoon's only moment of levity, prompting the
chief to snort out loud. The Grigios had responded by
coming as close to a smile as they ever would.

Burt had fought on valiantly, using his judicial skills
to probe the nuances of the translated answers. He
nearly had to force them to look at the photos of the
smiling team captains. They looked but didn't focus,
as if the nerves between their eyes and brain had been
temporarily severed.

The chief slurped from his tumbler of grappa, relish-
ing the harsh, potent remains of the season's first pressing. "I think you are wrong. No people here do work
like you say. To rob tourists? So what? But this is different." He expelled air through his lips, and a mist of
grappa sprayed across the photos.

We came all this way, Burt Baker thought. For nothing. But Martha had insisted, and truth to tell, he would
have felt guilty to be so close and not make the effort.

"We are an island," said the chief. "Like Corsica, Sar-
dinia. Smarter, yes. More handsome, a thousand times.
But we do for family. Not for friends, most times. And
for strangers, never."

He accepted another refill, starting and finishing it
as he rose slowly to his feet, then wiped his mouth with
an edge of the tablecloth. Seconds later and he had left

the taverna, not waiting for Burt's taxi and not thanking him for the drinks.

The judge ordered a bottle of mineral water to take the tannic taste out of his mouth. He'd grown dizzy from the grappa and the stuffy heat. His eyes were fuzzy. And so when he saw her face appear just a dozen feet away, he at first thought it was a hallucination. What could she possibly be doing here?

Amy had mentioned her name only this morning. And here she was, standing in the doorway, the afternoon sun illuminating her familiar profile. Well, familiar if, during the occasional break in court sessions, you occasionally returned to your chambers and caught the occasional episode of *The Roads We Choose.*

Betsy Caulfield continued to teeter on the threshold. With one hand, she shielded her violet eyes, peering shamelessly into the darkened, smoky interior. Burt and half a dozen Elban fishermen peered shamelessly back. And then, just as quickly, she vanished.

Burt shook his groggy head. "Miss Caulfield!" He slapped a twenty-euro note on the table, then pushed himself up on his crutches. "Miss Caulfield!"

She was out by the road, still shielding her eyes and looking back now toward the long arm of Hotel del Golfo, the resort that cradled the inner bend of the bay, greedily claiming for itself a perfect crescent of the sandy beach. She heard her name and turned. "Do you know anyplace nearby that sells sunglasses?" she asked. "This morning my favorite Guccis disappeared right off my chaise." She pointed vaguely toward the hotel. "The gift shop only has those cheap ones that ruin your eyes and look like shit."

"Betsy Caulfield. What are you—"

"They have sunglasses for me on the set. But the costume Nazi and the continuity Nazi joined forces and won't let me take them. As if I would lose a costume."

Burt smiled. She seemed remarkably like her character, Erica Knowles, only shorter. Perfectly proportioned, of course, which was probably the trick, but a little older and shorter. Brock and her other leading men couldn't be too much taller.

"Judge Burt Baker." He was still beaming as he balanced himself and held out a hand. "When you and Brock were going through that divorce, every day I would call a court recess at two o'clock sharp, just to keep up. Attorneys are still arguing over the significance of my behavior."

Betsy extended her free hand with a flourish. "What an honor! I hope no poor soul was rushed to conviction due to my distracting—how shall I say—artistry."

"What? No, no, nothing like that."

"Oh." She sounded disappointed. "We're over here taping, you know. Brock's obsession with Italy is tying in nicely with our producer's obsession with sweeps week."

"Brock? You two are back together?"

"Oops. Don't tell anyone. It's a whirlwind thing. Next month I think. We're over here for a kidnapping and our second honeymoon. Actually our third, if you count my amnesia." Betsy turned again to face the seaside road. "Oh, good. At last, a taxi." She waved at the green-and-white Fiat as it approached and began to slow down.

"I'm afraid that's mine," Burt apologized. "But I'll be happy to take you wherever you want."

"I can't believe you were with Georgina when she died." Betsy had repeated this several times throughout

the long afternoon. It was just about sunset now, and
Burt was barely listening. "What a small world."

They were in the taxi again, the same taxi, winding
back along the road toward Il Golfo. She had made the
driver wait for hours as they scoured the town for an acceptable pair of sunglasses. Burt had not brought up the
subject of Georgina right away, hoping not to spook her
into silence. Although spooking her into silence might
have been better.

Under different circumstances, the T.R.W.C. gossip
might have been fascinating. Today it had seemed dull.
And the banter about tints and frames had been inter-
minable. When Burt finally did manage to squeeze in a
mention of their mutual acquaintance, the subject flowed
freely. Betsy wanted as much information from him as he
wanted from her.

Patiently, he listened to what he already knew. The
actress had met Georgina through the Carvels. "I'd
known Fabian and Doris for ages. When my town house
was being redone, they were kind enough to put me up.
Every now and then I ran into Georgina when she
popped up from Palm Beach. Of course I was devas-
tated when I heard. I can't believe the police actually
think . . . Poor Marcus." Her voice was soft and teary,
but even years of acting experience couldn't disguise
the gossipmonger's glee. "Do you think he did it? You
were there. You must have an opinion."

Burt shifted uneasily beside her in the Fiat's cramped
rear. His arms were sore from supporting his weight all
afternoon, something that rarely happened anymore.
Most people were so sensitive and accommodating. Especially Martha.

Before he knew it, Betsy had made another verbal
circuit—murder, sunglasses, work, herself—and had re-

turned to the top of the list. "Such a shock to hear the news. T.R.W.C. was in Rome that very week, you know. Wonderful scenes."

"You were in Rome?" The judge perked up. "In Rome? At the same time Georgina was killed?"

"Can you believe it? News is so bad over here. I didn't find out until my sister telephoned from Vancouver. It happens a mere ten blocks away, and I have to find out from halfway around the world. Is that ironic?"

"I guess."

"Really? I've never been able to pinpoint the exact meaning of that word. *Ironic.*"

"Uh, yes. I think it is. Irony. Were you really in Rome? On the nineteenth?"

Betsy nodded, allowing the moment to lapse into an unfamiliar but not unwelcome lull.

Well, the day wasn't a total waste, Burt thought. He had met one of the actual players in the drama and had learned of her presence in Rome. A mere ten blocks away, as she'd put it.

The taxi slowed at the gates of the hotel resort, then turned up the drive. "Thanks again for keeping me company," Betsy said, flashing her famous Erica smile. "I'd ask you to join us for dinner, but unfortunately, we're taping tonight. Full moon. Can't waste a full moon."

"I understand." The words came out gravely but grateful.

"I can't believe we know so many of the same people. Ironic."

Betsy stood under the hotel's porte cochere and waved the taxi on its way. *What a nice man,* she thought. Something did seem to be wrong with his legs. She'd been meaning to ask, but it had kept slipping her mind.

CHAPTER 26

It was the first brutal day of autumn. Nature was blowing in off the river, erupting through the narrow streets and colliding with a steady stream of air, barreling up the canyons from the lower tip of Manhattan. The strongest of the gusts rattled the aging storefronts along Hudson Street. On the east side of the street, in the middle of a block in the heart of the Village, the words AMY'S TRAVEL shimmered in red. FROM THE ORDINARY TO THE EXOTIC, in smaller gray letters, danced below.

The travel agency was a cozy space, with both desks visible from the street. Or partly visible. Against her daughter's objection, Fanny had taken charge of the glass-paneled door, taping up the standard full-color window cards of Caribbean beaches or rafts tumbling down a white-water gulch in Borneo. There were two areas for doing business, one by Amy's desk, one by Fanny's. A few cushioned swivel chairs, a lamp, and an end table were arranged by each in an attempt to make the space feel homey.

Amy breathed on her Lafonts, cleaned each lens

with a wipe, then returned them to the bridge of her nose. Lou Halpern, now without smudges, sat opposite her. Lou and his sister were finally going to shut down the Cindilu Dairy for two weeks to visit their younger brother and his family.

"We just want some time in Shanghai with the niece and nephew. Cindy and I have never even seen Ling Ling and Lu Yi. Can you believe that?"

Amy vividly recalled their brother Gus, a college student in her grade school memories. Gus had been even more political and angry than their parents, arguing with them about why they stayed in a country that had treated them so badly. Their reply was simple. They loved this country, just not the system.

The twins, Cindy and Lou, sided with their parents, while the younger, headstrong Gus married a fellow revolutionary and moved to Shanghai to work for China Bank. The couple somehow managed to survive the political climate, Gus's inability to learn languages, and his wife's distaste for Chinese food. Their children, the Halpern niece and nephew, were in their twenties. Ling Ling, blond and blue-eyed like her mother, was a computer analyst for an export firm. Lu Yi, two years younger, was still at Shanghai University. Amy remembered their baby pictures: pale, open-faced Americans dressed in infant versions of the famous peasant-blue pajamas.

"On the phone, Ling Ling sounds just like the lady from the take-out Chinese. No lie. My half-Swedish niece has an accent you can cut with a knife. You know, that stuff with the *l*'s and *r*'s. I always thought that was genetic."

"Lou! You know better."

Lou bit the corner of his mouth. "Maybe."

Amy returned to her monitor. "Why don't we try

United to L.A., then Cathay Pacific to Shanghai?" While she began to block out the itinerary, Lou busied himself by swiveling his chair and peering out into the windstorm.

"So, what's the situation with your cop friend?"

Amy had to think. "Oh, Frank." Was it just a few days ago that she'd described Frank as a friend? "He's fine, I guess."

"You think he's going to come in or just keep sitting there?"

Amy thought for another second, then followed Lou's gaze.

"The green Camaro sitting down the block. He was driving it the other day. You under police protection or something? Whatever you do, don't go into the witness protection program. It's a crock."

Past the edge of a "white-water Borneo" window card, Amy could see the rear of Frank's Camaro. Sticking up from behind the wheel was a shock of the patrolman's salt-and-pepper hair, wavy and short.

"You didn't know he was there?" Lou chuckled. "I hate to tell you, but you're under surveillance. Don't be embarrassed. I was under surveillance once for five months. Waste of taxpayers' money."

Frank was slouched down in his seat, and Amy figured that his rearview mirror was adjusted to frame the shop-front door perfectly. "What the hell?" Amy was tempted to race right out and confront the man—after thinking of what to say, of course. And after putting on a coat and maybe a scarf. She was sorely tempted.

The temptation was pushed away by the sight of something else on the street, a few feet from the Camaro. Her mother had just emerged from the Armenian restaurant four doors down, bundled up against the wind and steadying herself on the arm of her lunchtime companion.

"Oh, my God!"

"What's the matter?" Lou swiveled again and nearly pressed his face up against the glass. "Your friend in the car is ducking down."

"I don't think I'm the one under surveillance."

"What do you mean? You think just because I'm going to China? Those paranoid jerks."

"Not you. Him." Amy was pointing at Marcus Alvarez, the man to Fanny's right. "Lou, do you mind if we do this some other time? I'll put together the flights and bring it over to the store. I've got the dates."

"You want me to go?" He sounded hesitant.

"I would appreciate it, yes."

"Well . . . sure."

"You know, Lou. The right to privacy?"

"Yeah, yeah." Lou rose without another word of protest. "I'll call Fanny tonight. She'll tell me."

Amy ushered Lou out and stood waiting for them at the door.

"Glad to see me?" Marcus caught Amy in a bear hug, pinning her arms to her sides. Somehow their lips touched, nothing too passionate, more like a prolonged cheek kiss that just happened to settle on her lips.

"I hope this isn't a jailbreak." Amy wriggled free, conscious of Frank's eyes on them. She pointed them inside and helped Fanny off with her coat.

"I was released Sunday morning. Flew home four hours later with Burt and Martha. They send their best."

"I'll call Burt tonight. Uh, why don't we go into the back office? It's so good to see you." She was already herding them away from the window, whispering to her mother as she passed. "You were answering my phone?"

"You left it in my living room."

"I did no such thing."

It was clear what had happened. While she'd been out last night, alone at a movie, her mother had wandered upstairs—to dust or rearrange the spice rack, whatever excuse. Marcus had called. Fanny had answered. The rest was history.

"He wanted to meet me," Fanny whispered.

"Right." One phone call and a lunch, and her mother had grown closer to Marcus than she had in two weeks. Amy led the way into a small back office.

"It was too bad you couldn't join us for lunch," said Marcus.

"I couldn't?"

A buzzer went off, and Amy turned to see a young couple entering the shop, the wind slamming the door behind them. "Mom, can you handle that? I'm worn out from all my lunchtime business."

Fanny delivered a mock-sour face, then beat a reluctant exit.

Marcus made himself at home in Amy's favorite leather chair. "I like Fanny."

"She's for sale."

Marcus leaned back, hands laced behind his head, looking carefree and delectable. "I got your note, by the way. After they fingerprinted me and took me away." Amy recalled the note and her use of a certain four-letter word. "It meant a lot, knowing you were on my side."

"No problem."

"Martha started telling me about your investigation. But she got distracted."

"I'll bet. How's Burt holding up?"

"Seems to be thriving."

Amy settled in across the desk and launched into a review, everything from Fanny's breaking and entering to her meeting with Rawlings, to her latest goal, investigating Betsy Caulfield. In the glow of his undivided attention, she spoke articulately, enjoying the moment, aware, as Marcus must have been aware, that she was doing it all for him.

"When Burt told me about Betsy being there . . ." She smiled. "Don't you think that's significant, her being both in Rome and Elba? That can't be a coincidence."

Marcus wasn't enthusiastic. "She's working. It's not as if she single-handedly planned the show's plotline."

"Maybe she did. She's a star."

"Even if she were somehow involved, she couldn't have killed Georgina. You were there. You saw."

With a sullen grunt, Amy gave it up. "Have the New York police been in touch?"

"No. Should I be worried about that? About not hearing from them?"

Amy thought of the green Camaro down the street. "When they want you, they'll let you know."

"Me killing Georgina because she supposedly killed Mr. Carvel? And poor Otto?"

"They say there's an extra twenty thousand in your bank account."

"They know about that? It's an inheritance. An aunt left each of us, all her nieces and nephews, twenty thousand."

"Oh." She was relieved. "That should be easy to prove."

"Otto had no idea who killed Carvel. He wasn't really

interested. The truth rarely makes a good game. Have you talked to Stu Romney?"

"Stew Rummy?" It never failed to amuse. "No. I left messages at his office, but he's always in some meeting. I wanted to ask him about a woman."

"What woman?"

"Mrs. Carvel let something slip, about a woman her husband was planning to give a large chunk of F.S.C. stock to."

"Yes. That was Mrs. Gray, the family cook."

"A cook?"

"This I know. Honest. I was right in the middle of the turmoil. She'd been with the Carvels forever."

"Why would he give a cook millions in stock?"

"No one knows. Honestly."

"I was hoping it might be Betsy Caulfield."

"I see." Marcus chuckled. "Mystery woman. A little romantic intrigue. Sorry. Just an old servant. She was getting ready to retire, and he wanted to give her the stock as a retirement package."

"But so much stock? No wonder Price got upset. I mean, what's-his-name, the son."

"Daniel. 'Price' was my invention. It seemed in keeping with his personality. Yes, Daniel and Stu talked Mr. Carvel out of the gift. They settled on a perfectly adequate retirement deal. Mrs. Gray seemed just as happy."

"I see." Amy glanced out the open office door and saw her mother leading the young couple toward the exit. She didn't have much time left. "And after Fabian disappeared, did Mrs. Gray also disappear? Or suddenly retire?"

"No. Oh, I see what you're getting at. The vengeful employee. No. Mrs. Gray stayed on the Long Island estate. About a year after the murder she finally retired."

"And as far as you know, she wasn't in San Diego at the time of the murder?"

"Correct."

"And she wasn't on the road rally with us."

"Of course not."

"Just checking." It felt like a game of Twenty Questions.

"Anything else you need to know?"

"Yes. Stu Romney. Is he any better off now than he was before Fabian's death? He's the chief financial officer. Was he perhaps fiddling with the books? Has he been out of the country in the past three weeks?"

"You'll have to ask him yourself."

"Right. The problem is how."

"What are you kids up to?" Fanny was racing in to join them in the rear office, nearly panting with exertion. "Honeymoon couple," she said, waving back over her shoulder. Amy could see them out on the street, the man carrying a plastic Amy's Travel bag. "I sold them an African safari."

Amy checked her watch. "Ten minutes? You sold them an African safari in ten minutes?"

"Why not?" She let out a satisfied sigh, then lit daintily on the arm of her daughter's chair. "So?"

"So." Amy was giving nothing away.

"So. Catching up on old times?"

Marcus studied the older woman's face. "Fanny, you may be able to help."

For God's sake, no, Amy thought but didn't dare say.

"We're in a bind about how to get information out of a suspect."

"A suspect?" In her excitement, Fanny slipped from the chair's arm, falling with a thud into Amy's lap. "Sorry, sweetie," she said, scrambling to her feet. "That wouldn't have happened if you'd been polite and given me your chair when I came in."

"Who asked you to come in?"

Before Amy knew it, Fanny had replaced her in the armchair. She leaned her compact frame forward, elbows on her knees, a study in concentration. "Tell me."

"Marcus. No!" Amy only realized she'd said it out loud when Marcus and Fanny turned her way.

"What do you mean?" Marcus seemed genuinely perplexed. "I'm just asking for ideas. Your mother—"

"You don't know what you're getting yourself into."

"Ignore her." Fanny leaned even farther toward Marcus and the desk. Another inch forward and she would topple right over. "So. Who exactly do you need to get information from?"

CHAPTER 27

"What I don't understand, Ms. Arbor, is why your client waited so long before coming forward. It's been over half a century since the alleged theft of her process, the process she claims as hers, took place. Allegedly."

Amy squirmed. "Yes," the fake Ms. Arbor said. "You see, my client was out of the country for quite a period of time. She was unaware of the situation until she returned just a few months ago."

The corporation lawyer regarded her curiously. He couldn't have been more than two years out of law school, she decided, forced to deal with only the most ridiculous claims against the food conglomerate. Amy felt sorry for him but even sorrier for herself.

Fanny, aka Amanda Steiner, sat beside her in the small, windowless office of the Lexington Avenue skyscraper, dressed in a black, shoulder-length wig that had been moldering in a closet since the 1980s. The absurdity of the patently false hair somehow worked. Combined with a darker shade of make-up, it had radically changed Fanny's appearance.

"She was unaware of the existence of Mexican fast food? That's a little hard to believe. We have Tico Taco stores in twenty-nine countries around the world."

"Twenty-nine. Imagine," said Fanny. She was enjoying this.

"Mrs. Steiner's family moved to Borneo. There are no Mexican restaurants in Borneo." Amy had checked this out with three different tourist boards. It was the one thing she said with any degree of certainty.

The young, slightly built man pressed a button on his intercom. "Helen. Check the international lists. Does Tico Taco or any competitor have operations in Borneo?" He lifted his finger. "Is that a country? Borneo? Forgive my ignorance."

"It's an island shared by three countries. It's part of Malaysia, Indonesia, and the entire country of Brunei."

The finger descended. "An island. Check Malaysia, Indonesia, Brunei."

Amy sat straight in her chair. "At this stage, all we want is a meeting with Stuart Romney. If anyone would recognize the validity of Mrs. Steiner's claim, it's him."

"Mr. Romney is our chief financial officer," the lawyer explained. "We don't like to bring him in, not in such early stages."

"You can call Doris Carvel," Fanny said cheerily. "I'm sure she remembers." Amy had ordered her to remain quiet but had never for an instant expected her to obey. "Little Amanda Steiner. My parents were friends of theirs."

The lawyer wrote himself a note. "San Diego friend," he mumbled.

"I was just a girl at the time."

Amy cleared her throat. "When we set up this ap-

pointment, it was with the understanding that we would
meet Mr. Romney personally."

"Is he out of town?" Fanny asked sweetly. "That might
explain why he hasn't returned our calls."

The lawyer looked uncomfortable. "Uh, no. Mr.
Romney's been in the office every day for as long as I've
been here. And that's over . . . well over six months."

"Six months," Fanny repeated, looking smugly at her
daughter and faux lawyer. "And not even a day away."

"Mrs. Steiner," Amy said between clenched teeth.

The intercom buzzed. "Yes, Helen?"

"There are two Tico Tacos in Jakarta, but that's not
on Borneo. None at all in Malaysia or Brunei."

"So the answer is no."

"That's correct, Mr. Weaver."

Weaver lifted his finger, then seriously locked eyes with
Amy. "And Mrs. Steiner never left Borneo? Not once?"

"Not for a second," Fanny swore. "I adore Borneo.
We have the best white-water rafting. It's on our travel
posters."

"All right, Ms. Arbor." The lawyer sighed. "If you'll
wait here, I'll be back."

Amy waited until the lawyer disappeared out the
door. "I thought I told you to stay quiet."

"What are you talking about? I was brilliant."

"That was the deal. I impersonate a lawyer and commit fraud and wind up in jail, and you stay quiet."

"Did you like the way I found out about Romney's
whereabouts for the past month? Pretty nifty."

"Nifty."

Fanny reached up under a corner of her wig and
scratched at her hairline. "You're taking all the fun out
of this. You know, Marcus wanted to be the lawyer. He
thought this was a great idea."

"That's because he knew he couldn't come. Romney would recognize him." She eyed the door. "Weaver's probably checking me out with the New York State Bar Association. I'll be going directly to jail, and I didn't even have the pleasure of seeing you stay quiet."

As promised, the lawyer returned. "Mr. Romney has a little time between appointments," he said grudgingly and ushered them out the door and down the hall.

Stuart Romney was waiting in a corner office, a big-windowed, architecturally pretentious room with double doors that opened onto an enclosed outer office, not just an assistant's desk in the hallway. His furnishings seemed out of place among all the chrome and glass. They were pieces from the 1950s, large, well maintained, expensive, and homey, not unlike the executive himself.

Romney appeared to be well past retirement age—a barrel-chested man, but thin through the limbs, if the cut of his suit was any indication. He was as tall as Amy, although an arthritic stoop made him seem shorter. His hair was full and white, which implied either great genes or a good wig, as opposed to Fanny's monstrosity.

He greeted Fanny warmly, calling her Amanda and embracing her hand in both of his. "So you knew Fabian and Doris from the old days. You're going to have to tell me what they were like."

"I was just a girl," Fanny said.

"What was the house like? Was it really as tiny as they say?"

"Well, to me it seemed huge," said Fanny without a hint of hesitation.

Amy would have loved to see her go on but figured that discretion probably trumped curiosity, at least in this case. "I'm sure we don't want to take up too much of Mr. Romney's time."

"Yes," Fanny agreed, "although I do love reminiscing."

"Yes." Romney paused and grew somber. "Weaver from legal says you have some kind of claim against Food Services Corporation. I have no idea what this could be."

Fanny turned to her lawyer with a tilt of the head. Amy cleared her throat. "Thank you for seeing us." She handed Romney a freshly minted business card. "Mrs. Steiner walked into my office with this amazing story. I was skeptical, of course, but she has the proof to back it up." Amy dried her palms on her black, slim, knee-length skirt.

It had happened over fifty years ago, she explained. Amanda's parents had been friends with the Carvels. The two wives often cooked for each other when their husbands had to work late. Simple, impromptu meals. And little Amanda helped. On the day when they experimented with Mexican cuisine, it was Amanda who accidentally changed the recipe for corn tortillas, and as the shells were cooling, it was she who folded the entire batch to save room on the kitchen counter. The shells, surprisingly, became hard and held their shape. As Amy elaborated on her lie, Romney nodded.

Amy went on. "Everyone ate them. They didn't want to hurt the child's feelings. Mrs. Carvel even took a few of the shells home to show her husband, Mr. Carvel."

Romney raised his hand. "I don't doubt this for a moment." He smiled. "What you're saying is that Fabian used Mrs. Steiner's childhood recipe for the hard, prefolded taco shell."

"Yes." Amy had been all set to argue. "You don't doubt this for a moment?"

"I don't. Amanda, I'm sure, is a reliable woman with a good memory. And if she has evidence, she has evidence. What exactly? A girlhood diary? Old letters?"

"I'm not at liberty to say."

"No, of course not."

Amy found new places on her skirt and dried her palms again. "Uh, shortly after this incident, the family moved from San Diego to Florida. And a year after that to Borneo. You're not doubting it for a moment?"

"No, I'm sure it's true."

"Oh."

This wasn't going according to plan. The plan, Fanny's brainstorm, had sounded almost reasonable yesterday. *Reasonable?* That in itself should have sent up warning flags.

By claiming to be the inventor of the prefolded taco, she had hoped to put him on the defensive. Amy the lawyer would threaten to make Romney a codefendant in the suit. And in defending himself, Romney would naturally divulge certain information. Did he have an equity position in F.S.C.? Would he be nervous about opening the company books for Mrs. Steiner's attorney? In short, in the inevitable scrutiny of a lawsuit, would he be anxious to hide anything?

"Just between us?" Romney shrugged. "No, I'm not surprised. From my first days with the company I suspected Fabian of stealing at least one of his ideas. You know what made me suspect?"

"Umm." Amy was at a loss.

"Milk allergies." Romney curved his mouth into a boyish grin. "Didn't know that, did you? Fabian was a smart food man and a true innovator. But he was extremely allergic to dairy. His whole life."

"Allergic," Amy repeated. "That doesn't make sense. How did he . . . ?"

"Good. You've done your homework. Yes, Ms. Arbor. On that glorious day, the day that's immortalized in every annual report, when Fabian first tasted an enchilada with sour cream folded inside . . . Well, I had my doubts."

"What?" Fanny rose dramatically to her feet. "Are you telling me people are making enchiladas with sour cream? My God. On that very same night, my mother put sour cream on our enchiladas. We're Jewish. Sour cream on everything."

Amy's teeth were clenching again. "Mrs. Steiner!" she warned.

"Makes perfect sense," Romney agreed. "The man stole two of your ideas."

"You're saying Carvel was lactose intolerant?" asked Fanny.

"I didn't say lactose intolerant." Romney steepled his fingers. "As Fabian once told me, there are three elements in milk that one can be allergic to." The steeple collapsed as he ticked off the list. "One can have trouble digesting lactose. One can be allergic to one or more of the milk proteins. Or one can be allergic to butterfat. Each allergy by itself can be fairly benign, or so I'm told. Compared to other food allergies."

"But Fabian had all three," Fanny guessed.

"They say he almost died as an infant. The merest taste of milk would give him violent cramps. For years, I kept expecting someone to come forward and take credit for the sour cream." He sighed. "But I'm afraid you don't have a claim."

Amy's mouth fell open. "Tico Taco's success was based on those two things. Of course we have a claim."

"Not really, Ms. Arbor." Romney's voice lost all traces of warmth. "Sour cream and a folded corn shell are not things you can patent. Believe me, we tried. And even if your client were somehow able to trace a direct link between her recipe and Fabian Carvel, something I genuinely doubt, you would also have to prove that she was intending to profit from her recipe. Otherwise there's no damage, is there? No basis for monetary compensation. You're a lawyer, Ms. Arbor. You follow my logic."

"Yes, I am. I mean, I do."

There was a light rap on the door. An assistant discreetly popped her head in. "Your two o'clock is here, Mr. Romney."

"Ah, the police officer. Thank you, Rita."

"Police officer?" Amy had a bad feeling.

"Yes. It seems an old acquaintance of mine recently died. Tragic." He led the way into his assistant's empty outer office. "I'm not sure what I can tell them, but anything to help the police."

Amy hung back, a move that Romney misinterpreted. "I'm afraid I can't give you any more time, Ms. Arbor. If you insist on pursuing this matter, which I frankly discourage, Mr. Weaver in legal would be your contact." Then he stepped out into the corridor and glanced left. "Be with you in a moment, Officer."

"Take your time, sir," boomed a familiar Bronx-bred voice.

"Come along, Amanda," Romney said. "I'll walk you to the elevator."

Instinctively, Amy sidestepped, putting herself in the path directly between Romney and Mrs. Steiner. It was a move that could have been called awkward or rude or perhaps, with some luck, communicative. "Uh, Mr. Romney, could we possibly make use of a telephone? Mrs. Steiner and I?"

"Use your cell, dear," her mother said.

"I can't. I forgot it," she said, measuring each word for meaning.

Romney regarded her curiously. "By all means. Use Rita's phone. Nine for an outside line."

"It was good of you to meet with us."

"Yes," Fanny agreed. "Thank you."

They all shook hands. Then Amy crossed to the console on Rita's desk, prepared to pantomime a phone conversation for as long as it would take to avoid Frank Loyola. The receiver was to her ear and her own home number dialed before she realized that Fanny had followed Romney out into the corridor. "Damn!"

Once, in a mystery novel—someone was tailing someone—she had read that in order to avoid detection, you should never peek around a corner with your head at eye level, since that was where your quarry's gaze would naturally fall. Amy obeyed this instruction and fell to her knees. Her eyes were just inches off the carpet when she poked her head around the doorjamb and gazed down the long corridor.

There it was, the dusty black wig, bobbing its way toward the elevator bank. Escorting the wig was the back half of Stu Romney's impeccably tailored suit. In the distance, standing by an open door, was the front of a decent but cheap suit, inhabited by a presentable Frank Loyola.

"Pleasure to meet you, Amanda. Take care." Romney leaned in to shake her hand. "Get rid of that lawyer," he hissed, loud enough for Amy to hear.

Frank was smiling and staring intently. The officer had previously seen Fanny only once, with different hair and from the driver's seat of a Camaro. But they had spoken at some length, and Fanny's voice was distinctive.

"Don't speak," Amy begged her mother telepathically.

"Can I help you? Ms. Arbor?" Rita was right there, by her office door, staring down.

Amy jumped, still on all fours, then pushed herself backward on her knees. "Lost one of my contact lenses," she whispered.

"I see," Rita whispered back. "Um . . . if you have contacts, why are you wearing glasses?"

"Oh, these." She laughed, fingering her round black frames. "They're just glass. I, uh, sometimes wear them to make me look, uh . . . something. Serious. They make me look serious."

"Contacts? Plus frames with clear glass?"

"They make me look serious."

"I see."

Amy stumbled to her feet and brushed off her knees. "Uh, don't worry about the lens. It's a disposable."

When Amy finally joined her mother by the elevator bank, she was practically homicidal. "You made me look like an idiot."

"Be specific, dear. When?"

"Never mind." She punched the DOWN button, even though it was lit. "Didn't you know what I meant?"

"When you jumped in front of me? Of course. Frank Loyola. I wanted to see what he looked like. Pretty much like he sounds. If you'd worn a disguise, like a proper detective, you would've been able to join me."

"Right." The elevator pinged brightly, and the doors flew open.

"That was an enjoyable afternoon."

"Enjoyable?"

"Yes, dear. Lighten up."

"We could have been arrested. And what did we find out? Nothing. He doesn't care if Carvel stole your precious recipe or not."

"Does this mean I don't get to sue?"

"Get in the elevator. Now."

CHAPTER 28

Marcus stood shirtless, the first time Amy had seen him this way. It was a nicer body than she'd suspected might lie beneath the usual T-shirts and the polos. His olive complexion always looked tan, and now, with a real tan, it looked even better. He was holding up two hangers, one with a black silk, long-sleeved shirt, the other with a gray silk polo.

"Either one," Amy advised.

Marcus frowned. "Did Vinny say anything about a dress code? These are my only unwrinkled pants."

How had she wound up here? Amy asked herself, trying not to stare. Well, it had started with Vinny organizing a reunion party, which was followed by her saying to Marcus, "I have a car. I'll pick you up."

His cute little two-bedroom was no smaller than most apartments in the Village, which made it preternaturally tiny to anyone outside New York City. One by one, Marcus held up the shirts. "Come in the bedroom so we can talk."

Amy followed him, seating herself on the edge of the bed. Marcus was already inside the squeeze-in closet, the door half closed. "Where do the Mrozeks live?" he asked.

"New Jersey. Not very far. But with rush hour . . . We should head out."

Marcus didn't seem to hear. "Fanny was so funny last night, describing your little adventure."

"Yeah, she's a hoot."

"The real problem, as I see it . . ." There came a pair of muffled grunts and the clattering of wooden hangers. "If we assume that Fabian's murder is connected to the other two . . ."

"And we do."

"Then we have a problem. None of the Fabian suspects were around for Georgina's murder, and none of Georgina's suspects have any connection to Fabian."

"None that we know of."

"True." Pronounced like another grunt. "But I'm thinking there must be two. Someone killed Fabian. And someone else killed to cover it up."

"Maybe." Amy repositioned herself on the bedspread and gained a partial view of the closet interior, the sight of clothes draped over hooks and hangers. A muscular back and two arms—now bare, now not. "It's so weird. Talking about murder suspects, and at the same time rushing off to break bread with them."

"They must feel the same way." Marcus emerged, wearing the black silk. "In or out?" he asked, pointing to the shirttail. Amy paused just long enough to give Marcus the wrong idea. He cocked his head quizzically, then crossed the few feet to where she was sitting. His fingers deftly unbuttoned what they'd buttoned just a second before. "How about off?"

"On," she said, choking in surprise. "Shirt on, please." Amy had nowhere to go and let herself fall back on her elbows. It created some distance between them but left her half reclined on the bedspread, which probably sent another wrong message. She countered with a firm "We're going to be late."

"Blame it on traffic," he said in a sexy whisper. Marcus knelt on the bed, his legs straddling her, and crawled forward until he was on his elbows, his face an inch from hers.

Amy adjusted her standard-issue, black-rimmed glasses but didn't take them off. "If we're going to do it, I don't want it to be a quickie." She breathed the words warmly.

"If we're going to do it, I want to do it."

They stared into each other's eyes. She was so tempted to remove the glasses. Then Marcus rolled away and lay beside her on the bed. Their hands touched in the silence, an electrical circuit that neither one chose to break. The gentle hum of an alarm clock filled the small room.

"Not like this," she finally said. "Not when we're racing out the door."

"I know," Marcus agreed. "When the time is right."

"The time's been right." She turned and again found her words tickling his ear. "I kept expecting once we got to Rome. Maybe. When things got less hectic."

"Less hectic." Marcus shook his head. "Gives me one more thing to hold against Georgina's killer. Come on," he said, breaking the moment for good. "Let's not be too late."

The Mrozek house was a low split-level, attached to a two-car garage, with a basketball hoop at the peak between the garage doors. In the fading light of a fall evening, Amy had joined the twins in doing what kids must have been doing in a million other driveways at that moment, shooting hoops and waiting for dinner.

Fifty feet away, in the kitchen, Vinny was powering his 250-pound frame from sink to counter to stove and back again in the graceful, practiced dance of a professional chef. Marcus sat out of harm's way on a bar stool, sipping white wine and enjoying the spectacle.

"Not fond of basketball?" Vinny asked. He was ladling a cream mixture into individual casseroles, each already inhabited by pan-seared scallops and mushrooms.

"Never got into sports," said Marcus.

"Me neither. We got a lot in common."

"Vinny, I've seen you with the boys. You love sports."

"I pretend to for the boys. It's amazing what you do when you have to." He slipped the nine casseroles under a cool broiler, then turned a black knob, igniting a whoosh of gas flames. "Guess what I'm making."

Marcus looked around, inspecting the bright, high-ceilinged room. A soup was bubbling on the stove, filling the air with the heady aroma of saffron and fish. The light in an eye-level convection oven illuminated a veal roast, and in the sink, a colander of green beans waited patiently to be emptied into a steamer. "French?" he guessed.

"Very French," Vinny teased. He glanced appraisingly over the cooking stations and preparation areas. "I think we're almost there."

"Anything I can do?" Marcus asked, setting aside his wine.

"Spoken like a smart guest. Wait until it's all done. You can put the perishables back in the fridge. I'm going to call the boys."

Vinny emptied the beans into the steamer, tossed on

a lid, and wiped his hands on his apron. By the time he was out the door, Marcus was circling the counters, picking up the cream carton and egg tray. He found places for everything in the misty bowels of the Sub-Zero, then continued to stand there, hands braced against the open double doors.

"Of course," he whispered, his mouth puckering into a grin. "That's what he meant."

"Dinnertime," Vinny called out from the edge of the court, and for once the boys didn't argue.

Dominick took a wild three-point shot from the oil spill line. He made it and let out a surprised whoop before batting the ball to his father. "Needs a little air."

"Amy. Good game," Donovan said over his shoulder with a generous smile, then joined his brother in barreling past Vinny into the house.

"Don't forget to wash." Vinny massaged the ball and watched as Amy retrieved her sweater from the top of an azalea bush. "Looks like they gave you the old runaround."

"It's hard to play point guard in a pencil skirt," she said, then spent a few seconds adjusting the skirt in question. Vinny tried not to look.

"So. So, what do you think?" He gestured like a game show hostess displaying the prizes. "Fifteen minutes out of the city."

"Remarkable," Amy said, thinking of the maddening rush-hour-and-a-half drive. It was one of the great lies of commuting. "Only fifteen minutes away." That and "We'll still pop into town whenever we feel like it." Amy had seen a dozen friends move fifteen minutes out of town. It might as well be the moon.

Vinny retrieved the car keys from his pocket and pressed a button on the key ring. With a whir, the left garage door began to rise. "Jolynn doesn't allow balls in the house," he explained. "Sometimes I think she barely allows the boys."

"Well, it must be hard taking over another woman's children. Are you and Jolynn planning kids of your own?"

"I did kind of want a girl, someone I could teach to cook. But Jolynn let me know from the start she couldn't." He pointed to the general region below the belt. And then, in a one-handed toss, he arced the ball into a tattered washing machine carton, one of the family's sports boxes. "So, what's the story with you and Marcus?" Vinny pushed his key ring button again and turned back toward the house.

"What do you mean, story? He needed a ride."

"You make sure you get to know each other, that's all." Vinny lingered by the kitchen door, lowering his voice both in pitch and volume. It was as close to meditative as Amy had ever seen him. "After their mother died, I guess I was kind of desperate. Wrong word. You know, a middle-aged man with teenage boys. And the restaurant. Not that Jolynn isn't great. Don't get me wrong. I mean, she's young and affectionate, and better looking than I deserve. And she's got no family. I tell you, that can be a plus. A lot of positive things."

Vinny crinkled his eyes into a grin and clamped a meaty hand on Amy's shoulder. "Hey, that was a great vacation." A second later his face went ashen. "I mean, apart from Georgina. What am I saying?"

"You had a good time?" Amy asked.

"Are you kidding? The food was exceptional. The boys had plenty to keep them busy. And I know Jolynn likes to complain, but the trip was great for her. She's been much more relaxed."

"Good. Good to hear. Oh, and thanks again for arranging this dinner."

"Our pleasure. It was Jolynn's idea, you know. I think she felt a little out of the loop. You know. Everyone else being so involved in the investigation."

"I'll make a point of thanking her."

"Please. She likes being appreciated."

"It means a lot to Marcus, knowing that you guys are sticking by him."

"Absolutely." Vinny opened the door and stepped inside. "So, you don't think Frank's going to be joining us?"

Amy took one last glance out at the darkening street. That had been her real reason for playing basketball in a pencil skirt, to keep an eye out for the green Camaro. It had never appeared. "I don't think so."

CHAPTER 29

Amy found the hostess and the three other guests in a formal living room that showed no signs of ever having been lived in. Martha and Burt sat side by side on a flawlessly white sofa, huddled over an iPad featuring the Mrozeks' digital memories.

"The Assisi dinner." Jolynn stood behind the couple, pointing between their heads to a group shot. "Right when we got our main courses. Look, you can see Frank's pigeon." The picture, taken by a waiter, showed the full length of the wooden table—Amy and the six captains, all pink-eyed and smiling. Jolynn chuckled.

"That was the same night Georgina got her brainstorm," Burt said. "Remember? We were all upset because we thought she'd solved the game. Of course she hadn't. How did the Dodos finish? Third? Fourth?"

"We would have finished first if you'd listened to me," said Holly Baker. "I told you it was Dodo from the start."

"No, you didn't," said Martha calmly and forcefully. "For the first week, you told everyone the killer had to be Bitsy. That's because I was Bitsy." Her tolerance of the younger generation had diminished noticeably since their return.

Marcus walked in from the hall, carrying candle-sticks for the table. "The boys are washing up. I think it's time to eat."

"You shouldn't be doing that," Jolynn scolded him. "You're the guest of honor. What else has Vinny been forcing you to do?"

"Nothing, I swear."

The clanging of an old-fashioned dinner triangle re-verberated through the house.

"Vinny, stop it!" screamed Jolynn. "It's uncouth. To the dining room, everyone."

It was just as Jolynn was guiding Marcus to his place at the head of the table that Vinny swung open the door from the kitchen. Cradled in his hands was a tureen of soup, the steam billowing up into his shaggy hair. "I know we don't have Daryl and family with us, but I did my best to bring back a few memories." He set the tureen in front of Marcus's plate and wafted a hand through the steam. "Some nice white fish with fennel and saffron . . ."

Seven faces stared blankly, except for Marcus, who had already guessed. Vinny tried another hint. "The next course is scallops and mushrooms. Followed by a nice veal roast with a garnish of tomato and basil."

"The opening night dinner," Jolynn said but added no inflection, nothing to indicate pleasure or apprecia-tion.

"Yes," Martha gasped, clasping her hands. "And you re-created all the dishes? From memory?"

"Hardly." Vinny ladled out the soup and passed the bowls to Holly, who passed them down the line. "French cooking is very standardized. A béarnaise sauce is almost always the same. As opposed to Italian, where you'll rarely get the same marinara twice, even from the same chef."

"Still, that's amazing." Martha turned to Burt. "Isn't that amazing?"

"I can't vouch that every ingredient is exact," Vinny added. "And I didn't use food coloring to write the team numbers into the shells of the strawberry tarts. Remember that?"

The meal turned out to be a pleasant one, given the situation and the cast. If the twins weren't on their best behavior, they at least toyed with the concept, paying enough attention to Holly to make her feel grown up and worthy of attention.

At the adults' end of the table there evolved a nice blend of subjects. The investigation did not go ignored. It was one of the few things they had in common, and the evening would have seemed stilted without it. But it wasn't the only or even the main topic. The meal drew to a relaxed, natural close, and with ice cream on the tarts, at Holly's request.

Amy fiddled with the crumbs of her shell, taking the time to observe her ex-guests. She was on equal footing with them, now that their complaints and problems were no longer the bane of her every waking moment. "It's funny, this dinner." She leaned diagonally toward Marcus, at the head of the table.

Marcus also leaned, the two of them forming a temporary island of privacy. "Funny how?"

"So many dinners. First night in Monte Carlo. That evening in Assisi. Georgina's murder. Even the Carvel dinner five years ago. As if dinners are the center of it all."

"Very much at the center."

Amy started. "What do you mean?"

Marcus glanced uneasily down the length of the table. It was a slight thing, a bare movement of the eye. "Later."

Yes, Amy reminded herself. This was yet another of those dinners. No matter how hard it might be to believe, one of them . . . one of them or Frank. She couldn't let herself forget Frank.

"Later what?" Martha drawled. She was leaning over the table, with a wink that tried its best to be sensual and wound up looking like an eye infection. "What's going on with you two? As if we didn't know."

"Know what?" Amy was a little slow on the uptake. "Oh, us?" She shot a glance at Marcus, then around the table, surprised to find herself facing down several sly little smiles. "Please, there's nothing to know."

It was Marcus who came to her rescue, deflecting the attention back to Martha. "Speaking of knowing something . . ." Marcus spread his arms wide, palms up, one in Burt's direction, the other in Martha's. "Don't think we haven't noticed the two of you."

The jurist and the decorator paused, then exchanged a conspiratorial nod.

"Touché." Burt laughed. "Caught red-handed. You see, unlike some, who neither admit nor deny, I will do the honest thing. Yes." He waved a strawberry-stained fork. "You caught us."

"Should we tell them now?" Martha murmured. She reached across the table, touching his free hand. "I know you wanted to inform your family first, but . . ."

"Oh, no," Holly moaned, anticipating the blow.

Martha went on. "These are the people who know us both. The ones who brought us together, you might say."

"Gag me," Holly added, and Martha seemed to be considering it.

"You're right, dear. Besides, from the way you're talking, they already know."

"I think we do." Vinny chuckled and beamed. "Congratulations."

"No, no. Let's do this properly." Burt pushed himself to his feet, his crutches hitting the edge of the linen-covered table. "My friends." He lifted his glass. "I am happy to announce that Ms. Martha Callas has foolishly consented to be my bride."

The suburban dining room echoed with a chorus of warm wishes. The twins whooped wildly, as if someone had scored a touchdown.

"You don't congratulate the bride," Jolynn said, chastising someone. "That's for the groom. You say 'Happiness' or "Best wishes' to the bride."

"To Burt and Martha." Vinny lifted his glass. The others followed suit. Wisely, no one waited for Holly. "To the happy couple."

"To the happy couple." Amy raised her own glass and had an immediate, unsettling flashback to their last group toast.

But this time, no one died.

Amy watched them in her rearview mirror, Vinny and Jolynn Mrozek, caught in a circle of porch light. The twins framed the mismatched couple like a pair of burly bookends. A warmly pleasant picture: the cozy, perfect house, the freshly mowed lawn, the smiling, waving family.

Amy negotiated the spirals of nearly identical streets,

all dedicated to trees or flowers or feminine first names. It was a confusing maze, made even more so by Marcus's lack of skill in reinterpreting—reverse interpreting—Vinny's original directions.

"When you get to Alice Avenue . . ."

"We're *on* Alice Avenue."

"Sorry. When you get to Hawthorne, make a right. No, that would be a left."

They finally encountered a sign for the Palisades Parkway, and Amy knew where they were. "Okay," she said and prepared to swing onto the leafy ribbon of road. "You were saying something about the dinners. How they're important." The evenly spaced streetlamps flashed a hypnotic pattern of lights and shadows through the Volvo's dim interior.

"Ah, yes." Marcus folded the sheet of directions and slipped it into the glove box. "I think I know why Fabian left the dinner table."

Amy lifted her foot from the gas and steered them into the slower, non-passing lane. "All right. I'm listening."

"Tonight wasn't the second time this menu's been served. It's the third."

Amy shrugged, not surprised. "The same dishes were served at the Carvel house five years ago."

"Right. The only difference might be the green beans. I don't remember . . ."

"Don't worry about the beans."

"Oh. Okay. Anyway, it was one of Otto's little touches, using the same menu. I'd almost forgotten. I mean, how could it be important?"

"But it is important. That's what you're saying?"

"Yes." Marcus twisted his body sideways, then propped his legs up in front of him, straining the seat belt's shoulder harness. He stared at Amy's profile. "Did you like the scallops in cream sauce?"

Amy gave him a fleeting glance, then looked back at the road. "They were fine."

"Just like you remembered them in Monte Carlo? Nice and creamy."

"I suppose."

"I didn't realize, either, until I thought about Mr. Carvel eating them."

"Oh, damn." Amy froze, her hands clutching the wheel.

"Pay attention. Amy, slow down."

They were heading into a series of S curves. Amy came back to reality just in time to ease on the brakes. "So, five years ago there was cream in Fabian Carvel's scallops. Do you remember that for sure?"

"Of course not. One dish? Five years ago? But there was cream in the scallops tonight. I saw Vinny put it in."

"Maybe Fabian's cook didn't use cream. I mean, he had the same cook for ages. Mrs. What's-her-name. She used some sort of cream substitute."

"Mrs. Gray. Yes, probably. But what if she didn't? It certainly would answer a few questions."

Amy veered off the Palisades Parkway and onto the approach ramp for the George Washington Bridge. As she did, Marcus laid out the scenario.

"It's like your mystery woman theory. Mrs. Gray was infuriated by Mr. Carvel's decision not to give her the company stock."

"So she put cream in his food."

"Why not? I didn't think about the scallops that night. If I had, I would have assumed it was a cream substitute. But Carvel knew. Why else would he have looked so odd just as he was eating it? Why else would he have left without a word? The woman who'd been his cook for decades had purposely made him sick."

Amy was skeptical. "So he runs away from his cook, a harmless old woman. She doesn't follow him, either. That's established. But he stays on the road for a week, then gets killed in San Diego. . . ." She merged into an E-ZPass lane and eased through the toll barrier to the upper level of the bridge. "Outrageous."

"It's not so outrageous."

"No. Sorry. I mean, thirteen bucks to cross a bridge."

Marcus waited until they were safely on the upper roadway's humming expanse. "Anyway, Georgina noticed the cream. She didn't instantly connect it to his disappearance. But at some point, she put it together."

Amy thought back to the dinner in Assisi. "Perhaps."

"And that's why she was killed."

"By the cook?" She maneuvered the Volvo into the far right lane. "The cook who wasn't in San Diego and wasn't in Rome? That cook?"

"All right, all right. But it does answer some questions."

Amy flashed back to that sunny afternoon on the roof garden when Georgina admitted knowing why Fabian had run off. "It wasn't anything," the heiress had said. A little inconsistency.

The car eased onto the mazelike exit ramp. "It answers some questions."

Marcus turned to face front, then adjusted his seat belt and settled into the cracked leather. "So . . ."

"We should give this information to the police."

"What information? You mean about an old cook and a milk allergy? Coming from their prime suspect? I think I'll skip that meeting."

They were on the Henry Hudson now, heading south

along the New York side of the river toward the Village and home. "So we don't tell the police. Or the team captains. If, by some miracle, we're right, then we're in just as much danger as Georgina." Amy frowned. "Killing her because she remembered cream in the scallops."

"That must be the loose thread. The loose thread that can unravel everything."

"Oh, a knitting metaphor."

"The killer knows that this thread will lead straight back to her. Or him. We must be close."

"We may be close." Amy glanced sideways. "Oh, and we do not tell this to my mother."

"Why not? If it weren't for Fanny, we wouldn't be this far along."

"Don't let her hear that. You'll be opening a whole Pandora's box."

"Now you're the one with the metaphors."

"It's a Pandora's box."

"You know what was at the bottom of the box?" Marcus's tone was playful and persuasive. Reaching over the gearshift, he placed a hand on Amy's knee. Her leg jerked, and the accelerator kicked in. "I learned this from a grade school comic book. At the bottom of Pandora's box, under all the troubles of the world, there was hope."

"Hope? With Fanny?" Amy eased off the pedal. "You're right. I used the wrong metaphor."

CHAPTER 30

Marcus climbed the stairs from the kitchen to the bedroom level, a cup of coffee in each hand. "Light, no sugar," he called out. "Right?"

By the time he reached the top, he could hear the shower running hard. On the far side of the bathroom door, Amy was singing. It was a cheery rock song from a million years ago about making love in a Mexican cantina.

Placing the steaming cups on a nightstand, he picked up his watch and slipped it on. He glanced around, then tiptoed to the center window of three and pulled down a slat of the venetian blind, just enough to see through. As always, except for a few hours twice a week, on the street cleaning days, Barrow Street was jammed with parked cars. But there weren't any here now that hadn't been here last night. Two grade school boys were running toward Seventh Avenue, dressed in uniforms and laughing. Other than that, the street was deserted.

He grabbed the moist bath towel draped over a bedpost. Toweling off his hair with one hand, he used the other to grab his phone and press a speed dial button.

His roommate picked up on the second ring. "Terry? Me again." Marcus tossed aside the towel and began to reach for his trousers, folded over a straight-backed chair. "Did they come back?"

"He was here a minute ago, just the one guy." Terry's voice seemed too loud, much louder than his own. Marcus cocked an ear—the singer was still on the floor of the Mexican cantina—then cupped a hand around the phone. "I can get into trouble, Marcus. He wants you to come in for questioning. That's all."

"Sure. That's why he was waiting at my door at ten thirty last night. For questioning?"

"You're going to have to come home sooner or later. I mean, if you don't . . . that's like being a fugitive."

"Not if I don't know about it. Did it sound like he was going to arrest me? Did he have a warrant? They can't force me to come in without a warrant, can they?"

"How should I know? On TV the police bring people in. Stuff like, 'You can answer my questions here or at the station house.' It sounds like they can force you."

"I don't think so, not without a warrant." Marcus cradled the phone in the crook of his neck as he slipped on the black trousers, followed by the black silk shirt from the other bedpost. He glanced around and was able to find only a small antique wall mirror. "She must be the only woman in America without a full-length mirror."

"You're in someone's apartment? Where are you?"

"It's better if you don't know."

Terry sighed. "What a mess."

Marcus sighed back. "Maybe I should have stuck around. But when I saw his car out front, I panicked. I've already spent a week in jail. It's no fun."

"Did you have an okay night?"

Marcus glanced toward the bathroom door. The water had stopped, and so had the singing. "I had a very nice night." He lowered his voice even more. "What did he say this morning? Same as before?"

"He asked if you came home at all and if I'd heard from you. His patience was pretty thin. He asked if you had a girlfriend."

"Girlfriend?"

"Someone named Amy. Is she the one who came over?"

"Damn. He must be on his way here. Gotta go."

By the time Amy, wearing only a towel and fogged-up glasses, emerged from the bathroom, Marcus was dressed and combing his hair. Amy came and kissed him shyly on the forehead. "Oh, coffee." Marcus watched as she strolled over to the nightstand, her face so open and warm and pleased. "Great. No sugar, I hope."

"We should go. We'll be late."

Amy eyed him over the rim of steam. Why was he acting like this? Was it just the awkwardness of the morning after? "Plenty of time to sit down with a cup of coffee." She smiled, hoping to put him at ease. "Don't you think? Traffic out to Long Island shouldn't be bad."

"I have to get home first, to change." And before Amy could object, he grabbed his coffee, still untasted, and his wallet and headed for the stairs.

Amy caught him by the arm, and a small wave of brown liquid sloshed out and onto the rug. "Sorry. Did it get you? Uh, I just wanted to say . . ." She had rehearsed this several different ways but never so rushed. "I'm glad you came over last night. I thought, after I dropped you off in front of the deli . . ."

"I told you. I needed milk."

"I know. But I thought . . . I assumed it was just an excuse not to ask me up. Anyway, thanks for changing your mind. When I looked out the window and saw you ringing the bell . . ."

Marcus kissed her lightly on the cheek and headed once more for the stairs. "I'll be downstairs talking to Fanny." It was a phrase designed to get Amy moving.

"Okay, I'm coming. Just a minute."

Fanny Abel was in the third-floor kitchen, Amy's kitchen, filching the last of the coffee. *Stronger than normal,* she thought curiously. The sound of footsteps made her look up, and her eyes widened in momentary shock. A second later and all was normal, as if handsome men in black descended every morning from her daughter's bedroom.

"Fanny, there's no time to explain."

"Explain? Sweetie, explain what?"

"No, no. This is an emergency."

The doorbell buzzed, a tinny blast exploding from the intercom beside the stove.

"Damn. Okay, okay." Marcus threw his hands to the sides of his head, as if physically trying to hold in his thoughts. "Okay. Quick. Yell upstairs. Tell Amy you'll answer the door."

Fanny barely skipped a beat. "Amy," she crooned in her piercing piccolo. "Don't answer that. I'm expecting Bernice Crenshaw. She hits your bell by mistake."

"Fine," came Amy's voice down the stairwell.

Fanny turned to Marcus. "Who is it? What do I do?"

"It's the police," Marcus said, biting his lower lip. "They're looking for me."

"Do they have a warrant?"

"I think it's just Frank Loyola. But Amy and I have some important things . . ."

"No need to explain." Fanny pushed a button on the intercom. "Who is it?" she asked.

"Police," a voice squawked almost indecipherably.

Fanny glanced up the stairs. "Bernice? Hello. Be down in a second." And before the voice could respond, Fanny released the button. "I'll get him into my living room. You and Amy take the stairs down. . . ."

"He may have another officer outside."

"Good point." Fanny began fixing her hair in the refrigerator chrome. "I know. Have Amy take you out through the garden. I saw Mrs. Pelegrino. She'll let you go through her house to Grove Street."

"Um." Marcus bit his lip. "I don't want Amy knowing about the police. You know how she gets."

"I do." Fanny paused. "Tell her you want to see the garden. Then say hello to Mrs. Pelegrino. She'll be there as soon as you poke your head out, the old snoop. Admire those dreadful cabbage flowers. Then ask for a drink of water or something. You've got an imagination, dear. Use it."

"Fanny, you're a wonder." Marcus bent down and kissed her on the cheek with more enthusiasm than he'd used on Amy just a minute before.

With the stairs tripping under her feet, Amy came racing down. She arrived just in time to see her mother scurrying down the next flight to her own half of the house.

"Bernice, keep your blouse on!" Then, with a halt and a quick pivot, "Marcus, dear, would you mind closing the door? No reason you two should eavesdrop on a couple of old biddies."

Amy waited until the kitchen door was firmly shut. "How did she take it?"

"Take . . . Oh, you mean seeing me come downstairs? She didn't mention it."

"I'll bet."

"You know, I think we do have some time, after all. No need to rush."

"Sure." Amy looked pleased. "How about more coffee? Damn. Fanny took the last of it, didn't she?"

"Oh, well." Marcus's air of disappointment lasted a second. "I know. Let's go out to the garden. I've never seen it by daylight. Do people here plant things in the fall? You know, like mums? Or those little purple ornamental cabbages?"

Amy's face lit up. "Yes, as a matter of fact. Mrs. Pelegrino. Come on. I'll show you."

CHAPTER 31

Marcus was enjoying this too much.

There was no other way to do it. They needed Doris Carvel to look at a photo and wanted to be together to gauge her reaction. This had been the most logical plan of attack. But Marcus was enjoying it too much.

"So romantic, you two meeting the way you did." Doris beamed up at Marcus on her left, then up at Amy on her right. The three of them were strolling arm in arm in arm along the banks of the Long Island Sound, at the edge of the lawn. Yellow and brown leaves crunched under their feet. "You'll have to let me throw a party."

"No, we can't let you do that." Amy twisted the ring on her finger and felt guilty about the whole sham.

"I insist. A small affair. A few of Marcus's friends from his days with us."

"That's not necessary."

"Sweetie, why not?" Marcus smiled and threw Amy a playful wink. What the hell did that mean? Was this hilariously funny somehow? He had already told Doris in exaggerated detail about how he'd proposed just a day after getting out of an Italian jail. And now he could barely keep from laughing. Was it really so comical to think that he could be in love with her, that the two of them could be engaged?

"Honey, it's too much trouble."

"It's no trouble at all," Doris interjected.

"You see?" Marcus agreed.

Amy stood her ground. "I don't want to make a fuss. Such busy people, like, for instance, Stu Romney . . ." Emphasis, emphasis. "He wouldn't be interested in spending an afternoon with me. Face-to-face?"

"How modest." Doris chuckled. "Stu would love to meet you. We spoke just the other day."

"Ah, yes." Marcus's grin faded as the memory of Amy's encounter with Stu clicked into place. "Maybe you shouldn't bother, Mrs. Carvel. Though it's a lovely thought."

"Nonsense." Doris was disappointed, but her mind had already turned elsewhere. "You know, it's funny, your mentioning Stu. He called the other day. I guess I said that. This woman, it seems, came into his office, claiming to be an old friend."

"Claiming to be?" Marcus asked. "You mean she wasn't?"

"I don't remember her at all. Amanda Steiner. She said her mother had been a friend of mine back in San Diego. I don't recall any Steiners. Of course, this was ages ago."

"Very strange," Amy said. "You don't remember her?"

"What did she want?" Marcus asked in a much more natural tone.

"Stu didn't say." Doris sighed. "It's so horrible, forgetting people. I mean, what do we have left after all these years but memories?" She let go of Marcus's arm and rearranged a shawl around her shoulders. "No. There wasn't any Steiner family. Why would she do that? Pretending to know us."

"I don't think you'll hear from her again," Amy said, meaning every word.

"Maybe she was a friend of Mrs. Gray's," Marcus proposed.

"Mrs. Gray?" Doris looked puzzled. "You didn't know her well, did you?"

"Barely. Mrs. Gray was the cook," Marcus explained to his fantasy fiancée, who already knew. "Tiny woman in black. Kept to herself."

"Kept very much to herself," Doris said. "Even in her young days in San Diego. The idea of her having friends . . . I suppose it's not impossible."

If there was one thing Marcus could do, besides lie, it was manipulate a situation. In some ways he reminded Amy of her mother, a comparison she preferred not to think about. "Maybe this Amanda character knew Mr. Gray," Amy suggested.

Doris looked uncomfortable. "There never was a Mr. Gray. Mrs. was just what we called her. Gray was her maiden name, although that's hard to believe, since she was Italian."

"Grigio," Amy translated. A fairly common name in Italy.

Marcus tilted his head to one side, as if dropping a half-forgotten memory out of his ear. "Didn't Mrs. Gray have a son? People used to talk about her son."

"Young folks like you. Is it so odd, having a child out of wedlock?" A sly smile crimped the corners of the old woman's mouth. "We called her Mrs. Gray for propriety's sake. We cared about propriety, God knows why. I'm not sure anyone ever knew who the father was. It was one of those things you didn't ask."

"You still don't," Marcus said.

Doris laughed, a vocal eruption more shrill than Amy would have expected. "How did we ever get on this subject? Discussing the help, for heaven's sake."

"We were speculating," said Amy. "How did this Amanda woman get to know so much about your family? If Mrs. Gray is still here, she might be able to tell us. . . ."

"Oh, no. She's long retired. About a year after . . ." Her face clouded over. Like many widows, Doris marked the passage of time with the date of her husband's death. Things happened so many years before or so many years after. "A year after Fabian left us," she continued, "I seem to recall her moving back to Italy. At least that was my takeaway." Doris glanced up, her eyes meeting Amy's. For a second, her face had a soft, gamine quality, the way it might have looked before life and her own personality had irretrievably imprinted themselves. "Fabian used that expression. Takeaway. 'What was your takeaway from the meeting?' Like it was packaged in those little Chinese containers."

In the distance, by the solarium, Kevin the butler had appeared. He was walking toward them. A purposeful walk, a "Please excuse us" walk. *Damn. One more minute,* Amy silently begged. That was all she needed. They might not get another chance.

Marcus sensed it, too. "You want to see a photo from our Italian trip?" Even as he spoke, he was fumbling frantically in the large pockets of his jacket.

"Oh, I love vacation photos. Is Georgina in the picture?"

"Yes," Amy said. "It is one of the last pictures taken of her."

In another second, the photo was out of its paper sleeve and crammed into Doris's arthritic hands. It was a six-by-nine shot of the captains, a "Here we are" photograph taken in front of the Rome finish line, enlarged from Amy's camera.

"Who are these people?" Doris asked.

The Irish butler from Boston was getting closer. Only his butler-like manners prevented him from interrupting them from a distance.

Marcus moved a foot to his left, positioning himself firmly between Kevin and his employer. "Those are some friends from the tour. See? There's Georgina."

"Georgina," Doris echoed sadly.

"Me. Burt Baker. He's a judge. Jolynn Mrozek, from New Jersey." As Marcus named them, Amy shoved a fingertip toward each, making sure that Doris had time to register the individual faces. "Frank Loyola, a policeman. Martha Callas from Dallas."

Doris followed the finger but was clearly losing interest. "Very nice. Very nice group." And then it came, an almost inaudible "Oh."

"Oh, what?" Amy had been alert for this, a glimmer of recognition flashing in the widow's eyes. "What is it?"

"Mrs. Carvel?" Kevin had arrived, just on the other side of Marcus's roadblock.

Amy held her ground. "Mrs. Carvel. Do you recognize one of these people? You look like you recognized someone. Another friend?"

Doris pursed her lips and emitted a noise, like a little grunt. "Uh, no. I thought for just a second . . . Silly me."

Kevin raised his voice and a hand. "Mrs. Carvel?"

"What's silly?" Amy asked. "What is it?"

Doris Carvel lowered the photograph and finally saw the butler. "Kevin?" She sounded almost relieved.

Marcus took back the photo. "Did one of these people look familiar?"

"What is it, Kevin?"

"Excuse me," Marcus insisted. Using both hands now, he thrust the six-by-nine once again into her line of sight. "Mrs. Carvel, please. If you do know one of these people, it's important. It could help solve your husband's murder."

"Solve my husband's . . ." For a woman who always tried to avoid the worst of life, such a claim had to be unsettling. "Is that why you came here? Fabian was killed by a mugger."

"Maybe he wasn't," Amy said evenly. "Is one of these faces familiar?"

"Please." Marcus was begging. "It would help me so much."

Doris considered it for a second, then raised her eyes and shook her head. "No, I'm sorry. I thought . . ." She seemed embarrassed by all the fuss. "I was wrong. My eyesight isn't what it used to be. Kevin?"

The butler spoke into Marcus's roadblock. "There's a police detective here to see you."

CHAPTER 32

"To see me?" The words were spoken twice and nearly in unison. Doris said them directly to Kevin in a kind of wide-eyed wonder, while Marcus's version was almost whispered.

"Yes, ma'am," Kevin answered. "He says it'll just take a minute."

Doris looked to Amy, as if expecting her to know. "Is this about Fabian?"

"He didn't say." Kevin offered his arm, and she took it.

Doris apologized to her guests in a way that made it clear that their time together was over. They accepted it with grace, emphasizing again that it had been a social call, nothing more, and they were glad to see her looking so well.

"It was so good seeing you," Marcus said as all four of them began walking up the lawn. Casually, he slipped his right hand into his jacket pocket, then stopped in his tracks. "Oh." He was already looking down, scouring the dried and varicolored leaves at their feet. "My house keys."

"They're not in your jacket?" Amy said.

"They must have fallen out."

"Oh, dear," Doris sighed. One more thing to sigh over.

"Maybe when we were sitting on the bench." Marcus looked back toward a stone bench fifty yards or so behind them, on a spit jutting out into the sound.

A good hostess by instinct, Doris turned back toward the bench.

"No, you go ahead," Marcus insisted. "You have people waiting. Amy and I will find them."

Doris hesitated. "Well, if you're sure you don't mind."

"Not at all," said Marcus and kissed her lightly on the cheek.

"Congratulations again," said Doris then accepted Kevin's arm and headed back toward the solarium.

Amy waited until they had disappeared inside. "You didn't lose anything."

"Of course not." Marcus pulled a set of keys out of his jacket as proof, then stepped behind the trunk of a hundred-year oak. Amy followed. "I didn't think we wanted to risk running into Sergeant Rawlings."

"You want to avoid Rawlings? Why? We have every right to be here."

"Does Frank know what your car looks like?"

"I don't know. You're afraid of running into Frank Loyola?"

"I've had enough police for a while."

"But we're doing nothing illegal—for a change. Visiting the wife of your old employer?" Amy was feeling bolder than usual, egged on by Marcus's uncharacteristic timidity. "It may not even be Rawlings. Crazy Doris may have a few speeding tickets she needs to make good on."

But Marcus was already on his way around to the left, passing assuredly between the rows of clipped hedges. Amy was reminded that the Carvel estate had once been his home.

"Marcus, what's the matter?" She raced to keep up.

They scurried between the last two hedges, and as they turned the corner, a figure was suddenly there, his bulk blocking the gravel path. "Marcus. I wanted to catch you."

Marcus let out a yelp and skidded to a halt. A second later he exhaled. "Kev. You scared me."

"Did you find your keys?"

"Yeah, found them."

The butler walked to the far side of the far hedge, out of sight of the solarium, and motioned for them to follow. "You were asking about the old man's death." He spoke directly to Marcus. For the first time, Amy noticed a familiarity between them, which was only natural, of course.

"Yes," Marcus said. "I suppose I should have come to you instead of bothering Mrs. Carvel."

"You can't visit a house just to talk to the butler. Why are you asking about Mr. Carvel? Does this have something to do with Italy?"

Amy and Marcus exchanged quick glances. "I suppose it doesn't matter," Amy muttered. "Go ahead."

Marcus gave Kevin the short version, changing a few facts here and there for simplicity's sake and because Kevin really didn't need to know. It actually made more sense in Marcus's shorthand. *Is this his normal rationale?* Amy wondered. *Editing the truth for the sake of brevity and discretion? It's probably what everyone does to some degree.*

Kevin was a quick study. "Right, right." He repeated this in the momentary lulls and didn't seem at all shocked or overwhelmed, an attitude that probably came with the job. "When I interrupted you to fetch the old lady, you had some picture you were showing her?"

"Please." Marcus removed the photo from its paper sleeve. "Take a look. I'm almost sure she recognized someone."

The burly butler took the photo, examined the faces and kept examining them as he shook his head. "Sorry."

"No one familiar? You're sure?"

"I've been with the family nine years, almost six as butler. Maybe before I came?" He handed it back. "If the old lady recognized someone, why wouldn't she say?"

"Good question," Amy said. Kevin glanced her way, as if startled by her existence. "We were also asking about the cook. Mrs. Gray."

"You remember Mrs. Gray." Kevin was once again addressing Marcus. "What can I tell you?"

Marcus took a step closer. "I was shocked when Mr. Carvel tried to give her all that stock. Remember?"

"We all were." A mischievous grin almost connected the freckles on his cheeks. "Rumors were flying thick. People were saying they'd been lovers at some point. Carvel and the cook."

"Who said that?" Marcus asked.

"You know. Tammy, upstairs."

"I remember Tammy. Is she still here?"

"Sure. Tammy was convinced that little Nardo was their love child."

"That's his name," said Marcus. "I was trying to remember. Leonardo. He was gone by the time I got here."

Amy took a strategic step back, almost vanishing into the sharply cut branches of a box hedge. It irked her, this fading into the background. But if that was what it took to facilitate the flow of information . . .

"You never met Nardo?" Kevin leaned in, amused. "Piece of work. He lived with his mom, not doing much of anything. Tiny thing like her. Weird kid. Always had this chip on his shoulder. I guess he must've been in his early twenties when he moved out. Tammy still keeps in touch with him. I think."

"Why did Mr. Carvel let him stay? I mean, if he wasn't working here . . ."

"That's what Tammy kept saying. That's why she thought he had to be the old man's love child. But Nardo didn't look a whit like Carvel. Not a whit."

"Did he ever come back to visit?" Amy asked.

Kevin didn't acknowledge the source but kept speaking to Marcus, as if he'd asked the question, as if he had, just for fun, thrown his voice. "Yeah. Couple of times. You know kids. When they get into trouble or need money. He came back once or twice while you were here. . . ."

This last sentence trailed off unexpectedly. It struck Amy as one of those sentences you regret halfway through, the kind you want to retract in midair but have to finish off and hope no one noticed. Amy looked at Marcus. He had noticed, too.

"Nardo came back to visit? While I was here?"

"He might have." Amy had no idea why Kevin was hedging, but he was.

Marcus stepped an inch closer. "Kev? Did Nardo happen to be around on the night Mr. Carvel disappeared?"

"Could've been. Who remembers? There was so much going on."

"My God. He was here, wasn't he?"

Kevin shrugged his beefy shoulders. "I said I don't remember. What's the big deal if he was?"

"It's no deal. I'm just trying to remember if I met him."

"You didn't. I mean . . ." Kevin stepped back, exhaling, then breathing deep. "Marcus, come on. You know the rules. Unauthorized people can't stay on the property, even if they used to live here."

"But you just said he visited. . . . Okay, you're right. I'm sorry." Amy was surprised that Marcus didn't press the point, but he didn't. "It's been great seeing you. You're looking good."

"Thanks. So, when are you two moving in?"

"Moving in?" Marcus looked blank.

"Together."

"Not until the wedding," Amy said, emerging from the box hedge. "You know how real estate is in New York. No one likes to give up a good apartment."

A quartet of beeps emanated from somewhere in Kevin's suit jacket. He ignored it. At the second series of beeps, he reached into a pocket. "Look," he said. "It was no big deal. Nardo staying with his mom. But after Mr. Carvel disappeared, with that private detective nosing around . . . I didn't want people getting into trouble."

"Sure," Marcus said. "I suppose you should answer those beeps."

"Right. Well, Mr. Alvarez . . ." Kevin stood there awkwardly, then grabbed Marcus by the upper arms, pulled him into his chest, and gave him a bear hug. "You take care of yourself."

"You, too," Marcus said from the muffled depths of the butler's jacket. Was he hugging back? Amy couldn't tell.

They watched Kevin walk quickly back into the house.

"If you're that hung up on each other, I'll call off the engagement."

"You work with what you got," Marcus replied.

They continued their way around the left side of the redbrick mansion, Marcus again in the lead.

"So, Nardo was hanging around on the night in question," he said.

"That's the takeaway I took away. Of course it could mean nothing."

"Shhh." Marcus had stopped at a corner yew tree. He raised a finger to his lips. Around the corner, Amy spied the crescent driveway, empty except for the cars—a RAV4 with New York police plates and, parked next to it, her old Volvo.

"Good." Marcus turned to Amy. "Get your keys ready."

"Why are we sneaking around?"

Marcus didn't answer but counted to three, then made a dash for the Volvo's passenger side, doing it in a crouched run.

"Marcus, buddy. Hello!"

The voice had come from the top of the marble steps, where Frank Loyola was pushing himself up to his feet with a grunt. He'd been patiently sitting there, hidden from view by a white marble column. "You've been giving us quite the runaround, buddy."

"Frank!" Marcus straightened up and tried to look happy, or at least not furtive. "What are you doing here?"

"Waiting for you." He was walking down the steps. "Actually, the sarge and me came to see Mrs. Carvel. But when I saw Amy's car, I thought it might pay to wait outside."

Marcus's smile hardened. "Does he ever let you sit in on the interviews? Or are you just the chauffeur?"

Frank returned the hardened smile. "You know we've been looking for you."

"I know no such thing."

"I should've figured you'd be hiding out at her place."

"I had no idea you were looking. . . ."

"Is that why you and Amy went running out through her backyard today? Don't think we didn't find out."

Amy remained uncharacteristically quiet through all this, and it grew increasingly hard for Marcus to avoid looking her way. "You wanted to see me? Here I am."

"Here you are. The sarge would like you to come down to the station to answer some questions."

"Do you have a warrant?"

"You're not under arrest. We don't need a warrant."

Marcus swallowed. Amy stayed silent. "You can't bring me in without a warrant. If I don't come voluntarily, you can't—"

"What's the matter? We thought you wanted to help solve Mr. Ingo's murder."

"Of course I do."

The ball went back and forth several more times. Marcus had the right to an attorney during questioning, although Frank made it clear that people were questioned all the time—witnesses, relatives—and only serious suspects were the ones who needed a lawyer. Was there any reason why he might need a lawyer? Although it was certainly his right to call one.

"I don't have a lawyer, not in New York." And for the first time he looked to Amy. "I don't suppose I really need one."

Amy didn't respond.

"Good." Frank pointed toward the door. "We can go inside and wait, or we can wait here. Rawlings shouldn't be too long. Whatever you prefer."

"I assume you don't need me anymore," Amy said flatly.

"Amy?" Marcus had packed a dozen questions into that word, and Amy ignored them all.

Frank curled the corner of his mouth. "You can go, Ms. Abel. We'll take care of Mr. Alvarez's transportation."

Amy kept her eyes lowered as she got into the Volvo. She removed the prop from her finger, Fanny's big, old-fashioned engagement ring, and tossed it into a cup holder. Then she slipped on her seat belt, started the engine, and drove slowly down the gravel drive. She did not look in the rearview mirror.

CHAPTER 33

The double bottom drawer of Amy's desk was, for all intents and purposes, a black hole, sucking in anything and everything, including two half-broken eyeglass frames that she couldn't bring herself to throw out. An informal storage system, it filled the gap between the formality of her files and the wastebasket.

At the moment, she was sitting cross-legged on the floor in front of the desk, the drawer pulled fully open, as she rummaged through a tangle of forgotten power cords, dull pencils, pages clipped from magazines. . . . Here was a *Travel + Leisure* piece, for example, four stapled pages, on the burgeoning popularity of road rallies. Amy ripped it into quarters and tossed it out. For as long as she could remember, either frustration or anger would prompt her to rummage through—about the only time she ever did so, except when she needed something. This situation fulfilled all three criteria: she was frustrated, angry, and needed something.

Near the bottom of the drawer she found a suitable manila envelope. It was just large enough and, unlike many of its mates, showed no signs of previous use. Amy crammed the red leather volume inside, then dove into the drawer again, hunting for an address that she was sure she'd seen back at the beginning of her search.

When she was finished, she reached for the phone and dialed. "Peter? Hi."

"Amy." There was lilt in the man's voice. A good sign. "How are you? How was the tour?"

"It went great," Amy said, both telling the truth and lying. "And you? How's business? I'm not interrupting anything?"

Like Amy, Peter Borg ran a travel business. Unlike Amy, he camped out in a mahogany-paneled storefront on the Upper East Side, drove a Porsche Boxster, and booked so many clients into the resorts of French Polynesia that authorities in the South Pacific joked about naming a small, uninhabited island after him.

They had met five months ago, on a fam tour of a new resort in Belize. On returning to New York, they'd gone out a handful of times—nothing very serious or passionate. He was too polished and East Side for her. And she supposed she was too Village for him. But they were friends. And Peter had the advantage of being just about the only man she knew who was not in Fanny's good graces, a considerable advantage, given her current mood.

Five minutes later, when Amy was at her liquor cabinet, pulling out the Campari bottle, Fanny's slow footsteps became audible on the stairs. She must have closed up early.

"I was going to stop by," Amy called out. "But we were making such progress on the case." She avoided facing her, even in the mirror above the bar. "Anyway, by the time we started back, the traffic on the expressway . . . I swear. They're never going to fix that road."

Fanny was putting her umbrella in Amy's umbrella stand. "Marcus called me at the office."

"Oh." She turned to face her mother. "Is it raining?"

"He thinks you may be mad at him."

"Doesn't miss a trick."

"So, what's the big deal?" Fanny made herself at home, settling into the sofa. "He came over last night because he was in trouble. Would you prefer him going to someone else?"

"I would prefer him telling me the truth."

"Well, hello, Miss Perfect."

"Is it raining hard? I've got a date."

"A date?" Fanny brushed this aside. "You know, if you weren't so judgmental, he might let himself be more honest." Fanny examined her daughter's face, like a mariner reading a map. "I hope you're not going to do anything foolish."

"No. For once, I'm not. I'm going to give up all this nonsense before I really get into trouble and wind up in jail as some sort of accessory after the fact."

"Accessory? Marcus didn't kill anyone."

"How do you know?" Amy demanded. "Why can't the police be right? Why can't it be the person who poured the poisoned wine?"

She waited for an answer. For once, Fanny was speechless. *Good.* "Marcus is an opportunist," Amy continued. "He's never had much of a profession—personal secretary, Otto's assistant, Georgina's companion. Well, that was made up, but you know what I mean. So he finds out about Georgina killing Fabian Carvel. He goes to the widow. And the widow pays him to kill Georgina."

"You mean the twenty thousand? That was an inheritance."

"The police haven't confirmed that."

"What about the sabotage on the tour?"

"Georgina did it. She took the tour because . . . well, she wanted to make sure the game didn't give away her perfect murder."

"And she arranged the break-ins on Elba?"

"She's rich. She paid someone."

Fanny took a few seconds to think it through, then shook her head. "No. Out of the question. It's not Marcus."

"Why not?"

"We don't know killers."

"Fine," said Amy. "I'm going back to my life, if I can remember where I left it."

"Oh, dear. You have a date with Peter Borg."

"Sheesh. I wonder what it's like to have a private thought."

"Well, you are predictable. You know, I'm starting to like Peter. He's got a lot going for him."

"Nice try." Amy gave up the idea of a drink and looked around the room for her wrap. It was under the manila envelope. Before she could reach it, Fanny had seen the name.

"What are you sending to Sergeant Rawlings?"

"Otto's script. He knows I have it."

"How does he know?"

"He just does. And since I'm not going to be needing it anymore . . ."

Fanny clucked her tongue. "So that's it? You're abandoning Marcus?"

"Absolutely." She looked at the stuffed envelope. "What do you think? Overnight delivery?"

"I can mail it. I have to get to the post office tomorrow morning."

"Yeah, right. You'll give it to Marcus."

"I won't give it to Marcus. Promise."

Amy threw up her hands. "Do whatever you want."

Fanny snatched up the envelope. "When he called, they were still questioning him. He needs you."

"Sure. Where else can he find a hideout? I even provided entertainment."

"Feeling cheap and used?" Her mother chuckled. "Sweetie, it comes with the territory."

"Really? Really? When did you ever feel cheap and used?"

"I've walked by my share of construction sites."

"Nice image, Mom. Thanks."

It was nearly an hour before her date and she had no place to go, but Amy grabbed her pashmina wrap and headed for the stairs. At the front door she automatically checked her bag. Keys. Wallet. And something else. By the glow of the vestibule's overhead light, she pulled out the photo, now folded and crumpled, and opened it like a greeting card.

There they were, six smiling faces in front of the finish line, one victim and her five suspects. Which one of these did Doris Carvel recognize? And why would she refuse to tell? "And why am I bothering?" she murmured aloud.

Amy stuffed the picture back in her bag, ignoring the wastebasket that was stationed right inside the door.

The date went better than expected. Peter had been glad to see her. He had asked all the right questions about the rally and had taken the answers at face value, showing just enough admiration and envy at Amy's achievement. Dinner was good. The conversation never lagged. And not once did Peter allude to the night's last-minute invitation and whatever might lie behind it. Amy returned home alone, and this seemed fine with Peter, but not so fine that she felt insulted. All in all, a decent evening.

In the morning Amy wandered into the sunroom office and realized she hadn't checked her phone since last night. There was a text from Burt Baker. She read the text, then pressed the CALL button.

"Amy. Thanks for getting back to me." There was a coolness in the judge's voice. "I got a lawyer to Marcus at about eight thirty last night. He was released around nine." A mutual pause. "Just thought you might like to know."

"I'm no longer involved in the investigation."

"I know. Fanny told me."

"Fanny?" At first she was mystified, then recalled that the judge had been Fanny's client, a friend of a mutual friend. "I suppose you know all about yesterday," she said.

"About the police picking him up?"

"No. About . . . Never mind."

"Look, Amy. I don't know what's going on with you two. I know you had a falling-out. But this isn't just about Marcus. A woman . . ." The words caught in his throat. "A woman we were all very fond of is dead. Could we meet someplace for lunch?"

Amy watched Lou walk away with the menus and wondered what the socialist would think if he knew that Amy's current tablemate was a federal court judge.

"Amy." Burt shifted uneasily in his half of the wooden booth, arranging one stiff leg out on the sawdust-covered floor. "There are lots of reasons not to quit. Now, I'm not trying to discount the skills of the Rome and New York and San Diego police departments . . ."

"But they're not mystery buffs like us."

Burt regarded his friend cautiously, then took a long drink from his water glass. "The police didn't witness the murder. You and I did."

"And what good is that? The only person who could have administered the poison is the very person who's been lying to me since day one."

"Let me tell you." Burt leaned across the table. "In my line, I hear a lot of defenses. Attention deficit disorder. Postpartum depression. Years ago we had a slew of PMS. But my favorite has to be the 'too bright' defense. 'Members of the jury, my client is not stupid. Why would he commit such a stupid crime?' "

"Criminals get caught precisely because they do stupid things."

"Exactly. Except in this case. I'm sorry, Amy. I just can't visualize Marcus killing someone so blatantly."

"Can you visualize Martha doing it? Can she visualize you?"

"Well . . ." Burt drained the last of his water. "I think we can."

"Oh." Finally she understood. "Oh." This wasn't just about Marcus and Georgina. She peered over the top of her glasses and into his eyes. "You think that Martha . . ."

The judge shrugged. "How well do I really know her? I'm no fool. I know there was a rivalry going on between them." He looked embarrassed. "You know . . ."

Amy almost burst out laughing. "Martha killed Georgina in order to get her out of the way? Well, someone thinks pretty highly of himself."

Burt had to smile. "I've been told I'm a pretty hot catch."

"Judge, come on. Martha wouldn't kill anyone."

"Martha wouldn't. You wouldn't. I wouldn't. But someone did. We're all living under a cloud. Railroading Marcus is not going to solve anything."

"Okay, I get it."

Lou had returned with their lunch. He arranged the plates on the narrow table, sandwich on the right, pickle on the left, and fixed a suspicious eye on the federal jurist.

"Was it something I said?" Burt hissed after they were left alone.

"Lou has this sixth sense about law enforcement." Amy reached across for her water glass and was surprised to find it empty.

"I can see why," Burt said, glancing around the Cindilu Dairy. "Cats in the windows. Sawdust on the floor. A dozen health code violations before you even get behind the counter."

Amy's eyes remained focused on the water glass, her mind suddenly whirling, her memory burrowing back to that warm, fateful evening in Rome. "Oh, my God."

"Oh, your God what?"

She was on the verge of blurting it out but stopped herself. "Nothing."

"It's not nothing. You just thought of something. What?"

"Nothing." She had more than once wondered about this moment. Would she ever have a breakthrough, as in an old-fashioned mystery novel? And if she did, would she be able to keep it from her friends, the actual suspects in the case? She looked at Burt. "Sorry. I thought I saw a bug in the water."

"I was drinking from this." Burt picked up the empty glass. "There's no bug." He lowered his voice. "Although this place is a death trap, I gotta tell you."

Amy smiled weakly, only half aware of what either of them was saying. Her eyes were glued, unblinking, to the glass. All she could think of was the seating arrangement. Who'd been sitting next to Georgina? Who'd been sitting across from her?

In two minutes she had it figured out.

CHAPTER 34

The buzzer zapped in a short, furious burst as Amy threw open the office door and strode in.

Fanny was at her desk, leaning forward on her elbows and chatting up a familiar-looking young couple. Out of the corner of her eye, she saw Amy and waved her over. "You'll just love the highland gorillas," she continued without missing a beat. "We were lucky to get you reservations. That camp is sold out months in advance. Amy can tell you. She's been there. Amy, come here." Amy stood her ground, motioning for Fanny to join her instead. "Excuse me, Matt. Wanda. I have to go humor the boss."

"Your honeymooners?" Amy whispered. "You're sending them to Rwanda?"

"First-class safari. Her family's footing the bill."

"You can't send them to Rwanda. Guerrillas."

"Yes, dear. They like gorillas."

Amy lowered her voice even further. "No, no, the human kind. Rebel forces. They're shooting people at the airport."

"No wonder reservations were easy."

"Mom, that package I gave you to mail this morning . . ."

"You wanted me to mail it? I mailed it. You want to see the postal receipt?"

"Damn!" Amy slapped her desktop. "Oh, it's not your fault. It's mine."

"What's the matter now? You didn't want me to mail it?"

"I did, but I don't now."

"Don't tell me you changed your mind?"

"Yeah." Amy was embarrassed. "I want to check out a few things."

"Oh, my," Fanny gasped. "You figured something out. I knew you would."

"Thanks. But I need to see Otto's research for the game."

"It's in the first-floor window seat at home, under a blanket. It might smell a bit. I put in new cedar blocks."

"What might smell? The master script?" Amy was confused. "You mean you didn't mail it?"

"I figured you might change your mind."

"You figured? You promised to mail it."

"Don't tell me you're upset?"

"No." She was shaking her head, half laughing with relief. "But you just swore. You had a receipt."

"Distrusting your mother enough to look at the receipt? Even you wouldn't do that."

"Bless your devious heart." Amy kissed her on the cheek, then headed for the door. "Thank you."

Fanny watched her leave, then crossed back to her clients, strutting all the way. "Bosses. Every now and then they appreciate you."

It was just a few blocks from the office to the brownstone, and Amy's pace slowed as she approached. She finally knew who had poisoned Georgina, at least who'd had an opportunity, the only person other than Marcus.

The envelope was just where Fanny had said, in the old cedar chest that doubled as a window seat. Amy tore open the envelope and pulled out the red script. It did smell a bit of cedar. She tucked it under her arm, then trudged up to the fourth-floor sunroom.

It shouldn't be impossible to connect the dots. Amy had a name now; she had a face and a personality and a past to delve into. She had a killer who had been ingenious and bold enough to poison a drink right under their noses. She just didn't have a motive.

Amy turned on her desk lamp and sat down with the script. She flipped to the back, to the section where Otto had compiled his notes from the San Diego investigation.

Okay, where do I start? What do I look for? The first thing that caught her eye was the credit card receipts. During Carvel's cross-country escapade from Long Island to San Diego, he periodically charged things. Or someone did. The police had determined that the signatures were forged. She inspected the signatures, then opened up her own files and tried to compare these to one of the signatures on a tour contract. There seemed to be no similarity, but maybe an expert could make a connection.

Next, she sought out the autopsy. After that, the crime scene report. Then the notes from the San Diego district attorney. When she finally looked up, it was already eight and darkness had settled over the communal garden. The sight magically triggered her appetite, and she reached for the phone.

"Leesa? Amy Abel. How are the boys? Good. You know, I saw Billy on the street the other day with his pals.

He was smoking." Amy nodded sadly into the cell phone. "Yeah, I know. What're you gonna do? Oh, just the usual. Nothing for Fanny." She hung up, safe in the knowledge that an order of steamed dumplings, sesame chicken, white rice, and a ripe orange would arrive at her door within fifteen minutes.

The next phone call was a bit more difficult. "Hi."

An eavesdropper on Amy's half of the conversation would have overheard little—long pauses interrupted by the usual "I'm still here" noises of a listener. "Uh-huh. Yeah. I know. I understand." And finally that most judgmental of phrases, "Look, I'm not blaming you."

"No, I don't think you're a killer." She listened for another minute, growing impatient with the excuses and explanations. "No, no, of course not." Another interruption. "They can't arrest you." She supposed it was just nerves that were making him go on and on like this. But still . . . "Because I know who the killer is." *Oops.* She shouldn't have said that.

"No, I won't tell you. It's really just a guess, but a good one. Give me a few hours to think about it." The intercom buzzed, and she knew it had to be Billy with her food. "I'm not telling anyone." She crossed to the intercom and, without a word, pressed the door release. "I don't know." She repeated this phrase twice more in response to different questions. "Look, Marcus, I gotta go. Someone's at the door." And she hung up.

Amy crossed to the stairs and waited at the top of the landing, listening to the slow patter of climbing feet. "Billy?"

Two flights below, a shadow moved in the stairwell. The shadow and the echoing footfalls and the solitude of the moment brought to mind the most clichéd of mystery conventions.

It was a scene distilled from a hundred worn-out plots. Early in the last reel or somewhere late in the novel, a witness—usually a woman—tells a friend that she knows the killer's identity but for some reason refuses to tell anyone. No, that would be too easy. In nine out of ten versions, this woman quickly becomes the final victim.

"Miss Abel?" asked a breathless voice.

Amy didn't reply but retreated a foot back toward the safety of her living room.

"You shouldn't have told."

A familiar voice, but Amy couldn't place it.

"You tell my mother I'm smoking?"

"Yes. Yes, I did," Amy yelled out through the open doorway.

A petulant Billy appeared from around the final mid-flight landing. "Why you do that?"

"Why?" She was almost giddy from relief. "Because smoking is dumb, that's why. Very dumb. You could die."

The stubby Chinese teenager climbed out of the shadows, waving one hand dismissively as the other held out a plastic shopping bag. "Agh, you can die from anything."

Right. She couldn't argue with that.

It was all together on one plate, more thrown together than mixed. One dumpling, soy sauce, a single piece of chicken, and a clump of white rice with square corners. Amy sat meditatively on a stool by the kitchen counter, clutching her coffee cup and watching through the lit window as the plate spun on the microwave turntable. Breakfast.

"Morning, Amy."

She didn't flinch, didn't even look up from her entertainment. She was too groggy to be surprised, not that Marcus could really surprise her anymore. "Morning."

"I rang Fanny's bell."

"Of course. Did you two have a nice chat?"

Marcus stood in the doorway, looking uncharacteristically sheepish. "Smells good." He wore blue jeans and a long-sleeved white T-shirt, the sleeves pushed up to expose his forearms. It was the simplest of outfits and made him look irresistible. Amy felt manipulated.

"How was your day with Frank and company? I'm sure you held your own."

"I survived. Want the gory details?"

"Sure."

Marcus ignored her frosty reception. Sergeant Rawlings, he explained, had eventually obtained a court order, allowing them to take fingerprints and handwriting samples. But most of his time at the station had been wasted, going over and over his alibi on the day of Otto's murder, a day that Marcus, along with millions of others, had spent relatively alone in the midst of the bustling city. "They seemed frustrated by the lack of evidence. I felt almost sorry for them."

"Me too."

"Amy." His composure was starting to crack. "I'm sorry. I should have told you. But I didn't want to hurt your feelings, and now I've done even worse. I was so afraid of being arrested."

"Any port in a storm."

"You know better."

"Oh, that's right. I know because you've always been so honest."

"Okay. You want to be mad at me. That's what this boils down to. You're glad for the excuse, so you won't have to deal with whatever might be happening between us."

"Whoa. You and Mom *did* have a chat."

"What was so wrong with me coming to you when I was in need? What? Would you prefer I went to someone else?"

Amy shook her head. "I don't want to discuss this." At the beep, she popped the door and used a pot holder to retrieve the plate. Steam fogged up her glasses, but she didn't take them off, just let them steam. "You're blocking the silverware drawer."

Marcus moved. "They sent men to search my place. And they spent a lot of time asking about the gun."

"I'd offer you some, but I don't feel like it." Amy stood at the counter and sliced her chicken. "Gun?"

"The gun used on Otto. It's probably the only piece of evidence that could connect me to his murder."

"Good point. The killer probably kept it. Just in case."

"There's a cheery thought." He waited patiently as Amy finished the chicken and started on the dumpling. "What you said last night, is that true? You know how she was poisoned?"

Amy chewed and nodded. "I'm going to see Rawlings this morning. It might be enough for him to get a search warrant. Maybe they'll find the gun."

"You think he'll listen?"

Amy looked doubtful. "I just wish I knew the motive."

"So you don't think it was about milk allergies and the vengeful cook?"

"I know that's your favorite theory."

"And not just because it's kind of wacky. It makes sense."

"I can't tell Rawlings about the milk. As it is, he'll probably laugh at me."

"Then why tell him? Tell me. We can smoke out this guy, you and me."

Amy chewed as she spoke. "You know what the definition of *farce* is? A farce is when someone says, 'Let's tell the police.' But no one does."

"Is that a quotation?"

"I think so. My point is, I'm not going to run around trying to trap a killer."

Marcus thought it over. "That's not the best definition of *farce*. There are plenty of farces where people call the police."

"You're missing the point."

"And a lot of farces are about sex, which wouldn't even entail calling the police."

"Please," Amy begged. "I'm still waking up."

"How can you eat that in the morning?"

No response.

"So, if you tell Rawlings, why won't you tell me?"

"Because. Because I promised myself I wouldn't."

"I see." He paused, as if to think it over. "Eat your breakfast."

Marcus backed up several steps, giving Amy the space she needed. As his eyes fell on the refrigerator door, he saw the photograph, the folded, wrinkled enlargement he had shown Doris Carvel. It was at eye level, held in place by palm tree magnets, preserved like a kid's first piece of art.

Six faces stared back from among the wrinkles. A discolored vertical fold obscured one of Burt's crutches, while a horizontal one made Jolynn a little fatter and Martha not quite so imposingly tall. A sudden flutter of light through the kitchen window played over the glossy surface, and it was this optical effect that gave enough shadow to one of the faces to send a chill of recognition through Marcus's frame.

He caught his breath and brushed his hair aside, hoping to hide the involuntary shudder. His mind was so completely occupied that he didn't even register the growing silence between them.

"What's the matter?"

"What?"

Amy had deposited her plate in the sink and was aiming hot water over the flecks of greasy rice. "I'm sorry if this is awkward," she said, still gazing into the sink.

"No, that's all right."

"There's no reason for me not to tell you, except pride."

"Good a reason as any." The words came out sounding more sarcastic than he'd intended.

"If you want me to tell you . . ."

"No. I don't need to know." He sounded sincere, if a little distracted. "I don't want to make you late for your meeting." Marcus was already heading for the stairs.

"Look, I'm sorry. Marcus, wait up."

But he didn't. A minute later and two flights down, he walked into another kitchen, this one filled with the smell of coffee and freshly unwrapped lox. "Can I borrow a car?"

"A car?" Fanny had already crossed to the cupboard and was reaching for another cup. "We only have one, dear. Well, Amy has one. Coffee?"

"No, thanks. She won't be using the Volvo today. She told me as much."

"Then go ask her for it," said Fanny. Then she saw Marcus's expression and understood. "Oh. Are we up to something Amy would disapprove of?"

"Absolutely."

"Wait a minute." She put the cup away and crossed to the stairwell. "Amy! I'm taking the car. Aunt Emily is leaving Uncle Joe again, and she needs to move a few things to Aunt Frieda's."

"Fine." Amy's voice echoed down the stairs. "Wish I could help, but I'm busy."

"Thanks, anyway." Fanny strolled back into the kitchen and unhooked a key from a row of nails above the stove. "So, when do we head out?"

"*We?* No, I'm sorry. This is more of a solo gig."

"Oh, I see." Fanny fingered the key. "No, I don't see. Why not? Are you meeting someone? I'm short, you know. I can squeeze under the dash, and they'll never see me."

Marcus gently pried the key ring from her fingers. "I would love having you along. But I need to have someone on the outside. In case things go wrong." Fanny stood there frowning, unconvinced. "Of course, you'll have to know exactly what I'm up to," he continued. "Do you mind if I tell you?"

Fanny brightened. "Try getting out of here without telling me. Just try."

CHAPTER 35

"You ever think about how much of life is mainte-nance? You know, cleaning stuff that just gets dirty. Cooking food that fills you up and just comes out the other end? I mean, I love cooking. Don't get me wrong. Raking leaves, there's an example. You can never rake them all. Even if you do, they're just gonna fall next year. Well, different leaves, but you know. All this work to stay one step ahead of decay."

"Maintenance is important," Marcus said, hoping to sound sympathetic. "Probably more important than building from scratch—maintaining what you have."

Vinny Mrozek stopped raking. He used a work glove to push back his hair. "I'm just a little down. No reason."

Marcus had taken a chance on catching the Mrozeks at home. When no one answered the bell, he performed the cautionary ritual of checking the yard. For once it paid off. Vinny had been by the back fence of his half acre, raking little piles of dead leaves into big piles. He seemed happy to see Marcus and didn't question his unexpected arrival.

"So, how's it going?"

"Fine." The day was overcast; the air moist and still. "Do you need some help? Plastic bags?"

Vinny set aside the rake. "Nah. It's illegal to burn, but . . ." He had already grabbed an armful of leaves and twigs and pinecones and was dropping them into the blackened mouth of a large steel drum. "What's autumn without the smell of burning leaves? The boys used to love this—before they figured out it was a chore."

"The boys are in school?"

He nodded. "And Jolynn's over at a neighbor's. I'll give her a call."

"Don't bother," Marcus said. This already felt like a bad idea. He had somehow expected to find the whole family here and to treat it as a social call. Now it didn't feel very social.

Vinny went back for another armful. "I hear Amy has abandoned the cause. Not that much is happening."

"Amy and I are just taking a break."

"I see." Vinny stood there, a silhouette between Marcus and the morning sun, cradling a bushel or more of leaves. "So what's up? She not really your type?"

Marcus nodded. "I don't think it's working out."

Vinny just stood there with his leaves. "Relationships are hard. Of course, a good-looking guy like yourself . . . You can have your pick."

"It's hard not having someone to talk to."

"You can talk to me," Vinny said. "Strictly confidential."

And without really thinking, he said it. "Look, Vinny, I think I've come up with an angle the police haven't considered."

"A new angle? Good for you." Vinny walked past him, then pushed the last of the leaves down into the steel drum and felt his pockets for a matchbook. "You know, Jolynn and I want to help."

"I do have a food question."

"Food question? You should have just called."

"I was impressed the other day by your memory for recipes."

Vinny chuckled modestly as he struck a match, used it to light the others, then tossed the matchbook and its sputtering flame into the drum. "It's a simple skill." The leaves crackled and blazed, giving off an almost immediate rush of heat. Vinny turned his back on the fire and made his way toward the kitchen door. "We'll keep an eye on it from the window."

Marcus followed. "Was there milk in the scallop dish? In Monte Carlo?"

"No. There was a touch of milk in the fish stock. But the coquilles Saint-Jacques had cream. Cream and butter. What's the deal with milk? Is this your new angle?"

"Believe it or not. Fabian Carvel had severe milk allergies. But he was served cream and butter in the scallops. I think that's what Georgina remembered."

Vinny mulled this over as they entered the house. He crossed to the open window above the sink and glanced out between the yellow flowered curtains at the flaring drum. "That's weird," he said and lowered the window with a single, firm shove. "In his own home? Maybe his cook didn't know."

"She'd been with him for decades."

"So she used dairy substitutes."

"She probably intended to. But her son was visiting. And I'm pretty sure he slipped in the real thing. That's why Fabian left the table—I think."

Vinny tugged at the left corner of his mustache, pulling his lip into a half frown. "A practical joke?"

"Or something more malicious. We won't know until we track down this son."

"You think you'll be able to find him?" Outside, the sun peeped through a thin spot in the cloud cover. Vinny squinted, then threw out a hand and pulled shut the field of yellow flowers.

Marcus felt suddenly cut off. "Maybe."

"Sounds like a long shot. You have any idea where this guy is?"

"I have an idea," said Marcus and instantly regretted it.

"Have you told anyone?"

Marcus found himself stepping to one side, placing the kitchen island between himself and Vinny. Could he have miscalculated the danger? He tried not to look as nervous as he felt. "We . . . uh, I, not we. Amy's no longer on the case. I really haven't discussed this with her." He fought his growing unease.

Vinny was edging toward him now. "So, this son of the cook? What did you say his name was?"

"He's not using his real name. I traced him to a hospital about four years ago." Marcus hadn't done any such thing, but it sounded good and it was logical, given what he'd seen in the Rome photograph. "But I lost him."

"Four years is a long time." Vinny was shuffling slowly around the marble-topped island. Marcus backed away. He tried to gauge the chef's size and heft and skill. "But this isn't what you came to see me about."

"I came to see you about the cream. I wanted an expert opinion."

"And that's all you wanted?" There was a strange expression on his face.

"Well, since I don't have Amy to talk this over with . . ."

"That's what I thought." Vinny was around the second edge surprisingly quick. His sizable right hand fell on Marcus's shoulder, swallowing it in a loose grip.

"Vinny!"

"That's not why you came." With his left hand he grabbed Marcus's arm.

Marcus tried to brush him off, but the grip had hardened. The man's intensity had been unexpected and Marcus felt paralyzed. Could he bluff his way out? Would he need a weapon? His eyes darted around the room. Where was the nearest door? The nearest knife?

And then his eyes settled on Vinny Mrozek's face and his narrowing gaze. It was a soft, embarrassed, vulnerable gaze. "Oh, Vinny!" He had to stop himself from laughing with relief. "That's not why I came."

"I'm up for it if you are." His tone was soft and pleading. "What do you say?"

"What the hell is this?" He tried to say it lightly. The grip had relaxed, and Marcus shrugged himself loose.

"I don't exactly know," said Vinny. "I've never done it with a guy."

"Me neither," said Marcus. "Believe me."

"I thought you were bi."

"I'm not gay, and I'm not bi."

"I have nothing against it," said Vinny. "It's just sex. Just human affection. I thought, you know, after our talk the other day . . . And then you come all the way out here, telling me about your breakup. . . . What was I supposed to think?"

"What about Jolynn?"

"You don't know what she's like." Vinny turned away. "Always so angry and cold. When we do have sex, it's always in the dark. And it's always the same way. I figured gay guys have more fun."

"Vinny, please. Even if I was gay and you didn't have a wife . . . Believe me, I'm not in the mood."

"You said you'd call by noon," Fanny scolded. "I was worried sick."

Marcus checked the dashboard. "What are you talking about? It's eleven fifty-two."

"I know. But if noon is the outside limit, then eleven thirty is normal. So, when eleven forty rolled around . . . what was I to think?"

"Right." Marcus was doing three things at once, driving, talking, and glancing down at the wrinkled set of directions Vinny had e-mailed Amy a few days ago. Four things, if you counted the translation of the directions from Manhattan–New Jersey to New Jersey–Manhattan. *Take Hawthorne Street, then a right to Alice Avenue. No, Alice to Hawthorne. Then a left . . .*

He put the phone down for a few seconds and pulled onto the shoulder of a suburban driveway.

"Hello?" Fanny's voice sounded anxious. "Are you all right?"

"Just a bit distracted. Sorry."

"Are you being held prisoner? Marcus, if you're being forced to make this call, work the word *cow* into a sentence."

"What?" He laughed and almost said the word accidentally. "I am not being held prisoner. Everything is fine, if you don't count Vinny's amorous advances."

"Really? Advances? Vinny is gay?"

"No. I think just starved for affection."

"Are you gay? If you don't want to say it, just say *cow*."

"I am not being held prisoner, and I'm not gay."

Fanny grunted. "Well, you can't blame me. This is a very suspicious conversation."

"I probably shouldn't have gone over, but the curiosity was too much."

"Are you calling the police?"

"Not before I see Jolynn. I mean, if I'm wrong? How embarrassing is that!"

"Pretty embarrassing," Fanny had to admit.

They spent another few minutes talking about the Mrozeks and their marriage, then about Amy. "Buy her something," Fanny suggested. "That's always a good first step."

Marcus hung up and deposited the phone in a cup holder. Then he pulled off the shoulder and tried once more to follow directions. Alice Avenue was curving gently into unfamiliar loops, if this was still Alice Avenue, which he doubted, since he hadn't seen a sign. This had never been one of his strengths. Amy had called it a revealing trait, the inability to follow other people's directions.

"How'd I get on Elm?" he asked himself, squinting at a lone street sign. His eyes scoured the thinning pattern of houses, looking for someone to point him toward Palisades Parkway. Why was no one ever on the streets here in suburbia? The sidewalk had just ended, too, which was not a good omen. He slowed even more and was barely aware that the car fifty yards behind him had also slowed. His mind wandered back to Amy and this morning and the picture on the refrigerator. *No wonder Doris Carvel didn't say anything,* Marcus thought. *I would have reacted the same way.*

The road took one more curve, then straightened out. Again, Marcus thought about the photo. It struck

him as ironic. He and Amy had each discovered different pieces of the puzzle, Amy from the dinner, he from
the photograph. Amy knew who'd poisoned the wine,
and he knew why. For a moment he regretted not having combined forces this morning. "Well, she wasn't in
the mood to listen."

Only four houses in sight, none of them showing
any sign of life. Maybe he should flag down the Grand
Cherokee behind him. He was just pulling up to a corner, was just beginning to roll down his window, when
half a block ahead a green metal rectangle popped up
from behind a golden-leafed tree. "Thank God." Marcus drove past the sign and made the suggested right
turn.

Once on the Palisades, he relaxed and allowed himself to think about the appliance outlet in Fort Lee.
They were bound to have a good selection of espresso ma-
chines, something fancy, on sale, and foolproof. Would
she be pleased about getting a present from him? Or
would she take it the wrong way, whichever way that
might be?

The same Jeep was still behind him, on his bumper,
causing him to flip on a turn signal and ease the Volvo
out of the passing lane. *We're the only two on the road,* he
thought, faintly annoyed. *Why can't he pass on the right?*

The forest-green vehicle pulled up beside him but
didn't pass, staying close enough and steady enough so
that Marcus could see his own reflection in the tinted
side window. Someone he knew had a green Grand
Cherokee. Who was it? Of course, half the Jeeps in the
world seemed to come in that shade.

The vehicles had just rounded a bend, still in tan-
dem, when the Jeep swerved over the dotted line. Marcus compensated, honking his horn. "Would you prefer

to hit that damned pothole or hit me?" They were on a straightaway now, and the northbound lanes, usually hidden by the rolling, tree-encrusted median, slipped momentarily into view. The Jeep edged back into its own lane. "That's better."

Barely had his eyes returned to the road when it happened again. The northbound lanes had just vanished behind a hillock when the Jeep swerved across the line. It was harder, more deliberate this time, forcing the Volvo off onto the thin shoulder.

In a gut-wrenching flash, he realized who owned the preppy-green Jeep. A surge of adrenaline pumped through his bloodstream, superseding all rational thought. Survival was the sole instinct. No anger, no panic, not even fear. To plan anything, to plan even a second ahead, seemed a luxurious impossibility.

Marcus slowed down, but the Jeep slowed, too. It was now halfway into his lane and edging closer. With a jolt, both his right tires lunged onto the high, grassy verge.

Instantly his car was at a twenty-degree angle, its roof tilting into the Jeep, almost close enough to scrape paint. He was leaning into his side window now but did his best to maintain control of the steering wheel, his knuckles so tight and white, they ached. But control came and went and came again in spurts too quick to pinpoint. The left tires began to skid on the gravel shoulder, while the rights bounced maniacally over rocks and holes and leafy brush. A row of four hefty sugar maples loomed directly ahead.

Marcus squeezed shut his eyes, and his hands moved reflexively, doing what his mind was too slow to tell them to do. The jerk of the wheel away from the trees made the Jeep also swerve and gave Marcus just enough leeway to avoid a direct hit. He heard both rearview mirrors snap off in shrieks, one metal against tree, the other metal against metal. His eyes flew back open. The maples' exposed roots shivered under his wheels.

When he realized he was still miraculously alive, actual thoughts began to return. *Slam on the brakes,* he told himself. But his instincts said no. *Control and survival.* To brake was to invite a host of uncontrolled possibilities. Swerving. Skidding. And even if he came safely to a stop, what then? A hit-and-run? A gunshot as he tried to escape into the woods on foot? *How?* he asked himself. *How had this happened so quickly?*

Another car was coming up from the rear. Marcus allowed himself a moment of hope. He turned his head in time to see something white speed by in the passing lane, honking its horn in a wail of irritation. It was gone in seconds. Tomorrow, when the irritated driver read about the accident in the news, would he even recall what he'd seen?

The shoulder widened. When the verge flattened, Marcus could finally lift his gaze from the immediate foreground. He had driven through one emergency turnout already, slamming down into the black roadway, only to be slammed back up, the wheel thrashing wildly in his hands. Ahead he could see a gap in the trees. Another turnout. And right in front of it . . . *No!* A road sign! EXIT GREENBROOK POND. He threw his foot to the other pedal. Again instinct. The brakes locked instantly, wrenching the car sideways.

The passenger door hammered into the sign, then through the sign, clipping off the yard-high aluminum supports as it went. The wide green rectangle slapped against the side windows, which were now the front window. Through the windshield, Marcus was relieved to see nothing. No Jeep. Only the two empty southbound lanes and the trees and the sky, all of them turning over and over in unison as the Volvo began to flip.

He reached for support to the ceiling and the door, then forced himself to pull back, grasping the shoulder harness instead. What was it they said? Drunks did better in crashes because their bodies were relaxed? Damn! Who could relax?

His foot was pushing through the brake pedal as the car flipped two complete revolutions, thrusting him to the right, to the ceiling, to the left and back. Then everything all over again, making the two rolls feel like ten.

The Volvo settled on four flat tires, flopping itself neatly onto the unpaved exit for Greenbrook Pond. A cloud of dust billowed around the wreck, swirling inside the car through a shattered rear window. He coughed fitfully, then cleared his throat, choking off his dry spasms.

Marcus sat there shivering, his throat clenched. Concentrating on each bone and joint, he waited for the dust to clear. A sprained right wrist from when he'd first reached up to the ceiling. A tender bruise across the torso, where the shoulder strap had caught him. Too traumatized to actually move, he flexed his arms, then his legs and feet. Nothing seemed broken.

The world outside the cloud was unnaturally quiet. A few gusts of sound whizzed by from the northbound lanes, but no such sounds from his own. Where the hell was New Jersey traffic when you needed it? His encounter with the Jeep seemed to have taken a lifetime, but he knew the whole thing couldn't have been more than sixty seconds.

And now? Was it over? As quickly as that? Had his attacker simply given up and driven on, afraid to take any more chances on a public parkway?

Marcus rolled down his window an inch. The soft

scent of pine played through the dust and helped to relax him, making him suddenly and strangely nostalgic for the childhood summers on his grandmother's farm. Marcus allowed himself one more cough, then took in his first deep breath.

He breathed in again. He exhaled. Then every muscle in his body clenched as an explosion ripped through the inch of air above his head. A second shot came a second later, shattering the driver's side glass, then the passenger glass, passing through the car as easily as it could have passed through him.

Marcus pulled himself down into the seat. *How easily could a bullet penetrate a Volvo?* he wondered. The shoulder harness caught him under the chin like a noose, keeping his head stubbornly above the door metal. With fast, feverish hands, he reached toward his right hip, seeking out the little red button. There it was. Why wouldn't it release? Again and again he punched it.

The third shot hit him. Marcus let out a muffled, strangled scream just as the buckle released.

CHAPTER 36

Amy pointed to an inside space on the bench. "You sit here, across from me. Frank can have the outside."

Sergeant Rawlings said nothing. But he traded places with Patrolman Loyola, scooting across to the inside of the wooden booth.

"There's a reason for this," Amy said, feeling foolish but determined. "Lou. Three orange juices."

"I can always eat," Frank said with a cautious eye to his superior. "Muffins here are pretty good."

Something close to a sneer wrinkled Rawlings's pale, young features. "You said you know who killed Ingo. That's the reason I'm here. Three hours ago I had breakfast."

"Then you must be hungry. And no. I said I know who killed Georgina Davis, though it's a safe bet it's the same person. As for Fabian Carvel, there I'm a mite shaky."

"If you're withholding evidence, Ms. Abel . . ."

"Whoa!" Amy was forcing herself to be loud and confident. If it came off a little obnoxious, so be it. "I don't know anything the police shouldn't know. For instance, Fabian Carvel had an allergy attack on the night of his disappearance. And the cook's son was in the house that night but was never questioned. And Carvel didn't voluntarily disappear. The credit card signatures on his cross-country trip were forged."

"That's not my case," Rawlings said.

"But they're all connected. Thanks, Lou." Lou had put the three glasses in front of his three customers. "Lou!" Amy took her orange juice and held it up to the light. "Is this fresh squeezed?"

"Don't push your luck." Lou dumped the menus and walked away.

Rawlings's patience was growing thin. "That thing about credit card receipts. You got that from Ingo's notes."

"No comment."

"Someone sent me that script. Overnight delivery."

"No comment." Amy sat up tall and lifted an orange juice. "To catching the killer."

Rawlings paused, examining Amy's face. "You're in a cocky mood, which is probably why I'm still listening."

Amy shrugged and toasted again. Rawlings reached for his juice. Frank followed suit, and all three touched glasses. The travel agent glanced over her rim as the homicide detective drank.

Rawlings caught the look. "What are you up to?" he demanded, then returned his juice. "What the hell!" He reached down in the glass and pulling out a red cat's-eye marble, half an inch across. "What the hell?"

"Think of it as a cyanide pill," Amy said with a nervous grin.

"I could've choked on this," Rawlings barked. "Waiter!"

"Lou didn't do it. I did." Lou was approaching with

an order pad, but Amy waved him away. "We're not ready."

"You? You mean, before we got here?"

"I mean just now." Amy took the wet marble from Rawlings and placed it on her place mat. "I held up my glass and asked about fresh squeezed. When you looked away, I dropped it in."

"But that was *your* glass."

"And just now, when we were toasting . . ." Amy pointed to a fresh water ring on the table. "I picked up yours. They were close together, so you assumed the remaining glass was yours. Even if you'd realized I'd taken the wrong one, the normal thing would be to just take mine. Neither one had been drunk from."

"Ooh!" Frank was excited, almost choking on his juice. "That's how she was poisoned."

"I could've bit into that damn marble."

"You bite your orange juice?"

"I could've swallowed it. Is that why you brought me here? To play a little parlor trick? Can you make a quarter come out of my ear?"

"Ooh." Frank was holding his temples in place with his fists. "Who was sitting across from Georgina?"

"The people on her left and right were too far away to do it unnoticed. Frank knows. He was there. But we always reach across the table for a glass. It's natural."

Rawlings gazed down at the wet marble, rolling it along the placemat with a fingertip. Amy knew enough not to push it further. "Okay," he said. "Tell me."

"Shouldn't we order first?" Amy asked with an eye cocked toward Lou, now a brooding presence behind the counter.

They ordered. And while they waited for, then ate

their muffins, Amy explained her theory, everything from Fabian's death to Otto's shooting and Georgina's poisoning. It all sounded good, Amy felt, until the moment when the big hole started to become apparent.

Rawlings saw it soon enough. "The murders aren't connected," he interrupted. "How is Carvel's killer, this Leonardo character that no one knows about . . . how is he connected to your poisoner?"

"I'm not quite sure," Amy mumbled. "But there's a connection."

"Connection, hell. It makes sense only if they're the same person."

"Not really. They could be related. You'll never know until you check it out."

"We did checks on everyone."

"Well, check this one again."

"Don't tell me what to do."

The two of them kept at it, with Frank sitting quietly by. Amy tried to emphasize other aspects, the logic, the personalities. But Rawlings kept returning to the hole, like a dog with a bone.

"All I'm asking for is a search warrant."

"That's all?"

"You'll find the gun that killed Otto."

Rawlings wiped his mouth. "Ms. Abel. This is not something I'm willing to act on right now. I appreciate your help, and I loved the magic trick. I really did. Lou, my man, the muffins were great." He slapped down a twenty and headed out the screen door.

Frank followed.

Lou crossed to the booth, took the bill, and began to wipe down, brushing the muffin crumbs into Amy's lap. "You and your pals might want to look for another spot. I got a reputation."

"Sorry, Lou. It won't happen again."

So that was it? Her great breakthrough? Amy knew she was right, but what good would that do her now?

Back out on the street, she was surprised to find Frank Loyola leaning against the shingle-sided building. Alone. "I told the sarge I had an errand to run."

"That's nice," Amy said, still mindful of their last encounter.

"Him and me came in separate cars, so . . ." Frank pointed to his green Camaro, parked by a hydrant. "You really think that's how it happened?"

"You were there."

Frank rubbed his chin. "It's possible. A couple of people picked up their king of Sweden wine and sniffed it. The pill could have gone in then."

Amy looked at the Camaro, then back at its owner. "So what's this errand?"

Frank kicked an old candy wrapper into the gutter. "I was thinking we might go visit someone. Nothing official. But I'm pretty good at throwing people off guard. What do you say?"

Amy shook her head. "I thought you were after Marcus."

"Yeah. But if Rawlings is right, then it's his collar and I'm still a flunky. If you're right . . ."

"Then it's your collar. No, thanks."

"Ah, come on." He was practically pleading. "If you must know, the sarge hasn't been too encouraging. Sure, he confers with me, but more like a witness than a fellow investigator. So, I was thinking if I showed a little more initiative . . . you know?"

"Unofficially? Without a warrant?"

"There are things we can do."

"Like making people vomit their muffins?"

"You're not making it easy." Frank bit his lower lip. "I'm sorry about that. But look what you got here. I'm an on-duty cop who half believes you, who's got a legal sidearm and knows what he can and can't do. You're not gonna do better. Not today."

"You're just doing this to get your gold shield."

"Yeah? Well, so what? I mean, so what?"

"So . . ." She mulled it over. "So you're right. Let's go."

For most of the drive they stayed silent, except for Amy's suggestion about the best approach to the Holland Tunnel, which Frank appreciated. Once in New Jersey, he headed north on the turnpike, weaving through steady traffic until the Palisades. From there on they expected clear sailing, and were surprised when the cars began slowing down and backing up.

Frank leaned out his window, regarded the flow with a practiced eye, then strained his neck to gaze at the nearly empty southbound lanes. "Feels like a rubbernecking delay."

The minutes crawled along with the traffic. Two miles later an access break between the wooded medians gave them a clear view. It was rubbernecking, as Frank had figured, caused by an accident in the southbound lanes. Everyone was ogling two highway patrol units, their reds flashing as they straddled an exit leading onto a dirt road. In the middle of the exit stood a battered Volvo sedan. A plume of light steam rose from its hood, and shrubs seemed to be growing out of the grille. Three windows had been broken or severely cracked, and all four tires were flat. A sign, EXIT GREENBROOK POND, lay crumpled nearby.

"How the Hector . . . ?"

Amy stared past Frank's head. "It's a Volvo like mine,"

she said as they crept toward a closer view. It had a Rye
Playland bumper sticker, too. And the license plate . . .
"Holy crap, it's my car."

Frank winced. "Are you sure?"

"It's my car."

Frank began to ease the Camaro across a lane and
through the access break. They pulled in behind the
patrol cars, and while Frank was busy showing his badge
to an officer, Amy jumped out and ran to the injured
Volvo. It was empty, with streaks of blood across the
driver's seat.

A minute later Frank joined her. "Someone dialed
nine-one-one about gunshots along this stretch. That
was maybe ten minutes ago. They say it probably got run
off the road. The boys are waiting for the locals. This
isn't really your car?"

"It is."

"Holy Hanna. Who else has keys? Your mom?"

"Yeah." Thirty yards in, the dirt road vanished around
a leafy bend. "I can't believe she . . . Can we drive back
in there?"

Frank shrugged. "It's a jurisdictional thing, you
know?"

"It's my mother."

"The Volvo's blocking the way. And we can't drive up
and around, 'cause my Camaro doesn't got enough
clearance."

"My mother gets run off the road, and you're talking
about clearance? She's in there."

"Not necessarily." But Frank was already talking to
Amy's back. "Hey!"

Amy had almost reached the bend in the dirt road
when the patrolman caught up. "All right," he hissed as

they fell in beside each other. "I guess there's nothing wrong with an off-duty New York cop taking a walk in the New Jersey woods."

"You're on duty."

"Sugar!" Frank stopped in his tracks, then started again. "Oh, what the Hector! But you follow my lead. This is my show."

It was Amy who first saw the Grand Cherokee parked in the middle of the road, near the spot where a footpath branched off and meandered into the brush. The two of them gazed silently. A breeze stirred the leaves at their feet, and Amy could swear she heard footsteps not far off, rhythmically crunching through the autumn debris. Frank heard them, too. He drew his service revolver and motioned for Amy to stay with the Grand Cherokee. Amy nodded.

She waited until Frank had turned down the footpath, not a second longer. Then she took the only other route, the dirt road beyond the Jeep, walking softly and listening through the dying breeze for the footsteps that might have been nothing more than the breeze. The road curved up an incline, and from the top Amy thought she could see the faint outline of the Empire State Building across the woods and the river.

Taking the curve down the other side, she was immediately faced with the kidney-shaped expanse of Greenbrook Pond. The road ended at the pond's edge, in a small gravel patch. Nearby, a graffiti-riddled storage shed leaned into a weeping willow, its chained and nailed-up boards serving to hold the structure together as much as to keep out intruders.

Amy felt a touch on her ankle, like the landing of an insect on skin, except that she was wearing trousers, not shorts. As she passed within a few yards of the shed, she felt another touch, this time more like a sharp pang, hitting her on the right hip. Amy stopped and inspected the spot and rubbed it.

"Amy," a voice whispered. She started, then spun clumsily in a circle. There was no one in sight, and she spun again. A third stone, this one too large to be a pebble, arched past her head and hit the ground. "Amy. The shed."

She hadn't even considered the shed. There seemed to be no way in and barely enough of it standing to accommodate a human being. As she stared, a narrow plank of rotting wood was lifted and moved aside, leaving a black hole about four inches wide. "Marcus?" Amy looked into the hole. "What are you doing in there?"

A pair of eyes inside the wedge of darkness reflected the cloudy daylight. "Get out of here now. Go." His voice was weak and shaky.

"Where's Fanny?"

"At home. I borrowed the car."

"Thanks for taking such good care of it."

"Amy, I've been shot."

CHAPTER 37

This had started out as a drive, going out to New Jersey to intimidate the Mrozeks and see what happened. Now, suddenly, it was a wrecked car—her car—and gunshots and the man she cared about, shot and bleeding in a tumbled-down shed.

"I'm bleeding like hell." Marcus moved his arm so that Amy could see it and the blood. So much blood.

"You should tie a tourniquet." Amy started unbuckling her belt. "Can you get out of there?"

"I'll take care of myself. Get help."

"I am help," she replied. "Frank's around, too. Somewhere."

"Does he have a gun? Nardo has a gun."

"Nardo shot you? He's here?"

"I recognized him in the Rome photo."

"I thought you never met him."

"I knew his mother. They look a lot alike, especially now. Oh, shit!" The hazel eyes had refocused somewhere behind Amy.

Too late she heard the crackling of leaves. "Turn around slowly," a voice said.

Amy obeyed and fixed her gaze on Jolynn Mrozek, walking down the slope, a tiny but lethal .22 pointed relentlessly at Amy's chest. *Well, this solves one problem,* she thought. *The murders are officially connected.*

"Leonardo Gray," Amy said, moving to her left, trying to cut off Jolynn's view of the hole between the boards in the shed.

"Jolynn Hanover Mrozek." Jolynn said the words with slow authority and kept coming up the slope. "Very much a woman, thank you. Of course, I can't have kids, which I call a blessing."

"Does Vinny know?"

She laughed. "Would you marry a transgendered? Well, maybe you would, but not Vinny. I know he's in the shed, so just step aside."

Amy held her ground and played for time. "Why did you kill Carvel?"

"So long ago," Jolynn said. "A lifetime." The small, bony woman glanced around, then shrugged. "It was more or less accidental. One thing leads to another. Events take on a life of their own, you know?"

"You sabotaged his food. He came back to the kitchen and found you."

Jolynn stopped in her tracks. "I knew it was just a matter of time. Either Otto would figure it out or Marcus would remember."

"What happened in the kitchen?"

"Questions, questions." Part of Jolynn seemed annoyed, and part of her seemed pleased. "I've never, ever talked about this. For obvious reasons." She settled gently onto a stump ten feet away, so feminine and proper, the muzzle of the .22 still trained on Amy's chest. "That bastard. If it wasn't for Mama . . . She was responsible for his success, you know. Of course you know."

"Sour cream and the prefolded taco."

"It was more than that," spat Jolynn. "She created all the early recipes. Everything. He promised to make it up, give us lots of stock. I was counting on that money for my operation." Here she smiled. "I told Mama I needed it for college."

"And then Carvel's family talked him out of it."

Jolynn's eyes narrowed. "Mama took it so good, like she was expecting it. That old Italian fishwife attitude where you figure you'll probably get screwed, anyway, so it doesn't matter."

"So you played a little prank on his food."

"That's all it was. A prank to get his attention." Jolynn was distracted now, waving her free hand at a persistent fly that was orbiting her black, lacquered hair. Amy felt an opportunity. But what could she do? A second later and the fly buzzed away.

"Anyway, he came fuming into the kitchen, yelling at Mama. I was yelling at him. Of course, that's just what he didn't want, someone yelling about his thievery. So, Mama stays to serve the next course. And he takes me by the neck and drags me off to the apartment above the garage. By now the asshole's threatening me with assault and battery charges. Assault with milk."

"And then he had his attack."

"You know a lot." The words were spoken as a threat.

"What's to know? He eats dairy. He has an attack."

Jolynn nodded. "It was damn scary. The mean old bastard is moaning, all bent over with cramps. And outside the window I see all these people running around, calling his name. I thought he was gonna die."

Yes, Amy thought, *events do take on a life of their own.* "So you got scared and hid out. And somehow that led to kidnapping him and driving cross-country."

Jolynn bristled, holding the pistol at arm's length and pointing it for emphasis. "It wasn't dumb. I'm not dumb."

Amy raised her hands to chest level. "I'm just trying to understand."

"Getting to San Diego was the only leverage I had. Mama left some stuff in the attic where we used to live. A diary, some old recipes, a thank-you letter from Fabian. Proof the inventions were really hers."

"You thought they'd still be in the attic?"

"It was a rental. No one used the attic. Anyway, I had no choice. This stuff would give me leverage. He'd have to forget about the kidnapping. And he'd give me money for the diary, just to not have it hanging over him. Mama would never do it. Too much of a victim. Well, Nardo wasn't gonna be a victim."

"So you had to get to San Diego and had to keep Carvel out of commission until you got there." Amy was beginning to fall in with the crazy logic. "I guess a car would be the only way. What? Tied up in the backseat?"

Jolynn regarded her with bemused disdain. "In the trunk. I'd buy ice cream cones along the way and feed them to him. God, that trunk smelled. I'd take him out at truck stops and try to clean him up. Poor slob barely knew where he was. We got to San Diego, and the stuff was in the attic, right where I knew it would be."

"Then you contacted Stu Romney."

"I figured he'd be the one to negotiate." Jolynn's eyes looked straight into Amy's, as if seeking approval or at least understanding. "I never meant to kill him. We were in our motel, and somehow he got out. I barely caught him. Sure, he was sick, but not as sick as he pretended. All I had on me was this pocketknife."

"You stabbed him to death with a pocketknife?"

"What else could I do?" She smirked, still a little proud of herself. "It wasn't easy. Afterward, I sold his watch and ring and cashed out as much as I could on his bank cards. Maybe a year later Mama moved back to Elba to live with her cousins, and I started to come out of my cocoon." Her free hand flew up in an almost joyous flourish. "Jolynn Hanover. On the prowl for a big brute of a man to make her happy." Her hand lost its flourish and fell to her side. "It's worked out okay. Once the twins get out of our hair."

The shrill call of a bird played in the empty air. Amy had warned herself not to let this happen, not to let the conversation lag. But her mind had been too busy weaving together the last of the threads.

Nardo Gray had been replaced by Jolynn, who, with each passing year, felt safer from Nardo's homicidal past. Until the rally, when she heard that Marcus was nosing around. Otto's involvement was a threat she couldn't ignore. What seemed like an unfathomable mystery to the overworked police might turn out to be child's play to a creature like Otto.

When Amy refocused her attention, Jolynn had just finished screwing a long black cylinder onto the pistol's snub nose. "I think this will be the end of it," Jolynn said, almost to herself. "Mind stepping aside? First come, first served."

"No." Amy stood her ground, squaring her body to block the shed's slab of open darkness.

"C'mon, girl. Move."

But Amy was frozen. Just like Monte Carlo. Like Minetta Lane two years ago. But now her inaction meant something different. It meant standing up to a cold-blooded killer. There was defiance in this frozen inaction.

"Well, have it your way." Without warning and in rapid succession, Jolynn fired four breathy, muffled shots.

Amy shut her eyes and heard a scream, unable to tell if it was her own or Marcus's. Shards of rotting wood splintered and flew, and she opened her eyes and turned to see two splintered, gaping holes on either side, waist high, just inches from her own trembling torso.

Jolynn cackled. "Believe it or not, I was aiming at you."

"Marcus!" Amy turned her back on the gun and started clawing at the gap in the boards, desperate to see if anything in the shed was still standing. "Marcus!" She looked downward into the shadows and saw nothing.

Jolynn stepped closer. "Bye-bye, Amy." Her tone was controlled and chilling.

It took every ounce of Amy's nerve to pivot slowly and face her. It wasn't so bad, after all, she discovered. Once she forced herself to actually turn and face her killer . . . it was actually quite a relief.

"Police. Drop the weapon."

Amy watched as Frank Loyola marched down the side of the hill, toward the pond, his service revolver drawn. Jolynn swiveled and a second later recovered her balance.

"Frankie, darling," she said in the mock-Bronx accent that she had used on him throughout the tour. "Fancy finding you here."

"Put down the gun, Jolynn."

She smiled, biting her lip and thinking. "The name's not Jolynn. It's Nardo."

Frank tried not to look confused. "Nardo?"

"Leonardo Gray. Amy must've told you."

"Nardo?" Frank glanced at Amy, then back. "The cook's son?"

"Yes, the cook's son. What's the matter?"

"You're not Nardo."

"That's the name I was born with."

"But you're a married woman."

"What's wrong, Frankie? I saw how you used to look at me. Don't think I didn't notice." And she clucked her tongue. "Tch, tch, tch."

Amy sneaked a step forward. A twig snapped under her weight, and she stepped back.

"Shame on you. Want to feel my titties?" Jolynn shoved her chest forward, as if to fill the twenty yards still between them. "They're really real." And she raised her gun.

"Whoever you are . . . whatever your name is . . ." The lumbering patrolman kept the revolver pointed and kept coming.

"My husband doesn't even know."

"This is your last warning. Drop the gun."

"I had my penis cut off, Frankie. Imagine having your penis cut off!" A millisecond later came the same breathy pop as before.

Frank collapsed to his knees, his own weapon falling into the leaves. He grabbed at his chest with both hands as Jolynn turned back to face the shed.

For Amy, the shot was like a starter pistol. With no more thought of consequences—damn the consequences—she was sprinting. Jolynn had just recovered and turned, her gun raised to shoot again, when Amy squeezed shut her eyes and leaped. She hit Jolynn squarely in the chest, throwing her eyes open as the two of them tumbled, Amy forward, Jolynn back, the .22 pistol lodged between them.

Amy spread herself on top of the small, writhing woman. She clutched at the gun barrel, then let go.

"Ow. Damn. Ow." It was searing hot. But she forced herself to grab again, and this time her hand found the cooler silencer. Gripping it with both hands, Amy pulled the gun off to one side. She was significantly stronger than Jolynn, and it would be just a matter of time before . . .

Jolynn concentrated all her strength on twisting the pistol sideways in a circle. At first Amy thought this was an attempt to aim it at her or wrench it out of her grasp. It wasn't until Jolynn had twisted it a full revolution and the silencer began to wobble in Amy's hands that she realized what Jolynn was doing. She was unscrewing it.

Jolynn smiled now. Short of letting go, there was nothing Amy could do. It was happening so fast. A second full twist.

Amy let go with one hand, then grabbed the barrel again. The shock of the heat sapped her strength just enough to allow Jolynn to turn the whole mechanism, pistol and wobbly silencer, away from the empty air and toward Amy's chest. It was at that same instant that the silencer snapped off, throwing Amy to one side and letting Jolynn start to wriggle out from under, the weapon now completely hers.

A second later and Amy found herself facing the muzzle, just inches from her face. She could see the hammer cocking back, as if in slow motion. Instinctively, she shut her eyes.

"Don't move!"

Amy stopped moving.

"I've got a gun."

Yes, of course she had a gun. And then Amy recognized the voice.

When she snapped open her eyes, Marcus was directly over them, legs spread on either side of their heads. He was wobbly on his feet and his left arm hung useless, dripping blood from the shoulder. In his right hand he held Frank's service revolver, aiming it straight down. Amy rolled away, leaving him an unobstructed target.

"You so much as twitch and I'll pull it. I'm not Frank. Don't think you can psyche me with penis talk."

Jolynn paused, considered her options, and slowly let go of the gun.

Marcus smiled.

So did Amy. "Penis talk?"

CHAPTER 38

"I thought those magic Kevlar vests protected you."
"Just because it didn't pierce the skin . . ." Frank was slurring his words. "Ain't you ever heard of trauma?"

"I live with my mother. I know trauma very well."

Frank lay back on his pillows and looked Amy in the eyes. "And I live with my dad. Nothing wrong with that." He managed a smile. At last they'd found a connection, one perhaps large enough to build a truce on. "Real heroes, that's what they're calling us. Did you hear?"

Amy didn't know what to say. Instead, she looked around for a vase. There were two of them in the private room, both filled with floral tributes from the PBAs of New Jersey and New York. It had been only a few hours since the shooting, and Amy was impressed by police efficiency, at least their florists' efficiency. She placed her own modest bouquet on Frank's meal tray. "These should get put in water."

"What's the matter, Abel? Don't like being a hero?"

Amy shrugged. "You and Marcus, maybe. I was just in the way."

"What're you saying? Marcus told me everything. Rambling on in the ambulance. How you blocked the shed with your body. You were ready to take a bullet."

"Jolynn shot anyway."

"Yeah. But those extra seconds. He was using them to squeeze out the back. If you'd have moved when Jolynn told you, he'd be dead. That's how he sees it."

"Really?" Amy mulled it over, trying hard to believe it. "Nah. I couldn't have moved if I wanted. I was too scared."

"Like the rest of us weren't. And then the way you jumped on her?"

"I distracted her while someone else got the gun."

"What're you talking? If it wasn't for that distraction . . ." Another wince forced Frank back into his pillows. "Have it your way. But I'm telling you, the press likes things nice and simple. We're heroes, and the bad guy is in jail. Bad girl," he corrected himself. "Jeez."

"Nice and simple."

"You see that kind of thing on talk shows, but you never expect . . . jeez." Frank squirmed. The angle of his neck looked uncomfortable. Amy gently lifted the officer's head and stuffed another pillow under it. "Thanks," Frank said. "Wanna be a real hero? Get me out of here."

"I'll do my best."

The first thing Amy saw when she left Frank's room was her mother pacing in the hall. In an instant she was being hugged, the short arms fiercely encircling her waist and cutting off her air.

"Are you all right?" Fanny let go her grip, then stepped back and examined her face. "You look pale."

"Oxygen deprivation," she wheezed. "I'm fine, really. Frank and Marcus, on the other hand . . ."

"I heard. They're letting Marcus see visitors. That's what I hear." Fanny grabbed Amy's hand and led her down the corridor. "Don't you ever scare me like that again."

"How did you get out here?"

"The sergeant drove me. You know this is only fifteen minutes out of the city?"

"I've been told."

"Sergeant Rawlings was very comforting. He explained as much as he could, which was awkward since I knew more than he did."

"That must have galled."

"It's a good lesson for the man. The next time Fanny and Amy Abel get involved in a murder, he should take us seriously."

"Next time? Mom, there wasn't a last time. There won't be a next."

"You never know. Travel can be very dangerous. Come on. We're going to see Marcus."

Amy stopped. "I'm not sure that's the best idea."

"Sure it is." Fanny dragged her daughter forward, expertly changing the subject as they walked. "The sergeant asked me about the tour."

"So he finally sees the connection."

" 'Did Jolynn come on the tour, planning to kill someone?' he asked me."

Amy had thought about this. "Well, she did follow us and throw the rock. At that point she had no idea what Marcus knew or didn't. But at the first dinner, when Jolynn saw the menu . . . You can imagine. Nardo's little prank, right there for everyone to eat."

"Yes, yes," Fanny said. "But she wasn't in any real danger."

"She didn't know that. I remember walking into my

room one night and smelling lilacs. I didn't connect it to Jolynn. But I'm sure she broke in regularly, checking the next day's game. That's how she found out about Elba."

"Right. She's the one who tried to have the rooms robbed."

"Her mother came from Elba. I imagine Jolynn got in touch with some relatives. She was hoping the robberies would make us cancel the game."

"And then Georgina finally remembered. Hey!" They stepped aside just in time as a pair of boys sped by in their wheelchairs. Fanny's eyes crinkled, and she was reminded of a world of more innocent pleasures. "When you had your tonsils out, you were the best wheelchair racer on the floor."

"I was nineteen."

"You never give yourself permission to feel proud. That's your problem."

Fanny had stopped at the door to room 426. There was no name penciled in on the sliding tag, no indication of the current occupant. "You stay on your best behavior. Remember, the two of you saved each other's lives. That's a bond."

Amy focused on the blank tag. "How did you know the room number? You were here? You already talked to him? Before you came to see me?"

"You were busy, and they said he could have visitors."

"I'm not sure I'm ready for this."

"Do what feels right. But you can't use the excuse of him being a killer."

"You don't waste any time, do you?"

"Amy, dear. I never make you do anything you don't want to. Eventually."

"Eventually."

"C'mon." Fanny had already pushed open the door and was ushering her daughter inside. "Look who's here," she called out in a sweet whisper. "Marcus, wake up." And with one more little push, Amy was in.

Fanny remained out in the hall and let the door swing gently shut.

FANNY'S FORTY FAVORITE TRAVEL TIPS

I know my daughter is the travel expert. But I've traveled a bit myself. Plus, I'm a true expert in giving advice. But please, you don't have to listen to any of my opinions if you don't want to. I'm just a mother with a lifetime of experience. Feel free to ignore me. That's all right.

1. Do a home exchange. I've never personally done this, but my sister-in-law Emily loves it. The concept is that you trade your home for someone else's home for a week or two. No money changes hands, but you get to live like a native rent-free while someone else lives like you in your home. There are several websites that show you photos and give you all the information and help you need to arrange a swap: homeexchange.com; onefinestay.com; and homeswap.com, to name a few. It's the only way Emily travels anymore. And it's not just because she's cheap.

2. Take along a power strip. Have you ever arrived at the airport only to find your phone battery low and all the electrical outlets being

used by other travelers? Well, go right up to
that nice businessman and ask if you can borrow his outlet and plug him into your power
strip instead. You'll make a lot of instant
friends. And the power strip will be useful in
your hotel room. You can never have too
many outlets.

3. Always pack a hat. Even if you're not a hat
    person, it will come in handy. You'll wind up
    using it for sun protection and light drizzles
    and—in Amy's case, not mine—the occa-
    sional bad-hair day.

4. Make a packing list. I know this sounds bor-
    ing and anal. But once you do it, you'll never
    have to do it again. Then, as you're unpack-
    ing at the end of each trip, add items to the
    list that you wish you'd taken and cross off
    items that you took and never used. You can
    store your packing list in your empty suitcase
    until the next time.

5. Take only clothes that go together. Every-
    thing you pack should be in the same general
    palate. If not, you'll wind up with one clean
    blouse (a print) and one clean skirt (a con-
    trasting print), and you'll wish you'd listened
    to me. My rule is bring all solid colors for
    bottoms and colorful ones for tops.

6. Bring at least two books to read on the plane.
    No matter how many online reviews you read,
    one of your books is going to be a clunker.

Just give it away and start on the second. Or better, bring an e-reader. And don't forget your e-reader charger.

7. Bring a bag for dirty laundry. I know it sounds like a waste of packing space, but it beats sniffing through your underwear every morning. If your hotel has placed a plastic laundry bag in your room, you can steal it. They won't mind.

8. Use a weekly pill container for your jewelry. Earrings, little bracelets and necklaces, they can all fit inside the compartments of a pill container. This way, they'll all stay organized and untangled.

9. Bring hand sanitizer and duct tape. This is really two tips, but I felt guilty about listing two such obvious things, so I lumped them together. You can have a perfectly fine time without either one. But if you remember to bring them, you'll be surprised how often you use them—especially the duct tape.

10. Don't pack that second dress-up outfit. First, no one at that fancy Paris bistro is going to care that you wore the same outfit last week to the theatre in London. And second, travel is a lot more casual than it used to be. Be sure to pack a stain stick, just in case.

11. Don't pack anything you haven't worn before. Those new shoes you couldn't resist or that

last-minute sweater purchase can turn out to be disappointing. The shoes will pinch and the sweater will wind up draping all wrong and make you look ten pounds heavier. Take only what you know is comfortable and looks good on you.

12. Buy a hanging toiletry kit. This is Amy's favorite, a real lifesaver, she says. These bags unzip, fold out and can be hung from a shower door or a hook or any doorframe. You don't ever have to unpack the contents, just use your toiletries and return them to the bag. Given the size of most hotel bathrooms, a hanging kit keeps you organized and cuts down on bathroom clutter. Go online and check out "hanging toiletry kits," and you'll see what I mean.

13. Roll up your clothes instead of folding them. I don't know why a rolled up shirt takes up less space in a suitcase than a folded shirt, but it does. Rolling your clothes also cuts down on fold marks and wrinkles.

14. Use plastic wrap for liquid containers. If you've ever placed liquids in your checked luggage, you know there's the possibility that the caps will leak and your favorite pashmina will get covered in your favorite shampoo. To avoid this, unscrew the lid, place a layer of plastic wrap over the mouth, then screw or snap the cap back on. No leaks!

15.   Take plenty of zip-lock bags. Amy says these
      sealable plastic baggies are perfect for pre-
      serving crime scene evidence. But they also
      have a thousand other uses, from packing a
      wet swimsuit to keep your extra batteries dry.

16.   Use a shower cap on your shoes. When you
      pack your shoes, cover the soles with a shower
      cap to keep the rest of your things clean. A lot
      of hotels still give away shower caps. Take
      them.

17.   Add a dryer sheet for freshness. Always un-
      fold a fresh dryer sheet in the bottom of your
      bag. It takes up no room. And it leaves your
      clothes smelling clean, with fewer wrinkles.

18.   Lost luggage. Take a selfie standing beside
      your luggage. It's next to no effort, and if
      your bag gets lost on a flight, you'll have a pic-
      ture to share with the person in charge. In-
      clude yourself in the photo in order to show
      scale—and to remind them how sweet and
      desperate you are.

19.   Bring an empty water bottle in your carry-on.
      You can fill it once you pass security and avoid
      having to buy one at that overpriced airport
      store with the rude service.

20.   Ask to buy a last-minute upgrade. I do this at
      the ticket counter as I'm checking in. If the
      flight has any leftover business class seats, the

agent is authorized to sell them at a steep discount. If you don't ask, you don't get.

21. Fragile luggage. Amy says I shouldn't mention this one, but she's way too stodgy. Whenever I know I'm going to be in a rush at my destination city, I ask the nice people at check-in to mark my luggage with a big red "fragile" sticker. The bag actually does get better treatment, and they put it on top of the pile when they unload the plane. That means it comes out earlier on the conveyor belt.

22. Try for extra elbow room. If you're traveling with a friend, book an aisle and a window seat, with an empty seat in-between. This will discourage anyone else from booking the dreaded middle seat and give you some extra elbow room. If the flight is full and someone winds up sitting there, you can always lay on the charm and ask them to switch, so you and your friend can sit together.

23. Forgot the charger for your electronics? Before you spend half a day trying to buy a new charger, ask at your hotel's front desk. They will often have a box full of orphan chargers that previous guests have left behind.

24. Alert your credit card company. The banks are a lot more vigilant about fraud than they used to be, even a few years ago. The moment they see an ATM withdrawal in Valparaiso,

they will freeze your account and you'll have to spend an hour of your valuable vacation on the phone trying to undo it. To avoid this, call them before leaving and let them know your destination.

25. Bring at least two credit cards. And be sure to keep one of them in your luggage. This can help prevent a whole slew of disasters, from an ATM eating your only card, to losing it if your wallet is lost or stolen.

26. Wear something dark on the plane. You will spill food on yourself in those cramped spaces. Guaranteed. And then you'll be stuck carrying around a stained white blouse for the entire trip.

27. Buy duty-free cocktails. If Amy and I wind up in a hotel room with a little balcony, we will often sit out with a glass of wine or a cocktail before venturing off to dinner. But the hotel minibar selections are always expensive and mediocre. And finding a liquor store is not easy. In some places, like India, they're nearly nonexistent. My solution is to buy a bottle of something at the duty-free shop before leaving the U.S. Then you're all set for your first evening, gazing out over a new vista and planning tomorrow.

28. Avoid the hotel breakfast. I know the hotel is convenient when you're hungry and only half-awake. But it will be cheaper and a lot more

fun to go out the front door and eat where the locals do.

29. Buy event tickets online. If you're planning to go to a major museum or site, buy your tickets online. It will save you from having to stand in a long line in the blistering sun and you may even get some discounts or special packages.

30. Don't ask the concierge. If your hotel has a concierge service, you'll be tempted to use them to answer every possible question, especially if the concierges are cute. But it's not a good idea to ask them for recommendations. In most cases, the concierge gets a kickback for everything they book for you—tours, shows, cooking classes, even restaurants—so it's in their best interest to recommend the ones that pay them. Instead, go online yourself and check things out.

31. Get lost. Amy and I never purposely set out to get lost. But every now and then, we'll head out late and try to find a restaurant that we know is impossible to locate, or wander through the old section of town without a map, or rent a canoe on a river and get carried away by the current. The results are never perfect and never predictable. But they've supplied us with some of our best memories.

32. Don't throw out your travel-size containers. Before each new trip refill these tiny contain-

ers with ingredients from your regular bathroom supply. You'll wind up saving a bunch.

33. Never go to a restaurant with a menu in three
or more languages. More than two languages
on a menu is a sure indication of a tourist
trap. Many of my best dining experiences
were in places where the waiters and I had to
play charades in order to communicate. Don't
be afraid to take a chance—unless you have
major food allergies, of course.

34. Don't be afraid of a B&B. Staying at a bed
and breakfast instead of a hotel gives you a
lot more bang for the buck. The downside is
that you don't have a hotel staff to do your
bidding. The upside is that you get breakfast!
And you'll get a real sense of what it's like to
live like a local. Many of the new generation
of B&Bs are quite luxurious, but be sure to
check with a site like Tripadvisor to make
sure you're not walking into a surprise.

35. Don't overtip. People in most countries don't
tip like Americans, except Canadians, who are
just like Americans, only nicer. It's not a matter of being stingy or generous. It's a cultural
thing. They don't expect it. In most regions
of the world, the waiters will be thrilled if you
leave between five and ten percent of the
restaurant check. But you'll have to leave it
in cash, since there's usually no line for it on
your credit card receipt.

36. Before leaving for the day, write down your
hotel's name and address. I know you're not
a five-year-old, or an eighty-five-year old with
dementia. But you'd be surprised how many
hotels have similar names or how easy it is to
forget all the places you've been staying during your whirlwind travels. It's also helpful to
show the name to your cab driver if you can't
pronounce the street name.

37. Cull through your photos every night. This
will help you eliminate the bad ones before
the prospect becomes overwhelming. It will
also let you label the good ones while your
memory of the day is still fresh. I can't tell
you how many times Amy has turned to me
and said, "What was the name of that church
we went to three days ago?"

38. Equip your phone. There are all sorts of
phone apps these days to help the curious
traveler: translation apps, GPS apps, apps
for walking tours, even audio guides that you
can use instead of renting a headset at a museum. Just be careful to turn your phone fea-
ture off when you're not using it. Those
roaming charges can kill you.

39. Go to a cemetery. Just about every great city
has a great cemetery and they're definitely
worth a visit, from London's Highgate, which
has been used in dozens of horror flicks, to
New Orleans, where most of the graves are

built aboveground. I know it sounds morbid, but there's no better way to immerse yourself in the history and culture of a town than to pay a visit to its late inhabitants.

40. Don't put off travel. If you've always wanted to hike the Inca Trail, or drive through the wilds of New Zealand, start making your plans. You're not getting any younger, dear. At some point, you're going to lose your energy and wanderlust and be content to just sit in a rocking chair. So go out and travel while you can.

Fanny and Amy Abel, the dynamic mother-and-daughter owners of a NYC travel agency, have just booked their biggest trip yet. But with danger in the air, the itinerary may include murder . . .

Don't miss the second book in the
Amy's Travel Mystery series,

Dearly Departed

On sale in February 2016!

CHAPTER 1

At the sound of the electronic buzz, Amy Abel glanced up and let out a little moan. This wasn't her usual reaction to the sight of two smiling people bouncing into her travel agency and waving a check, but she couldn't help herself.

"We're so excited," said Donna Petronia. "Aren't you excited?"

Amy stood to greet them, stretching to her full height of five feet ten, then slipping off her heels, an almost unconscious reaction when people shorter than her walked into the office. She picked up her favorite red Lafonts from the desk, and the couple came more clearly into focus.

"The second annual mystery road rally," Donna chirped.

"I know you can't guarantee us a real murder this time," said Daryl.

Donna slapped his arm playfully. "He doesn't mean that. It must have been perfectly awful for you. And those poor people."

"I was just being naughty," Daryl apologized. "Still . . .

seeing someone actually killed while you're playing a mystery game . . . That must have been a once-in-a-life-time thing."

"For the victim, yes." Amy tried not to sound judgmental. After all, Daryl and Donna were just a couple of bored, rich New Yorkers looking for a thrill. "And you should be careful what you wish for."

Donna laughed. "Oh, we really don't want a murder, especially not one of us."

"No one wants to kill us," said Daryl with a kind of false modesty. "It's just the possibility that's so fascinating, isn't it? The feeling of danger."

"Donna and Daryl, about the tour . . ." There was no easy way for her to say this. "I know I told you . . ."

"It's not fully booked?" Daryl's smile dimmed by several watts. "Because we would've paid earlier. I offered to put a deposit down. On more than one occasion." He pushed the check across the desk.

"I know." Amy's eyes drifted past the shedding ficus toward the bathroom in the corner. Her mother had disappeared in there right before the couple arrived. Amy figured she had anywhere from another minute to ten. "Look." She spoke quickly now. "I'm not sure this is going to work out." She tried pushing the check back.

"What do you mean, not work out?" Donna pushed it back again. "Is this tour happening or not?"

"Um . . . it's not." Amy hadn't firmly decided, not until the moment she said it. "It's probably not in the best of taste for me to organize another murder mystery, considering what happened." She tried pushing again, but now three hands were on the check, and it was two against one. She hadn't seen such fighting over a check since the last time her uncles were in a restaurant.

"But it's such a hot ticket," Daryl argued. "That write-up in the *Times* . . ."

"I know," Amy said. "All the calls and the press. But I don't think I can do it again."

"Don't do this to yourself," Donna murmured, trying her best to look motherly. "For your own good, dear. You have to get back up on the horse. . . ."

"On the dead horse," Daryl interjected. "Isn't that the expression?"

"No," Donna said, turning on her husband. "You beat a dead horse. You get back up on a live one."

"We're not doing anything with horses, alive or dead." It was a fourth voice, and for a moment Amy couldn't tell whose side it was on. Fanny Abel had stepped around the ficus, pasting on a smile that was broad, artificial and, to Amy at least, frightening. She was nearly a foot shorter than her daughter and weighed perhaps a few pounds less. "Sorry to interrupt—Donna and Daryl, hello—but it's probably easier, sweetie, to tell them the truth." She paused now, running her fingers dramatically through her auburn pageboy. "We are being sued."

"Sued?" All three of them said it at once, although Amy tried to hide her surprise.

"Yes." Fanny adjusted her smile to look apologetic. "I'm afraid the victim's family has slapped an injunction on all future mystery tours. Cease and desist. Something to do with intellectual property and how another tour would do irrevocable harm to the victim's reputation."

Donna's fleshy face contorted. "That doesn't make sense. First off, being killed has nothing to do with your reputation. Plus, Amy has every right to do another mystery. Otherwise, there wouldn't be any mystery games at all."

Fanny held up a red polished fingernail. "Then there's the suit from the accused's lawyers, saying how another mystery tour would be prejudicial to their defense case, since the real-life case mirrored a mystery game in which their client was involved. Did I say one cease and desist order? I meant two."

"But that makes even less sense," Daryl said.

"Well, don't look at me," Fanny shot back. "I'm not a lawyer."

Amy allowed herself a crooked smile. She was in safe hands. Fanny, bless her, was definitely on her side. And that gave Amy an advantage of about 1,000 percent. No one could beat her mother in a fight like this, especially when she only half understood the argument and was making things up as she went.

By the end of five more minutes, the Petronias had beat a confused, ignominious retreat, and the check lay torn in the bottom of a rattan wastebasket. Fanny had even had an extra minute at the end to fill the electric teapot and bring out the Earl Grey.

"I'll take care of the other cancellations," Fanny said. "To tell you the truth, I kind of enjoy it, except for the money part."

"I don't know what got into me," Amy said as she watched her mother push aside her keyboard and arrange the bone china she kept stored in the bottom right of the file cabinet. "I know we need the money."

"I'm the one who should apologize." The words sounded strange coming from Fanny's lips, unexpected and foreign, as if she had learned them phonetically. "I shouldn't have pushed you to do another mystery rally. But that's all my readers on TrippyGirl wanted to talk about."

TrippyGirl was the blog Fanny had started shortly

after her daughter's European escapades, a combination of a little fact and a lot of fiction that followed a girl nicknamed Trippy, loosely based on Amy, and her adventures around the world.

"I thought I could do it," said the real Amy. "I did. But the idea of getting up every day and facing vultures like Donna and Daryl and treating death as some form of entertainment, which it is, of course—between books and TV and the news . . ."

"But you've had to face the real thing, dear, more than once. You know what? I think you should forget about murders. Don't even read those cozies you're so fond of. It's not good." The tea bags were in the cups; the pot was whistling. Amy watched, the calmness growing inside her, as Fanny Abel eased the hot water over the bags.

Amy's Travel was the name on the door. Her first impulse had been to name it Amy and Eddie's Travel, except that people would always ask who Eddie was, and she didn't think she could bear that.

Travel had been their shared passion. Amy loved the exotic and the history of it, like the Edwardian splendor of the Victoria Falls Hotel in the heart of Africa, where they'd been given the honeymoon suite, even though he had just proposed. Eddie had enjoyed all this, plus the thrill of bungee jumping from the staggering height of a bridge just downriver from the falls.

"How many times will you get to do something like this?" he'd asked as a pair of sketchy-looking entrepreneurs tied the frayed bungee rope around his feet and nudged him out onto the platform.

"You mean jumping off a bridge on the border between two third world countries, over the friggin' Victoria Falls?"

"Exactly." Eddie laughed. Then, without another thought, he turned and whooped and dove out over the rapids. A world-embracing swan dive. "Whoooo!"

On that afternoon, he jumped the falls twice and talked her into doing it once. She was sick for the next four hours. No one had told her there would be so much bouncing and spinning involved, and that wasn't even counting the free fall and the snap. But it would become one of her proudest moments and fondest memories.

The memories all changed one month later, when Eddie was killed by muggers just a few blocks from their Greenwich Village apartment.

Nearly two years after the mind-numbing horror of that night, after retrenching completely from life and moving back into the comfort of her childhood home, Amy finally made another daring leap and opened up shop. Eddie would have loved it.

"If we don't do this," Amy murmured, blowing steam off the rim of the dainty white cup, "are we broke? Are we going to have to close the doors?"

"Yes, we are broke," her mother replied. "I mean, a travel agency in this day and age? But we're building some momentum with TrippyGirl. Some of them are booking little trips. Of course, everyone got very excited about the next rally, which apparently is not happening."

Amy sighed. "Mother, please."

"I can't help making you feel a little guilty. It's my job."

Before Amy could retaliate, the phone rang, the actual landline reserved for business. It was an odd enough occurrence that it galvanized their focus. Fanny lifted a finger, counted silently to three, and answered. "Amy's Travel. From the ordinary to the exotic. How may I direct . . . Oh, hello, Peter." Her enthusiasm dipped. "She's not here at the moment."

Amy held out her hand for the receiver. Fanny ignored her. "Yes, I gave her your message, and she wants to call you back. But you know the travel business. Busy, busy. Yes, I'll tell her you need to speak to her. Bye-bye."

Amy watched her mother hang up, then cleared her throat. "How long has Peter been calling?"

"Two days. He says it's business and urgent, but I don't believe a thing that man says."

"Why?" Any normal woman, she thought, would be incensed that her mother was screening her calls. But that battle had been fought and lost years ago. "Has Peter ever lied to you?" Amy asked. "No. You just don't like him. Unlike some men who lie all the time and you still like him."

"There's more to honesty than telling the truth."

"Excuse me. Sorry to interrupt." It was Peter Borg himself, standing in the front doorway, tall, bland, and blond, but looking good today in a narrow-cut Marc Jacobs suit. "The door buzzed," he said, pointing behind him with one hand. In his other was his iPhone. "I guess you didn't hear."

"I told you she wasn't here," Fanny said without batting an eye.

"I know," Peter apologized. "But I was in the neighborhood."

Any normal mother, Amy thought again, would be embarrassed to be caught in a lie mere moments after telling it. Not Fanny.

"In the neighborhood?" she mocked and pointed a fat, accusing finger. "It's not bad enough that he makes me fib. No, he has to rub it in my face. If that's not dishonest, I don't know what is." And with that, she pivoted and marched off to the back office, slamming the door behind her.

Amy watched her go, then sighed. "I have no control over her. None."

"Why doesn't Fanny like me?" Peter asked. Tentatively, he sat down in a client chair, all the while keeping one eye on the back office door.

"Take it as a compliment." Amy pushed over her mother's untouched cup of Earl Grey. Peter picked it up without comment and sipped. Peter Borg was everything a normal mother could want for her daughter: handsome, hard-working and well-to-do. He was also devoted to Amy, although she'd given him very little encouragement. They had dated once or twice and been on a Caribbean tour together, for business. But there had never been that spark. For Fanny—and to a slightly lesser extent for Amy—it was all about the spark.

"I hope you're not going to do another mystery rally," he said, lowering the half-empty cup. "No matter how popular . . . it won't be good for your reputation."

"You're right." Amy hadn't thought of that angle. She knew only that she couldn't go through with it. "I know you never approved, but . . . it's not happening."

"Good." Peter scooted his chair forward, closer, planted his elbows on her desk, and steepled his long, thin fingers. "Because I have another proposal. Less work, more interesting, and probably just as lucrative."

And with that, Peter proceeded to outline his meeting two weeks ago with Paisley MacGregor.

Amy listened, her interest growing with each odd little revelation. She vaguely recalled the large, informal woman in her formal whites serving lunch one day, when Peter had persuaded Amy to come over. She'd known Peter was just showing off the maid. MacGregor had known. Everyone had known, and everyone had played along.

"And you fired her?" That was a detail Amy had never heard.

"I made up some excuse," Peter said. "But it doesn't matter, does it? She got sick and quit working. Then she died."

"Oh." Amy was taken aback. "I'm sorry."

"Oops. I should have said that at the beginning. She died three days ago."

"I'm sorry," Amy repeated, although it wasn't a surprise, given the story that he'd just told. "Did she have family?"

"MacGregor?" It was almost a snort. "No. Just her beloved employers. So, what do you say? I checked with her lawyers. I'm also a guest, so that gives me the right to involve another tour operator. You'll be paid well and get an around-the-world trip."

Amy hesitated. "I don't know."

"I'll split my commissions with you. Fifty-fifty."

"Why would you do that?"

"I need the help. You've worked with the rich and fussy. And I need someone who isn't attached to MacGregor. Even now it's a handful, contacting everyone and getting them on board. You've always wanted to see the Taj Mahal. Right?"

She must have mentioned this dream to him at some point. "You're spreading ashes at the Taj Mahal?"

"We'll be throwing MacGregor right into it."

"Eddie and I always wanted to go."

"The Taj Mahal at dawn. Something you'll never forget. And we're going to be flying private." There was a sharp gleam in his eyes.

"I've never flown private," Amy had to admit.

"A reconfigured seven-fifty-seven. I'm leasing it from some oil sheik. It seats twenty, with a crew of six. Everyone practically has a room. Of course, with us, they'll be only eight. Nine if you come along."

Amy was prepared to hear more. But then Fanny reemerged from the inner office. She was emotionally composed now, fluffing out the ruffles on her favorite beige blouse and checking the time on her Lady Hamilton.

"Hey, Fanny," Peter said smoothly. "How is Trippy-Girl? I'm a huge fan, by the way."

Amy was surprised. "You are?"

"It's a great blog," Peter said, aiming the words at Fanny. "Although I think you may be getting some traffic from people who think it's about drugs."

"We get a bit of that," Amy admitted. "But Mom likes the name."

Fanny's eyes were still on Lady Hamilton. "Amy, dear," she said. "Don't you have to be somewhere for Marcus?"

"Damn it." Amy checked her own watch, then gathered her things—her shoulder bag from the desktop, her keys, and a newly purchased pair of Bebe Misfits, black and tortoiseshell. "Peter, I have to get moving. It's Marcus's birthday. Marcus Alvarez?"

"I know who Marcus is. Wish him a happy birthday for me." Peter was already walking her toward the door. He stopped her in the middle of the door's electric eye, and the door started to buzz. It kept buzzing as he looked deep into her eyes. "Promise you'll think about my offer?"

"Yes, of course. Although I'm not sure—"

"Think about it."

Grab These Cozy Mysteries
from
Kensington Books

Follow P.I. Savannah Reid
with
G.A. McKevett